PENGUIN CLASSICS

THE FIGURE IN THE CARPET
AND OTHER STORIES

HENRY JAMES was born in 1843 in Washington Place, New York, of Scottish and Irish ancestry. His father was a prominent theologian and philosopher, and his elder brother, William, is also famous as a philosopher. He attended schools in New York and later in London, Paris and Geneva, entering the Law School at Harvard in 1862. In 1865 he began to contribute reviews and short stories to American journals. In 1875, after two prior visits to Europe, he settled for a year in Paris, where he met Flaubert, Turgenev and other literary figures. However, the next year he moved to London, where he became so popular in society that in the winter of 1878–9 he confessed to accepting 107 invitations. In 1898 he left London and went to live at Lamb House, Rye, Sussex. Henry James became a naturalized citizen in 1915, was awarded the Order of Merit, and died in 1916.

In addition to many short stories, plays, books of criticism, autobiography and travel, he wrote some twenty novels, the first published being *Roderick Hudson* (1875). They include *The Europeans*, *Washington Square*, *The Portrait of a Lady*, *The Bostonians*, *The Princess Casamassima*, *The Tragic Muse*, *The Spoils of Poynton*, *The Awkward Age*, *The Wings of the Dove*, *The Ambassadors* and *The Golden Bowl*.

FRANK KERMODE was born in 1919 and educated at Douglas High School and Liverpool University. From 1974 to 1982 he was King Edward VII Professor of English Literature at Cambridge University. He is an Honorary Fellow of King's College, Cambridge, and holds honorary doctorates from Chicago, Liverpool, Newcastle, Yale, Wesleyan, Sewanee and Amsterdam universities. He is a Fellow of the British Academy and of the Royal Society of Literature, an Honorary Member of the American Academy of Arts and Sciences and of the American Academy of Arts and Letters, and an Officier de l'Ordre des Arts et des Sciences. He was knighted in 1991. Professor Kermode's publications include *Romantic Image*, *The Sense of an Ending*, *Puzzles and Epiphanies*, *Continuities*, *Shakespeare*, *Spenser*, *Donne*, *The Classic*, *The Genesis of Secrecy*, *Essays on Fiction 1971–82*, *Forms of Attention*, *History and Value*, *An Appetite for Poetry*, *The Uses of Error*, *Shakespeare's Language* (Penguin, 2000), *Pleasing Myself* (Penguin, 2001), and an autobiography, *Not Entitled*. He has also edited *He Knew He Was Right* and *The Way We Live Now* by Anthony Trollope for Penguin Classics.

GEOFFREY MOORE was General Editor for the works of Henry James in Penguin Classics. He died in 1999.

HENRY JAMES

THE FIGURE
IN THE CARPET
AND OTHER STORIES

**EDITED WITH AN INTRODUCTION
AND NOTES BY
FRANK KERMODE**

PENGUIN BOOKS

PENGUIN BOOKS

Published by the Penguin Group
Penguin Books Ltd, 80 Strand, London WC2R 0RL, England
Penguin Putnam Inc., 375 Hudson Street, New York, New York 10014, USA
Penguin Books Australia Ltd, Ringwood, Victoria, Australia
Penguin Books Canada Ltd, 10 Alcorn Avenue, Toronto, Ontario, Canada M4V 3B2
Penguin Books India (P) Ltd, 11 Community Centre, Panchsheel Park, New Delhi – 110 017, India
Penguin Books (NZ) Ltd, Cnr Rosedale and Airborne Roads, Albany, Auckland, New Zealand
Penguin Books (South Africa) (Pty) Ltd, 24 Sturdee Avenue, Rosebank 2196 South Africa

Penguin Books Ltd, Registered Offices: 80 Strand, London WC2R 0RL, England

www.penguin.com

This edition first published 1986

24

Introduction and notes copyright © Frank Kermode, 1986
All rights reserved

Printed in England by Clays Ltd, St Ives plc
Filmset in Monophoto Sabon

Except in the United States of America, this book is sold subject
to the condition that it shall not, by way of trade or otherwise, be lent,
re-sold, hired out, or otherwise circulated without the publisher's
prior consent in any form of binding or cover other than that in
which it is published and without a similar condition including this
condition being imposed on the subsequent purchaser

www.greenpenguin.co.uk

Penguin Books is committed to a sustainable future
for our business, our readers and our planet.
The book in your hands is made from paper
certified by the Forest Stewardship Council.

Contents

INTRODUCTION
7

NOTE ON THE TEXT
31

SELECTIONS FROM HENRY JAMES'S
PREFACES TO THE NEW YORK EDITION
33

THE AUTHOR OF BELTRAFFIO
57

THE LESSON OF THE MASTER
113

THE PRIVATE LIFE
189

THE MIDDLE YEARS
233

THE DEATH OF THE LION
259

THE NEXT TIME
305

THE FIGURE IN THE CARPET
355

JOHN DELAVOY
401

NOTES
445

With the exception of 'The Author of Beltraffio' the stories here collected were written between 1888 and 1897, when James was in his late forties and early fifties. He was not exactly a popular writer, and during this period in particular he could say, and repeat, that he had fallen on evil days. The failure of his play *Guy Domville* in 1895, when he was hissed and booed at the curtain call, gave him one of his worst moments, and confirmed his scepticism as to the existence of any considerable literate public – a public capable of that measure of cooperation an artist might reasonably look for. He valued the respect of the few, and would still have liked the approval of the many; but he was absolutely unwilling (perhaps, like his hero Limbert in 'The Next Time', quite unable) to change his ways in order to bring about that desired end. Again and again in these tales we are asked, from one angle or another, to contemplate the position of the artist in an 'age of trash triumphant', and we need not be coy about suggesting that they allude, however guardedly, to James's view of his own plight.

It would, however, be easy to be too solemn about these stories, for they are mostly comic or even farcical in tone, a fact sometimes overlooked by interpreters, and especially in the case of 'The Figure in the Carpet'. There is an element of game or even joke in the working out of the given themes or situations, and we shall always miss the point if we ignore this fact. On the other hand it is true that the stories all have some bearing on a subject James took with perfect seriousness. Fiction, according to James, was an art, or not worth bothering about. Unfortunately this was a view the public at large did not share. The artist, at any rate as James and some contemporaries understood his role, could not quite ignore this difference of opinion, since after all the public provided him with a living and the means to carry on being an artist. But he could not but be aware of a distance between them, and even, on his side, of a certain contempt. On the other side one may suppose a reciprocal suspicion, of personal eccentricity and dubious morality. The aesthetic distance expressed itself as an ethical one. The artist took a view of life more specialized, loftier perhaps, and requiring a notion of the vitality of art inaccessible to the crowd; the crowd thought of him as a self-centred and probably self-destructive misfit.

These ideas have Romantic origins. To be endowed with more than usual 'organic sensibility', to know how the imagination creates life and meaning, is to be set apart. The belief that art therefore imposes alienation and suffering – that the price of this higher kind of life is isolation – was not only maintained but lived through by many nineteenth-century artists; and in the years of these tales it had become almost fashionable, for this was the period of Yeats's 'tragic generation' and the symbolic trial of Wilde.

James considered the relation between artist and public from many angles, though never with the abandon of the Bohemian or of the *poète maudit*. He wrote a good deal about painters and painting, and saw the novelist's struggle for formal power and life as analogous to that of the visual artist. His Prefaces glory in the recollection of efforts to establish true 'relations', efforts that would mean little to casual novel-readers or indeed to most novelists. As he says in the Preface to *The American* (1877),

I am willing to grant, assuredly, that this interest, in a given relation, will nowhere so effectually kindle as on the artist's own part. And I am afraid that after all even his best excuse for it must remain the highly personal plea – the joy of living over, as a chapter of experience, the particular intellectual adventure. Here lurks an immense homage to the general privilege of the artist, to that constructive, that creative passion – portentous words, but they are convenient – the exercise of which finds so many an occasion for appearing to him the highest of human fortunes, the rarest boon of the gods. He values it, all sublimely and perhaps a little fatuously, for itself – as the great extension, great beyond all others, of experience and of consciousness.

And he goes on to dismiss the idea that 'the partaker of the "life of art"' should repine at the lack of rewards.

Much rather should he endlessly wonder at his not having to pay half his substance for his luxurious immersion ... the torment of expression, of which we have heard in our time so much, being after all but the last refinement of his privilege. It may leave him weary and worn; but how, after his fashion, he will have lived! As if one were to expect at once freedom and ease! That silly safety is but the sign of bondage and forfeiture.

Here we have a sane account of that condition of the artist that others might represent as a Faustian bargain; yet it yields nothing of their highest claims, except perhaps in the concessive phrase 'perhaps a little fatuously'. Perfection of the work is, for the artist, an ethical imperative, for to attain it is quite simply his life. In *The Tragic Muse*, a novel published in 1890, James treats at length of 'the "artist-life" and of the difficult terms on which it is at the best secured and enjoyed'; he adds that 'the conflict between art and the "world"' strikes him 'as one of the half-dozen great primary motives'. 'We must recognise,' says one of the characters, 'our particular form, the instrument that each of us who carries anything – carries in his being. Mastering this instrument, learning to play it to perfection – that's what I call duty, what I call conduct, what I call success.' It is in the Preface to that book that he criticizes Thackeray, Dumas and Tolstoy for producing 'large loose baggy monsters', though by some they are thought 'superior to art'. He cannot understand that expression. 'There is life and life, and as waste is only life sacrificed and thereby prevented from "counting", I delight in a deep-breathing economy and an organic form.' To neglect the art of fiction is to waste life.

These and related ideas are given memorable expression in James's essay on 'The Art of Fiction', published in 1884 (the year of 'The Author of Beltraffio'). But he ridicules the consumer's view of the novel – 'a novel is a novel, as a pudding is a pudding, and ... our only business with it [is] to swallow it'. He hopes for a change in this view, but fears that a puritanical fear of the form – an 'evangelical hostility' – prevents novelists themselves from taking fiction seriously as one of the fine arts. Moreover the enormous output of novels totally indifferent to art prejudices the chances of the few that are not, the few that seek 'the strange irregular rhythm of life'. He defends the view that 'the province of art is all life' and not just the parts of it thought suitable by evangelicals and Grundyites; but he is not by any means defending mere naturalism or even mere candour. What he wants is completeness; and completeness without waste entails that harmony of relations he calls 'organic'. To the young novelists he says, '... all life belongs to you, but you must be as complete as possible'; he bids them be 'generous and delicate' but by no means diffident or cautiously unwilling, when the need exists, to represent on the page what people know well enough but do not wish to read about. All 'life' becomes the material necessary to the life of the work of art.

That James never really changes these views is obvious from his later novels, and, most poignantly, from his quarrel with H. G. Wells. James was surprised when Wells, with whom he had long been on friendly terms, lampooned him in *Boon* precisely on the score of his dedication to fiction as an art. He made a dignified protest, but Wells continued to maintain, not very apologetically, that the difference between them on the subject of life and literature was a fundamental one. 'To you literature like painting is an end, to me literature like architecture is a means, it has a use.' James's view of the matter, said Wells, had become 'too dominant in the world of criticism'. It did not appear to James that this was so; in any case he felt obliged to re-state his opinion. Neither architecture nor fiction were to be thought of as mere 'means'. Whatever the novel had to give to life – whatever its 'use' – had to come from its being art. And in a famous sentence James added: 'It is art that *makes* life, makes interest, makes importance, for our consideration and application of these things, and I know of no substitute whatever for the force and beauty of its process.' It was his final statement of an unwavering belief.

All about him was the evidence that trash was triumphant. He observed, for example, the lonely struggles of Conrad, the miseries of Gissing; he observed the success of formless, conventional best-sellers; and in between he saw people of talent, Arnold Bennett for instance, content themselves (as he thought) with work much less 'done', much more negligent of form and 'interest', than it should have been. *Clayhanger*, he observed, was 'describable through its being a monument exactly not to an idea, a pursued and captured meaning, or in short *to* anything whatever, but just simply *of* the quarried and gathered material it happens to contain'. Without form, in short, there is no real interest, and even no meaning. Strether's celebrated advice in *The Ambassadors*, 'Live all you can', if addressed to an artist, is a sentence: delicious hard labour for life.

The eighties and nineties saw a huge expansion in the reading public, or, if you like, an enlarged market for trash. At the same time the myth of the artist as isolated, even accursed, waxed strongly; and in particular there was a new

or renewed disposition among some practitioners to take
the novel seriously as art. The examples of Flaubert and
Turgenev were much cited, the large loose baggy monsters
of the English tradition deplored. James seems to have
suffered few of the agonies of Conrad, and private means
kept him from the desperate straits of Gissing; but the
relation of artist to public was none the less of high interest
to him, as the Preface to *The Tragic Muse* expressly states.
So it is not surprising that in these years, more especially in
the last decade of the century, he should look again and
again at this and related subjects.

'The Author of Beltraffio' is a treatment of the topic he
touched upon, as we have seen, in 'The Art of Fiction' in
the same year: a narrow public morality as the enemy of the
art of fiction. In a notebook entry* for 26 March 1884 he
records a remark passed by Edmund Gosse about the
historian and poet J. A. Symonds, whose 'extreme and
somewhat hysterical aestheticism' was compounded by
illness, and by worse misfortunes; his wife thought his books
'immoral, pagan, hyper-aesthetic, etc.'. This was what
James called the *donnée* – ' the air-blown grain' – from
which the story, in the manner of all James's works, was to
grow. (In this case there would be a clash of moralities, a
clash all the more intense in that their representatives were
husband and wife.) Once this had been established the
author had next to decide on the treatment. The speck, the
donnée 'scarcely visible to the common eye', the 'single
small seed ... a mere floating particle in the stream of talk',
might grow to be a very long novel, or a *nouvelle*, or a
story so brief as to deserve only to be called an anecdote.
Sometimes what was planned first as a short story grew in
the treatment and became a novel. James always felt the

* This and all following entries are taken from *The Notebooks of Henry
James*, edited by F. O. Matthiessen and Kenneth B. Murdock (Oxford
University Press, 1947).

difficulty of keeping things short, and he had a particular affection for the intermediate length of the novella or *nouvelle*. But circumstances often required him to write short stories, and the formal conditions of these were very different from those governing other forms. It is noticeable that many of the stories collected in this volume were written very quickly, and very shortly after the reception of the *donnée*; their development terminated very early. They lack the elaborate exfoliation we associate with the longer works of the mature James, and are more obviously schematic, anecdotal and pointed. They are virtuoso exercises, games, even in some instances jokes. Of 'The Middle Years', the shortest of the stories here collected, James reflected that the 'struggle to keep compression rich' might be compared with 'the anxious effort of some warden of the insane engaged at a critical moment in making fast a victim's straitjacket', but the others run to a length he found more comfortable, and 'The Author of Beltraffio' is of that kind.

In this story the conflict between husband and wife called for an observer, and the observer was characterized as young, 'ingenuous' and American, a dedicated admirer of the great Mark Ambient. The battle between husband and wife was to be fought out, naturally enough, over a child. James considered several possible fates for the child, but settled for his death as 'a victim to his parents' fight for him; or perhaps the mother can deliberately sacrifice him'. Once these pieces were in play he introduced another, the sister of Ambient. This done, he wrote the 'gruesome' tale at once.

The scheme of the story is simple and virtually allegorical: the life of art versus the life of evangelical conscience, ending in the sacrifice of life. But the development of the implicit 'relations' greatly complicates the issue. Ambient is seen through the eyes of his young, ardent guest; he has 'a brush of the Bohemian' but also appears to be an English gentleman. His house, his child and his sister all have, in the narrator's view, an 'aesthetic' quality, the sister not at all admirably so. Of the child we may make what we like; he seems well but is sick, is described as beautiful and beautifully dressed, yet is made to seem grotesque. With the child's mother the young man lamentably fails to reach anything like an understanding, though he keeps her appalling secret from Ambient. Does the infant's 'more than mortal bloom' lie rather in the unreliable eye of the beholder, or is it a romantic–decadent corruption genuinely there, and the signal to the mother that he should not survive to express, under his father's influence, the evil that, for her, animates all art? At any rate, the 'perfect little work of art' who looks even 'more exquisitely beautiful in death' has a dangerously Paterian air in the young man's account of him. Indeed, most of the young man's standards are impregnated with contemporary doctrines of art. Miss Ambient is a Rossetti, Mrs Ambient a Reynolds; the house belongs to a picture, and the novelist himself (who has few admirers) almost fits a stereotype (velvet jacket, loose shirt-collars, wide-awake hat, candid conversation), though with a touch of what to the visitor is also foreign, the style of an English gentleman.

It is indeed extraordinary that James, despite the gruesome ending of the story, with its demonstration of the destructiveness of the enemies of art, should in its small compass have found and developed so many ambiguities, such baffling uncertainties of focus. The original diagram remains just visible, and the story says something about a condition of life, the passionate hatred of literature. But the complications are immense, and include the secret fears of the narrator that his attempt to 'convert' Mrs Ambient was the 'proximate cause' of the boy's dying as she read the proof-sheets of Ambient's new novel. Does he suspect that such art may after all prey upon life, that the party of Mrs Ambient is right?

'The Author of Beltraffio' is a story Ambient himself might have written, and James cannot have been amazed at the response of the '*bonnes gens*' who found it 'painful and repulsive'. 'Shine on putrescence as genius may,' cried one reviewer, 'it cannot glorify it'; and another deplored its 'cast-off purple patches of a fast-decaying Frenchy school'. He was accustomed to these elementary mistakes, and frequently deplored the feebleness of criticism; for after all it was written by some of the very few who had a duty to understand the art of fiction.

'The Lesson of the Master', written four years later, has been described as the first of James's fully ambiguous stories – those works like 'The Turn of the Screw' (1898) and *The Sacred Fount* (1901) in which mutually exclusive interpretations co-exist. The production of such narratives undoubtedly interested James as a technical problem, though as such it is only a formalization of tendencies inherent in all highly developed works of fiction. The origin of 'The Lesson of the Master' was somebody's remarking that Alphonse Daudet would not have written his *Trente Áns de Paris* had he not married. As James notes,

It occurred to me that a very interesting situation would be that of an elder artist or writer, who has been ruined (in his own sight) by his marriage and its forcing him to produce promiscuously and cheaply – his position in regard to a young *confrère* whom he sees on the brink of the same disaster, and whom he endeavours to save, to rescue, by some act of bold interference – breaking off the marriage, annihilating the wife, making trouble between the parties.

Once he saw that the decisive act could be the older man marrying the girl, the tale was already fully ambiguous, since his motive for doing so might be totally selfish or totally unselfish.

It is evident from these and from other stories that James's was a doubling imagination. Here an older man spoiled by marriage is doubled by a young man of equal promise on the verge of marrying. In this instance all remains on the level of the reasonably plausible, though doubles can easily produce more fantastic plots, as in 'The Private Life' and, later, in 'The Jolly Corner'. In this story the doubling of the writers, and the doubling of the interpretation, are tethered to the unfantastic realities of contemporary London.

This was the London of Gissing and Wilde, but it was also the London of Henry St George's grand friends; the story opens in one of their grand country houses. Writers and artists perhaps mixed in 'society' rather more than they do nowadays, but to do so called for a certain income. To be married – to have, as St George has, a dragon – also called more firmly for a reasonable establishment than it now does. It is a plight we see illustrated once more in the story of Ralph Limbert in 'The Next Time', and James himself calls St George 'in *essence* ... an observed reality'. He was unabashed by the criticism that such heroes of the artistic life as Paraday (in 'The Death of the Lion') or Limbert, or Paul Overt or the young St George, did not actually exist. His job was 'to imagine ... the honourable, the producible case'. And it was common enough at the time to declare that marriage and children were the ruin of the artist. The intention of the tale is not of course, simply to say this. Any such simplicity is ruled out by the introduction of the youthful double, to bring in what James called 'the precious element of contrast'. What we have now is not a statement but a composition.

Overt – James took care over his characters' names – has been open to influence; he has absorbed some of the artistic prejudice against marriage. St George's wife, on her own proud admission, had once induced him to burn a manuscript; Overt knows at once that it was one of his best things. The joke about St George's attachment to Miss Fancourt prompts him to say that he hopes *she* won't burn any of his books. Fascinated as he is by the *life* she embodies, Overt can still notice that she congratulates him on his *book*, though he has written three or four. It is permissible to believe that he was lucky to misread the clues, fall for the older man's arguments, go abroad and miss marriage with this person; that to him living and blooming must turn out to be precisely a matter of hammering out 'headachy fancies with a bent back at an ink-stained table'. In these stories women are not presented as the kind of readers an artist needs; their interest is held to be in another kind of life altogether, a kind which for all its beauty is more easily incorporated into the ménage of somebody who is, or like St George resembles, 'a lucky stockbroker'. As James himself remarked,

... we are, as a public, chalk-marked by nothing of such values [the values set upon art by genius] any more than ... we are susceptible of consciousness of such others (these in the sphere of literary eminence) as my Neil Paraday in 'The Death of the Lion', as my Hugh Vereker in 'The Figure in the Carpet', as my Ralph Limbert, above all, in 'The Next Time', as sundry unprecedented and unmatched heroes and martyrs of the artistic ideal, in short, elsewhere exemplified in my pages.

Women constituted a large part of that public, and might stand for the whole, for 'our so marked collective mistrust of anything like close or analytic appreciation', for 'this odd numbness of the general sensibility ... in presence of a work of art, to a view scarce of half the intentions embodied, and moreover but to the scantest measure of these'. That is why St George can tell Overt that even if he strayed from perfection only two or three people would notice. And yet to do so would be to betray the spirit of art and to regret it 'as a man thinks of a woman he has in some detested hour of his youth loved and forsaken'. This striking metaphor links the two lives – 'there is life and life' – in an ambiguous intimacy, and honours both lives; if there are 'no women who really understand', the reason is that they are concerned with other perfections. Thus the man who is also an artist is necessarily 'in a false position'. St George can even say that we should be better off without art. 'Happy the societies in which it hasn't made its appearance, for from the moment it comes they have a consuming ache, they have an incurable corruption, in their breast.' Of course all this may be a part of St George's special pleading, and is borrowed from the talk of the time. But it also expresses the situation of the artist who must give himself to his unregarded work, and yet in some degree belong to the society which neglects or resents it.

'The Private Life' considers the contrast between the artist alone and at work, and the behaviour of the same person as a man in society. James got the idea of Clare Vawdrey from the poet Browning and the contrast between his work and his commonplace, though persistent, social presence. Having arrived at this double, he doubled it again, and added, on the basis of the painter Frederick Lord Leighton, an artist, a superb social presence, who existed only when in company and disappeared altogether when alone. The notion is of course a fantasy and James so describes it in his notebook; it might also be treated farcically, but he avoids doing that because he believes the idea can be made 'amusing and pretty'. He saw the tale as needing to be very brief, but, as he says in the Preface, it 'fairly thickened'. It did so in the development of the contrast between 'a highly distinguished man, constantly to be encountered, whose fortune and whose peculiarity it was to bear out personally as little as possible ... the high denotements, the rich implications and rare associations, of the genius to which he owed his position and his renown', and another of an accomplished and dazzling personality whose manner so precluded the supposition of an inner self that one could not imagine 'any private and domestic *ego* at all'. So the second man not only has no *alter ego* but no ego at all; and it is in terms of these antithetical identities that the tale is worked out.

'The Private Life' is a *jeu d'esprit*, indeed James more or less apologizes for the 'small game' it plays; but it is, as he claims, thickened, fleshed out; the conspiracy between Blanche Adney and the narrator works well, and even Lady Mellifont, whose private life must be rather blank, is made interesting. The thing is, as James might say, *done*, and its life comes from the doing rather than from the *donnée*; nor is it all joke, for the image of the artist Vawdrey working alone in the dark is genuinely a figure for the operation of the imagination as James understood it. Again it is the composition that creates interpretative depth.

'The idea of the old artist, or man of letters, who, at the end, feels a kind of anguish of desire for a respite, a prolongation – another period of life to do the *real* thing that he has in him – the thing for which all the others have been but a slow preparation' – that is how James notes the conception of 'The Middle Years' (a title, incidentally, given also to a posthumous fragment of his autobiography). If only this artist could begin again, with the benefit of all he has learned in one life, he might show in another all he is capable of. What James needs is 'some incident ... to show that what he *has* done *is* that of which he is capable' or alternatively an incident 'showing what he might do, just when he must give up forever. The last idea the best.' Having so decided, James, his invention following a track we are already aware of, conjures up first the author's young medical admirer and then the main content of the tale. As the editors of the notebooks point out,* the story, first

The Notebooks of Henry James, ed. F. O. Matthiessen and Kenneth B. Murdock (Oxford University Press, 1947).

published in 1893, reflects both James's deepening anxiety about himself – his sense of not being wanted, of having missed the way – and also his melancholy, compounded by the death in 1892 of his sister Alice.

Commenting with some pride on the brevity of the story, James remarks also that it cost him unusual effort and time. Technically, and perhaps in other ways, the tale seems to have meant a good deal to him. The foundation, as I have noted already, is a familiar one: the ageing, disappointed author and the youthful admirer, here offering the comfort of medical attention as well as informed admiration.

Dencombe is of all these writers the one whose meditations most resemble those of his author, as if James were indeed imagining his life cut short without an opportunity to develop a 'last manner'. The young man chooses him rather than the rich Countess, and his admiration for Dencombe's *The Middle Years* is entirely disinterested, since at first he does not know he is addressing the author. He is, moreover, capable of the subtlest consolation: 'What people "could have done" is mainly what they've in fact done.' Dencombe is partly persuaded: 'A second chance – *that's* the delusion. There never was to be but one. We work in the dark – we do what we can – we give what we have.' But he is 'poor Dencombe' in the last as he was in the first sentence, and he has used up 'his first and only chance'.

'The Middle Years' stands somewhat apart from the other stories of the literary life; the tone is darker, the ironies less vivid, the relation between old and young more intimate and more understanding. 'The Death of the Lion', though it also deals with the last years of a great writer, is written in a manner more appropriate to its setting; it appeared in the *Yellow Book*. James has some sharply satirical portraits of journal editors – Mr Beston in 'John Delavoy', Mr Pinhorn in this story – but he thought kindly of the young American Henry Harland, editor of the dashing new magazine, which had Aubrey Beardsley as its art editor and a brilliant array of contributors. James was a little dubious about a close association with Beardsley, but cheered up when he discovered that his own contributions would not be illustrated, and praised the journal (and its editor) for its 'bright young defiance' of the conventions in allowing him all the space he needed to get 'the true form' of what he was doing. Beardsley soon left, however, and the whole bright venture did not in fact survive the trial of Oscar Wilde, who, when arrested, was carrying a yellow book, though not the *Yellow Book*. But James wrote three long stories for it: 'The Death of the Lion' in the first number, 'The Coxon Fund' in the second, and 'The Next Time' in the sixth. ('The Coxon Fund' is missing from the present volume, for reasons of space.) There could have been no more suitable medium for them, for the *Yellow Book* was, as everyone knows, the flagship periodical of the English Nineties, and the position of the artist in relation to society was in those years a fashionable topic.

Could not something be done with the idea of the great (the distinguished, the celebrated) artist – man of letters he must, in the case, be – who is tremendously made up to, fêted, written to for his autograph, portrait, etc., and yet with whose work, in this age of advertisement and newspaperism, this age of interviewing, not one of the persons concerned has the smallest acquaintance? It would have the merit, at least, of corresponding to an immense reality – a reality that strikes me every day of my life.

So James meditates in his notebook. Artists are cultivated if they are celebrities; art is ignored. How to turn this into 'a little concrete drama'? There will be a lion, and lionizers, who know nothing of his work. 'They must *kill him, hein*? – kill him with the very fury of their selfish exploitation . . .' Nothing is more extraordinary in the entire history of authors' notebooks than the speed with which James, pen in hand, sometimes reaches his 'little concrete situation'. He now sees a writer come late in life to fame; he already understands that 'the whole intention of the tale should be admirably satiric, ironic', and 'the *consciousness of the moral* should probably reside only in the person telling the story'. The country-house party and the 'ultra-modern hostess' now come into view, as does the male writer who uses a woman's name, and his counterpart (rather more usual), the woman novelist who uses a man's name – like, for instance, John Oliver Hobbes, really Pearl Craigie, a writer then enjoying some success. Having here performed in a farcical mode his usual trick of double and antithesis, James, just as characteristically, conceives the plot mechanism: the new, great, incomplete manuscript that will be lost. A week later he understands the role of his narrator, 'my critical *reflector* of the whole thing, a young intending interviewer who has repented, come to consciousness, fallen away'. And the opening sentence presents itself to him almost in the form in which it is eventually to appear.

How exactly these intentions were realized in the 'doing' will be obvious to readers of the story. Mr Pinhorn will allow the young critic – something of a hack, as his opening remarks suggest – to interview and 'write up' Neil Paraday, that virtually unknown genius; but he cannot allow him to write up the author's genius, his books. Mr Pinhorn wants 'the genuine article'. The young man, now converted, is present to observe the beginning of Paraday's lionization, effected by the correspondent of the *Empire* whose notion of a literary topic is 'the permissibility of the larger latitude', as exemplified by the works of the male Dora Forbes and the female Guy Walsingham. When the young man suggests that Mr Morrow of the *Empire* will find more 'revelations' in Paraday's new book than in an interview, the best Mr Morrow can do is to pick up the second volume and 'insincerely' thumb it, before tossing it away. Soon Paraday is king of the beasts, fêted by all and read by none; after a life of neglect and solitude he does not resist, though well aware that 'No one has the faintest conception of what I'm trying for'. The sequence of events which results in Paraday's death and the loss through carelessness of his manuscript is managed in the way James had initially prescribed. Only the young American lady who agrees to forego the writer's acquaintance as a mark of reverence for his work has intruded into the original situation. It is a surprising role for a woman in a James story about writing, but it affords another contrast and aids him in the achievement of rendering a tragic *donnée* in the mode of irony and even, at moments, of farce.

'The Next Time', our second *Yellow Book* story, was conceived immediately after the débâcle of *Guy Domville*, as an idea for a story about a man of letters 'who is all his life trying – if only to get a living – to do something *vulgar*, to take the measure of the huge, flat foot of the public'. James hoped for this beginning to provide 'a mate to "The Death of the Lion" '. His hero's troubles with the *Blackport Beacon* were suggested by James's own experience as writer of Paris letters for the *New York Tribune* twenty years earlier; he had been insufficiently 'vulgar', insufficiently 'personal'. *Guy Domville* belatedly confirmed his inability to make, as it were, 'a sow's ear out of a silk purse'. Having arrived at this general notion, James at once, in his usual way, balanced his silk-purse failure with a sow's-ear success, and postulated a profoundly vulgar best-selling author (a woman, either to sharpen the antithesis or for the sake of realism) who wished for a *succès d'estime*.

This scheme took a few months to mature, and James dropped the idea of using the best-selling lady as his narrator. The great man is given an obvious motive for desiring popular sales: he wants to marry, but 'the worst he could do for the money wasn't bad enough'. The narrator, it is

decided, shall be 'I', and very aware of the contrasts and
ironies in what is going on. The other necessary agents then
appeared: the fiancée's mother, 'grim, vulgar, worldly',
selfish and forbidding. The bad novelist is the fiancée's
sister. The narrator, a failed suitor of the chosen girl,
becomes deeply involved in the action; he is an unsuccessful
literary critic, whose work actually damages the prospects
of his friend. There will be a marriage, to make the production of sows' ears a more urgent necessity. The vulgar
best-seller will ask the critic to write up her attempt at a silk
purse, certain that his intervention will procure the desired
failure. And so on: it is another privileged view of James at
work, never losing sight of the original, rather abstract, idea
as he forms his schemes, and peoples those schemes with
contrasts and characters, and the multiple ironies attaching
to the frustration of their aims. As the manifold compo-
sitional possibilities declare themselves, we see James fuss-
ing about the length of the finished work, which he says
'will take 10,000 words'. It took almost twice as many, yet
there is not too much of it. It deserves to be catalogued
under the classification of 'the beautiful and blest *nouvelle*',
an area opened up by the generosity of the *Yellow Book*. In
the story of Ray Limbert, James treats many of the topics
we have noted as characteristic of this group of tales.
Limbert is a devotee of his art, one of the elect who cannot
escape from grace. The world, society, marriage, try to
seduce but only succeed in killing him; even his friendly critic
becomes, willy-nilly but in the manner of his profession, an
enemy. Yet although greed and incompetence and vulgarity
have to be displayed in it, the story is again told without
gloom, a social comedy – as if the plight of the artist in an
uncomprehending, ruthless and exploitative world were
seen by one who takes that world as it is, and as it includes,
without visible remorse, provision for the extinction of
artists and the neglect of art.

The critic as enemy recurs in the next story, 'The Figure in the Carpet'. In 'The Art of Fiction' James had said of the novelist that 'his manner is his secret, not necessarily a jealous one. He cannot disclose it as a general thing if he would; he would be at a loss to teach it to others.' But he would have liked to find critics, expert readers, who could disclose it, or something of it; and the failure of any such to appear was a cause of frequent lamentation. This is the broad idea behind 'The Figure in the Carpet'. Reflecting on it later, James speaks first of the lack of 'anything like close or analytic appreciation' – a passage I have already quoted – and puts the case for Hugh Vereker's story as a fit instance of this defect. The quest for Vereker's 'undiscovered, not to say undiscoverable, secret' is therefore, in James's intention, a figure for a more general critical failure, the failure to find out (as Paraday put it) what the artist–writer was 'trying for'. In his notebook, James imagines the possessor of the secret as believing 'that they don't *know* his work who don't know, who haven't felt, or guessed, or perceived, this interior thought – this special *beauty* (that is mainly the just word) that pervades and controls and animates them'. So his 'I' shall be a critic – 'another little writer' – who is told by the author of the existence of 'the latent beauty' which is 'the very soul and core of the work'. In the usual way the details of the story now work themselves out in the pages of the notebook: the role of Gwendolen, her marriage and death, her ignorant widower. In his later discussion of the tale James says he remembers an impulse 'to reinstate analytic appreciation, by some ironic or fantastic stroke, so far as possible, in its virtually forfeited rights and dignities'. In a curious passage he develops this idea. He had imagined an artist whose intentions had 'all vainly' taken for granted 'the public, or at the worst the not unthinkable private, exercise of penetration'. He repeats that in 'what we call criticism' curiosity never emerges 'from the limp state'; but in Vereker's young critic he aims to show 'that at a given moment the limpness begins vaguely to throb and heave, to become conscious of a comparative tension'. The test undergone by the questers of his story is a test of critical potency.

When James speaks of the 'intention' of his work, he is not suggesting that there is some simply apprehensible design to which correct interpretation must exactly conform; and as he remarks in his retrospective glance at the story, something is left for the reader to decide. It would certainly not be incorrect to say that in one light 'The Figure in the Carpet' is an elaborate skit on ineffectual criticism, on the failure of professional commentators – 'little writers' – to make out what one is trying to do. That was a situation with which James was all too familiar. But the odd sexuality of the language in the passage I have quoted from the Preface may serve to remind us that 'The Figure in the Carpet' is far too complicated in tone and composition to be dealt with so summarily. Indeed it is itself so impenetrable that of all these stories it is the one that has attracted the most elaborate and conflicting interpretations. Critics of many nationalities and persuasions have lately tried their hand at 'the all-ingenious "Figure in the Carpet"', as James called it, all of them interested in different kinds of critical interpretation – psychoanalytical, narratological, 'reader-response', and all with variations of emphasis. I cannot here discuss their interpretations, except to say that all are opposed to any deflatingly 'referential' explanation; that Tzvetan Todorov declares the secret to be the existence of a secret; and that Shlomith Rimmon, in the most exhaustive of these studies, finds the tale to be fully ambiguous, and the reader's quest for James's 'figure in the carpet' to be parallel to that of the critics inside the story.

The point may seem too simple to make in such company, but it occurs to me that analyses of this kind tend to overlook the fact that 'The Figure in the Carpet' is the funniest, the most 'wicked', of these stories. In 'The Aspern Papers' (1888) – a major work that belongs to this group of stories of the literary life, but is to be found in another Penguin volume (Henry James, *The Aspern Papers and The Turn of the Screw*, 1984) – the quester after the secret is obliged to decide whether he wishes to acquire it at the cost of marrying a woman in other respects undesirable. His motive is, of course, selfish, and so is that of the narrator in the present story. In due course he also is required to speculate whether he should pay the same price, that is, marry the young widow Gwendolen. He expects Drayton Deane, who did marry her, to possess the secret of Vereker. He can conceive of no other motive for marriage except the acquisition of the secret. One of the jokes in the story is, as the Preface hints, the confusion in the narrator's mind between two sorts of penetration and two sorts of secret; for him the secret of the bridal chamber can only be Vereker's secret. Perhaps his error in that matter represents his mistake about the nature of the secret; his wrong-headed quest for the secret is a sort of prurience, a kind of perversion, a vulgar ignorance at best, of the kind Vereker warned him against in their first conversation.

The other running joke is about death. Will Mrs Erme pull round? If so Corvick can marry Gwendolen, authoress of *Deep Down*. Despite her denial of an engagement, he does so; and having discovered the secret – in India – he communicates it to her; he will not tell her before. No sooner has he done so, under the seal of marriage, than James casually kills him off by overturning a dog-cart. The secret now rests with Gwendolen, for she must have 'seen the idol unveiled . . . For what else but that ceremony had the nuptials taken place?' Vereker himself, who did not believe a woman would ever find it out, thought that marriage might 'help' the Corvicks. But once her husband is dead Gwendolen makes the treasure inaccessible; she has enjoyed with him 'a pastime too precious to be shared with the crowd', and whatever that pastime was the secret remains too precious to impart, even, in the fantasy of the frustrated narrator, to a second husband.

It seems likely that James nowhere else used such a series of *double entendres*. They are jokes about something serious, as we know; for the life-work of the artist is greeted only by the 'twaddle' of the critics and the smothering embrace of 'society', which, by drawing him into itself, ends his life and his work. And we might think also that the bright young man's misapprehensions concerning the secrets of marriage – of the growing point of one kind of life – are matched by his ignorance – accompanied by an excessive, impotent interest – in another kind of creative secret. Vereker's secret – 'the thing for the critic to find' – is not, we infer, the sort of thing the celibate and impotent may look for when they speculate about sex. It is a triumph of patience, a quality pervading the life of the subject, like marriage. It is not the subject but the treatment, which is why it is a suffusing presence in all of Vereker's work, and not a nugget hidden here or there. It is a matter of life and death and a matter of jokes and games. The error of criticism is a ludicrous one; it is also tragic.

'John Delavoy' is not the last story of the literary life – there were, later, 'The Birthplace' and 'The Velvet Glove', each of which, in its way, made a contribution to the subject. But 'John Delavoy' is a good enough conclusion. In the early days of 1896 James had an essay on Dumas returned by an editor as shocking to the 'prudery' of his paper. In this act he saw the possibility of adding to his 'series of *small* things on the life and experiences of men of letters'. It seems the editor would have preferred something 'merely personal'. The 'sneakingness and baseness' of the editor represents that of his public, and it should be open to ironic representation in 'some illustrative little action'. So James imagines a distinguished writer, whose work is thought scandalous; editors want to *seem* to deal with him simply because he is famous, but his fame depends on what they won't print. 'So they desire the clap-trap tribute of an *intimate* portrait . . .' Since there must be opposition, the story will be of a serious, intelligent young critic and a vulgar editor. The latter must win. At once James imagines the dead great man's daughter, the portrait, and her relations with the two men. The tale is ready to be *done*. He gives the figure of the editor a maturity and authority not suggested in the draft, and makes the daughter intelligent; for she must be able to see that only the young man's essay is equal to its subject.

James left 'John Delavoy' out of Scribner's New York Edition; one can only guess why. Perhaps the combination of great, misunderstood author, young devotee and vast venal public had occurred too often in the 'series'. Perhaps, on re-reading the story, he found the composition, the relations, inadequate. Yet the story has great merit and interest. It opens with the disastrous failure of a friend's first night; *Guy Domville* was not forgotten. It discusses the difficulties of authors, even of critics, who are 'too good' for the rulers of the literary world. In Mr Beston it offers a strong satirical portrait of a powerful and dangerous type, one of the princes of the new Grub Street, protectors of their subscription lists at the expense of art, which is to say of life. Their own version of life is a false one, for their notion of human interest is life, intimate life, without sex; they are the enemies of the creative wherever found. Once more, however, merely by specifying the serious subject one betrays the tone of the thing; for, as usual in these stories, James treats it in a bantering, ironic way, missing no opportunity to produce civilized amusement where, in his shoes, others would be rancorous. So 'John Delavoy', like all these tales, is a small monument to the humour of civility

in what seemed to its author, and not without reason, to be
an encroaching desert of literary barbarism.

FRANK KERMODE

Selections from Henry James's Prefaces to the New York Edition

THE LESSON OF THE MASTER, THE DEATH OF THE LION, THE NEXT TIME, THE FIGURE IN THE CARPET

My clearest remembrance of any provoking cause connected with the matter of the present volume applies, not to the composition at the head of my list – which owes that precedence to its greatest length and earliest date – but to the next in order, an effort embalmed, to fond memory, in a delightful association. I make the most of this passage of literary history – I like so, as I find, to recall it. It lives there for me in old Kensington days; which, though I look back at them over no such great gulf of years – 'The Death of the Lion' first appeared but in 1894 – have already faded for me to the complexion of ever so long ago. It was of a Sunday afternoon early in the spring of that year: a young friend, a Kensington neighbour and an ardent man of letters, called on me to introduce a young friend of his own and to bespeak my interest for a periodical about to take birth, in his hands, on the most original 'lines' and with the happiest omens. What omen could be happier for instance than that this infant *recueil*,[1] joyously christened even before reaching the cradle, should take the name of *The Yellow Book*? – which so certainly would command for it the liveliest attention. What, further, should one rejoice more to hear than that this venture was, for all its constitutional gaiety, to brave the quarterly form, a thing hitherto of austere, of awful tradition, and was indeed in still other ways to sound the note of bright young defiance? The project, modestly and a little vaguely but all communicatively set forth, amused me, charmed me, on the spot – or at least the touchingly

York Edition incorporates James's own last thoughts on his texts, though they are sometimes expressed in the more elaborate and idiosyncratic later manner. The third option provides a text of undoubted authority, and the alterations are not, in these cases, such as greatly change the manner of the originals, so I have given the New York rendering; except, of course, in the case of 'John Delavoy', for which I have used the version published in the collection called *The Soft Side* (Methuen & Co., London, 1900). I have altered James's text only to eliminate typographical errors and oddities.

James himself wrote twice about most of these stories: first in his notebooks, then, much later (but again with the exception of 'John Delavoy') in the splendid Prefaces to the New York Edition. These are conveniently assembled by R. P. Blackmur in *The Art of the Novel* (Scribner's, 1934 and later editions).

NOTE ON THE TEXT

These stories first appeared in periodicals: 'The Author of Beltraffio' in the *English Illustrated Magazine*, June/July 1884; 'The Lesson of the Master' in *Universal Review*, July/August 1888; 'The Private Life' in *Atlantic Monthly*, April 1892; 'The Middle Years' in *Scribner's*, May 1893; 'The Death of the Lion' in the *Yellow Book*, April 1894; 'The Next Time' in the *Yellow Book*, July 1895; 'The Figure in the Carpet' in *Cosmopolis*, January/February 1896; and 'John Delavoy' in *Cosmopolis*, January/February 1898. All appeared, quite soon after their periodical publication, in various collections of stories by James; and all save 'John Delavoy' are included in Scribner's New York Edition (1907–9) of his collected works ('The Lesson of the Master', 'The Death of the Lion', 'The Next Time' and 'The Figure in the Carpet' in Volume XV; 'The Author of Beltraffio' and 'The Middle Years' in Volume XVI; 'The Private Life' in Volume XVII).

James, as is well known, was, like Dencombe in 'The Middle Years', an inveterate reviser of his work, the revisions varying from mere touching up to quite substantial rewriting. In making a collection of this sort one has therefore to choose among three possible texts: that of the first (periodical) publication; that of the first appearance in book form; and that of the New York Edition. Arguments are available to support any one of these choices. The original version may be preferred for its freshness; the second may, not too heavily, correct lapses due to the haste of the first publication or slips in proof-reading; the New convinced and inflamed projector did. It was the happy fortune of the late Henry Harland to charge everything he touched, whether in life or in literature, with that influence – an effect by which he was always himself the first to profit. If he came to me, about *The Yellow Book*, amused, he pursued the enterprise under the same hilarious star; its difficulties no less than its felicities excited, in the event, his mirth; and he was never more amused (nor, I may certainly add, more amusing) than when, after no very prolonged career, it encountered suddenly and all distressfully its term. The thing had then been to him, for the few years, a humorous uneasy care, a business attended both with other troubles and other pleasures; yet when, before the too prompt harshness of his final frustration, I reflect that he had adventurously lived, wrought and enjoyed, the small square lemon-coloured quarterly, 'failure' and all, figures to me perhaps his most beguiling dream and most rewarding hours.

The bravest of the portents that Sunday afternoon – the intrinsic, of course I mean; the only ones today worth speaking of – I have yet to mention; for I recall my rather embarrassed inability to measure as yet the contributory value of Mr Aubrey Beardsley, by whom my friend was accompanied and who, as his prime illustrator, his perhaps even quite independent picture-maker, was to be in charge of the 'art department.' This young man, slender, pale, delicate, unmistakably intelligent, somehow invested the whole proposition with a detached, a slightly ironic and melancholy grace. I had met him before, on a single occasion, and had seen an example or two of his so curious and so disconcerting talent – my appreciation of which seems to me, however, as I look back, to have stopped quite short. The young *recueil* was to have pictures, yes, and they were to be as often as possible from Beardsley's hand; but they were to wear this unprecedented distinction, and were to scatter it all about them, that they should have nothing to do with the text – which put the whole matter on an ideal basis. To those who remember the short string of numbers of *The Yellow Book* the spasmodic independence of these contributions will still be present. They were, as illustrations, related surely to nothing else in the same pages – save once or twice, as I imperfectly recall, to some literary effort of Beardsley's own that matched them in perversity; and I might well be at peace as to any disposition on the part of the strange young artist ever to emulate *my* comparatively so incurious text. There would be more to say about him, but he must not draw me off from a greater relevance – my point being simply that he had associated himself with Harland that brave day to dangle before me the sweetest aid to inspiration ever snatched by a poor scribbler from editorial lips. I should sooner have come to this turn of the affair, which at once bathed the whole prospect in the rosiest glow.

I was invited, and all urgently, to contribute to the first number, and was regaled with the golden truth that my composition might absolutely assume, might shamelessly parade in, its own organic form. It was disclosed to me, wonderfully, that – so golden the air pervading the enterprise – any projected contribution might conform, not only unchallenged but by this circumstance itself the more esteemed, to its true intelligible nature. For any idea I might wish to express I might have space, in other words, elegantly to express it – an offered licence that, on the spot, opened up the millennium to the 'short story.' One had so often known this product to struggle, in one's hands, under the rude prescription of brevity at any cost, with the opposition so offered to its really becoming a story, that my friend's emphasised indifference to the arbitrary limit of length struck me, I remember, as the fruit of the finest artistic intelligence. We had been at one – that we already knew –

on the truth that the forms of wrought things, in this order, *were*, all exquisitely and effectively, the things; so that, for the delight of mankind, form might compete with form and might correspond to fitness; might, that is, in the given case, have an inevitability, a marked felicity. Among forms, moreover, we had had, on the dimensional ground – for length and breadth – our ideal, the beautiful and blest *nouvelle*;[2] the generous, the enlightened hour for which appeared thus at last to shine. It was under the star of the *nouvelle* that, in other languages, a hundred interesting and charming results, such studies on the minor scale as the best of Turgenieff's, of Balzac's, of Maupassant's, of Bourget's, and just lately, in our own tongue, of Kipling's,[3] had been, all economically, arrived at – thanks to their authors', as 'contributors,' having been able to count, right and left, on a wise and liberal support. It had taken the blank misery of our Anglo-Saxon sense of such matters to organise, as might be said, the general indifference to this fine type of composition. In that dull view a 'short story' was a 'short story,' and that was the end of it. Shades and differences, varieties and styles, the value above all of the idea happily *developed*, languished, to extinction, under the hard-and-fast rule of the 'from six to eight thousand words' – when, for one's benefit, the rigour was a little relaxed. For myself, I delighted in the shapely *nouvelle* – as, for that matter, I had from time to time and here and there been almost encouraged to show.

However, these are facts quite of the smaller significance and at which I glance only because I seem still to recognise in those of my three bantlings held by Harland at the baptismal font – 'The Death of the Lion' (1894), 'The Coxon Fund' (1894), 'The Next Time' (1895), *plus* a paper not here to be reproduced – something of the less troubled confidence with which they entered on their first state of being. These pieces have this in common that they deal all with the literary life, gathering their motive, in each case, from some noted adventure, some felt embarrassment, some extreme predicament, of the artist enamoured of perfection, ridden by his idea or paying for his sincerity. They testify indeed, as they thus stand together, to no general intention – they minister only, I think, to an emphasised effect. The particular case, in respect to each situation depicted, appealed to me but on its merits; though I was to note with interest, as my sense more and more opened itself, that situations of the order I speak of might again and again be conceived. They rose before me, in fine, as numerous, and thus, here, even with everything not included, they have added themselves up. I must further mention that if they enjoy in common their reference to the troubled artistic consciousness, they make together, by the same stroke, this other rather blank profession, that few of them recall to me, however dimly, any scant pre-natal phase.

In putting them sundry such critical questions so much after the fact I find it interesting to make out – critically interesting of course, which is all our interest here pretends to be – that whereas any anecdote about life pure and simple, as it were, proceeds almost as a matter of course from some good jog of fond fancy's elbow, some pencilled note on somebody else's case, so the material for any picture of personal states so specifically complicated as those of my hapless friends in the present volume will have been drawn preponderantly from the depths of the designer's own mind. This, amusingly enough, is what, on the evidence before us, I seem critically, as I say, to gather – that the states represented, the embarrassments and predicaments studied, the tragedies and comedies recorded, can be intelligibly fathered but on his own intimate experience. I have already mentioned the particular rebuke once addressed me on all this ground, the question of where on earth, where roundabout us at this hour, I had 'found' my Neil Paradays, my Ralph Limberts, my Hugh Verekers and other such supersubtle fry. I was reminded then, as I have said, that these represented eminent cases fell to the ground, as by their foolish weight, unless I could give chapter and verse for the eminence. I was reduced to confessing I couldn't, and yet must repeat again here how little I was so abashed. On going over these things I see, to our critical edification, exactly why – which was because I was able to plead that my postulates, my animating presences, were all, to their great enrichment, their intensification of value, ironic; the strength of applied irony being surely in the sincerities, the lucidities, the utilities that stand behind it. When it's not a campaign, of a sort, on behalf of the something better (better than the obnoxious, the provoking object) that blessedly, as is assumed, *might* be, it's not worth speaking of. But this is exactly what we mean by operative irony. It implies and projects the possible other case, the case rich and edifying where the actuality is pretentious and vain. So it plays its lamp; so, essentially, it carries that smokeless flame, which makes clear, with all the rest, the good cause that guides it. My application of which remarks is that the studies here collected have their justification in the ironic spirit, the spirit expressed by my being able to reply promptly enough to my friend: 'If the life about us for the last thirty years refuses warrant for these examples, then so much the worse for that life. The *constatation* would be so deplorable that instead of making it we must dodge it: there are decencies that in the name of the general self-respect we must take for granted, there's a kind of rudimentary intellectual honour to which we must, in the interest of civilisation, at least pretend.' But I must really reproduce the whole passion of my retort.

'What does your contention of non-existent conscious *exposures*, in the midst of all the stupidity and vulgarity and hypocrisy, imply but that we have been, nationally, so to speak, graced with no instance of recorded sensibility fine enough to react against these things? – an admission too distressing. What one would accordingly fain do is to baffle any such calamity, to *create* the record, in default of any other enjoyment of it; to imagine, in a word, the honourable, the producible case. What better example than this of the high and helpful public and, as it were, civic use of the imagination? – a faculty for the possible fine employments of which in the interest of morality my esteem grows every hour I live. How can one consent to make a picture of the preponderant futilities and vulgarities and miseries of life without the impulse to exhibit as well from time to time, in its place, some fine example of the reaction, the opposition or the escape? One does, thank heaven, encounter here and there symptoms of immunity from the general infection; one recognises with rapture, on occasion, signs of a protest against the rule of the cheap and easy; and one sees thus that the tradition of a high aesthetic temper needn't, after all, helplessly and ignobly perish. These reassurances are one's warrant, accordingly, for so many recognitions of the apparent doom and the exasperated temper – whether with the spirit and the career fatally bruised and finally broken in the fray, or privileged but to gain from it a finer and more militant edge. I have had, I admit, to project *signal* specimens – have had, naturally, to make and to keep my cases interesting; the only way to achieve which was to suppose and represent them eminent. In other words I was inevitably committed, always, to the superior case; so that if this is what you reprehensively mean, that I have been thus beguiled into citing celebrities without analogues and painting portraits without models, I plead guilty to the critical charge. Only what I myself mean is that I carry my guilt lightly and have really in face of each perpetrated licence scarce patience to defend myself.' So I made my point and so I continued.

'I can't tell you, no, who it is I "aimed at" in the story of Henry St George; and it wouldn't indeed do for me to name his exemplar publicly even were I able. But I none the less maintain his situation to have been in *essence* an observed reality – though I should be utterly ashamed, I equally declare, if I hadn't done quite my best for it. It was the fault of this notable truth, and not my own, that it too obscurely lurked – dim and disengaged; but where is the work of the intelligent painter of life if not precisely in some such aid given to true meanings to be born? He must bear up as he can if it be in consequence laid to him that the flat grows salient and the tangled clear, the common – worst of all! – even amusingly rare, by passing through his hands. Just so when you ask who in the world I had in mind for a victim, and what in the world for a treasure, so sacrificed to the advertisement not even of their own merits but of all sorts of independent, of really indifferent, exhibitory egotism, as the practically harried and hunted Neil Paraday and his borrowed, brandished and then fatally mislaid manuscript, I'm equally confident of having again and again closely noted in the social air all the elements of such a drama. I've put these elements together – that was my business, and in doing this wished of course to give them their maximum sense, which depended, for irony, for comedy, for tragedy, in other words for beauty, on the "importance" of the poor foredoomed monarch of the jungle. And then, I'm not ashamed to allow, it was *amusing* to make these people "great," so far as one could do so without making them intrinsically false. (Yes – for the mere accidental and relative falsity I don't care.) It was amusing because it was more difficult – from the moment, of course I mean, that one worked out at all their greatness; from the moment one didn't simply give it to be taken on trust. Working out economically almost anything is the very life of the art of representation; just as the request to take on trust, tinged with the least extravagance, is the very death of the same. (There may be such a state of mind brought about on the reader's part, I think, as a positive desire to take on trust; but that is only the final fruit of insidious proceedings, operative to a sublime end, on the author's side; and is at any rate a different matter.) As for the all-ingenious "Figure in the Carpet", let me perhaps a little pusillanimously conclude, nothing would induce me to come into close quarters with you on the correspondences of this anecdote. Here exactly is a good example for you of the virtue of your taking on trust – when I have artfully begotten in you a disposition. All I can at this point say is that if ever I was aware of ground and matter for a significant fable, I was aware of them in that connection.'

My plea for 'correspondences' will perhaps, however, after all, but bring my reader back to my having, at the outset of these remarks, owned to full unconsciousness of seed dropped here by that quick hand of occasion that had elsewhere generally operated; which comes to saying, no doubt, that in the world of letters things don't at this time of day very strikingly happen. Suggestive and illuminating incident is indeed scarce frequent enough to be referred to as administering the shake that starts up afresh the stopped watch of attention. I shouldn't therefore probably have accumulated these illustrations without the sense of something interchangeable, or perhaps even almost indistinguishable, between my own general adventure and the more or less lively illustration into which I was to find this experiment so repeatedly flower. Let it pass that if I am so oddly unable to say here, at any point, 'what gave me my idea', I must just a trifle freely have helped myself to it from hidden stores. But, burdened thus with the imputation of that irregularity, I shall give a poor account of my homogeneous group without the charity of a glance, however brief, at its successive components. However I might have been introduced in fact to Henry St George, of 'The Lesson of the Master', or however I might have been deprived of him, my complete possession of him, my active sympathy with him as a known and understood and admired and pitied, in fine as a fully measured, quantity, hangs about the pages still as a vague scent hangs about thick orchard trees. The great sign of a grasped warrant – for identification, arrest or whatever – is, after all, in the confidence that dissipates vagueness; and the logic of such developed situations as those of the pair commemorated at the head of my list imposed itself all triumphantly. Hadn't one again and again caught 'society' in the very fact of not caring in the least what might become of the subject, however essentially fine and fragile, of a patronage reflecting such credit on all concerned, so long as the social game might be played a little more intensely, and if possible more irrelevantly, by this unfortunate's aid? Given the Lion, his 'death' was but too conceivably the issue of the cruel exposure thus involved for him; and if it be claimed by what I can but feel rather a pedantic view that so precious an animal exactly *couldn't*, in our conditions, have been 'given', I must reply that I yet had met him – though in a preserve not perhaps known in all its extent to geographers.

Of such a fantasy as 'The Next Time' the principle would surely soon turn up among the consulted notes of any sincere man of letters – taking literature, that is, on the side of the money to be earned by it. There are beautiful talents the exercise of which yet isn't lucrative, and there are pressing needs the satisfaction of which may well appear difficult under stress of that failure of felicity. Just so there are other talents that leave any fine appreciation mystified and gaping, and the active play of which may yet be observed to become on occasion a source of vast pecuniary profit. Nothing then is at moments more attaching, in the light of 'comparative' science, than the study of just where and when, just how and why recognition denies itself to the appeal at all artfully, and responds largely to the appeal coarsely enough, commingled. The critical spirit – with leisure indeed to spare – may well, in its restlessness, seek to fix a bit exactly the point at which a beautiful talent, as I have called it, ceases, when imperilled by an empty pocket, to be a 'worldly' advantage. The case in which impunity, for the *malheureux*⁴ ridden by that questionable boon, insists on breaking down would seem thus to become susceptible of much fine measurement. I don't know, I confess, that it proveably is; but the critical spirit at all afraid of so slight a misadventure as a waste of curiosity is of course deplorably false to its nature. The difficulty here, in truth, is that, from the moment a straight dependence on the broad-backed public is a part of the issue, the explicative quantity to be sought is precisely the mood of that monster – which, consistently and consummately unable to give the smallest account of itself, naturally renders no grain of help to enquiry. Such a study as that of Ray Limbert's so prolonged, so intensified, but so vain continuance in hope (hope of successfully growing in his temperate garden some specimen of the rank exotic whose leaves are rustling cheques) is in essence a 'story about the public', only wearing a little the reduced face by reason of the too huge scale, for direct portrayal, of the monstrous countenance itself. Herein resides, as I have hinted, the anxious and easy interest of almost any sincere man of letters in the mere vicinage, even if that be all, of such strained situations as Ray Limbert's. They speak of the public, such situations, to whoever it may concern. They at all events had from far back insidiously beset the imagination of the author of 'The Next Time', who can scarce remember the day when he wasn't all sympathetically, all tenderly occupied with some presumed literary watcher – and quite of a sublime constitution – for that postponed redress. Therefore in however developed a state the image in question was at last to hover before him, some form of it had at least never been far to seek.

I to *this* extent recover the acute impression that may have given birth to 'The Figure in the Carpet', that no truce, in English-speaking air, had ever seemed to me really struck, or even approximately strikeable, with our so marked collective mistrust of anything like close or analytic appreciation – appreciation, to *be* appreciation, implying of course some such rudimentary zeal; and this though that fine process be the Beautiful Gate itself of enjoyment. To have become consistently aware of this odd numbness of the general sensibility, which seemed ever to condemn it, in presence of a work of art, to a view scarce of half the intentions embodied, and moreover but to the scantest measure of these, was to have been directed from an early day to some of the possible implications of the matter, and so to have been led on by seductive steps, albeit perhaps by devious ways, to such a congruous and, as I would fain call it, fascinating case as that of Hugh Vereker and his undiscovered, not to say undiscoverable, secret. That strikes me, when all is said, as an ample indication of the starting-point of this particular portrayal. There may be links missing between the chronic consciousness I have glanced at – that of Hugh Vereker's own analytic projector,[5] speaking through the mouth of the anonymous scribe – and the poor man's attributive dependence, for the sense of being understood and enjoyed, on some responsive reach of critical perception that he is destined never to waylay with success; but even so they scarce signify, and I may not here attempt to catch them. This too in spite of the amusement almost always yielded by such recoveries and reminiscences, or to be gathered from the manipulation of any string of evolutionary pearls. What I most remember of my proper process is the lively impulse, at the root of it, to reinstate analytic appreciation, by some ironic or fantastic stroke, so far as possible, in its virtually forfeited rights and dignities. Importunate to this end had I long found the charming idea of some artist whose most characteristic intention, or cluster of intentions, should have taken all vainly for granted the public, or at the worst the not unthinkable private, exercise of penetration. I couldn't, I confess, be indifferent to those rare and beautiful, or at all events odd and attaching, elements that might be imagined to grow in the shade of so much spent intensity and so much baffled calculation. The mere quality and play of an ironic consciousness in the designer left wholly alone, amid a chattering unperceiving world, with the thing he has most wanted to do, with the design more or less realised – some effectual glimpse of that might by itself, for instance, reward one's experiment. I came to Hugh Vereker, in fine, by this travelled road of a generalisation; the habit of having noted for many years how strangely and helplessly, among us all, what we call criticism – its curiosity never emerging from the limp state – is apt to stand off from the intended sense of things, from such finely-attested matters, on the artist's part, as a spirit and a form, a bias and a logic, of his own. From my definite preliminary it was no far cry to the conception of an intent worker who should find himself to the very end in presence but of the limp curiosity. Vereker's drama indeed – or I should perhaps rather say that of the aspiring young analyst whose report we read and to whom, I ruefully grant, I have ventured to impute a developed wit – is that at a given moment the limpness begins vaguely to throb and heave, to become conscious of a comparative tension. As an effect of this mild convulsion acuteness, at several points, struggles to enter the field, and the question that accordingly comes up, the issue of the affair, can be but whether the very secret of perception hasn't been lost. That is the situation, and

'The Figure in the Carpet' exhibits a small group of well-meaning persons engaged in a test. The reader is, on the evidence, left to conclude.

THE AUTHOR OF BELTRAFFIO,
THE MIDDLE YEARS

What I had lately and most particularly to say of 'The Coxon Fund' is no less true of 'The Middle Years', first published in *Scribner's Magazine* (1893) – that recollection mainly and most promptly associates with it the number of times I had to do it over to make sure of it. To get it right was to squeeze my subject into the five or six thousand words I had been invited to make it consist of – it consists, in fact, should the curious care to know, of some 5550 – and I scarce perhaps recall another case, with the exception I shall presently name, in which my struggle to keep compression rich, if not, better still, to keep accretions compressed, betrayed for me such community with the anxious effort of some warden of the insane engaged at a critical moment in making fast a victim's straitjacket. The form of 'The Middle Years' is not that of the *nouvelle*, but that of the concise anecdote; whereas the subject treated would perhaps seem one comparatively demanding 'developments' – if indeed, amid these mysteries, distinctions were so absolute. (There is of course neither close nor fixed measure of the reach of a development, which in some connections seems almost superfluous and then in others to represent the whole sense of the matter; and we should doubtless speak more thoroughly by book had we some secret for exactly tracing deflexions and returns.) However this may be, it was as an anecdote, an anecdote only, that I was determined my little situation here should figure; to which end my effort was of course to follow it as much as possible from its outer edge in, rather than from its centre outward. That fond formula, I had alas already discovered, may set as many traps in the garden as its opposite may set in the wood; so that after boilings and reboilings of the contents of my small cauldron, after added pounds of salutary sugar, as numerous as those prescribed in the choicest recipe for the thickest jam, I well remember finding the whole process and act (which, to the exclusion of everything else, dragged itself out for a month) one of the most expensive of its sort in which I had ever engaged.

But I recall, by good luck, no less vividly how much finer a sweetness than any mere spooned-out saccharine dwelt in the fascination of the questions involved. Treating a theme that 'gave' much in a form that, at the best, would give little, might indeed represent a peck of troubles; yet who, none the less, beforehand, was to pronounce with authority such and such an idea anecdotic and such and such another developmental? One had, for the vanity of *a priori* wisdom here, only to be so constituted that to see any form of beauty, for a particular application, proscribed or even questioned, was forthwith to covet that form more than any other and to desire the benefit of it exactly there. One had only to be reminded that for the effect of quick roundness the small smooth situation, though as intense as one will, is prudently indicated, and that for a fine complicated entangled air nothing will serve that doesn't naturally swell and bristle – one had only, I say, to be so warned off or warned on, to see forthwith no beauty for the simple thing that shouldn't, and even to perversity, enrich it, and none for the other, the comparatively intricate, that shouldn't press it out as a mosaic. After which fashion the careful craftsman would have prepared himself the special inviting treat of scarce being able to say, at his highest infatuation, before any series, which might be the light thing weighted and which the dense thing clarified. The very attempt so to discriminate leaves him in fact at moments even a little ashamed; whereby let him shirk here frankly certain of the issues presented by the remainder of our company – there being, independently of these mystic matters, other remarks to make. Blankness overtakes me, I confess, in connection with the brief but concentrated 'Greville Fane' – *that* emerges, how concentrated I tried to make it – which must have appeared in a London weekly journal at the beginning of the 'nineties'; but as to which I further retain only a dim warm pleasantness as of old Kensington summer hours. I re-read, ever so kindly, to the promotion of a mild aftertaste – that of a certain feverish pressure, in a cool north room resorted to in heavy London Augusts, with stray, rare echoes of the town, beyond near roofs and chimneys, making harmless detonations, and with the perception, over my page, as I felt poor Greville grow, that her scant record, to be anything at all, would have to be a minor miracle of foreshortening. For here is exactly an illustrative case: the subject, in this little composition, is 'developmental' enough, while the form has to make the anecdotic concession; and yet who shall say that for the right effect of a small harmony the fusion has failed? We desire doubtless a more detailed notation of the behaviour of the son and daughter, and yet had I believed the right effect missed 'Greville Fane' wouldn't have figured here.

Nothing, by the same stroke, could well have been condemned to struggle more for that harmony than 'The Abasement of the Northmores' and 'The Tree of Knowledge': the idea in these examples (1900) being developmental with a vengeance and the need of an apparent ease and a general congruity having to enforce none the less – as on behalf of some victim of the income-tax who would minimise his 'return' – an almost heroic dissimulation of capital. These things, especially the former, are novels intensely compressed, and with that character in them yet keeping at bay, under stress of their failing else to be good short stories, any air of mutilation. They had had to be good short stories in order to earn, however precariously, their possible wage and 'appear' – so certain was it that there would be no appearance, and consequently no wage, for them as frank and brave *nouvelles*. They could but conceal the fact that they *were* 'nouvelles'; they could but masquerade as little anecdotes. I include them here by reason of that successful, that achieved and consummate – as it strikes me – duplicity: which, however, I may add, was in the event to avail them little – since they were to find nowhere, the unfortunates, hospitality and the reward of their effort. It is to 'The Tree of Knowledge' I referred just above, I may further mention, as the production that had cost me, for keeping it 'down', even a greater number of full revolutions of the merciless screw than 'The Middle Years'. On behalf also of this member of the group, as well as for 'The Author of Beltraffio', I recover exceptionally the sense of the grain of suggestion, the tiny air-blown particle. In presence of a small interesting example of a young artist long dead, and whom I had yet briefly seen and was to remember with kindness, a friend had made, thanks to a still greater personal knowledge of him and of his quasi-conspicuous father, likewise an artist, one of those brief remarks that the dramatist feels as fertilising. 'And then,' the lady I quote had said in allusion to certain troubled first steps of the young man's career, to complications of consciousness that had made his early death perhaps less strange and less lamentable, even though superficially more tragic; 'and then he had found his father out, artistically: having grown up in so happy a personal relation with him only to feel, at last, quite awfully, that he didn't and couldn't believe in him.' That fell on one's ear of course only to prompt the inward cry: 'How can there possibly *not* be all sorts of good things in it?' Just so for 'The Author of Beltraffio' – long before this and some time before the first appearance of the tale in

The English Illustrated Magazine (1884): it had been said to me of an eminent author, these several years dead and on some of the embarrassments of whose life and character a common friend was enlarging: 'Add to them all, moreover, that his wife objects intensely to what he writes. She can't bear it (as you can for that matter rather easily conceive) and that naturally creates a tension –!' *There* had come the air-blown grain which, lodged in a handful of kindly earth, was to produce the story of Mark Ambient.

Elliptic, I allow, and much of a skipping of stages, so bare an account of such performances; yet with the constitutive process for each idea quite sufficiently noted by my having had, always, only to say to myself sharply enough: 'Dramatise it, dramatise it!' That answered, in the connection, always, all my questions – that provided for all my 'fun'. The two tales I have named but represent therefore their respective grains of seed dramatically handled.

THE PRIVATE LIFE

I proceed almost eagerly, in any case, to 'The Private Life' – and at the cost of reaching for a moment over 'The Jolly Corner': I find myself so fondly return to ground on which the history even of small experiments may be more or less written. This mild documentation fairly thickens for me, I confess, the air of the first-mentioned of these tales; the scraps of records flit through that medium, to memory, as with the incalculable brush of wings of the imprisoned bat at eventide. This piece of ingenuity rests for me on such a handful of acute impressions as I may not here tell over at once; so that, to be brief, I select two of the sharpest. Neither of these was, in old London days, I make out, to be resisted even under its single pressure; so that the hour struck with a vengeance for 'Dramatise it, dramatise it!' (dramatise, that is, the combination) from the first glimpse of a good way to work together two cases that happened to have been given me. They were those – as distinct as possible save for belonging alike to the 'world', the London world of a time when Discrimination still a little lifted its head – of a highly distinguished man, constantly to be encountered, whose fortune and whose peculiarity it was to bear out personally as little as possible (at least to *my* wondering sense) the high denotements, the rich implications and rare associations, of the genius to which he owed his position and his renown. One may go, naturally, in such a connection, but by one's own applied measure; and I have never ceased to ask myself, in this particular loud, sound, normal, hearty presence, all so assertive and so whole, all bristling with prompt responses and expected opinions and usual views, radiating all a broad daylight equality of emphasis and impartiality of address (for most relations) – I never ceased, I say, to ask myself what lodgement, on such premises, the rich proud genius one adored could ever have contrived, what domestic commerce the subtlety that was its prime ornament and the world's wonder have enjoyed, under what shelter the obscurity that was its luckless drawback and the world's despair have flourished. The whole aspect and *allure* of the fresh sane man, illustrious and undistinguished – no 'sensitive poor gentleman' he! – was mystifying; they made the question of who then had written the immortal things such a puzzle.

So at least one could but take the case – though one's need for relief depended, no doubt, on what one (so to speak) suffered. The writer of these lines, at any rate, suffered so much – I mean of course but by the unanswered question – that light *had* at last to break under pressure of the whimsical theory of two distinct and alternate presences, the assertion of either of which on any occasion directly involved the entire extinction of the other. This explained to the imagination the mystery: our delightful inconceivable celebrity was *double*, constructed in two quite distinct and 'watertight' compartments – one of these figures by the gentleman who sat at a table all alone, silent and unseen, and wrote admirably deep and brave and intricate things; while the gentleman who regularly came forth to sit at a quite different table and substantially and promiscuously and multitudinously dine stood for its companion. They had nothing to do, the so dissimilar twins, with each other; the diner could exist but by the cessation of the writer, whose emergence, on his side, depended on his – and our! – ignoring the diner. Thus it was amusing to think of the real great man as a presence known, in the late London days, all and only to himself – unseen of other human eye and converted into his perfectly positive, but quite secondary, *alter ego* by any approach to a social contact. To the same tune was the social personage known all and only to society, was he conceivable but as 'cut dead', on the return home and the threshold of the closed study, by the waiting spirit who would flash at that signal into form and possession. Once I had so seen the case I couldn't see it otherwise; and so to see it moreover was inevitably to feel in it a situation and a motive. The ever-importunate murmur, 'Dramatise it, dramatise it!' haunted, as I say, one's perception; yet without giving the idea much support till, by the happiest turn, the whole possibility was made to glow.

For didn't there immensely flourish in those very days and exactly in that society the apparition the most qualified to balance with the odd character I have referred to and to supply to 'drama', if 'drama' there was to be, the precious element of contrast and antithesis? – that most accomplished of artists and most dazzling of men of the world whose effect on the mind repeatedly invited to appraise him was to beget in it an image of representation and figuration so exclusive of any possible inner self that, so far from there being here a question of an *alter ego*, a double personality, there seemed scarce a question of a real and single one, scarce foothold or margin for any private and domestic *ego* at all. Immense in this case too, for any analytic witness, the solicitation of wonder – which struggled all the while, not less amusingly than in the other example, towards the explanatory secret; a clear view of the perpetual, essential performer, consummate, infallible, impeccable, and with his high shining elegance, his intensity of presence, on these lines, involving to the imagination an absolutely blank reverse or starved residuum, no *other* power of presence whatever. One said it under one's breath, one really yearned to know: was he, such an embodiment of skill and taste and tone and composition, of every public gloss and grace, thinkable even as occasionally single? – since to be truly single is to be able, under stress, to be separate, to be *solus*, to know at need the interlunar swoon of *some* independent consciousness. Yes, *had* our dazzling friend any such alternative, could he so unattestedly exist, and was the withdrawn, the sequestered, the unobserved and unhonoured condition so much as imputable to him? Wasn't his potentiality of existence public, in fine, to the last squeeze of the golden orange, and when he passed from our admiring sight into the chamber of mystery what, the next minute, was on the other side of the door? It was irresistible to believe at last that there was at such junctures inveterately nothing; and the more so, once I had begun to dramatise, as this supplied the most natural opposition in the world to my fond companion-view – the other side of the door *only* cognisant of the true Robert Browning.[6] One's harmless formula for the poetic employment of this pair of conceits couldn't go much further than 'Play them against each other' – the ingenuity of which small game 'The Private Life' reflects as it can.

THE AUTHOR
OF BELTRAFFIO

THE AUTHOR
OF BEL TRAFFIO

*

THE AUTHOR OF BELTRAFFIO

I

Much as I wished to see him I had kept my letter of introduction three weeks in my pocket-book. I was nervous and timid about meeting him – conscious of youth and ignorance, convinced that he was tormented by strangers, and especially by my country-people, and not exempt from the suspicion that he had the irritability as well as the dignity of genius. Moreover, the pleasure, if it should occur – for I could scarcely believe it was near at hand – would be so great that I wished to think of it in advance, to feel it there against my breast, not to mix it with satisfactions more superficial and usual. In the little game of new sensations that I was playing with my ingenuous mind I wished to keep my visit to the author of 'Beltraffio' as a trump-card. It was three years after the publication of that fascinating work, which I had read over five times and which now, with my riper judgement, I admire on the whole as much as ever. This will give you about the date of my first visit – of any duration – to England; for you will not have forgotten the commotion, I may even say the scandal, produced by Mark Ambient's masterpiece. It was the most complete presentation that had yet been made of the gospel of art; it was a kind of aesthetic war-cry. People had endeavoured to sail nearer to 'truth' in the cut of their sleeves and the shape of their sideboards;[1] but there had not as yet been, among English novels, such an example of beauty of execution and 'intimate' importance of theme. Nothing had been done in that line from the point of view of art for art. That served me as a fond formula, I may mention, when I was twenty-five; how much it still serves I won't take upon myself to say – especially as the discerning reader will be able to judge for himself. I had been in England, briefly, a twelvemonth before the time to which I began by alluding, and had then learned that Mr Ambient was in distant lands – was making a considerable tour in the East; so that there was nothing to do but to keep my letter till I should be in London again. It was of little use to me to hear that his wife had not left England and was, with her little boy, their only child, spending the period of her husband's absence – a good many months – at a small place they had down in Surrey. They had a house in London, but actually in the occupation of other persons. All this I had picked up, and also that Mrs Ambient was charming – my friend the American poet, from whom I had my introduction, had never seen her, his relations with the great man confined to the exchange of letters; but she wasn't, after all, though she had lived so near the rose, the author of 'Beltraffio', and I didn't go down into Surrey to call on her. I went to the Continent, spent the following winter in Italy and returned to London in May. My visit to Italy had opened my eyes to a good many things, but to nothing more than the beauty of certain pages in the works of Mark Ambient. I carried his productions about in my trunk – they are not, as you know, very numerous, but he had preluded to 'Beltraffio' by some exquisite things – and I used to read them over in the evening at the inn. I used profoundly to reason that the man who drew those characters and wrote that style understood what he saw and knew what he was doing. This is my sole ground for mentioning my winter in Italy. He had been there much in former years – he was saturated with what painters call the 'feeling' of that classic land. He expressed the charm of the old hill-cities of Tuscany, the look of certain lonely grass-grown places which, in the past, had echoed with life; he understood the great artists, he understood the spirit of the Renaissance; he understood everything. The scene of one of his earlier novels was laid in Rome, the scene of another in Florence, and I had moved through these cities in company with the figures he set so firmly on their feet. This is why I was now so much happier even than before in the prospect of making his acquaintance.

At last, when I had dallied with my privilege long enough, I dispatched to him the missive of the American poet. He had already gone out of town; he shrank from the rigour of the London 'season',[2] and it was his habit to migrate on the first of June. Moreover I had heard he was this year hard at work on a new book, into which some of his impressions of the East were to be wrought, so that he desired nothing so much as quiet days. That knowledge, however, didn't prevent me – *cet âge est sans pitié*[3] – from sending with my friend's letter a note of my own, in which I asked his leave to come down and see him for an hour or two on some day to be named by himself. My proposal was accompanied with a very frank expression of my sentiments, and the effect of the entire appeal was to elicit from the great man the kindest possible invitation. He would be delighted to see me, especially if I should turn up on the following Saturday and would remain till the Monday morning. We would take a walk over the Surrey commons, and I could tell him all about the other great man, the one in America. He indicated to me the best train, and it may be imagined whether on the Saturday afternoon I was punctual at Waterloo. He carried his benevolence to the point of coming to meet me at the little station at which I was to alight, and my heart beat very fast as I saw his handsome face, surmounted with a soft wide-awake[4] and which I knew by a photograph long since enshrined on my mantel-shelf, scanning the carriage-windows as the train rolled up. He recognised me as infallibly as I had recognised himself; he

appeared to know by instinct how a young American of
critical pretensions, rash youth, would look when much
divided between eagerness and modesty. He took me by the
hand and smiled at me and said: 'You must be – a – *you*, I
think!' and asked if I should mind going on foot to his house,
which would take but a few minutes. I remember feeling it
a piece of extraordinary affability that he should give
directions about the conveyance of my bag; I remember
feeling altogether very happy and rosy, in fact quite trans-
ported, when he laid his hand on my shoulder as we came
out of the station.

I surveyed him, askance, as we walked together; I had
already, I had indeed instantly, seen him as all delightful.
His face is so well known that I needn't describe it; he looked
to me at once an English gentleman and a man of genius,
and I thought that a happy combination. There was a brush
of the Bohemian⁵ in his fineness; you would easily have
guessed his belonging to the artist guild. He was addicted
to velvet jackets, to cigarettes, to loose shirt-collars, to
looking a little dishevelled. His features, which were firm
but not perfectly regular, are fairly enough represented in
his portraits; but no portrait I have seen gives any idea of
his expression. There were innumerable things in it, and
they chased each other in and out of his face. I have seen
people who were grave and gay in quick alternation; but
Mark Ambient was grave and gay at one and the same
moment. There were other strange oppositions and contra-
dictions in his slightly faded and fatigued countenance. He
affected me somehow as at once fresh and stale, at once
anxious and indifferent. He had evidently had an active
past, which inspired one with curiosity; yet what was that
compared to his obvious future? He was just enough above
middle height to be spoken of as tall, and rather lean and
long in the flank. He had the friendliest frankest manner
possible, and yet I could see it cost him something. It

cost him small spasms of the self-consciousness that is an
Englishman's last and dearest treasure – the thing he pays
his way through life by sacrificing small pieces of even as
the gallant but moneyless adventurer in 'Quentin Durward'⁶
broke off links of his brave gold chain. He had been thirty-
eight years old at the time 'Beltraffio' was published. He
asked me about his friend in America, about the length of
my stay in England, about the last news in London and the
people I had seen there; and I remember looking for the
signs of genius in the very form of his questions and thinking
I found it. I liked his voice as if I were somehow myself
having the use of it.

There was genius in his house too I thought when we got
there; there was imagination in the carpets and curtains, in
the pictures and books, in the garden behind it, where
certain old brown walls were muffled in creepers that
appeared to me to have been copied from a masterpiece of
one of the pre-Raphaelites.⁷ That was the way many things
struck me at that time, in England – as reproductions of
something that existed primarily in art or literature. It was
not the picture, the poem, the fictive page, that seemed to
me a copy; these things were the originals, and the life of
happy and distinguished people was fashioned in their
image. Mark Ambient called his house a cottage, and I saw
afterwards he was right; for if it hadn't been a cottage it
must have been a villa,⁸ and a villa, in England at least, was
not a place in which one could fancy him at home. But it
was, to my vision, a cottage glorified and translated; it was
a palace of art,⁹ on a slightly reduced scale – and might
besides have been the dearest haunt of the old English *genius
loci*.¹⁰ It nestled under a cluster of magnificent beeches, it
had little creaking lattices that opened out of, or into,
pendent mats of ivy, and gables, and old red tiles, as well as
a general aspect of being painted in water-colours and
inhabited by people whose lives would go on in chapters

and volumes. The lawn seemed to me of extraordinary extent, the garden-walls of incalculable height, the whole air of the place delightfully still, private, proper to itself. 'My wife must be somewhere about,' Mark Ambient said as we went in. 'We shall find her perhaps – we've about an hour before dinner. She may be in the garden. I'll show you my little place.'

We passed through the house and into the grounds, as I should have called them, which extended into the rear. They covered scarce three or four acres, but, like the house, were very old and crooked and full of traces of long habitation, with inequalities of level and little flights of steps – mossy and cracked were these – which connected the different parts with each other. The limits of the place, cleverly dissimulated, were muffled in the great verdurous screens. They formed, as I remember, a thick loose curtain at the further end, in one of the folds of which, as it were, we presently made out from afar a little group. 'Ah there she is!' said Mark Ambient; 'and she has got the boy.' He noted that last fact in a slightly different tone from any in which he yet had spoken. I wasn't fully aware of this at the time, but it lingered in my ear and I afterwards understood it.

'Is it your son?' I enquired, feeling the question not to be brilliant.

'Yes, my only child. He's always in his mother's pocket. She coddles him too much.' It came back to me afterwards too – the sound of these critical words. They weren't petulant; they expressed rather a sudden coldness, a mechanical submission. We went a few steps further, and then he stopped short and called the boy, beckoning to him repeatedly.

'Dolcino, come and see your daddy!' There was something in the way he stood still and waited that made me think he did it for a purpose. Mrs Ambient had her arm round the child's waist, and he was leaning against her knee;

but though he moved at his father's call she gave no sign of releasing him. A lady, apparently a neighbour, was seated near her, and before them was a garden-table on which a tea-service had been placed.

Mark Ambient called again, and Dolcino struggled in the maternal embrace; but, too tightly held, he after two or three fruitless efforts jerked about and buried his head deep in his mother's lap. There was a certain awkwardness in the scene; I thought it odd Mrs Ambient should pay so little attention to her husband. But I wouldn't for the world have betrayed my thought and, to conceal it, I began loudly to rejoice in the prospect of our having tea in the garden. 'Ah she won't let him come!' said my host with a sigh; and we went our way till we reached the two ladies. He mentioned my name to his wife, and I noticed that he addressed her as 'My dear,' very genially, without a trace of resentment at her detention of the child. The quickness of the transition made me vaguely ask myself if he were perchance hen-pecked – a shocking surmise which I instantly dismissed. Mrs Ambient was quite such a wife as I should have expected him to have; slim and fair, with a long neck and pretty eyes and an air of good breeding. She shone with a certain coldness and practised in intercourse a certain bland detach-ment, but she was clothed in gentleness as in one of those vaporous redundant scarves that muffle the heroines of Gainsborough and Romney.[11] She had also a vague air of race, justified by my afterwards learning that she was 'connected with the aristocracy'. I have seen poets married to women of whom it was difficult to conceive that they should gratify the poetic fancy – women with dull faces and glutinous minds, who were none the less, however, excellent wives. But there was no obvious disparity in Mark Ambi-ent's union. My hostess – so far as she could be called so – delicate and quiet, in a white dress, with her beautiful child at her side, was worthy of the author of a work so distinguished as 'Beltraffio'. Round her neck she wore a black velvet ribbon, of which the long ends, tied behind, hung down her back, and to which, in front, was attached a miniature portrait of her little boy. Her smooth shining hair was confined in a net. She gave me an adequate greeting and Dolcino – I thought this small name of endearment delightful[12] – took advantage of her getting up to slip away from her and go to his father, who seized him in silence and held him high for a long moment, kissing him several times.

I had lost no time in observing that the child, not more than seven years old, was extraordinarily beautiful. He had the face of an angel – the eyes, the hair, the smile of innocence, the more than mortal bloom. There was something that deeply touched, that almost alarmed, in his beauty, composed, one would have said, of elements too fine and pure for the breath of this world. When I spoke to him and he came and held out his hand and smiled at me I felt a sudden strange pity for him – quite as if he had been an orphan or a changeling or stamped with some social stigma. It was impossible to be in fact more exempt from these misfortunes, and yet, as one kissed him, it was hard to keep from murmuring all tenderly 'Poor little devil!' though why one should have applied this epithet to a living cherub is more than I can say. Afterwards indeed I knew a trifle better; I grasped the truth of his being too fair to live, wondering at the same time that his parents shouldn't have guessed it and have been in proportionate grief and despair. For myself I had no doubt of his evanescence, having already more than once caught in the fact the particular infant charm that's as good as a death-warrant.

The lady who had been sitting with Mrs Ambient was a jolly ruddy personage in velveteen and limp feathers, whom I guessed to be the vicar's wife – our hostess didn't introduce me – and who immediately began to talk to Ambient about chrysanthemums. This was a safe subject, and yet there was a certain surprise for me in seeing the author of 'Beltraffio' even in such superficial communion with the Church of England. His writings implied so much detachment from that institution, expressed a view of life so profane, as it were, so independent and so little likely in general to be thought edifying, that I should have expected to find him an object of horror to vicars and their ladies – of horror repaid on his own part by any amount of effortless derision. This proved how little I knew as yet of the English people and their extraordinary talent for keeping up their forms, as well as of some of the mysteries of Mark Ambient's hearth and home. I found afterwards that he had, in his study, between nervous laughs and free cigar-puffs, some wonderful comparisons for his clerical neighbours; but meanwhile the chrysanthemums were a source of harmony, as he and the vicaress were equally attached to them, and I was surprised at the knowledge they exhibited of this interesting plant. The lady's visit, however, had presumably been long, and she presently rose for departure and kissed Mrs Ambient. Mark started to walk with her to the gate of the grounds, holding Dolcino by the hand.

'Stay with me, darling,' Mrs Ambient said to the boy, who had surrendered himself to his father.

Mark paid no attention to her summons, but Dolcino turned and looked at her in shy appeal. 'Can't I go with papa?'

'Not when I ask you to stay with me.'

'But please don't ask me, mamma,' said the child in his small clear new voice.

'I must ask you when I want you. Come to me, dearest.' And Mrs Ambient, who had seated herself again, held out her long slender slightly too osseous hands.

Her husband stopped, his back turned to her, but without releasing the child. He was still talking to the vicaress, but this good lady, I think, had lost the thread of her attention.

She looked at Mrs Ambient and at Dolcino, and then looked at me, smiling in a highly amused cheerful manner and almost to a grimace.

'Papa,' said the child, 'mamma wants me not to go with you.'

'He's very tired – he has run about all day. He ought to be quiet till he goes to bed. Otherwise he won't sleep.' These declarations fell successively and very distinctly from Mrs Ambient's lips.

Her husband, still without turning round, bent over the boy and looked at him in silence. The vicaress gave a genial irrelevant laugh and observed that he was a precious little pet. 'Let him choose,' said Mark Ambient. 'My dear little boy, will you go with me or will you stay with your mother?'

'Oh it's a shame!' cried the vicar's lady with increased hilarity.

'Papa, I don't think I can choose,' the child answered, making his voice very low and confidential. 'But I've been a great deal with mamma today,' he then added.

'And very little with papa! My dear fellow, I think you *have* chosen!' On which Mark Ambient walked off with his son, accompanied by re-echoing but inarticulate comments from my fellow visitor.

His wife had seated herself again, and her fixed eyes, bent on the ground, expressed for a few moments so much mute agitation that anything I could think of to say would be but a false note. Yet she none the less quickly recovered herself, to express the sufficiently civil hope that I didn't mind having had to walk from the station. I reassured her on this point, and she went on: 'We've got a thing that might have gone for you, but my husband wouldn't order it.' After which and another longish pause, broken only by my plea that the pleasure of a walk with our friend would have been quite what I would have chosen, she found for reply: 'I believe the Americans walk very little.'

'Yes, we always run,' I laughingly allowed.

She looked at me seriously, yet with an absence in her pretty eyes. 'I suppose your distances are so great.'

'Yes, but we break our marches! I can't tell you the pleasure to me of finding myself here,' I added. 'I've the greatest admiration for Mr Ambient.'

'He'll like that. He likes being admired.'

'He must have a very happy life then. He has many worshippers.'

'Oh yes, I've seen some of them,' she dropped, looking away, very far from me, rather as if such a vision were before her at the moment. It seemed to indicate, her tone, that the sight was scarcely edifying, and I guessed her quickly enough to be in no great intellectual sympathy with the author of 'Beltraffio'. I thought the fact strange, but somehow, in the glow of my own enthusiasm, didn't think it important: it only made me wish rather to emphasise that homage.

'For me, you know,' I returned – doubtless with a due *suffisance*[13] – 'he's quite the greatest of living writers.'

'Of course I can't judge. Of course he's very clever,' she said with a patient cheer.

'He's nothing less than supreme, Mrs Ambient! There are pages in each of his books of a perfection classing them with the greatest things. Accordingly for me to see him in this familiar way, in his habit as he lives, and apparently to find the man as delightful as the artist – well, I can't tell you how much too good to be true it seems and how great a privilege I think it.' I knew I was gushing, but I couldn't help it, and what I said was a good deal less than what I felt. I was by no means sure I should dare to say even so much as this to the master himself, and there was a kind of rapture in speaking it out to his wife which was not affected by the fact that, as a wife, she appeared peculiar. She listened to me with her face grave again and her lips a little compressed, listened as if in no doubt, of course, that her husband was remarkable, but as if at the same time she had heard it frequently enough and couldn't treat it as stirring news. There was even in her manner a suggestion that I was so young as to expose myself to being called forward – an imputation and a word I had always loathed; as well as a hinted reminder that people usually got over their early extravagance. 'I assure you that for me this is a red-letter day,' I added.

She didn't take this up, but after a pause, looking round her, said abruptly and a trifle dryly: 'We're very much afraid about the fruit this year.'

My eyes wandered to the mossy mottled garden-walls, where plum-trees and pears, flattened and fastened upon the rusty bricks, looked like crucified figures with many arms. 'Doesn't it promise well?'

'No, the trees look very dull. We had such late frosts.'

Then there was another pause. She addressed her attention to the opposite end of the grounds, kept it for her husband's return with the child. 'Is Mr Ambient fond of gardening?' it occurred to me to ask, irresistibly impelled as I felt myself, moreover, to bring the conversation constantly back to him.

'He's very fond of plums,' said his wife.

'Ah well then I hope your crop will be better than you fear. It's a lovely old place,' I continued. 'The whole impression's that of certain places he has described. Your house is like one of his pictures.'

She seemed a bit frigidly amused at my glow. 'It's a pleasant little place. There are hundreds like it.'

'Oh it has his *tone*,' I laughed, but sounding my epithet and insisting on my point the more sharply that my companion appeared to see in my appreciation of her simple establishment a mark of mean experience.

It was clear I insisted too much. 'His tone?' she repeated with a harder look at me and a slightly heightened colour.

'Surely he has a tone, Mrs Ambient.'

'Oh yes, he has indeed! But I don't in the least consider that I'm living in one of his books at all. I shouldn't care for that in the least,' she went on with a smile that had in some degree the effect of converting her really sharp protest into an insincere joke. 'I'm afraid I'm not very literary. And I'm not artistic,' she stated.

'I'm very sure you're not ignorant, not stupid,' I ventured to reply, with the accompaniment of feeling immediately afterwards that I had been both familiar and patronising. My only consolation was in the sense that she had begun it, had fairly dragged me into it. She had thrust forward her limitations.

'Well, whatever I am I'm very different from my husband. If you like him you won't like me. You needn't say anything. Your liking me isn't in the least necessary!'

'Don't defy me!' I could but honourably make answer.

She looked as if she hadn't heard me, which was the best thing she could do; and we sat some time without further speech. Mrs Ambient had evidently the enviable English quality of being able to be mute without unrest. But at last she spoke – she asked me if there seemed many people in town. I gave her what satisfaction I could on this point, and we talked a little of London and of some of its characteristics at that time of the year. At the end of this I came back irrepressibly to Mark.

'Doesn't he like to be there now? I suppose he doesn't find the proper quiet for his work. I should think his things had been written for the most part in a very still place. They suggest a great stillness following on a kind of tumult. Don't you think so?' I laboured on. 'I suppose London's a tremendous place to collect impressions, but a refuge like this, in the country, must be better for working them up.

Does he get many of his impressions in London, should you say?' I proceeded from point to point in this malign enquiry simply because my hostess, who probably thought me an odious chattering person, gave me time; for when I paused – I've not represented my pauses – she simply continued to let her eyes wander while her long fair fingers played with the medallion on her neck. When I stopped altogether, however, she was obliged to say something, and what she said was that she hadn't the least idea where her husband got his impressions. This made me think her, for a moment, positively disagreeable; delicate and proper and rather aristocratically fine as she sat there. But I must either have lost that view a moment later or been goaded by it to further aggression, for I remember asking her if our great man were in a good vein of work and when we might look for the appearance of the book on which he was engaged. I've every reason now to know that she found me insufferable.

She gave a strange small laugh as she said; 'I'm afraid you think I know much more about my husband's work than I do. I haven't the least idea what he's doing,' she then added in a slightly different, that is a more explanatory, tone and as if from a glimpse of the enormity of her confession. 'I don't read what he writes.'

She didn't succeed, and wouldn't even had she tried much harder, in making this seem to me anything less than monstrous. I stared at her and I think I blushed. 'Don't you admire his genius? Don't you admire "Beltraffio"?'

She waited, and I wondered what she could possibly say. She didn't speak, I could see, the first words that rose to her lips; she repeated what she had said a few minutes before. 'Oh of course he's very clever!' And with this she got up; our two absentees had reappeared.

II

Mrs Ambient left me and went to meet them; she stopped and had a few words with her husband that I didn't hear and that ended in her taking the child by the hand and returning with him to the house. Her husband joined me in a moment, looking, I thought, the least bit conscious and constrained, and said that if I would come in with him he would show me my room. In looking back upon these first moments of my visit I find it important to avoid the error of appearing to have at all fully measured his situation from the first or made out the signs of things mastered only afterwards. This later knowledge throws a backward light and makes me forget that, at least on the occasion of my present reference – I mean that first afternoon – Mark Ambient struck me as only enviable. Allowing for this he must yet have failed of much expression as we walked back to the house, though I remember well the answer he made to a remark of mine on his small son.

'That's an extraordinary little boy of yours. I've never seen such a child.'

'Why,' he asked while we went, 'do you call him extraordinary?'

'He's so beautiful, so fascinating. He's like some perfect little work of art.'

He turned quickly in the passage, grasping my arm. 'Oh don't call him that, or you'll – you'll –!' But in his hesitation he broke off suddenly, laughing at my surprise. Immediately afterwards, however, he added: 'You'll make his little future very difficult.'

I declared that I wouldn't for the world take any liberties with his little future – it seemed to me to hang by threads of such delicacy. I should only be highly interested in watching it.

'You Americans are very keen,' he commented on this. 'You notice more things than we do.'

'Ah if you want visitors who aren't struck with you,' I cried, 'you shouldn't have asked me down here!'

He showed me my room, a little bower of chintz, with open windows where the light was green, and before he left me said irrelevantly: 'As for my small son, you know, we shall probably kill him between us before we've done with him!' And he made this assertion as if he really believed it, without any appearance of jest, his fine near-sighted expressive eyes looking straight into mine.

'Do you mean by spoiling him?'

'No, by fighting for him!'

'You had better give him to me to keep for you,' I said. 'Let me remove the apple of discord!'

It was my extravagance of course, but he had the air of being perfectly serious. 'It would be quite the best thing we could do. I should be all ready to do it.'

'I'm greatly obliged to you for your confidence.'

But he lingered with his hands in his pockets. I felt as if within a few moments I had, morally speaking, taken several steps nearer to him. He looked weary, just as he faced me then, looked preoccupied and as if there were something one might do for him. I was terribly conscious of the limits of my young ability, but I wondered what such a service might be, feeling at bottom nevertheless that the only thing I could do for him was to like him. I suppose he guessed this and was grateful for what was in my mind, since he went on presently: 'I haven't the advantage of being an American, but I also notice a little, and I've an idea that' – here he smiled and laid his hand on my shoulder – 'even counting out your nationality you're not destitute of intelligence. I've only known you half an hour, but –!' For which again he pulled up. 'You're very young after all.'

'But you may treat me as if I could understand you!' I said; and before he left me to dress for dinner he had virtually given me a promise that he would.

When I went down into the drawing-room – I was very punctual – I found that neither my hostess nor my host had appeared. A lady rose from the sofa, however, and inclined her head as I rather surprisedly gazed at her. 'I dare say you don't know me,' she said with the modern laugh. 'I'm Mark Ambient's sister.' Whereupon I shook hands with her, saluting her very low. Her laugh was modern – by which I mean that it consisted of the vocal agitation serving between people who meet in drawing-rooms as the solvent of social disparities, the medium of transitions; but her appearance was – what shall I call it? – medieval. She was pale and angular, her long thin face was inhabited by sad dark eyes and her black hair intertwined with golden fillets and curious clasps. She wore a faded velvet robe which clung to her when she moved and was 'cut', as to the neck and sleeves, like the garments of old Italians. She suggested a symbolic picture, something akin even to Dürer's Melancholia,[14] and was so perfect an image of a type which I, in my ignorance, supposed to be extinct, that while she rose before me I was almost as much startled as if I had seen a ghost. I afterwards concluded that Miss Ambient wasn't incapable of deriving pleasure from this weird effect, and I now believe that reflexion concerned in her having sunk again to her seat with her long lean but not ungraceful arms locked together in an archaic manner on her knees and her mournful eyes addressing me a message of intentness which foreshadowed what I was subsequently to suffer. She was a singular fatuous artificial creature, and I was never more than half to penetrate her motives and mysteries. Of one thing I'm sure at least: that they were considerably less insuperable than her appearance announced. Miss Ambient was a restless romantic disappointed spinster, consumed with the love of Michael-Angelesque attitudes[15] and mystical robes; but I'm now convinced she hadn't in her nature those depths of unutterable thought which, when you first knew her, seemed to look out from her eyes and to prompt her complicated gestures. Those features in especial had a misleading eloquence; they lingered on you with a far-off dimness, an air of obstructed sympathy, which was certainly not always a key to the spirit of their owner; so that, of a truth, a young lady could scarce have been so dejected and disillusioned without having committed a crime for which she was consumed with remorse, or having parted with a hope that she couldn't sanely have entertained. She had, I believe, the usual allowance of rather vain motives: she wished to be looked at, she wished to be married, she wished to be thought original.

It cost me a pang to speak in this irreverent manner of one of Ambient's name, but I shall have still less gracious things to say before I've finished my anecdote, and moreover – I confess it – I owe the young lady a bit of a grudge. Putting aside the curious cast of her face she had no natural aptitude for an artistic development, had little real intelligence. But her affectations rubbed off on her brother's renown, and as there were plenty of people who darkly disapproved of him they could easily point to his sister as a person formed by his influence. It was quite possible to regard her as a warning, and she had almost compromised him with the world at large. He was the original and she the inevitable imitation. I suppose him scarce aware of the impression she mainly produced, beyond having a general idea that she made up very well as a Rossetti;[16] he was used to her and was sorry for her, wishing she would marry and observing how she didn't. Doubtless I take her too seriously, for she did me no harm, though I'm bound to allow that I can only half-account for her. She wasn't so mystical as she looked, but was a strange indirect uncomfortable embarrassing woman. My story gives the reader at best so very small a knot to untie that I needn't hope to excite his curiosity by delaying to remark that Mrs Ambient hated her sister-in-law. This I learned but later on, when other matters came to my knowledge. I mention it, however, at once, for I shall perhaps not seem to count too much on having beguiled him if I say he must promptly have guessed it. Mrs Ambient, a person of conscience, put the best face on her kinswoman, who spent a month with her twice a year; but it took no great insight to recognise the very different personal paste of the two ladies, and that the usual feminine hypocrisies would cost them on either side much more than the usual effort. Mrs Ambient, smooth-haired, thin-lipped, perpetually fresh, must have regarded her crumpled and dishevelled visitor as an equivocal joke; she herself so the opposite of a Rossetti, she herself a Reynolds or a Lawrence,[17] with no more far-fetched note in her composition than a cold ladylike candour and a well-starched muslin dress.

It was in a garment and with an expression of this kind that she made her entrance after I had exchanged a few words with Miss Ambient. Her husband presently followed her and, there being no other company, we went to dinner. The impressions I received at that repast are present to me still. The elements of oddity in the air hovered, as it were, without descending – to any immediate check of my delight. This came mainly of course from Ambient's talk, the easiest and richest I had ever heard. I mayn't say today whether he laid himself out to dazzle a rather juvenile pilgrim from over the sea; but that matters little – it seemed so natural to him to shine. His spoken wit or wisdom, or whatever, had thus a charm almost beyond his written; that is if the high finish of his printed prose be really, as some people have maintained, a fault. There was such a kindness in him, however, that I've no doubt it gave him ideas for me, or about me, to see me sit as open-mouthed as I now figure myself. Not so the two ladies, who not only were very nearly dumb from beginning to end of the meal, but who hadn't even the air of being struck with such an exhibition of fancy and taste. Mrs Ambient, detached, and inscrutable, met neither my eye nor her husband's: she attended to her dinner, watched her servants, arranged the puckers in her dress, exchanged at wide intervals a remark with her sister-in-law and, while she slowly rubbed her lean white hands between the courses, looked out of the window at the first signs of evening – the long June day allowing us to dine without candles. Miss Ambient appeared to give little direct heed to anything said by her brother; but on the other hand she was much engaged in watching its effect upon me. Her 'die-away'[18] pupils continued to attach themselves to my countenance, and it was only her air of belonging to another century that kept them from being importunate. She seemed to look at me across the ages, and the interval of time diminished for me the inconvenience. It was as if she knew in a general way that he must be talking very well, but she herself was so at home among such allusions that she had no need to pick them up and was at liberty to see what would become of the exposure of a candid young American to a high aesthetic temperature.

The temperature was aesthetic certainly, but it was less so than I could have desired, for I failed of any great success in making our friend abound about himself. I tried to put him on the ground of his own genius, but he slipped through my fingers every time and shifted the saddle on one or other of his contemporaries. He talked about Balzac and Browning, about what was being done in foreign countries, about his recent tour in the East and the extraordinary forms of life to be observed in that part of the world. I felt he had reasons for holding off from a direct profession of literary faith, a full consistency or sincerity, and therefore dealt instead with certain social topics, treating them with extraordinary humour and with a due play of that power of ironic evocation in which his books abound. He had a

deal to say about London as London appears to the observer
who has the courage of some of his conclusions during the
high-pressure time – from April to July – of its gregarious
life. He flashed his faculty of playing with the caught image
and liberating the wistful idea over the whole scheme of
manners or conception of intercourse of his compatriots,
among whom there were evidently not a few types for which
he had little love. London in short was grotesque to him,
and he made capital sport of it; his only allusion that I can
remember to his own work was his saying that he meant
some day to do an immense and general, a kind of epic,
social satire. Miss Ambient's perpetual gaze seemed to put
to me: 'Do you perceive how artistic, how very strange and
interesting, we are? Frankly now is it possible to be *more*
artistic, *more* strange and interesting, than this? You surely
won't deny that we're remarkable.' I was irritated by her
use of the plural pronoun, for she had no right to pair herself
with her brother; and moreover of course I couldn't see my
way to – at all genially – include Mrs Ambient. Yet there
was no doubt they were, taken together, unprecedented
enough, and, with all allowances, I had never been left, or
condemned, to draw so many rich inferences.

After the ladies had retired my host took me into his study
to smoke, where I appealingly brought him round, or so
tried, to some disclosure of fond ideals. I was bent on
proving I was worthy to listen to him, on repaying him for
what he had said to me before dinner, by showing him how
perfectly I understood. He liked to talk; he liked to defend
his convictions and his honour (not that I attacked them);
he liked a little perhaps – it was a pardonable weakness –
to bewilder the youthful mind even while wishing to win it
over. My ingenuous sympathy received at any rate a shock
from three or four of his professions – he made me occasionally gasp and stare. He couldn't help forgetting, or rather
couldn't know, how little, in another and dryer clime, I had

ever sat in the school in which he was master; and he promoted me as at a jump to a sense of its penetralia. My trepidations, however, were delightful; they were just what I had hoped for, and their only fault was that they passed away too quickly; since I found that for the main points I was essentially, I was quite constitutionally, on Mark Ambient's 'side'. This was the taken stand of the artist to whom every manifestation of human energy was a thrilling spectacle and who felt for ever the desire to resolve his experience of life into a literary form. On that high head of the passion for form – the attempt at perfection, the quest for which was to his mind the real search for the holy grail – he said the most interesting, the most inspiring things. He mixed with them a thousand illustrations from his own life, from other lives he had known, from history and fiction, and above all from the annals of the time that was dear to him beyond all periods, the Italian cinquecento.[19] It came to me thus that in his books he had uttered but half his thought, and that what he had kept back – from motives I deplored when I made them out later – was the finer, and braver part. It was his fate to make a great many still more 'prepared' people than me not inconsiderably wince; but there was no grain of bravado in his ripest things (I've always maintained it, though often contradicted), and at bottom the poor fellow, disinterested to his finger-tips and regarding imperfection not only as an aesthetic but quite also as a social crime, had an extreme dread of scandal. There are critics who regret that having gone so far he didn't go further; but I regret nothing – putting aside two or three of the motives I just mentioned – since he arrived at a noble rarity and I don't see how you can go beyond that. The hours I spent in his study – this first one and the few that followed it; they were not after all so numerous – seem to glow, as I look back on them, with a tone that is partly that of the brown old room, rich, under the shaded candle-light where we sat and smoked, with the dusky delicate bindings of valuable books; partly that of his voice, of which I still catch the echo, charged with the fancies and figures that came at his command. When we went back to the drawing-room we found Miss Ambient alone in possession and prompt to mention that her sister-in-law had a quarter of an hour before been called by the nurse to see the child, who appeared rather unwell – a little feverish.

'Feverish! how in the world comes he to be feverish?' Ambient asked. 'He was perfectly right this afternoon.'

'Beatrice says you walked him about too much – you almost killed him.'

'Beatrice must be very happy – she has an opportunity to triumph!' said my friend with a bright bitterness which was all I could have wished it.

'Surely not if the child's ill,' I ventured to remark by way of pleading for Mrs Ambient.

'My dear fellow, you aren't married – you don't know the nature of wives!' my host returned with spirit.

I tried to match it. 'Possibly not; but I know the nature of mothers.'

'Beatrice is perfect as a mother,' sighed Miss Ambient quite tremendously and with her fingers interlaced on her embroidered knees.

'I shall go up and see my boy,' her brother went on. 'Do you suppose he's asleep?'

'Beatrice won't let you see him, dear' – as to which our young lady looked at me, though addressing our companion.

'Do you call that being perfect as a mother?' Ambient asked.

'Yes, from her point of view.'

'Damn her point of view!' cried the author of 'Beltraffio'. And he left the room; after which we heard him ascend the stairs.

I sat there for some ten minutes with Miss Ambient, and

we naturally had some exchange of remarks, which began,
I think, by my asking her what the point of view of her
sister-in-law could be.

'Oh it's so very odd. But we're so very odd altogether.
Don't you find us awfully unlike others of our class? – which
indeed mostly, in England, is awful. We've lived so much
abroad. I adore "abroad". Have you people like us in
America?'

'You're not all alike, you interesting three – or, counting
Dolcino, four – surely, surely; so that I don't think I
understand your question. We've no one like your brother –
I may go so far as that.'

'You've probably more persons like his wife,' Miss Ambient desolately smiled.

'I can tell you that better when you've told me about her
point of view.'

'Oh yes – oh yes. Well,' said my entertainer, 'she doesn't
like his ideas. She doesn't like them for the child. She thinks
them undesirable.'

Being quite fresh from the contemplation of some of
Mark Ambient's *arcana* I was particularly in a position to
appreciate this announcement. But the effect of it was to
make me, after staring a moment, burst into laughter which
I instantly checked when I remembered the indisposed child
above and the possibility of parents nervously or fussily
anxious.

'What has that infant to do with ideas?' I asked. 'Surely
he can't tell one from another. Has he read his father's
novels?'

'He's very precocious and very sensitive, and his mother
thinks she can't begin to guard him too early.' Miss Ambient's head drooped a little to one side and her eyes fixed
themselves on futurity. Then of a sudden came a strange
alteration; her face lighted to an effect more joyless than
any gloom, to that indeed of a conscious insincere grimace,

and she added: 'When one has children what one writes becomes a great responsibility.'

'Children are terrible critics,' I prosaically answered. 'I'm really glad I haven't any.'

'Do you also write then? And in the same style as my brother? And do you like that style? And do people appreciate it in America? I don't write, but I think I feel.' To these and various other enquiries and observations my young lady treated me till we heard her brother's step in the hall again and Mark Ambient reappeared. He was so flushed and grave that I supposed he had seen something symptomatic in the condition of his child. His sister apparently had another idea; she gazed at him from afar – as if he had been a burning ship on the horizon – and simply murmured 'Poor old Mark!'

'I hope you're not anxious,' I as promptly pronounced.

'No, but I'm disappointed. She won't let me in. She has locked the door, and I'm afraid to make a noise.' I dare say there might have been a touch of the ridiculous in such a confession, but I liked my new friend so much that it took nothing for me from his dignity. 'She tells me – from behind the door – that she'll let me know if he's worse.'

'It's very good of her,' said Miss Ambient with a hollow sound.

I had exchanged a glance with Mark in which it's possible he read that my pity for him was untinged with contempt, though I scarce know why he should have cared; and as his sister soon afterwards got up and took her bedroom candlestick he proposed we should go back to his study. We sat there till after midnight; he put himself into his slippers and an old velvet jacket, he lighted an ancient pipe, but he talked considerably less than before. There were longish pauses in our communion, but they only made me feel we had advanced in intimacy. They helped me further to understand my friend's personal situation and to imagine it by no means the happiest possible. When his face was quiet it was vaguely troubled, showing, to my increase of interest – if that was all that was wanted! – that for him too life was the same struggle it had been for so many another man of genius. At last I prepared to leave him, and then, to my ineffable joy, he gave me some of the sheets of his forth-coming book – which, though unfinished, he had indulged in the luxury, so dear to writers of deliberation, of having 'set up', from chapter to chapter, as he advanced. These early pages, the *prémices*,[20] in the language of letters, of that new fruit of his imagination, I should take to my room and look over at my leisure. I was in the act of leaving him when the door of the study noiselessly opened and Mrs Ambient stood before us. She observed us a moment, her candle in her hand, and then said to her husband that as she supposed he hadn't gone to bed she had come down to let him know Dolcino was more quiet and would probably be better in the morning. Mark Ambient made no reply; he simply slipped past her in the doorway, as if for fear she might seize him in his passage, and bounded upstairs to judge for himself of his child's condition. She looked so frankly discomfited that I for a moment believed her about to give him chase. But she resigned herself with a sigh and her eyes turned, ruefully and without a ray, to the lamplit room where various books at which I had been looking were pulled out of their places on the shelves and the fumes of tobacco hung in mid-air. I bade her good-night and then, without intention, by a kind of fatality, a perversity that had already made me address her overmuch on that question of her husband's powers, I alluded to the precious proof-sheets with which Ambient had entrusted me and which I nursed there under my arm. 'They're the opening chapters of his new book,' I said. 'Fancy my satisfaction at being allowed to carry them to my room!'

She turned away, leaving me to take my candlestick from

the table in the hall; but before we separated, thinking it apparently a good occasion to let me know once for all – since I was beginning, it would seem, to be quite 'thick' with my host – that there was no fitness in my appealing to her for sympathy in such a case; before we separated, I say, she remarked to me with her quick fine well-bred inveterate curtness: 'I dare say you attribute to me ideas I haven't got. I don't take that sort of interest in my husband's proof-sheets. I consider his writings most objectionable!'

III

I had an odd colloquy the next morning with Miss Ambient, whom I found strolling in the garden before breakfast. The whole place looked as fresh and trim, amid the twitter of the birds, as if, an hour before, the housemaids had been turned into it with their dust-pans and feather-brushes. I almost hesitated to light a cigarette and was doubly startled when, in the act of doing so, I suddenly saw the sister of my host, who had, at the best, something of the weirdness of an apparition, stand before me. She might have been posing for her photograph. Her sad-coloured robe arranged itself in serpentine folds at her feet; her hands locked themselves listlessly together in front; her chin rested on a cinquecento ruff. The first thing I did after bidding her good-morning was to ask her for news of her little nephew – to express the hope she had heard he was better. She was able to gratify this trust – she spoke as if we might expect to see him during the day. We walked through the shrubberies together and she gave me further light on her brother's household, which offered me an opportunity to repeat to her what his wife had so startled and distressed me with the night before. *Was* it the sorry truth that she thought his productions objectionable?

'She doesn't usually come out with that so soon!' Miss Ambient returned in answer to my breathlessness.

'Poor lady,' I pleaded, 'she saw I'm a fanatic.'

'Yes, she won't like you for that. But you mustn't mind, if the rest of us like you! Beatrice thinks a work of art ought to have a "purpose". But she's a charming woman – don't you think her charming? I find in her quite the grand air.'

'She's very beautiful,' I produced with an effort; while I reflected that though it was apparently true that Mark Ambient was mismated it was also perceptible that his sister was perfidious. She assured me her brother and his wife had no other difference but this one – that she thought his writings immoral and his influence pernicious. It was a fixed idea; she was afraid of these things for the child. I answered that it was in all conscience enough, the trifle of a woman's regarding her husband's mind as a well of corruption, and she seemed much struck with the novelty of my remark. 'But there hasn't been any of the sort of trouble that there so often is among married people,' she said. 'I suppose you can judge for yourself that Beatrice isn't at all – well, whatever they call it when a woman kicks over! And poor Mark doesn't make love to other people either. You might think he would, but I assure you he doesn't. All the same of course, from her point of view, you know, she has a dread of my brother's influence on the child – on the formation of his character, his "ideals", poor little brat, his principles. It's as if it were a subtle poison or a contagion – something that would rub off on his tender sensibility when his father kisses him or holds him on his knee. If she could she'd prevent Mark from even so much as touching him. Every one knows it – visitors see it for themselves; so there's no harm in my telling you. Isn't it excessively odd? It comes from Beatrice's being so religious and so tremendously moral – so *à cheval*[21] on fifty thousand *riguardi*.[22] And then of course we mustn't forget,' my companion added, a little unexpectedly, to this polyglot proposition, 'that some of Mark's ideas are – well, really – rather impossible, don't you know?'

I reflected as we went into the house, where we found Ambient unfolding *The Observer* at the breakfast-table, that none of them were probably quite so 'impossible, don't you know?' as his sister. Mrs Ambient, a little 'the worse', as was mentioned, for her ministrations, during the night to Dolcino, didn't appear at breakfast. Her husband described her however as hoping to go to church. I afterwards learnt that she did go, but nothing naturally was less on the cards than that we should accompany her. It was while the church-bell droned near at hand that the author of 'Beltraffio' led me forth for the ramble he had spoken of in his note. I shall attempt here no record of where we went or of what we saw. We kept to the fields and copses and commons, and breathed the same sweet air as the nibbling donkeys and the browsing sheep, whose woolliness seemed to me, in those early days of acquaintance with English objects, but part of the general texture of the small dense landscape, which looked as if the harvest were gathered by the shears and with all nature bleating and braying for the violence. Everything was full of expression for Mark Ambient's visitor – from the big bandy-legged geese whose whiteness was a 'note' amid all the tones of green as they wandered beside a neat little oval pool, the foreground of a thatched and whitewashed inn, with a grassy approach and a pictorial sign – from these humble wayside animals to the crests of high woods which let a gable or a pinnacle peep here and there and looked even at a distance like trees of good company, conscious of an individual profile. I admired the hedge-rows, I plucked the faint-hued heather, and I was for ever stopping to say how charming I thought the threadlike footpaths across the fields, which wandered in a diagonal of finer grain from one smooth stile to another. Mark

Ambient was abundantly good-natured and was as much struck, dear man, with some of my observations as I was with the literary allusions of the landscape. We sat and smoked on stiles, broaching paradoxes in the decent English air; we took short cuts across a park or two where the bracken was deep and my companion nodded to the old woman at the gate; we skirted rank coverts which rustled here and there as we passed, and we stretched ourselves at last on a heathery hillside where if the sun wasn't too hot neither was the earth too cold, and where the country lay beneath us in a rich blue mist. Of course I had already told him what I thought of his new novel, having the previous night read every word of the opening chapters before I went to bed.

'I'm not without hope of being able to make it decent enough,' he said as I went back to the subject while we turned up our heels to the sky. 'At least the people who dislike my stuff – and there are plenty of them, I believe – will dislike this thing (if it does turn out well) most.' This was the first time I had heard him allude to the people who couldn't read him – a class so generally conceived to sit heavy on the consciousness of the man of letters. A being organised for literature as Mark Ambient was must certainly have had the normal proportion of sensitiveness, of irritability; the artistic *ego*, capable in some cases of such monstrous development, must have been in his composition sufficiently erect and active. I won't therefore go so far as to say that he never thought of his detractors or that he had any illusions with regard to the number of his admirers – he could never so far have deceived himself as to believe he was popular, but I at least then judged (and had occasion to be sure later on) that stupidity ruffled him visibly but little, that he had an air of thinking it quite natural he should leave many simple folk, tasting of him, as simple as ever he found them, and that he very seldom talked about the newspapers, which, by the way, were always even abnormally vulgar about him. Of course he may have thought them over – the newspapers – night and day; the only point I make is that he didn't show it; while at the same time he didn't strike one as a man actively on his guard. I may add that, touching his hope of making the work on which he was then engaged the best of his books, it was only partly carried out. That place belongs incontestably to 'Beltraffio', in spite of the beauty of certain parts of its successor. I quite believe, however, that he had at the moment of which I speak no sense of having declined; he was in love with his idea, which was indeed magnificent, and though for him, as I suppose for every sane artist, the act of execution had in it as much torment as joy, he saw his result grow like the crescent of the young moon and promise to fill the disk. 'I want to be truer than I've ever been,' he said, settling himself on his back with his hands clasped behind his head; 'I want to give the impression of life itself. No, you may say what you will, I've always arranged things too much, always smoothed them down and rounded them off and tucked them in – done everything to them that life doesn't do. I've been a slave to the old superstitions.'

'You a slave, my dear Mark Ambient? You've the freest imagination of our day!'

'All the more shame to me to have done some of the things I have! The reconciliation of the two women in "Natalina", for instance, which could never really have taken place. That sort of thing's ignoble – I blush when I think of it! This new affair must be a golden vessel, filled with the purest distillation of the actual; and oh how it worries me, the shaping of the vase, the hammering of the metal! I have to hammer it so fine, so smooth; I don't do more than an inch or two a day. And all the while I have to be so careful not to let a drop of the liquor escape! When I see the kind of things Life herself, the brazen hussy, does, I despair of ever catching her peculiar trick. She has an impudence, Life! If one risked a fiftieth part of the effects she risks! It takes ever so long to believe it. You don't know yet, my dear youth. It isn't till one has been watching her some forty years that one finds out half of what she's up to! Therefore one's earlier things must inevitably contain a mass of rot. And with what one sees, on one side, with its tongue in its cheek, defying one to be real enough, and on the other the *bonnes gens*[23] rolling up their eyes at one's cynicism, the situation has elements of the ludicrous which the poor reproducer himself is doubtless in a position to appreciate better than any one else. Of course one mustn't worry about the *bonnes gens*,' Mark Ambient went on while my thoughts reverted to his ladylike wife as interpreted by his remarkable sister.

'To sink your shaft deep and polish the plate through which people look into it – that's what your work consists of,' I remember ingeniously observing.

'Ah polishing one's plate – that's the torment of execution!' he exclaimed, jerking himself up and sitting forward. 'The effort to arrive at a surface, if you think anything of that decent sort necessary – some people don't, happily for them! My dear fellow, if you could see the surface I dream of as compared with the one with which I've to content myself. Life's really too short for art – one hasn't time to make one's shell ideally hard. Firm and bright, firm and bright is very well to say – the devilish thing has a way sometimes of being bright, and even of being hard, as mere tough frozen pudding is hard, without being firm. When I rap it with my knuckles it doesn't give the right sound. There are horrible sandy stretches where I've taken the wrong turn because I couldn't for the life of me find the right. If you knew what a dunce I am sometimes! Such things figure to me now base pimples and ulcers on the brow of beauty!'

'They're very bad, very bad,' I said as gravely as I could. 'Very bad? They're the highest social offence I know; it ought – it absolutely ought; I'm quite serious – to be capital. If I knew I should be publicly thrashed else I'd manage to find the true word. The people who can't – some of them don't so much as know it when they see it – would shut their inkstands, and we shouldn't be deluged by this flood of rubbish!'

I shall not attempt to repeat everything that passed between us, nor to explain just how it was that, every moment I spent in his company, Mark Ambient revealed to me more and more the consistency of his creative spirit, the spirit in him that felt all life as plastic material. I could but envy him the force of that passion, and it was at any rate through the receipt of this impression that by the time we returned I had gained the sense of intimacy with him that I have noted. Before we got up for the homeward stretch he alluded to his wife's having once – or perhaps more than once – asked him whether he should like Dolcino to read 'Beltraffio'. He must have been unaware at the moment of all that this conveyed to me – as well doubtless of my extreme curiosity to hear what he had replied. He had said how much he hoped Dolcino would read *all* his works – when he was twenty; he should like him to know what his father had done. Before twenty it would be useless; he wouldn't understand them.

'And meanwhile do you propose to hide them – to lock them up in a drawer?' Mrs Ambient had proceeded.

'Oh no – we must simply tell him they're not intended for small boys. If you bring him up properly after that he won't touch them.'

To this Mrs Ambient had made answer that it might be very awkward when he was about fifteen, say; and I asked her husband if it were his opinion in general that young people shouldn't read novels.

'Good ones – certainly not!' said my companion. I suppose
I had had other views, for I remember saying that for myself
I wasn't sure it was bad for them if the novels were 'good'
to the right intensity of goodness. 'Bad for *them*, I don't say
so much!' my companion returned. 'But very bad, I'm afraid,
for the poor dear old novel itself.' That oblique accidental
allusion to his wife's attitude was followed by a greater
breadth of reference as we walked home. 'The difference
between us is simply the opposition between two distinct
ways of looking at the world, which have never succeeded
in getting on together, or in making any kind of common
household, since the beginning of time. They've borne all
sorts of names, and my wife would tell you it's the difference
between Christian and Pagan. I may be a pagan, but I don't
like the name; it sounds sectarian. She thinks me at any rate
no better than an ancient Greek. It's the difference between
making the most of life and making the least, so that you'll
get another better one in some other time and place. Will it
be a sin to make the most of that one too, I wonder; and
shall we have to be bribed off in the future state as well as
in the present? Perhaps I care too much for beauty – I don't
know, I doubt if a poor devil *can*; I delight in it, I adore it,
I think of it continually, I try to produce it, to reproduce it.
My wife holds that we shouldn't cultivate or enjoy it without
extraordinary precautions and reserves. She's always afraid
of it, always on her guard. I don't know what it can
ever have done to her, what grudge it owes her or what
resentment rides. And she's so pretty too herself! Don't you
think she's lovely? She was at any rate when we married.
At that time I wasn't aware of that difference I speak
of – I thought it all came to the same thing: in the end,
as they say. Well, perhaps it will in the end. I don't know
what the end will be. Moreover I care for seeing things
as they are; that's the way I try to show them in any professed picture. But you mustn't talk to Mrs Ambient about

things as they are. She has a mortal dread of things as they are.'

'She's afraid of them for Dolcino,' I said: surprised a moment afterwards at being in a position – thanks to Miss Ambient – to be so explanatory; and surprised even now that Mark shouldn't have shown visibly that he wondered what the deuce I knew about it. But he didn't; he simply declared with a tenderness that touched me: 'Ah nothing shall ever hurt *him*!'

He told me more about his wife before we arrived at the gate of home, and if he be judged to have aired overmuch his grievance I'm afraid I must admit that he had some of the foibles as well as the gifts of the artistic temperament; adding, however, instantly that hitherto, to the best of my belief, he had rarely let this particular cat out of the bag. 'She thinks me immoral – that's the long and short of it,' he said as we paused outside a moment and his hand rested on one of the bars of his gate; while his conscious expressive perceptive eyes – the eyes of a foreigner, I had begun to account them, much more than of the usual Englishman – viewing me now evidently as quite a familiar friend, took part in the declaration. 'It's very strange when one thinks it all over, and there's a grand comicality in it that I should like to bring out. She's a very nice woman, extraordinarily well-behaved, upright and clever and with a tremendous lot of good sense about a good many matters. Yet her conception of a novel – she has explained it to me once or twice, and she doesn't do it badly as exposition – is a thing so false that it makes me blush. It's a thing so hollow, so dishonest, so lying, in which life is so blinked and blinded, so dodged and disfigured, that it makes my ears burn. It's two different ways of looking at the whole affair,' he repeated, pushing open the gate. 'And they're irreconcileable!' he added with a sigh. We went forward to the house, but on the walk, halfway to the door, he stopped and said

to me: 'If you're going into this kind of thing there's a
fact you should know beforehand; it may save you some
disappointment. There's a hatred of art, there's a hatred of
literature – I mean of the genuine kind. Oh the shams –
those they'll swallow by the bucket!' I looked up at the
charming house, with its genial colour and crookedness,
and I answered with a smile that those evil passions might
exist, but that I should never have expected to find them
there. 'Ah it doesn't matter after all,' he a bit nervously
laughed; which I was glad to hear, for I was reproaching
myself with having worked him up.

If I had it soon passed off, for at luncheon he was
delightful; strangely delightful considering that the difference between himself and his wife was, as he had said,
irreconcileable. He had the art, by his manner, by his smile,
by his natural amenity, of reducing the importance of it in
the common concerns of life; and Mrs Ambient, I must add,
lent herself to this transaction with a very good grace. I
watched her at table for further illustrations of that fixed
idea of which Miss Ambient had spoken to me; for in the
light of the united revelations of her sister-in-law and her
husband she had come to seem to me almost a sinister
personage. Yet the signs of a sombre fanaticism were not
more immediately striking in her than before; it was only
after a while that her air of incorruptible conformity, her
tapering monosyllabic correctness, began to affect me as in
themselves a cold thin flame. Certainly, at first, she re-
sembled a woman with as few passions as possible; but if
she had a passion at all it would indeed be that of Philistin-
ism. She might have been (for there are guardian-spirits, I
suppose, of all great principles) the very angel of the pink
of propriety – putting the pink for a principle, though
I'd rather put some dismal cold blue. Mark Ambient,
apparently, ten years before, had simply and quite inevitably
taken her for an angel, without asking himself for what. He

had been right in calling my attention to her beauty. In looking for some explanation of his original surrender to her I saw more than before that she was, physically speaking, a wonderfully cultivated human plant – that he might well have owed her a brief poetic inspiration. It was impossible to be more propped and pencilled, more delicately tinted and petalled.

If I had had it in my heart to think my host a little of a hypocrite for appearing to forget at table everything he had said to me in our walk, I should instantly have cancelled such a judgement on reflecting that the good news his wife was able to give him about their little boy was ground enough for any optimistic reaction. It may have come partly too from a certain compunction at having breathed to me at all harshly on the cool fair lady who sat there – a desire to prove himself not after all so mismated. Dolcino continued to be much better, and it had been promised him he should come downstairs after his dinner. As soon as we had risen from our own meal Mark slipped away, evidently for the purpose of going to his child; and no sooner had I observed this than I became aware his wife had simultaneously vanished. It happened that Miss Ambient and I, both at the same moment, saw the tail of her dress whisk out of a doorway; an incident that led the young lady to smile at me as if I now knew all the secrets of the Ambients. I passed with her into the garden and we sat down on a dear old bench that rested against the west wall of the house. It was a perfect spot for the middle period of a Sunday in June, and its felicity seemed to come partly from an antique sundial which, rising in front of us and forming the centre of a small intricate parterre,[24] measured the moments ever so slowly and made them safe for leisure and talk. The garden bloomed in the suffused afternoon, the tall beeches stood still for an example, and, behind and above us, a rose-tree of many seasons, clinging to the faded grain of the brick, expressed the whole character of the scene in a familiar exquisite smell. It struck me as a place to offer genius every favour and sanction – not to bristle with challenges and checks. Miss Ambient asked me if I had enjoyed my walk with her brother and whether we had talked of many things.

'Well, of most things,' I freely allowed, though I remembered we hadn't talked of Miss Ambient.

'And don't you think some of his theories are very peculiar?'

'Oh I guess I agree with them all.' I was very particular, for Miss Ambient's entertainment, to guess.

'Do you think art's everything?' she put to me in a moment.

'In art, of course I do!'

'And do you think beauty's everything?'

'Everything's a big word, which I think we should use as little as possible. But how can we not want beauty?'

'Ah there you are!' she sighed, though I didn't quite know what she meant by it. 'Of course it's difficult for a woman to judge how far to go,' she went on. 'I adore everything that gives a charm to life. I'm intensely sensitive to form. But sometimes I draw back – don't you see what I mean? – I don't quite see where I shall be landed. I only want to be quiet, after all,' Miss Ambient continued as if she had long been baffled at this modest desire. 'And one must be good, at any rate, must not one?' she pursued with a dubious quaver – an intimation apparently that what I might say one way or the other would settle it for her. It was difficult for me to be very original in reply, and I'm afraid I repaid her confidence with an unblushing platitude. I remember moreover attaching to it an enquiry, equally destitute of freshness and still more wanting perhaps in tact, as to whether she didn't mean to go to church, since that was an obvious way of being good. She made answer that she had performed this duty in the morning, and that for her, of

Sunday afternoons, supreme virtue consisted in answering the week's letters. Then suddenly and without transition she brought out: 'It's quite a mistake about Dolcino's being better. I've seen him and he's not at all right.'

I wondered, and somehow I think I scarcely believed. 'Surely his mother would know, wouldn't she?'

She appeared for a moment to be counting the leaves on one of the great beeches. 'As regards most matters one can easily say what, in a given situation, my sister-in-law will, or would, do. But in the present case there are strange elements at work.'

'Strange elements? Do you mean in the constitution of the child?'

'No, I mean in my sister-in-law's feelings.'

'Elements of affection of course; elements of anxiety,' I concurred. 'But why do you call them strange?'

She repeated my words. 'Elements of affection, elements of anxiety. She's very anxious.'

Miss Ambient put me indescribably ill at ease; she almost scared me, and I wished she would go and write her letters. 'His father will have seen him now,' I said, 'and if he's not satisfied he will send for the doctor.'

'The doctor ought to have been here this morning,' she promptly returned. 'He lives only two miles away.'

I reflected that all this was very possibly but a part of the general tragedy of Miss Ambient's view of things; yet I asked her why she hadn't urged that view on her sister-in-law. She answered me with a smile of extraordinary significance and observed that I must have very little idea of her 'peculiar' relations with Beatrice; but I must do her the justice that she re-enforced this a little by the plea that any distinguishable alarm of Mark's was ground enough for a difference of his wife's. He was always nervous about the child, and as they were predestined by nature to take opposite views, the only thing for the mother was to cultivate a false optimism. In Mark's absence and that of his betrayed fear she would have been less easy. I remembered what he had said to me about their dealings with their son – that between them they'd probably put an end to him; but I didn't repeat this to Miss Ambient: the less so that just then her brother emerged from the house, carrying the boy in his arms. Close behind him moved his wife, grave and pale; the little sick face was turned over Ambient's shoulder and towards the mother. We rose to receive the group, and as they came near us Dolcino twisted himself about. His enchanting eyes showed me a smile of recognition, in which, for the moment, I should have taken a due degree of comfort. Miss Ambient, however, received another impression, and I make haste to say that her quick sensibility, which visibly went out to the child, argues that in spite of her affectations she might have been of some human use. 'It won't do at all – it won't do at all,' she said to me under her breath. 'I shall speak to Mark about the Doctor.'

Her small nephew was rather white, but the main difference I saw in him was that he was even more beautiful than the day before. He had been dressed in his festal garments – a velvet suit and a crimson sash – and he looked like a little invalid prince too young to know condescension and smiling familiarly on his subjects.

'Put him down, Mark, he's not a bit at his ease,' Mrs Ambient said.

'Should you like to stand on your feet, my boy?' his father asked.

He made a motion that quickly responded. 'Oh yes; I'm remarkably well.'

Mark placed him on the ground; he had shining pointed shoes with enormous bows. 'Are you happy now, Mr Ambient?'

'Oh yes, I'm particularly happy,' Dolcino replied. But the words were scarce out of his mouth when his mother caught

him up and, in a moment, holding him on her knees, took
her place on the bench where Miss Ambient and I had been
sitting. This young lady said something to her brother, in
consequence of which the two wandered away into the
garden together.

IV

I remained with Mrs Ambient, but as a servant had brought
out a couple of chairs I wasn't obliged to seat myself beside
her. Our conversation failed of ease, and I, for my part, felt
there would be a shade of hypocrisy in my now trying
to make myself agreeable to the partner of my friend's
existence. I didn't dislike her – I rather admired her; but I
was aware that I differed from her inexpressibly. Then I
suspected, what I afterwards definitely knew and have
already intimated, that the poor lady felt small taste for her
husband's so undisguised disciple; and this of course was
not encouraging. She thought me an obtrusive and design-
ing, even perhaps a depraved, young man whom a perverse
Providence had dropped upon their quiet lawn to flatter his
worst tendencies. She did me the honour to say to Miss
Ambient, who repeated the speech, that she didn't know
when she had seen their companion take such a fancy to a
visitor; and she measured apparently my evil influence by
Mark's appreciation of my society. I had a consciousness,
not oppressive but quite sufficient, of all this; though I must
say that if it chilled my flow of small-talk it yet didn't prevent
my thinking the beautiful mother and beautiful child, interlaced there against their background of roses, a picture
such as I doubtless shouldn't soon see again. I was free, I
supposed, to go into the house and write letters, to sit in the
drawing-room, to repair to my own apartment and take a
nap; but the only use I made of my freedom was to linger
still in my chair and say to myself that the light hand of Sir

Joshua[25] might have painted Mark Ambient's wife and son.
I found myself looking perpetually at the latter small mortal,
who looked constantly back at me, and that was enough to
detain me. With these vaguely-amused eyes he smiled, and
I felt it an absolute impossibility to abandon a child with
such an expression. His attention never strayed; it attached
itself to my face as if among all the small incipient things of
his nature throbbed a desire to say something to me. If I
could have taken him on my own knee he perhaps would
have managed to say it; but it would have been a critical
matter to ask his mother to give him up, and it has remained
a constant regret for me that on that strange Sunday afternoon I didn't even for a moment hold Dolcino in my arms.
He had said he felt remarkably well and was especially
happy; but though peace may have been with him as he
pillowed his charming head on his mother's breast, dropping
his little crimson silk legs from her lap, I somehow didn't
think security was. He made no attempt to walk about; he
was content to swing his legs softly and strike one as languid
and angelic.

Mark returned to us with his sister; and Miss Ambient,
repeating her mention of the claims of her correspondence,
passed into the house. Mark came and stood in front of his
wife, looking down at the child, who immediately took hold
of his hand and kept it while he stayed. 'I think Mackintosh
ought to see him,' he said; 'I think I'll walk over and fetch
him.'

'That's Gwendolen's idea, I suppose,' Mrs Ambient replied very sweetly.

'It's not such an out-of-the-way idea when one's child's
ill,' he returned.

'I'm not ill, papa; I'm much better now,' sounded in the
boy's silver pipe.

'Is that the truth, or are you only saying it to be agreeable?
You've a great idea of being agreeable, you know.'

The child seemed to meditate on this distinction, this imputation, for a moment; then his exaggerated eyes, which had wandered, caught my own as I watched him. 'Do *you* think me agreeable?' he enquired with the candour of his age and with a look that made his father turn round to me laughing and ask, without saying it, 'Isn't he adorable?'

'Then why don't you hop about, if you feel so lusty?' Ambient went on while his son swung his hand.

'Because mamma's holding me close!'

'Oh yes; I know how mamma holds you when I come near!' cried Mark with a grimace at his wife.

She turned her charming eyes up to him without deprecation or concession. 'You can go for Mackintosh if you like. I think myself it would be better. You ought to drive.'

'She says that to get me away,' he put to me with a gaiety that I thought a little false; after which he started for the Doctor's.

I remained there with Mrs Ambient, though even our exchange of twaddle had run very thin. The boy's little fixed white face seemed, as before, to plead with me to stay, and after a while it produced still another effect, a very curious one, which I shall find it difficult to express. Of course I expose myself to the charge of an attempt to justify by a strained logic after the fact a step which may have been on my part but the fruit of a native want of discretion; and indeed the traceable consequences of that perversity were too lamentable to leave me any desire to trifle with the question. All I can say is that I acted in perfect good faith and that Dolcino's friendly little gaze gradually kindled the spark of my inspiration. What helped it to glow were the other influences – the silent suggestive garden-nook, the perfect opportunity (if it was not an opportunity for that it was an opportunity for nothing) and the plea I speak of, which issued from the child's eyes and seemed to make him say: 'The mother who bore me and who presses me here to her bosom – sympathetic little organism that I am – has really the kind of sensibility she has been represented to you as lacking, if you only look for it patiently and respectfully. How is it conceivable she shouldn't have it? How is it possible that *I* should have so much of it – for I'm quite full of it, dear strange gentleman – if it weren't also in some degree in her? I'm my great father's child, but I'm also my beautiful mother's, and I'm sorry for the difference between them!' So it shaped itself before me, the vision of reconciling Mrs Ambient with her husband, of putting an end to their ugly difference. The project was absurd of course, for had I not had his word for it – spoken with all the bitterness of experience – that the gulf dividing them was well-nigh bottomless? Nevertheless, a quarter of an hour after Mark had left us, I observed to my hostess that I couldn't get over what she had told me the night before about her thinking her husband's compositions 'objectionable.' I had been so very sorry to hear it, had thought of it constantly and wondered whether it mightn't be possible to make her change her mind. She gave me a great cold stare, meant apparently as an admonition to me to mind my business. I wish I had taken this mute counsel, but I didn't take it. I went on to remark that it seemed an immense pity so much that was interesting should be lost on her.

'Nothing's lost upon me,' she said in a tone that didn't make the contradiction less. 'I know they're very interesting.'

'Don't you like papa's books?' Dolcino asked, addressing his mother but still looking at me. Then he added to me: 'Won't you read them to me, American gentleman?'

'I'd rather tell you some stories of my own,' I said. 'I know some that are awfully good.'

'When will you tell them? Tomorrow?'

'Tomorrow with pleasure, if that suits you.'

His mother took this in silence. Her husband, during our

walk, had asked me to remain another day; my promise to
her son was an implication that I had consented, and it
wasn't possible the news could please her. This ought
doubtless to have made me more careful as to what I said
next, but all I can plead is that it didn't. I soon mentioned
that just after leaving her the evening before, and after
hearing her apply to her husband's writings the epithet
already quoted, I had on going up to my room sat down to
the perusal of those sheets of his new book that he had been
so good as to lend me. I had sat entranced till nearly three
in the morning – I had read them twice over. 'You say you
haven't looked at them. I think it's such a pity you shouldn't.
Do let me beg you to take them up. They're so very
remarkable. I'm sure they'll convert you. They place him
in – really – such a dazzling light. All that's best in him is
there. I've no doubt it's a great liberty, my saying all this;
but pardon me, and *do* read them!'

'Do read them, mamma!' the boy again sweetly shrilled.
'Do read them!'

She bent her head and closed his lips with a kiss. 'Of
course I know he has worked immensely over them,' she
said; after which she made no remark, but attached her eyes
thoughtfully to the ground. The tone of these last words
was such as to leave me no spirit for further pressure, and
after hinting at a fear that her husband mightn't have caught
the Doctor I got up and took a turn about the grounds.
When I came back ten minutes later she was still in her place
watching her boy, who had fallen asleep in her lap. As I
drew near she put her finger to her lips and a short time
afterwards rose, holding him; it being now best, she said,
that she should take him upstairs. I offered to carry him and
opened my arms for the purpose; but she thanked me and
turned away with the child in her embrace, his head on her
shoulder. 'I'm very strong,' was her last word as she passed
into the house, her slim flexible figure bent backward

with the filial weight. So I never laid a longing hand on Dolcino.

I betook myself to Ambient's study, delighted to have a quiet hour to look over his books by myself. The windows were open to the garden; the sunny stillness, the mild light of the English summer, filled the room without quite chasing away the rich dusky tone that was a part of its charm and that abode in the serried shelves where old morocco[26] exhaled the fragrance of curious learning, as well as in the brighter intervals where prints and medals and miniatures were suspended on a surface of faded stuff. The place had both colour and quiet; I thought it a perfect room for work and went so far as to say to myself that, if it were mine to sit and scribble in, there was no knowing but I might learn to write as well as the author of 'Beltraffio'. This distinguished man still didn't reappear, and I rummaged freely among his treasures. At last I took down a book that detained me a while and seated myself in a fine old leather chair by the window to turn it over. I had been occupied in this way for half an hour – a good part of the afternoon had waned – when I became conscious of another presence in the room and, looking up from my quarto, saw that Mrs Ambient, having pushed open the door quite again in the same noiseless way marking or disguising her entrance the night before, had advanced across the threshold. On seeing me she stopped; she had not, I think, expected to find me. But her hesitation was only of a moment; she came straight to her husband's writing-table as if she were looking for something. I got up and asked her if I could help her. She glanced about an instant and then put her hand upon a roll of papers which I recognised, as I had placed it on that spot at the early hour of my descent from my room.

'Is this the new book?' she asked, holding it up.

'The very sheets,' I smiled; 'with precious annotations.'

'I mean to take your advice' – and she tucked the little

bundle under her arm. I congratulated her cordially and
ventured to make of my triumph, as I presumed to call it, a
subject of pleasantry. But she was perfectly grave and
turned away from me, as she had presented herself, without
relaxing her rigour; after which I settled down to my quarto
again with the reflexion that Mrs Ambient was truly an
eccentric. My triumph too suddenly seemed to me rather
vain. A woman who couldn't unbend at a moment exquisitely indicated would never understand Mark Ambient. He
came back to us at last in person, having brought the Doctor
with him. 'He was away from home,' Mark said, 'and I
went after him to where he was supposed to be. He had left
the place, and I followed him to two or three others, which
accounts for my delay.' He was now with Mrs Ambient,
looking at the child, and was to see Mark again before
leaving the house. My host noticed at the end of two minutes
that the proof-sheets of his new book had been removed
from the table; and when I told him, in reply to his question
as to what I knew about them, that Mrs Ambient had carried
them off to read he turned almost pale with surprise. 'What
has suddenly made her so curious?' he cried; and I was
obliged to tell him that I was at the bottom of the mystery.
I had had it on my conscience to assure her that she really
ought to know of what her husband was capable. 'Of what
I'm capable? Elle ne s'en doute que trop!'²⁷ said Ambient
with a laugh; but he took my meddling very good-naturedly
and contented himself with adding that he was really much
afraid she would burn up the sheets, his emendations and
all, of which latter he had no duplicate. The Doctor paid
a long visit in the nursery, and before he came down I retired to my own quarters, where I remained till dinner-
time. On entering the drawing-room at this hour I found
Miss Ambient in possession, as she had been the evening
before.

'I was right about Dolcino,' she said, as soon as she saw

me, with an air of triumph that struck me as the climax of perversity. 'He's really very ill.'

'Very ill! Why when I last saw him, at four o'clock, he was in fairly good form.'

'There has been a change for the worse, very sudden and rapid, and when the Doctor got here he found diphtheritic symptoms. He ought to have been called, as I knew, in the morning, and the child oughtn't to have been brought into the garden.'

'My dear lady, he was very happy there,' I protested with horror.

'He would be very happy anywhere. I've no doubt he's very happy now, with his poor little temperature –!' She dropped her voice as her brother came in, and Mark let us know that as a matter of course Mrs Ambient wouldn't appear. It was true the boy had developed diphtheritic symptoms, but he was quiet for the present and his mother earnestly watching him. She was a perfect nurse, Mark said, and Mackintosh would come back at ten. Our dinner wasn't very gay – with my host worried and absent; and his sister annoyed me by her constant tacit assumption, conveyed in the very way she nibbled her bread and sipped her wine, of having 'told me so.' I had had no disposition to deny anything she might have told me, and I couldn't see that her satisfaction in being justified by the event relieved her little nephew's condition. The truth is that, as the sequel was to prove, Miss Ambient had some of the qualities of the sibyl and had therefore perhaps a right to the sibylline contortions. Her brother was so preoccupied that I felt my presence an indiscretion and was sorry I had promised to remain over the morrow. I put it to Mark that clearly I had best leave them in the morning; to which he replied that, on the contrary, if he was to pass the next days in the fidgets my company would distract his attention. The fidgets had already begun for him, poor fellow; and as we sat in his study with our cigars after dinner he wandered to the door whenever he heard the sound of the Doctor's wheels. Miss Ambient, who shared this apartment with us, gave me at such moments significant glances; she had before rejoining us gone upstairs to ask about the child. His mother and his nurse gave a fair report, but Miss Ambient found his fever high and his symptoms very grave. The Doctor came at ten o'clock, and I went to bed after hearing from Mark that he saw no present cause for alarm. He had made every provision for the night and was to return early in the morning.

I quitted my room as eight struck the next day and when I came downstairs saw, through the open door of the house, Mrs Ambient standing at the front gate of the grounds in colloquy with Mackintosh. She wore a white dressing-gown, but her shining hair was carefully tucked away in its net, and in the morning freshness, after a night of watching, she looked as much 'the type of the lady' as her sister-in-law had described her. Her appearance, I suppose, ought to have reassured me; but I was still nervous and uneasy, so that I shrank from meeting her with the necessary challenge. None the less, however, was I impatient to learn how the new day found him; and as Mrs Ambient hadn't seen me I passed into the grounds by a roundabout way and, stopping at a further gate, hailed the Doctor just as he was driving off. Mrs Ambient had returned to the house before he got into his cart.

'Pardon me, but as a friend of the family I should like very much to hear about the little boy.'

The stout sharp circumspect man looked at me from head to foot and then said: 'I'm sorry to say I haven't seen him.'

'Haven't seen him?'

'Mrs Ambient came down to meet me as I alighted, and told me he was sleeping so soundly, after a restless night, that she didn't wish him disturbed. I assured her I wouldn't disturb him, but she said he was quite safe now and she could look after him herself.'

'Thank you very much. Are you coming back?'

'No sir; I'll be hanged if I come back!' cried the honest practitioner in high resentment. And the horse started as he settled beside his man.

I wandered back into the garden, and five minutes later Miss Ambient came forth from the house to greet me. She explained that breakfast wouldn't be served for some time and that she desired a moment herself with the Doctor. I let her know that the good vexed man had come and departed, and I repeated to her what he had told me about his dismissal. This made Miss Ambient very serious, very serious indeed, and she sank into a bench, with dilated eyes, hugging her elbows with crossed arms. She indulged in many strange signs, she confessed herself immensely distressed, and she finally told me what her own last news of her nephew had been. She had sat up very late – after me, after Mark – and before going to bed had knocked at the door of the child's room, opened to her by the nurse. This good woman had admitted her and she had found him quiet, but flushed and 'unnatural,' with his mother sitting by his bed. 'She held his hand in one of hers,' said Miss Ambient, 'and in the other – what do you think? – the proof-sheets of Mark's new book! She was reading them there intently: did you ever hear of anything so extraordinary? Such a very odd time to be reading an author whom she never could abide!' In her agitation Miss Ambient was guilty of this vulgarism of speech, and I was so impressed by her narrative that only in recalling her words later did I notice the lapse. Mrs Ambient had looked up from her reading with her finger on her lips – I recognised the gesture she had addressed me in the afternoon – and, though the nurse was about to go to rest, had not encouraged her sister-in-law to relieve her of any part of her vigil. But certainly at that time the boy's state was far from reassuring – his poor little breathing so painful; and what change could have taken place in him in those few hours that would justify Beatrice in denying Mackintosh access? This was the moral of Miss Ambient's anecdote, the moral for herself at least. The moral for me, rather, was that it *was* a very singular time for Mrs Ambient to be going into a novelist she had never appreciated and who had simply happened to be recommended to her by a young American she disliked. I thought of her sitting there in the sick-chamber in the still hours of the night and after the nurse had left her, turning and turning those pages of genius and wrestling with their magical influence.

I must be sparing of the minor facts and the later emotions of this sojourn – it lasted but a few hours longer – and devote but three words to my subsequent relations with Ambient. They lasted five years – till his death – and were full of interest, of satisfaction and, I may add, of sadness. The main thing to be said of these years is that I had a secret from him which I guarded to the end. I believe he never suspected it, though of this I'm not absolutely sure. If he had so much as an inkling the line he had taken, the line of absolute negation of the matter to himself, shows an immense effort of the will. I may at last lay bare my secret, giving it for what it is worth; now that the main sufferer has gone, that he has begun to be alluded to as one of the famous early dead and that his wife has ceased to survive him; now too that Miss Ambient, whom I also saw at intervals during the time that followed, has, with her embroideries and her attitudes, her necromantic glances and strange intuitions, retired to a Sisterhood, where, as I am told, she is deeply immured and quite lost to the world.

Mark came in to breakfast after this lady and I had for some time been seated there. He shook hands with me in silence, kissed my companion, opened his letters and newspapers and pretended to drink his coffee. But I took

these movements for mechanical and was little surprised
when he suddenly pushed away everything that was before
him and, with his head in his hands and his elbows on the
table, sat staring strangely at the cloth.

'What's the matter, *caro fratello mio*?'[28] Miss Ambient
quavered, peeping from behind the urn.

He answered nothing, but got up with a certain violence
and strode to the window. We rose to our feet, his relative
and I, by a common impulse, exchanging a glance of some
alarm; and he continued to stare into the garden. 'In heaven's
name what has got possession of Beatrice?' he cried at
last, turning round on us a ravaged face. He looked from
one of us to the other – the appeal was addressed to us
alike.

Miss Ambient gave a shrug. 'My poor Mark, Beatrice is
always – Beatrice!'

'She has locked herself up with the boy – bolted and
barred the door. She refuses to let me come near him!' he
went on.

'She refused to let Mackintosh see him an hour ago!' Miss
Ambient promptly returned.

'Refused to let Mackintosh see him? By heaven I'll smash
in the door!' And Mark brought his fist down upon the
sideboard, which he had now approached, so that all the
breakfast-service rang.

I begged Miss Ambient to go up and try to have speech
of her sister-in-law, and I drew Mark out into the garden.
'You're exceedingly nervous, and Mrs Ambient's probably
right,' I there undertook to plead. 'Women know; women
should be supreme in such a situation. Trust a mother – a
devoted mother, my dear friend!' With such words as these
I tried to soothe and comfort him, and, marvellous to relate,
I succeeded, with the help of many cigarettes, in making
him walk about the garden and talk, or suffer me at least to
do so for near an hour. When about that time had elapsed his

sister reappeared, reaching us rapidly and with a convulsed face while she held her hand to her heart.

'Go for the Doctor, Mark – go for the Doctor this moment!'

'Is he dying? Has she killed him?' my poor friend cried, flinging away his cigarette.

'I don't know what she has done! But she's frightened, and now she wants the Doctor.'

'He told me he'd be hanged if he came back!' I felt myself obliged to mention.

'Precisely – therefore Mark himself must go for him, and not a messenger. You must see him and tell him it's to save your child. The trap has been ordered – it's ready.'

'To save him? I'll save him, please God!' Ambient cried, bounding with his great strides across the lawn.

As soon as he had gone I felt I ought to have volunteered in his place, and I said as much to Miss Ambient; but she checked me by grasping my arm while we heard the wheels of the dog-cart rattle away from the gate. 'He's off – he's off – and now I can think! To get him away – while I think – while I think!'

'While you think of what, Miss Ambient?'

'Of the unspeakable thing that has happened under this roof!'

Her manner was habitually that of such a prophetess of ill that I at first allowed for some great extravagance. But I looked at her hard, and the next thing felt myself turn white. 'Dolcino *is* dying then – he's dead?'

'It's too late to save him. His mother has let him die! I tell you that because you're sympathetic, because you've imagination,' Miss Ambient was good enough to add, interrupting my expression of horror. 'That's why you had the idea of making her read Mark's new book!'

'What has that to do with it? I don't understand you. Your accusation's monstrous.'

'I see it all – I'm not stupid,' she went on, heedless of my emphasis. 'It was the book that finished her – it was that decided her!'

'Decided her? Do you mean she has murdered her child?' I demanded, trembling at my own words.

'She sacrificed him; she determined to do nothing to make him live. Why else did she lock herself in, why else did she turn away the Doctor? The book gave her a horror; she determined to rescue him – to prevent him from ever being touched. He had a crisis at two o'clock in the morning. I know that from the nurse, who had left her then, but whom, for a short time, she called back. The darling got much worse, but she insisted on the nurse's going back to bed, and after that she was alone with him for hours.'

I listened with a dread that stayed my credence, while she stood there with her tearless glare. 'Do you pretend then she has no pity, that she's cruel and insane?'

'She held him in her arms, she pressed him to her breast, not to see him; but she gave him no remedies; she did nothing the Doctor ordered. Everything's there untouched. She has had the honesty not even to throw the drugs away!'

I dropped upon the nearest bench, overcome with my dismay – quite as much at Miss Ambient's horrible insistence and distinctness as at the monstrous meaning of her words. Yet they came amazingly straight, and if they did have a sense I saw myself too woefully figure in it. Had I been then a proximate cause –? 'You're a very strange woman and you say incredible things,' I could only reply.

She had one of her tragic headshakes. 'You think it necessary to protest, but you're really quite ready to believe me. You've received an impression of my sister-in-law – you've guessed of what she's capable.'

I don't feel bound to say what concession on this score I made to Miss Ambient, who went on to relate to me that within the last half-hour Beatrice had had a revulsion, that she was tremendously frightened at what she had done; that her fright itself betrayed her; and that she would now give heaven and earth to save the child. 'Let us hope she will!' I said, looking at my watch and trying to time poor Ambient; whereupon my companion repeated all portentously 'Let us hope so!' When I asked her if she herself could do nothing, and whether she oughtn't to be with her sister-in-law, she replied: 'You had better go and judge! She's like a wounded tigress!'

I never saw Mrs Ambient till six months after this, and therefore can't pretend to have verified the comparison. At the latter period she was again the type of the perfect lady. 'She'll treat him better after this,' I remember her sister-in-law's saying in response to some quick outburst, on my part, of compassion for her brother. Though I had been in the house but thirty-six hours this young lady had treated me with extraordinary confidence, and there was therefore a certain demand I might, as such an intimate, make of her. I extracted from her a pledge that she'd never say to her brother what she had just said to me, that she'd let him form his own theory of his wife's conduct. She agreed with me that there was misery enough in the house without her contributing a new anguish, and that Mrs Ambient's proceedings might be explained, to her husband's mind, by the extravagance of a jealous devotion. Poor Mark came back with the Doctor much sooner than we could have hoped, but we knew five minutes afterwards that it was all too late. His sole, his adored little son was more exquisitely beautiful in death than he had been in life. Mrs Ambient's grief was frantic; she lost her head and said strange things. As for Mark's – but I won't speak of that. *Basta, basta,*[29] as he used to say. Miss Ambient kept her secret – I've already had occasion to say that she had her good points – but it rankled in her conscience like a guilty participation and, I imagine, had something to do with her ultimately retiring from the world. And, apropos of consciences, the reader is now in a position to judge of my compunction for my effort to convert my cold hostess. I ought to mention that the death of her child in some degree converted her. When the new book came out (it was long delayed) she read it over as a whole, and her husband told me that during the few supreme weeks before her death – she failed rapidly after losing her son, sank into a consumption and faded away at Mentone – she even dipped into the black 'Beltraffio'.

THE LESSON OF THE MASTER

He had been told the ladies were at church, but this was corrected by what he saw from the top of the steps – they descended from a great height in two arms, with a circular sweep of the most charming effect – at the threshold of the door which, from the long bright gallery, overlooked the immense lawn. Three gentlemen, on the grass, at a distance, sat under the great trees, while the fourth figure showed a crimson dress that told as a 'bit of colour' amid the fresh rich green. The servant had so far accompanied Paul Overt as to introduce him to this view, after asking him if he wished to go to his room. The young man declined that privilege, conscious of no disrepair from so short and easy a journey and always liking to take at once a general perceptive possession of a new scene. He stood there a little with his eyes on the group and on the admirable picture, the wide grounds of an old country-house near London – that only made it better – on a splendid Sunday in June. 'But that lady, who's *she*?' he said to the servant before the man left him.

'I think she's Mrs St George, sir.'

'Mrs St George the wife of the distinguished –'
Then Paul Overt checked himself, doubting if a footman would know.

'Yes, sir – probably, sir,' said his guide, who appeared to wish to intimate that a person staying at Summersoft would naturally be, if only by alliance, distinguished. His tone,

THE LESSON OF
THE
MASTER

�

however, made poor Overt himself feel for the moment scantly so.

'And the gentlemen?' Overt went on.

'Well, sir, one of them's General Fancourt.'

'Ah yes, I know; thank you.' General Fancourt was distinguished, there was no doubt of that, for something he had done, or perhaps even hadn't done – the young man couldn't remember which – some years before in India. The servant went away, leaving the glass doors open into the gallery, and Paul Overt remained at the head of the wide double staircase, saying to himself that the place was sweet and promised a pleasant visit, while he leaned on the balustrade of fine old ironwork which, like all the other details, was of the same period as the house. It all went together and spoke in one voice – a rich English voice of the early part of the eighteenth century. It might have been church-time on a summer's day in the reign of Queen Anne: the stillness was too perfect to be modern, the nearness counted so as to distance, and there was something so fresh and sound in the originality of the large smooth house, the expanse of beautiful brickwork that showed for pink rather than red and that had been kept clear of messy creepers by the law under which a woman with a rare complexion disdains a veil. When Paul Overt became aware that the people under the trees had noticed him he turned back through the open doors into the great gallery which was the pride of the place. It marched across from end to end and seemed – with its bright colours, its high panelled windows, its faded flowered chintzes, its quickly-recognised portraits and pictures, the blue-and-white china of its cabinets and the attenuated festoons and rosettes of its ceiling – a cheerful upholstered avenue into the other century.

Our friend was slightly nervous; that went with his character as a student of fine prose, went with the artist's general disposition to vibrate; and there was a particular thrill in the idea that Henry St George might be a member of the party. For the young aspirant he had remained a high literary figure, in spite of the lower range of production to which he had fallen after his three first great successes, the comparative absence of quality in his later work. There had been moments when Paul Overt almost shed tears for this; but now that he was near him – he had never met him – he was conscious only of the fine original source and of his own immense debt. After he had taken a turn or two up and down the gallery he came out again and descended the steps. He was but slenderly supplied with a certain social boldness – it was really a weakness in him – so that, conscious of a want of acquaintance with the four persons in the distance, he gave way to motions recommended by their not committing him to a positive approach. There was a fine English awkwardness in this – he felt that too as he sauntered vaguely and obliquely across the lawn, taking an independent line. Fortunately there was an equally fine English directness in the way one of the gentlemen presently rose and made as if to 'stalk' him, though with an air of conciliation and reassurance. To this demonstration Paul Overt instantly responded, even if the gentleman were not his host. He was tall, straight and elderly and had, like the great house itself, a pink smiling face, and into the bargain a white moustache. Our young man met him halfway while he laughed and said: 'Er – Lady Watermouth told us you were coming; she asked me just to look after you.' Paul Overt thanked him, liking him on the spot, and turned round with him to walk towards the others. 'They've all gone to church – all except us,' the stranger continued as they went; 'we're just sitting here – it's so jolly.' Overt pronounced it jolly indeed: it was such a lovely place. He mentioned that he was having the charming impression for the first time.

'Ah you've not been here before?' said his companion.

'It's a nice little place – not much to *do*, you know.' Overt wondered what he wanted to 'do' – he felt that he himself was doing so much. By the time they came to where the others sat he had recognised his initiator for a military man and – such was the turn of Overt's imagination – had found him thus still more sympathetic. He would naturally have a need for action, for deeds at variance with the pacific pastoral scene. He was evidently so good-natured, however, that he accepted the inglorious hour for what it was worth. Paul Overt shared it with him and with his companions for the next twenty minutes; the latter looked at him and he looked at them without knowing much who they were, while the talk went on without much telling him even what it meant. It seemed indeed to mean nothing in particular; it wandered, with casual pointless pauses and short terrestrial flights, amid names of persons and places – names which, for our friend, had no great power of evocation. It was all sociable and slow, as was right and natural of a warm Sunday morning.

His first attention was given to the question, privately considered, of whether one of the two younger men would be Henry St George. He knew many of his distinguished contemporaries by their photographs, but had never, as happened, seen a portrait of the great misguided novelist. One of the gentlemen was unimaginable – he was too young; and the other scarcely looked clever enough, with such mild undiscriminating eyes. If those eyes were St George's the problem presented by the ill-matched parts of his genius would be still more difficult of solution. Besides, the deportment of their proprietor was not, as regards the lady in the red dress, such as could be natural, towards the wife of his bosom, even to a writer accused by several critics of sacrificing too much to manner. Lastly Paul Overt had a vague sense that if the gentleman with the expressionless eyes bore the name that had set his heart beating faster (he also had contradictory conventional whiskers – the young admirer of the celebrity had never in a mental vision seen *his* face in so vulgar a frame) he would have given him a sign of recognition or of friendliness, would have heard of him a little, would know something about 'Ginistrella,' would have an impression of how that fresh fiction had caught the eye of real criticism. Paul Overt had a dread of being grossly proud, but even morbid modesty might view the authorship of 'Ginistrella' as constituting a degree of identity. His soldierly friend became clear enough: he was 'Fancourt,' but was also 'the General'; and he mentioned to the new visitor in the course of a few moments that he had but lately returned from twenty years' service abroad.

'And now you remain in England?' the young man asked.

'Oh yes; I've bought a small house in London.'

'And I hope you like it,' said Overt, looking at Mrs St George.

'Well, a little house in Manchester Square – there's a limit to the enthusiasm *that* inspires.'

'Oh I meant being at home again – being back in Piccadilly.'

'My daughter likes Piccadilly – that's the main thing. She's very fond of art and music and literature and all that kind of thing. She missed it in India and she finds it in London, or she hopes she'll find it. Mr St George has promised to help her – he has been awfully kind to her. She has gone to church – she's fond of that too – but they'll all be back in a quarter of an hour. You must let me introduce you to her – she'll be so glad to know you. I dare say she has read every blest word you've written.'

'I shall be delighted – I haven't written so very many,' Overt pleaded, feeling, and without resentment, that the General at least was vagueness itself about that. But he wondered a little why, expressing this friendly disposition, it didn't occur to the doubtless eminent soldier to pronounce the word that would put him in relation with Mrs St George. If it was a question of introductions Miss Fancourt – apparently as yet unmarried – was far away, while the wife of his illustrious confrère was almost between them. This lady struck Paul Overt as altogether pretty, with a surprising juvenility and a high smartness of aspect, something that – he could scarcely have said why – served for mystification. St George certainly had every right to a charming wife, but he himself would never have imagined the important little woman in the aggressively Parisian dress the partner for life, the *alter ego*, of a man of letters. That partner in general, he knew, that second self, was far from presenting herself in a single type: observation had taught him that she was not inveterately, not necessarily plain. But he had never before seen her look so much as if her prosperity had deeper foundations than an ink-spotted study-table littered with proof-sheets. Mrs St George might have been the wife of a gentleman who 'kept' books rather than wrote them, who carried on great affairs in the City and made better bargains than those that poets mostly make with publishers. With this she hinted at a success more personal – a success peculiarly stamping the age in which society, the world of conversation, is a great drawing-room with the City for its antechamber. Overt numbered her years at first as some thirty, and then ended by believing that she might approach her fiftieth. But she somehow in this case juggled away the excess and the difference – you only saw them in a rare glimpse, like the rabbit in the conjuror's sleeve. She was extraordinarily white, and her every element and item was pretty; her eyes, her ears, her hair, her voice, her hands, her feet – to which her relaxed attitude in her wicker chair gave a great publicity – and the numerous ribbons and trinkets with which she was bedecked. She looked as if she had put on her best clothes to go to church and then had decided they were too good for that and had stayed at home. She

told a story of some length about the shabby way Lady Jane
had treated the Duchess, as well as an anecdote in relation
to a purchase she had made in Paris – on her way back from
Cannes; made for Lady Egbert, who had never refunded the
money. Paul Overt suspected her of a tendency to figure
great people as larger than life, until he noticed the manner
in which she handled Lady Egbert, which was so sharply
mutinous that it reassured him. He felt he should have
understood her better if he might have met her eye; but she
scarcely so much as glanced at him. 'Ah here they come –
all the good ones!' she said at last; and Paul Overt admired
at his distance the return of the churchgoers – several
persons, in couples and threes, advancing in a flicker of sun
and shade at the end of a large green vista formed by the
level grass and the overarching boughs.

'If you mean to imply that *we're* bad, I protest,' said one
of the gentlemen – 'after making one's self agreeable all the
morning!'

'Ah if they've found you agreeable –!' Mrs St George gaily
cried. 'But if we're good the others are better.'

'They must be angels then,' said the amused General.

'Your husband was an angel, the way he went off at your
bidding,' the gentleman who had first spoken declared to
Mrs St George.

'At my bidding?'

'Didn't you make him go to church?'

'I never made him do anything in my life but once – when
I made him burn up a bad book. That's all!' At her 'That's
all!' our young friend broke into an irrepressible laugh; it
lasted only a second, but it drew her eyes to him. His own
met them, though not long enough to help him to understand
her; unless it were a step towards this that he saw on the
instant how the burnt book – the way she alluded to it! –
would have been one of her husband's finest things.

'A bad book?' her interlocutor repeated.

'I didn't like it. He went to church because your daughter went,' she continued to General Fancourt. 'I think it my duty to call your attention to his extraordinary demonstrations to your daughter.'

'Well, if you don't mind them I don't!' the General laughed.

'Il s'attache à ses pas.[1] But I don't wonder – she's so charming.'

'I hope she won't make him burn any books!' Paul Overt ventured to exclaim.

'If she'd make him write a few it would be more to the purpose,' said Mrs St George. 'He has been of a laziness of late – !'

Our young man stared – he was so struck with the lady's phraseology. Her 'Write a few' seemed to him almost as good as her 'That's all.' Didn't she, as the wife of a rare artist, know what it was to produce *one* perfect work of art? How in the world did she think they were turned off? His private conviction was that, admirably as Henry St George wrote, he had written for the last ten years, and especially for the last five, only too much, and there was an instant during which he felt inwardly solicited to make this public. But before he had spoken a diversion was effected by the return of the absentees. They strolled up dispersedly – there were eight or ten of them – and the circle under the trees rearranged itself as they took their place in it. They made it much larger, so that Paul Overt could feel – he was always feeling that sort of thing, as he said to himself – that if the company had already been interesting to watch the interest would now become intense. He shook hands with his hostess, who welcomed him without many words, in the manner of a woman able to trust him to understand and conscious that so pleasant an occasion would in every way speak for itself. She offered him no particular facility for sitting by her, and when they had all subsided again he found himself still next General Fancourt, with an unknown lady on his other flank.

'That's my daughter – that one opposite,' the General said to him without loss of time. Overt saw a tall girl, with magnificent red hair, in a dress of a pretty grey-green tint and of a limp silken texture, a garment that clearly shirked every modern effect. It had therefore somehow the stamp of the latest thing, so that our beholder quickly took her for nothing if not contemporaneous.

'She's very handsome – very handsome,' he repeated while he considered her. There was something noble in her head, and she appeared fresh and strong.

Her good father surveyed her with complacency, remarking soon: 'She looks too hot – that's her walk. But she'll be all right presently. Then I'll make her come over and speak to you.'

'I should be sorry to give you that trouble. If you were to take me over *there* –!' the young man murmured.

'My dear sir, do you suppose I put myself out that way? I don't mean for you, but for Marian,' the General added.

'*I* would put myself out for her soon enough,' Overt replied; after which he went on: 'Will you be so good as to tell me which of those gentlemen is Henry St George?'

'The fellow talking to my girl. By Jove, he *is* making up to her – they're going off for another walk.'

'Ah is that he – really?' Our friend felt a certain surprise, for the personage before him seemed to trouble a vision which had been vague only while not confronted with the reality. As soon as the reality dawned the mental image, retiring with a sigh, became substantial enough to suffer a slight wrong. Overt, who had spent a considerable part of his short life in foreign lands, made now, but not for the first time, the reflexion that whereas in those countries he had almost always recognised the artist and the man of letters by his personal 'type', the mould of his face, the character of his head,[2] the expression of his figure and even the indications of his dress, so in England this identification was as little as possible a matter of course, thanks to the greater conformity, the habit of sinking the profession instead of advertising it, the general diffusion of the air of the gentleman – the gentleman committed to no particular set of ideas. More than once, on returning to his own country, he had said to himself about people met in society: 'One sees them in this place and that, and one even talks with them; but to find out what they *do* one would really have to be a detective.' In respect to several individuals whose work he was the opposite of 'drawn to'– perhaps he was wrong – he found himself adding 'No wonder they conceal it – when it's so bad!' He noted that oftener than in France and in Germany his artist looked like a gentleman – that is like an English one – while, certainly outside a few exceptions, his gentleman didn't look like an artist. St George was not one of the exceptions; that circumstance he definitely apprehended before the great man had turned his back to walk off with Miss Fancourt. He certainly looked better behind than any foreign man of letters – showed for beautifully correct in his tall black hat and his superior frock coat. Somehow, all the same, these very garments – he wouldn't have minded them so much on a weekday – were disconcerting to Paul Overt, who forgot for the moment that the head of the profession was not a bit better dressed than himself. He had caught a glimpse of a regular face, a fresh colour, a brown moustache and a pair of eyes surely never visited by a fine frenzy, and he promised himself to study these denotements on the first occasion. His superficial sense was that their owner might have passed for a lucky stockbroker – a gentleman driving eastward every morning from a sanitary suburb in a smart dog-cart. That carried out the impression already derived from his wife. Paul's glance, after a moment, travelled back to this lady, and he saw how her own had followed her husband as he moved off with Miss Fancourt. Overt permitted himself to wonder a little if she were jealous when another woman took him away. Then he made out that Mrs St George wasn't glaring at the indifferent maiden. Her eyes rested but on her husband, and with unmistakeable serenity. That was the way she wanted him to be – she liked his conventional uniform. Overt longed to hear more about the book she had induced him to destroy.

II

As they all came out from luncheon General Fancourt took hold of him with an 'I say, I want you to know my girl!' as if the idea had just occurred to him and he hadn't spoken of it before. With the other hand he possessed himself all paternally of the young lady. 'You know all about him. I've seen you with his books. She reads everything – everything!' he went on to Paul. The girl smiled at him and then laughed at her father. The General turned away and his daughter spoke – 'Isn't papa delightful?'

'He is indeed, Miss Fancourt.'

'As if I read you because I read "everything"!'

'Oh I don't mean for saying that,' said Paul Overt. 'I liked him from the moment he began to be kind to me. Then he promised me this privilege.'

'It isn't for you he means it – it's for me. If you flatter yourself that he thinks of anything in life but me you'll find you're mistaken. He introduces every one. He thinks me insatiable.'

'You speak just like him,' laughed our youth.

'Ah but sometimes I want to'– and the girl coloured. 'I don't read everything – I read very little. But I *have* read you.'

'Suppose we go into the gallery,' said Paul Overt. She

pleased him greatly, not so much because of this last remark – though that of course was not too disconcerting –
as because, seated opposite to him at luncheon, she had
given him for half an hour the impression of her beautiful
face. Something else had come with it – a sense of generosity,
of an enthusiasm which, unlike many enthusiasms, was not
all manner. That was not spoiled for him by his seeing that
the repast had placed her again in familiar contact with
Henry St George. Sitting next her this celebrity was also
opposite our young man, who had been able to note that he
multiplied the attentions lately brought by his wife to the
General's notice. Paul Overt had gathered as well that this
lady was not in the least discomposed by these fond excesses
and that she gave every sign of an unclouded spirit. She had
Lord Masham on one side of her and on the other the
accomplished Mr Mulliner, editor of the new high-class
lively evening paper which was expected to meet a want felt
in circles increasingly conscious that Conservatism must be
made amusing, and unconvinced when assured by those of
another political colour that it was already amusing enough.
At the end of an hour spent in her company Paul Overt
thought her still prettier than at the first radiation, and if
her profane allusions to her husband's work had not still
rung in his ears he should have liked her – so far as it could
be a question of that in connexion with a woman to whom
he had not yet spoken and to whom probably he should
never speak if it were left to her. Pretty women were a clear
need to this genius, and for the hour it was Miss Fancourt
who supplied the want. If Overt had promised himself a
closer view the occasion was now of the best, and it brought
consequences felt by the young man as important. He saw
more in St George's face, which he liked the better for its
not having told its whole story in the first three minutes.
That story came out as one read, in short instalments – it
was excusable that one's analogies should be somewhat

professional – and the text was a style considerably involved, a language not easy to translate at sight. There were shades of meaning in it and a vague perspective of history which receded as you advanced. Two facts Paul had particularly heeded. The first of these was that he liked the measured mask much better at inscrutable rest than in social agitation; its almost convulsive smile above all displeased him (as much as any impression from that source could), whereas the quiet face had a charm that grew in proportion as stillness settled again. The change to the expression of gaiety excited, he made out, very much the private protest of a person sitting gratefully in the twilight when the lamp is brought in too soon. His second reflexion was that, though generally averse to the flagrant use of ingratiating arts by a man of age 'making up' to a pretty girl, he was not in this case too painfully affected: which seemed to prove either that St George had a light hand or the air of being younger than he was, or else that Miss Fancourt's own manner somehow made everything right.

Overt walked with her into the gallery, and they strolled to the end of it, looking at the pictures, the cabinets, the charming vista, which harmonised with the prospect of the summer afternoon, resembling it by a long brightness, with great divans and old chairs that figured hours of rest. Such a place as that had the added merit of giving those who came into it plenty to talk about. Miss Fancourt sat down with her new acquaintance on a flowered sofa, the cushions of which, very numerous, were tight ancient cubes of many sizes, and presently said: 'I'm so glad to have a chance to thank you.'

'To thank me –?' He had to wonder.

'I liked your book so much. I think it splendid.'

She sat there smiling at him, and he never asked himself which book she meant; for after all he had written three or four. That seemed a vulgar detail, and he wasn't even gratified by the idea of the pleasure she told him – her handsome bright face told him – he had given her. The feeling she appealed to, or at any rate the feeling she excited, was something larger, something that had little to do with any quickened pulsation of his own vanity. It was responsive admiration of the life she embodied, the young purity and richness of which appeared to imply that real success was to resemble *that*, to live, to bloom, to present the perfection of a fine type, not to have hammered out headachy fancies with a bent back at an ink-stained table. While her grey eyes rested on him – there was a wideish space between these, and the division of her rich-coloured hair, so thick that it ventured to be smooth, made a free arch above them – he was almost ashamed of that exercise of the pen which it was her present inclination to commend. He was conscious he should have liked better to please her in some other way. The lines of her face were those of a woman grown, but the child lingered on in her complexion and in the sweetness of her mouth. Above all she was natural – that was indubitable now; more natural than he had supposed at first, perhaps on account of her aesthetic toggery, which was conventionally unconventional, suggesting what he might have called a tortuous spontaneity. He had feared that sort of thing in other cases, and his fears had been justified; for, though he was an artist to the essence, the modern reactionary nymph, with the brambles of the woodland caught in her folds and a look as if the satyrs had toyed with her hair, made him shrink not as a man of starch and patent leather, but as a man potentially himself a poet or even a faun. The girl was really more candid than her costume, and the best proof of it was her supposing her liberal character suited by any uniform. This was a fallacy, since if she was draped as a pessimist he was sure she liked the taste of life. He thanked her for her appreciation – aware at the same time that he didn't appear to thank her enough and that she might think him ungracious. He was afraid she would ask him to explain something he had written, and he always winced at that – perhaps too timidly – for to his own ear the explanation of a work of art sounded fatuous. But he liked her so much as to feel a confidence that in the long run he should be able to show her he wasn't rudely evasive. Moreover she surely wasn't quick to take offence, wasn't irritable; she could be trusted to wait. So when he said to her 'Ah don't talk of anything I've done, don't talk of it *here*; there's another man in the house who's the actuality!'– when he uttered this short sincere protest it was with the sense that she would see in the words neither mock humility nor the impatience of a successful man bored with praise.

'You mean Mr St George – isn't he delightful?'

Paul Overt met her eyes, which had a cool morning-light that would have half-broken his heart if he hadn't been so young. 'Alas I don't know him. I only admire him at a distance.'

'Oh you *must* know him – he wants so to talk to you,' returned Miss Fancourt, who evidently had the habit of saying the things that, by her quick calculation, would give people pleasure. Paul saw how she would always calculate on everything's being simple between others.

'I shouldn't have supposed he knew anything about me,' he professed.

'He does then – everything. And if he didn't I should be able to tell him.'

'To tell him everything?' our friend smiled.

'You talk just like the people in your book,' she answered.

'Then they must all talk alike.'

She thought a moment, not a bit disconcerted. 'Well, it must be so difficult. Mr St George tells me it *is* – terribly. I've tried too – and I find it so. I've tried to write a novel.'

'Mr St George oughtn't to discourage you,' Paul went so far as to say.

'You do much more – when you wear that expression.'

'Well, after all, why try to be an artist?' the young man pursued. 'It's so poor – so poor!'

'I don't know what you mean,' said Miss Fancourt, who looked grave.

'I mean as compared with being a person of action – as living your works.'

'But what's art but an intense life – if it be real?' she asked. 'I think it's the only one – everything else is so clumsy!' Her companion laughed, and she brought out with her charming serenity what next struck her. 'It's so interesting to meet so many celebrated people.'

'So I should think – but surely it isn't new to you.'

'Why I've never seen any one – any one: living always in Asia.'

The way she talked of Asia somehow enchanted him. 'But doesn't that continent swarm with great figures? Haven't you administered provinces in India and had captive rajahs and tributary princes chained to your car?'[3]

It was as if she didn't care even *should* he amuse himself at her cost. 'I was with my father, after I left school to go out there. It was delightful being with him – we're alone together in the world, he and I – but there was none of the society I like best. One never heard of a picture – never of a book, except bad ones.'

'Never of a picture? Why, wasn't all life a picture?'

She looked over the delightful place where they sat. 'Nothing to compare to this. I adore England!' she cried.

It fairly stirred in him the sacred chord. 'Ah of course I don't deny that we must do something with her, poor old dear, yet!'

'She hasn't been touched, really,' said the girl.

'Did Mr St George say that?'

There was a small and, as he felt, harmless spark of irony in his question; which, however, she answered very simply, not noticing the insinuation. 'Yes, he says England hasn't been touched – not considering all there is,' she went on eagerly. 'He's so interesting about our country. To listen to him makes one want so to do something.'

'It would make *me* want to,' said Paul Overt, feeling strongly, on the instant, the suggestion of what she said and that of the emotion with which she said it, and well aware of what an incentive, on St George's lips, such a speech might be.

'Oh you – as if you hadn't! I should like so to hear you talk together,' she added ardently.

'That's very genial of you; but he'd have it all his own way. I'm prostrate before him.'

She had an air of earnestness. 'Do you think then he's so perfect?'

'Far from it. Some of his later books seem to me of a queerness – !'

'Yes, yes – he knows that.'

Paul Overt stared. 'That they seem to me of a queerness – ?'

'Well yes, or at any rate that they're not what they should be. He told me he didn't esteem them. He has told me such wonderful things – he's so interesting.'

There was a certain shock for Paul Overt in the knowledge that the fine genius they were talking of had been reduced to so explicit a confession and had made it, in his misery, to the first comer; for though Miss Fancourt was charming what was she after all but an immature girl encountered at a country-house? Yet precisely this was part of the sentiment he himself had just expressed: he would make way completely for the poor peccable great man not because he didn't read him clear, but altogether because he did. His consideration was half composed of tenderness for superficialities which he was sure their perpetrator judged privately, judged more ferociously than any one, and which represented some tragic intellectual secret. He would have his reasons for his psychology *à fleur de peau*,⁴ and these reasons could only be cruel ones, such as would make him dearer to those who already were fond of him. 'You excite my envy. I have my reserves, I discriminate – but I love him,' Paul said in a moment. 'And seeing him for the first time this way is a great event for me.'

'How momentous – how magnificent!' cried the girl. 'How delicious to bring you together!'

'*Your* doing it – that makes it perfect,' our friend returned.

'He's as eager as you,' she went on. 'But it's so odd you shouldn't have met.'

'It's not really so odd as it strikes you. I've been out of England so much – made repeated absences all these last years.'

She took this in with interest. 'And yet you write of it as well as if you were always here.'

'It's just the being away perhaps. At any rate the best bits, I suspect, are those that were done in dreary places abroad.'

'And why were they dreary?'

'Because they were health-resorts – where my poor mother was dying.'

'Your poor mother?'– she was all sweet wonder.

'We went from place to place to help her to get better. But she never did. To the deadly Riviera, (I hate it!) to the high Alps, to Algiers, and far away – a hideous journey – to Colorado.'

'And she isn't better?' Miss Fancourt went on.

'She died a year ago.'

'Really? – like mine! Only that's years since. Some day you must tell me about your mother,' she added.

He could at first, on this, only gaze at her. 'What right things you say! If you say them to St George I don't wonder he's in bondage.'

It pulled her up for a moment. 'I don't know what you mean. He doesn't make speeches and professions at all – he isn't ridiculous.'

'I'm afraid you consider then that I am.'

'No, I don't' – she spoke it rather shortly. And then she added: 'He understands – understands everything.'

The young man was on the point of saying jocosely: 'And I don't – is that it?' But these words, in time, changed themselves to others slightly less trivial. 'Do you suppose he understands his wife?'

Miss Fancourt made no direct answer, but after a moment's hesitation put it: 'Isn't she charming?'

'Not in the least!'

'Here he comes. Now you must know him,' she went on. A small group of visitors had gathered at the other end of the gallery and had been there overtaken by Henry St George, who strolled in from a neighbouring room. He stood near them a moment, not falling into the talk but taking up an old miniature from a table and vaguely regarding it. At the end of a minute he became aware of Miss Fancourt and her companion in the distance; whereupon, laying down his miniature, he approached them with the same procrastinating air, his hands in his pockets and his eyes turned, right and left, to the pictures. The gallery was so long that this transit took some little time, especially as there was a moment when he stopped to admire the fine Gainsborough. 'He says Mrs St George has been the making of him,' the girl continued in a voice slightly lowered.

'Ah he's often obscure!' Paul laughed.

'Obscure?' she repeated as if she heard it for the first time. Her eyes rested on her other friend, and it wasn't lost upon Paul that they appeared to send out great shafts of softness. 'He's going to speak to us!' she fondly breathed. There was a sort of rapture in her voice, and our friend was startled. 'Bless my soul, does she care for him like *that*? – is she in love with him?' he mentally enquired. 'Didn't I tell you he was eager?' she had meanwhile asked of him.

'It's eagerness dissimulated,' the young man returned as the subject of their observation lingered before his Gainsborough. 'He edges towards us shyly. Does he mean that she saved him by burning that book?'

'That book? what book did she burn?' The girl quickly turned her face to him.

'Hasn't he told you then?'

'Not a word.'

'Then he doesn't tell you everything!' Paul had guessed that she pretty much supposed he did. The great man had now resumed his course and come nearer; in spite of which his more qualified admirer risked a profane observation. 'St George and the Dragon is what the anecdote suggests!'

His companion, however, didn't hear it; she smiled at the dragon's adversary. 'He *is* eager – he is!' she insisted.

'Eager for you – yes.'

But meanwhile she had called out: 'I'm sure you want to know Mr Overt. You'll be great friends, and it will always be delightful to me to remember I was here when you first met and that I had something to do with it.'

There was a freshness of intention in the words that carried them off; nevertheless our young man was sorry for Henry St George, as he was sorry at any time for any person publicly invited to be responsive and delightful. He would have been so touched to believe that a man he deeply admired should care a straw for him that he wouldn't play with such a presumption if it were possibly vain. In a single glance of the eye of the pardonable master he read – having the sort of divination that belonged to his talent – that this personage had ever a store of friendly patience, which was part of his rich outfit, but was versed in no printed page of a rising scribbler. There was even a relief, a simplification, in that: liking him so much already for what he had done, how could one have liked him any more for a perception which must at the best have been vague? Paul Overt got up, trying to show his compassion, but at the same instant he found himself encompassed by St George's happy personal art – a manner of which it was the essence to conjure away false positions. It all took place in a moment. Paul was conscious that he knew him now, conscious of his handshake and of the very quality of his hand; of his face, seen nearer and consequently seen better, of a general fraternising assurance, and in particular of the circumstance that St George didn't dislike him (as yet at least) for being imposed by a charming but too gushing girl, attractive enough without such danglers. No irritation at any rate was reflected in the voice with which he questioned Miss Fancourt as to some project of a walk – a general walk of the company round the park. He had soon said something to Paul about a talk –'We must have a tremendous lot of talk; there are so many things, aren't there?'– but our friend could see this idea wouldn't in the present case take very immediate effect. All the same he was extremely happy, even after the matter of the walk had been settled – the three presently passed back to the other part of the gallery, where it was discussed with several members of the party; even when, after they had all gone out together, he found himself for half an hour conjoined with Mrs St George. Her husband had taken the advance with Miss Fancourt, and this pair were quite out of sight. It was the prettiest of rambles for a summer afternoon – a grassy circuit, of immense extent, skirting the limit of the park within. The park was completely surrounded by its old mottled but perfect red wall, which, all the way on their left, constituted in itself an object of interest. Mrs St George mentioned to him the surprising number of acres thus enclosed, together with numerous other facts relating to the property and family, and the family's other properties: she couldn't too strongly urge on

him the importance of seeing their other houses. She ran
over the names of these and rang the changes on them with
the facility of practice, making them appear an almost
endless list. She had received Paul Overt very amiably on
his breaking ground with her by the mention of his joy in
having just made her husband's acquaintance, and struck
him as so alert and so accommodating a little woman that
he was rather ashamed of his *mot*[5] about her to Miss
Fancourt; though he reflected that a hundred other people,
on a hundred occasions, would have been sure to make it.
He got on with Mrs St George, in short, better than he
expected; but this didn't prevent her suddenly becoming
aware that she was faint with fatigue and must take her way
back to the house by the shortest cut. She professed that she
hadn't the strength of a kitten and was a miserable wreck;
a character he had been too preoccupied to discern in her
while he wondered in what sense she could be held to have
been the making of her husband. He had arrived at a
glimmering of the answer when she announced that she
must leave him, though this perception was of course
provisional. While he was in the very act of placing himself
at her disposal for the return the situation underwent a
change; Lord Masham had suddenly turned up, coming back
to them, overtaking them, emerging from the shrubbery –
Overt could scarcely have said how he appeared – and Mrs
St George had protested that she wanted to be left alone
and not to break up the party. A moment later she was
walking off with Lord Masham. Our friend fell back and
joined Lady Watermouth, to whom he presently mentioned
that Mrs St George had been obliged to renounce the attempt
to go further.

'She oughtn't to have come out at all,' her ladyship rather
grumpily remarked.

'Is she so very much of an invalid?'

'Very bad indeed.' And his hostess added with still greater

austerity: 'She oughtn't really to come to one!' He wondered what was implied by this, and presently gathered that it was not a reflexion on the lady's conduct or her moral nature: it only represented that her strength was not equal to her aspirations.

III

The smoking-room at Summersoft was on the scale of the rest of the place – high light commodious and decorated with such refined old carvings and mouldings that it seemed rather a bower for ladies who should sit at work at fading crewels than a parliament of gentlemen smoking strong cigars. The gentlemen mustered there in considerable force on the Sunday evening, collecting mainly at one end, in front of one of the cool fair fireplaces of white marble, the entablature of which was adorned with a delicate little Italian 'subject.'[6] There was another in the wall that faced it, and, thanks to the mild summer night, a fire in neither; but a nucleus for aggregation was furnished on one side by a table in the chimney-corner laden with bottles, decanters and tall tumblers. Paul Overt was a faithless smoker; he would puff a cigarette for reasons with which tobacco had nothing to do. This was particularly the case on the occasion of which I speak; his motive was the vision of a little direct talk with Henry St George. The 'tremendous' communion of which the great man had held out hopes to him earlier in the day had not yet come off, and this saddened him considerably, for the party was to go its several ways immediately after breakfast on the morrow. He had, how-ever, the disappointment of finding that apparently the author of 'Shadowmere' was not disposed to prolong his vigil. He wasn't among the gentlemen assembled when Paul entered, nor was he one of those who turned up, in bright habiliments, during the next ten minutes. The young man waited a little, wondering if he had only gone to put on something extraordinary; this would account for his delay as well as contribute further to Overt's impression of his tendency to do the approved superficial thing. But he didn't arrive – he must have been putting on something more extraordinary than was probable. Our hero gave him up, feeling a little injured, a little wounded, at this loss of twenty coveted words. He wasn't angry, but he puffed his cigarette sighingly, with the sense of something rare possibly missed. He wandered away with his regret and moved slowly round the room, looking at the old prints on the walls. In this attitude he presently felt a hand on his shoulder and a friendly voice in his ear. 'This is good. I hoped I should find you. I came down on purpose.' St George was there without a change of dress and with a fine face – his graver one – to which our young man all in a flutter responded. He explained that it was only for the Master – the idea of a little talk – that he had sat up, and that, not finding him, he had been on the point of going to bed.

'Well, you know, I don't smoke – my wife doesn't let me,' said St George, looking for a place to sit down. 'It's very good for me – very good for me. Let us take that sofa.'

'Do you mean smoking's good for you?'

'No no – her not letting me. It's a great thing to have a wife who's so sure of all the things one can do without. One might never find them out one's self. She doesn't allow me to touch a cigarette.' They took possession of a sofa at a distance from the group of smokers, and St George went on: 'Have you got one yourself?'

'Do you mean a cigarette?'

'Dear no – a wife!'

'No; and yet I'd give up my cigarette for one.'

'You'd give up a good deal more than that,' St George returned. 'However, you'd get a great deal in return. There's a something to be said for wives,' he added, folding his arms and crossing his outstretched legs. He declined tobacco altogether and sat there without returning fire. His companion stopped smoking, touched by his courtesy; and after all they were out of the fumes, their sofa was in a far-away corner. It would have been a mistake, St George went on, a great mistake for them to have separated without a little chat; 'for I know all about you,' he said, 'I know you're very remarkable. You've written a very distinguished book.'

'And how do you know it?' Paul asked.

'Why, my dear fellow, it's in the air, it's in the papers, it's everywhere.' St George spoke with the immediate familiarity of a confrère – a tone that seemed to his neighbour the very rustle of the laurel.[7] 'You're on all men's lips and, what's better, on all women's. And I've just been reading your book.'

'Just? You hadn't read it this afternoon,' said Overt.

'How do you know that?'

'I think you should know how I know it,' the young man laughed.

'I suppose Miss Fancourt told you.'

'No indeed – she led me rather to suppose you had.'

'Yes – that's much more what she'd do. Doesn't she shed a rosy glow over life? But you didn't believe her?' asked St George.

'No, not when you came to us there.'

'Did I pretend? did I pretend badly?' But without waiting for an answer to this St George went on: 'You ought always to believe such a girl as that – always, always. Some women are meant to be taken with allowances and reserves; but you must take *her* just as she is.'

'I like her very much,' said Paul Overt.

Something in his tone appeared to excite on his companion's part a momentary sense of the absurd; perhaps it was the air of deliberation attending this judgement. St George broke into a laugh to reply. 'It's the best thing you can do with her. She's a rare young lady! In point of fact, however, I confess I hadn't read you this afternoon.'

'Then you see how right I was in this particular case not to believe Miss Fancourt.'

'How right? how can I agree to that when I lost credit by it?'

'Do you wish to pass exactly for what she represents you? Certainly you needn't be afraid,' Paul said.

'Ah, my dear young man, don't talk about passing – for the likes of me! I'm passing away – nothing else than that. She has a better use for her young imagination (isn't it fine?) than in "representing" in any way such a weary wasted used-up animal!' The Master spoke with a sudden sadness that produced a protest on Paul's part; but before the protest could be uttered he went on, reverting to the latter's striking novel: 'I had no idea you were so good – one hears of so many things. But you're surprisingly good.'

'I'm going to be surprisingly better,' Overt made bold to reply.

'I see that, and it's what fetches me. I don't see so much else – as one looks about – that's going to be surprisingly better. They're going to be consistently worse – most of the things. It's so much easier to be worse – heaven knows I've found it so. I'm not in a great glow, you know, about what's breaking out all over the place. But you *must* be better, you really must keep it up. I haven't of course. It's very difficult – that's the devil of the whole thing, keeping it up. But I see you'll be able to. It will be a great disgrace if you don't.'

'It's very interesting to hear you speak of yourself; but I don't know what you mean by your allusions to your having fallen off,' Paul Overt observed with pardonable hypocrisy. He liked his companion so much now that the fact of any decline of talent or of care had ceased for the moment to be vivid to him.

'Don't say that – don't say that,' St George returned gravely, his head resting on the top of the sofa-back and his eyes on the ceiling. 'You know perfectly what I mean. I haven't read twenty pages of your book without seeing that you can't help it.'

'You make me very miserable,' Paul ecstatically breathed.

'I'm glad of that, for it may serve as a kind of warning. Shocking enough it must be, especially to a young fresh mind, full of faith – the spectacle of a man meant for better things sunk at my age in such dishonour.' St George, in the same contemplative attitude, spoke softly but deliberately, and without perceptible emotion. His tone indeed suggested an impersonal lucidity that was practically cruel – cruel to himself – and made his young friend lay an argumentative hand on his arm. But he went on while his eyes seemed to follow the graces of the eighteenth-century ceiling: 'Look at me well, take my lesson to heart – for it *is* a lesson. Let that good come of it at least that you shudder with your pitiful impression, and that this may help to keep you straight in the future. Don't become in your old age what I have in mine – the depressing, the deplorable illustration of the worship of false gods!'

'What do you mean by your old age?' the young man asked.

'It has made me old. But I like your youth.'

Paul answered nothing – they sat for a minute in silence. They heard the others going on about the governmental majority. Then 'What do you mean by false gods?' he enquired.

His companion had no difficulty whatever in saying, 'The idols of the market; money and luxury and "the world"; placing one's children and dressing one's wife; everything that drives one to the short and easy way. Ah the vile things they make one do!'

'But surely one's right to want to place one's children.'

'One has no business to have any children,' St George placidly declared. 'I mean of course if one wants to do anything good.'

'But aren't they an inspiration – an incentive?'

'An incentive to damnation, artistically speaking.'

'You touch on very deep things – things I should like to discuss with you,' Paul said. 'I should like you to tell me volumes about yourself. This is a great feast for *me*!'

'Of course it is, cruel youth. But to show you I'm still not incapable, degraded as I am, of an act of faith, I'll tie my vanity to the stake for you and burn it to ashes. You must come and see me – you must come and see us,' the Master quickly substituted. 'Mrs St George is charming; I don't know whether you've had any opportunity to talk with her. She'll be delighted to see you; she likes great celebrities, whether incipient or predominant. You must come and dine – my wife will write to you. Where are you to be found?'

'This is my little address'– and Overt drew out his pocketbook and extracted a visiting-card. On second thoughts, however, he kept it back, remarking that he wouldn't trouble his friend to take charge of it but would come and see him straightway in London and leave it at his door if he should fail to obtain entrance.

'Ah you'll probably fail; my wife's always out – or when she isn't out is knocked up from having *been* out. You must come and dine – though that won't do much good either, for my wife insists on big dinners.' St George turned it over further, but then went on: 'You must come down and see us in the country, that's the best way; we've plenty of room and it isn't bad.'

'You've a house in the country?' Paul asked enviously.

'Ah not like this! But we have a sort of place we go to – an hour from Euston. That's one of the reasons.'

'One of the reasons?'

'Why my books are so bad.'

'You must tell me all the others!' Paul longingly laughed. His friend made no direct rejoinder to this, but spoke again abruptly. 'Why have I never seen you before?'

The tone of the question was singularly flattering to our hero, who felt it to imply the great man's now perceiving he had for years missed something. 'Partly, I suppose, because there has been no particular reason why you should see me. I haven't lived in the world – in your world. I've spent many years out of England, in different places abroad.'

'Well, please don't do it any more. You must do England – there's such a lot of it.'

'Do you mean I must write about it?'– and Paul struck the note of the listening candour of a child.

'Of course you must. And tremendously well, do you mind? That takes off a little of my esteem for this thing of yours – that it goes on abroad. Hang "abroad"! Stay at home and do things here – do subjects we can measure.'

'I'll do whatever you tell me,' Overt said, deeply attentive. 'But pardon me if I say I don't understand how you've been reading my book,' he added. 'I've had you before me all the afternoon, first in that long walk, then at tea on the lawn, till we went to dress for dinner, and all evening at dinner and in this place.'

St George turned his face about with a smile. 'I gave it but a quarter of an hour.'

'A quarter of an hour's immense, but I don't understand where you put it in. In the drawing-room after dinner you weren't reading – you were talking to Miss Fancourt.'

'It comes to the same thing, because we talked about "Ginistrella". She described it to me – she lent me her copy.'

'Lent it to you?'

'She travels with it.'

'It's incredible,' Paul blushed.

'It's glorious for you, but it also turned out very well for me. When the ladies went off to bed she kindly offered to send the book down to me. Her maid brought it to me in the hall, and I went to my room with it. I hadn't thought of coming here, I do that so little. But I don't sleep early, I always have to read an hour or two. I sat down to your novel on the spot, without undressing, without taking off anything but my coat. I think that's a sign my curiosity had been strongly roused about it. I read a quarter of an hour, as I tell you, and even in a quarter of an hour I was greatly struck.'

'Ah the beginning isn't very good – it's the whole thing!' said Overt, who had listened to this recital with extreme interest. 'And you laid down the book and came after me?' he asked.

'That's the way it moved me. I said to myself "I see it's off his own bat, and he's there, by the way, and the day's over, and I haven't said twenty words to him." It occurred to me that you'd probably be in the smoking-room and that it wouldn't be too late to repair my omission. I wanted to do something civil to you, so I put on my coat and came down. I shall read your book again when I go up.'

Our friend faced round in his place – he was touched as he had scarce ever been by the picture of such a demonstration in his favour. 'You're really the kindest of men. Cela s'est passé comme ça?⁸ – and I've been sitting here with you all this time and never apprehended it and never thanked you!'

'Thank Miss Fancourt – it was she who wound me up. She has made me feel as if I had read your novel.'

'She's an angel from heaven!' Paul declared.

'She is indeed. I've never seen any one like her. Her interest in literature's touching – something quite peculiar to herself;

she takes it all so seriously. She feels the arts and she wants to feel them more. To those who practise them it's almost humiliating – her curiosity, her sympathy, her good faith. How can anything be as fine as she supposes it?'

'She's a rare organisation,' the younger man sighed.

'The richest I've ever seen – an artistic intelligence really of the first order. And lodged in such a form!' St George exclaimed.

'One would like to represent such a girl as that,' Paul continued.

'Ah there it is – there's nothing like life!' said his companion. 'When you're finished, squeezed dry and used up and you think the sack's empty, you're still appealed to, you still get touches and thrills, the idea springs up – out of the lap of the actual – and shows you there's always something to be done. But I shan't do it – she's not for me!'

'How do you mean, not for you?'

'Oh it's all over – she's for you, if you like.'

'Ah much less!' said Paul. 'She's not for a dingy little man of letters; she's for the world, the bright rich world of bribes and rewards. And the world will take hold of her – it will carry her away.'

'It will try – but it's just a case in which there may be a fight. It would be worth fighting, for a man who had it in him, with youth and talent on his side.'

These words rang not a little in Paul Overt's consciousness – they held him briefly silent. 'It's a wonder she has remained as she is; giving herself away so – with so much to give away.'

'Remaining, you mean, so ingenuous – so natural? Oh she doesn't care a straw – she gives away because she overflows. She has her own feelings, her own standards; she doesn't keep remembering that she must be proud. And then she hasn't been here long enough to be spoiled; she has picked up a fashion or two, but only the amusing ones. She's a provincial – a provincial of genius,' St George went on; 'her very blunders are charming, her mistakes are interesting. She has come back from Asia with all sorts of excited curiosities and unappeased appetites. She's first-rate herself and she expends herself on the second-rate. She's life herself and she takes a rare interest in imitations. She mixes all things up, but there are none in regard to which she hasn't perceptions. She sees things in a perspective – as if from the top of the Himalayas – and she enlarges everything she touches. Above all she exaggerates – to herself, I mean. She exaggerates you and me!'

There was nothing in that description to allay the agitation caused in our younger friend by such a sketch of a fine subject. It seemed to him to show the art of St George's admired hand, and he lost himself in gazing at the vision – this hovered there before him – of a woman's figure which should be part of the glory of a novel. But at the end of a moment the thing had turned into smoke, and out of the smoke – the last puff of a big cigar – proceeded the voice of General Fancourt, who had left the others and come and planted himself before the gentlemen on the sofa. 'I suppose that when you fellows get talking you sit up half the night.'

'Half the night? – jamais de la vie! I follow a hygiene' – and St George rose to his feet.

'I see – you're hothouse plants,' laughed the General. 'That's the way you produce your flowers.'

'I produce mine between ten and one every morning – I bloom with a regularity!' St George went on.

'And with a splendour!' added the polite General, while Paul noted how little the author of 'Shadowmere' minded, as he phrased it to himself, when addressed as a celebrated story-teller. The young man had an idea *he* should never get used to that; it would always make him uncomfortable – from the suspicion that people would think they had to – and he would want to prevent it. Evidently his great colleague had toughened and hardened – had made himself a surface. The group of men had finished their cigars and taken up their bedroom candlesticks; but before they all passed out Lord Watermouth invited the pair of guests who had been so absorbed together to 'have' something. It happened that they both declined; upon which General Fancourt said: 'Is that the hygiene? You don't water the flowers?'

'Oh I should drown them!' St George replied; but, leaving the room still at his young friend's side, he added whimsically, for the latter's benefit, in a lower tone: 'My wife doesn't let me.'

'Well I'm glad I'm not one of you fellows!' the General richly concluded.

The nearness of Summersoft to London had this consequence, chilling to a person who had had a vision of sociability in a railway-carriage, that most of the company, after breakfast, drove back to town, entering their own vehicles, which had come out to fetch them, while their servants returned by train with their luggage. Three or four young men, among whom was Paul Overt, also availed themselves of the common convenience; but they stood in the portico of the house and saw the others roll away. Miss Fancourt got into a victoria[10] with her father after she had shaken hands with our hero and said, smiling in the frankest way in the world, 'I *must* see you more. Mrs St George is so nice; she has promised to ask us both to dinner together.' This lady and her husband took their places in a perfectly-appointed brougham – she required a closed carriage – and as our young man waved his hat to them in response to their nods and flourishes he reflected that, taken together, they were an honourable image of success, of the material rewards and the social credit of literature. Such things were not the full measure, but he nevertheless felt a little proud for literature.

IV

Before a week had elapsed he met Miss Fancourt in Bond Street, at a private view of the works of a young artist in 'black-and-white'[11] who had been so good as to invite him to the stuffy scene. The drawings were admirable, but the crowd in the one little room was so dense that he felt himself up to his neck in a sack of wool. A fringe of people at the outer edge endeavoured by curving forward their backs and presenting, below them, a still more convex surface of resistance to the pressure of the mass, to preserve an interval between their noses and the glazed mounts of the pictures; while the central body, in the comparative gloom projected by a wide horizontal screen hung under the skylight and allowing only a margin for the day, remained upright dense and vague, lost in the contemplation of its own ingredients. This contemplation sat especially in the sad eyes of certain female heads, surmounted with hats of strange convolution and plumage, which rose on long necks above the others. One of the heads, Paul perceived, was much the most beautiful of the collection, and his next discovery was that it belonged to Miss Fancourt. Its beauty was enhanced by the glad smile she sent him across surrounding obstructions, a smile that drew him to her as fast as he could make his way. He had seen for himself at Summersoft that the last thing her nature contained was an affectation of indifference; yet even with this circumspection he took a fresh satisfaction in her not having pretended to await his arrival with composure. She smiled as radiantly as if she wished to make him hurry, and as soon as he came within earshot she broke out in her voice of joy: 'He's here – he's here; he's coming back in a moment!'

'Ah your father?' Paul returned as she offered him her hand.

'Oh dear no, this isn't in my poor father's line. I mean

Mr St George. He has just left me to speak to some one –
he's coming back. It's he who brought me – wasn't it
charming?'

'Ah that gives him a pull over me – I couldn't have
"brought" you, could I?'

'If you had been so kind as to propose it – why not you
as well as he?' the girl returned with a face that, expressing
no cheap coquetry, simply affirmed a happy fact.

'Why he's a *père de famille*.[12] They've privileges,' Paul
explained. And then quickly: 'Will you go to see places with
me?' he asked.

'Anything you like,' she smiled. 'I know what you mean,
that girls have to have a lot of people – !' Then she broke
off: 'I don't know; I'm free. I've always been like that – I
can go about with any one. I'm so glad to meet you,' she
added with a sweet distinctness that made those near her
turn round.

'Let me at least repay that speech by taking you out of
this squash,' her friend said. 'Surely people aren't happy
here!'

'No, they're awfully *mornes*,[13] aren't they? But I'm very
happy indeed and I promised Mr St George to remain on
this spot till he comes back. He's going to take me away.
They send him invitations for things of this sort – more than
he wants. It was so kind of him to think of me.'

'They also send me invitations of this kind – more than *I*
want. And if thinking of *you* will do it – !' Paul went on.

'Oh I delight in them – everything that's life, everything
that's London!'

'They don't have private views in Asia, I suppose,' he
laughed. 'But what a pity that for this year, even in this
gorged city, they're pretty well over.'

'Well, next year will do, for I hope you believe we're
going to be friends always. Here he comes!' Miss Fancourt
continued before Paul had time to respond.

He made out St George in the gaps of the crowd, and this perhaps led to his hurrying a little to say: 'I hope that doesn't mean I'm to wait till next year to see you.'

'No, no – aren't we to meet at dinner on the twenty-fifth?' she panted with an eagerness as happy as his own.

'That's almost next year. Is there no means of seeing you before?'

She stared with all her brightness. 'Do you mean you'd *come*?'

'Like a shot, if you'll be so good as to ask me!'

'On Sunday then – this next Sunday?'

'What have I done that you should doubt it?' the young man asked with delight.

Miss Fancourt turned instantly to St George, who had now joined them, and announced triumphantly: 'He's coming on Sunday – this next Sunday!'

'Ah my day – my day too!' said the famous novelist, laughing, to their companion.

'Yes, but not yours only. You shall meet in Manchester Square; you shall talk – you shall be wonderful!'

'We don't meet often enough,' St George allowed, shaking hands with his disciple. 'Too many things – ah too many things! But we must make it up in the country in September. You won't forget you've promised me that?'

'Why he's coming on the twenty-fifth – you'll see him then,' said the girl.

'On the twenty-fifth?' St George asked vaguely.

'We dine with you; I hope you haven't forgotten. He's dining out that day,' she added gaily to Paul.

'Oh bless me, yes – that's charming! And you're coming? My wife didn't tell me,' St George said to him. 'Too many things – too many things!' he repeated.

'Too many people – too many people!' Paul exclaimed, giving ground before the penetration of an elbow.

'You oughtn't to say that. They all read you.'

'Me? I should like to see them! Only two or three at most,' the young man returned.

'Did you ever hear anything like that? He knows, haughtily, how good he is!' St George declared, laughing, to Miss Fancourt. 'They read *me*, but that doesn't make me like them any better. Come away from them, come away!' And he led the way out of the exhibition.

'He's going to take me to the Park,' Miss Fancourt observed to Overt with elation as they passed along the corridor that led to the street.

'Ah does he go there?' Paul asked, taking the fact for a somewhat unexpected illustration of St George's *mœurs*.[14]

'It's a beautiful day – there'll be a great crowd. We're going to look at the people, to look at types,'[15] the girl went on. 'We shall sit under the trees; we shall walk by the Row.'

'I go once a year – on business,' said St George, who had overheard Paul's question.

'Or with a country cousin, didn't you tell me? I'm the country cousin!' she continued over her shoulder to Paul as their friend drew her towards a hansom to which he had signalled. The young man watched them get in; he returned, as he stood there, the friendly wave of the hand with which, ensconced in the vehicle beside her, St George took leave of him. He even lingered to see the vehicle start away and lose itself in the confusion of Bond Street. He followed it with his eyes; it put to him embarrassing things. 'She's not for *me*!' the great novelist had said emphatically at Summersoft; but his manner of conducting himself towards her appeared not quite in harmony with such a conviction. How could he have behaved differently if she *had* been for him? An indefinite envy rose in Paul Overt's heart as he took his way on foot alone; a feeling addressed alike, strangely enough, to each of the occupants of the hansom. How much he should like to rattle about London with such a girl! How much he should like to go and look at 'types' with St George!

The next Sunday at four o'clock he called in Manchester Square, where his secret wish was gratified by his finding Miss Fancourt alone. She was in a large bright friendly occupied room, which was painted red all over, draped with the quaint cheap florid stuffs that are represented as coming from southern and eastern countries, where they are fabled to serve as the counterpanes of the peasantry, and bedecked with pottery of vivid hues, ranged on casual shelves, and with many water-colour drawings from the hand (as the visitor learned) of the young lady herself, commemorating with a brave breadth the sunsets, the mountains, the temples and palaces of India. He sat an hour – more than an hour, two hours – and all the while no one came in. His hostess was so good as to remark, with her liberal humanity, that it was delightful they weren't interrupted: it was so rare in London, especially at that season, that people got a good talk. But luckily now, of a fine Sunday, half the world went out of town, and that made it better for those who didn't go, when these others were in sympathy. It was the defect of London – one of two or three, the very short list of those she recognised in the teeming world-city she adored – that there were too few good chances for talk: you never had time to carry anything far.

'Too many things, too many things!' Paul said, quoting St George's exclamation of a few days before.

'Ah yes, for him there are too many – his life's too complicated.'

'Have you seen it *near*? That's what I should like to do; it might explain some mysteries,' her visitor went on. She asked him what mysteries he meant, and he said: 'Oh peculiarities of his work, inequalities, superficialities. For one who looks at it from the artistic point of view it contains a bottomless ambiguity.'

She became at this, on the spot, all intensity. 'Ah do describe that more – it's so interesting. There are no such suggestive questions. I'm so fond of them. He thinks he's a failure – fancy!' she beautifully wailed.

'That depends on what his ideal may have been. With his gifts it ought to have been high. But till one knows what he really proposed to himself – ! Do *you* know by chance?' the young man broke off.

'Oh he doesn't talk to me about himself. I can't make him. It's too provoking.'

Paul was on the point of asking what then he did talk about, but discretion checked it and he said instead: 'Do you think he's unhappy at home?'

She seemed to wonder. 'At home?'

'I mean in his relations with his wife. He has a mystifying little way of alluding to her.'

'Not to me,' said Marian Fancourt with her clear eyes. 'That wouldn't be right, would it?' she asked gravely.

'Not particularly; so I'm glad he doesn't mention her to you. To praise her might bore you, and he has no business to do anything else. Yet he knows you better than me.'

'Ah but he respects *you*!' the girl cried as with envy.

Her visitor stared a moment, then broke into a laugh. 'Doesn't he respect you?'

'Of course, but not in the same way. He respects what you've done – he told me so the other day.'

Paul drank it in, but retained his faculties. 'When you went to look at types?'

'Yes – we found so many: he has such an observation of them! He talked a great deal about your book. He says it's really important.'

'Important! Ah the grand creature!'– and the author of the work in question groaned for joy.

'He was wonderfully amusing, he was inexpressibly droll, while we walked about. He sees everything; he has so many comparisons and images, and they're always exactly right. C'est d'un trouvé,[16] as they say!'

'Yes, with his gifts, such things as he ought to have done!' Paul sighed.

'And don't you think he *has* done them?'

Ah it was just the point. 'A part of them, and of course even that part's immense. But he might have been one of the greatest. However, let us not make this an hour of qualifications. Even as they stand,' our friend earnestly concluded, 'his writings are a mine of gold.'

To this proposition she ardently responded, and for half an hour the pair talked over the Master's principal productions. She knew them well – she knew them even better than her visitor, who was struck with her critical intelligence and with something large and bold in the movement in her mind. She said things that startled him and that evidently had come to her directly; they weren't picked-up phrases – she placed them too well. St George had been right about her being first-rate, about her not being afraid to gush, not remembering that she must be proud. Suddenly something came back to her, and she said: 'I recollect that he did speak of Mrs St George to me once. He said, apropos of something or other, that she didn't care for perfection.'

'That's a great crime in an artist's wife,' Paul returned.

'Yes, poor thing!' and the girl sighed with a suggestion of many reflections, some of them mitigating. But she presently added: 'Ah perfection, perfection – how one ought to go in for it! I wish *I* could.'

'Every one can in his way,' her companion opined.

'In *his* way, yes – but not in hers. Women are so hampered – so condemned! Yet it's a kind of dishonour if you don't, when you want to *do* something, isn't it?' Miss Fancourt pursued, dropping one train in her quickness to take up another, an accident that was common with her. So these two young persons sat discussing high themes in their eclectic drawing-room, in their London 'season' –

discussing, with extreme seriousness, the high theme of perfection. It must be said in extenuation of this eccentricity that they were interested in the business. Their tone had truth and their emotion beauty; they weren't posturing for each other or for some one else.

The subject was so wide that they found themselves reducing it; the perfection to which for the moment they agreed to confine their speculations was that of the valid, the exemplary work of art. Our young woman's imagination, it appeared, had wandered far in that direction, and her guest had the rare delight of feeling in their conversation a full interchange. This episode will have lived for years in his memory and even in his wonder; it had the quality that fortune distils in a single drop at a time – the quality that lubricates many ensuing frictions. He still, whenever he likes, has a vision of the room, the bright red sociable talkative room with the curtains that, by a stroke of successful audacity, had the note of vivid blue. He remembers where certain things stood, the particular book open on the table and the almost intense odour of the flowers placed, at the left, somewhere behind him. These facts were the fringe, as it were, of a fine special agitation which had its birth in those two hours and of which perhaps the main sign was in its leading him inwardly and repeatedly to breathe 'I had no idea there was any one like this – I had no idea there was any one like this!' Her freedom amazed him and charmed him – it seemed so to simplify the practical question. She was on the footing of an independent personage – a motherless girl who had passed out of her teens and had a position and responsibilities, who wasn't held down to the limitations of a little miss. She came and went with no dragged duenna, she received people alone, and, though she was totally without hardness, the question of protection or patronage had no relevancy in regard to her. She gave such an impression of the clear and the noble combined with the easy and the natural that in spite of her eminent modern situation she suggested no sort of sisterhood with the 'fast' girl. Modern she was indeed, and made Paul Overt, who loved old colour, the golden glaze of time, think with some alarm of the muddled palette of the future. He couldn't get used to her interest in the arts he cared for; it seemed too good to be real – it was so unlikely an adventure to tumble into such a well of sympathy. One might stray into the desert easily – that was on the cards and that was the law of life; but it was too rare an accident to stumble on a crystal well. Yet if her aspirations seemed at one moment too extravagant to be real they struck him at the next as too intelligent to be false. They were both high and lame, and, whims for whims, he preferred them to any he had met in a like relation. It was probable enough she would leave them behind – exchange them for politics or 'smartness' or mere prolific maternity, as was the custom of scribbling daubing educated flattered girls in an age of luxury and a society of leisure. He noted that the water-colours on the walls of the room she sat in had mainly the quality of being naïves, and reflected that naïveté in art is like a zero in a number: its importance depends on the figure it is united with. Meanwhile, however, he had fallen in love with her. Before he went away, at any rate, he said to her: 'I thought St George was coming to see you today, but he doesn't turn up.'

For a moment he supposed she was going to cry 'Comment donc?'[17] Did you come here only to meet him?' But the next he became aware of how little such a speech would have fallen in with any note of flirtation he had as yet perceived in her. She only replied: 'Ah yes, but I don't think he'll come. He recommended me not to expect him.' Then she gaily but all gently added: 'He said it wasn't fair to you. But I think I could manage two.'

'So could I,' Paul Overt returned, stretching the point a

little to meet her. In reality his appreciation of the occasion was so completely an appreciation of the woman before him that another figure in the scene, even so esteemed a one as St George, might for the hour have appealed to him vainly. He left the house wondering what the great man had meant by its not being fair to him; and, still more than that, whether he had actually stayed away from the force of that idea. As he took his course through the Sunday solitude of Manchester Square, swinging his stick and with a good deal of emotion fermenting in his soul, it appeared to him he was living in a world strangely magnanimous. Miss Fancourt had told him it was possible she should be away, and that her father should be, on the following Sunday, but that she had the hope of a visit from him in the other event. She promised to let him know should their absence fail, and then he might act accordingly. After he had passed into one of the streets that open from the Square he stopped, without definite intentions, looking sceptically for a cab. In a moment he saw a hansom roll through the place from the other side and come a part of the way towards him. He was on the point of hailing the driver when he noticed a 'fare' within; then he waited, seeing the man prepare to deposit his passenger by pulling up at one of the houses. The house was apparently the one he himself had just quitted; at least he drew that inference as he recognised Henry St George in the person who stepped out of the hansom. Paul turned off as quickly as if he had been caught in the act of spying. He gave up his cab – he preferred to walk; he would go nowhere else. He was glad St George hadn't renounced his visit altogether – that would have been too absurd. Yes, the world was magnanimous, and even he himself felt so as, on looking at his watch, he noted but six o'clock, so that he could mentally congratulate his successor on having an hour still to sit in Miss Fancourt's drawing-room. He himself might use that hour for another visit, but by the time he reached the Marble Arch the idea of such a course had become incongruous to him. He passed beneath that architectural effort and walked into the Park till he had got upon the spreading grass. Here he continued to walk; he took his way across the elastic turf and came out by the Serpentine. He watched with a friendly eye the diversions of the London people, he bent a glance almost encouraging on the young ladies paddling their sweethearts about the lake and the guardsmen tickling tenderly with their bearskins[18] the artificial flowers in the Sunday hats of their partners. He prolonged his meditative walk; he went into Kensington Gardens, he sat upon the penny chairs, he looked at the little sail-boats launched upon the round pond and was glad he had no engagement to dine. He repaired for this purpose, very late, to his club, where he found himself unable to order a repast and told the waiter to bring whatever there was. He didn't even observe what he was served with, and he spent the evening in the library of the establishment, pretending to read an article in an American magazine. He failed to discover what it was about; it appeared in a dim way to be about Marian Fancourt.

Quite late in the week she wrote to him that she was not to go into the country – it had only just been settled. Her father, she added, would never settle anything, but put it all on her. She felt her responsibility – she had to – and since she was forced this was the way she had decided. She mentioned no reasons, which gave our friend all the clearer field for bold conjecture about them. In Manchester Square on this second Sunday he esteemed his fortune less good, for she had three or four other visitors. But there were three or four compensations; perhaps the greatest of which was that, learning how her father had after all, at the last hour, gone out of town alone, the bold conjecture I just now spoke of found itself becoming a shade more bold. And then her presence was her presence, and the personal red room was there and was full of it, whatever phantoms passed and vanished, emitting incomprehensible sounds. Lastly, he had the resource of staying till every one had come and gone and of believing this grateful to her, though she gave no particular sign. When they were alone together he came to his point. 'But St George did come – last Sunday. I saw him as I looked back.'

'Yes, but it was the last time.'

'The last time?'

'He said he would never come again.'

Paul Overt stared. 'Does he mean he wishes to cease to see you?'

'I don't know what he means,' the girl bravely smiled. 'He won't at any rate see me here.'

'And pray why not?'

'I haven't the least idea,' said Marian Fancourt, whose visitor found her more perversely sublime than ever yet as she professed this clear helplessness.

V

'Oh I say, I want you to stop a little,' Henry St George said to him at eleven o'clock the night he dined with the head of the profession. The company – none of it indeed *of* the profession – had been numerous and was taking its leave; our young man, after bidding good night to his hostess, had put out his hand in farewell to the master of the house. Besides drawing from the latter the protest I have cited this movement provoked a further priceless word about their chance now to have a talk, their going into his room, his having still everything to say. Paul Overt was all delight at this kindness; nevertheless he mentioned in weak jocose qualification the bare fact that he had promised to go to another place which was at a considerable distance.

'Well then you'll break your promise, that's all. You quite

awful humbug!' St George added in a tone that confirmed our young man's ease.

'Certainly I'll break it – but it was a real promise.'

'Do you mean to Miss Fancourt? You're following her?' his friend asked.

He answered by a question. 'Oh is *she* going?'

'Base imposter!' his ironic host went on. 'I've treated you handsomely on the article of that young lady: I won't make another concession. Wait three minutes – I'll be with you.' He gave himself to his departing guests, accompanied the long-trained ladies to the door. It was a hot night, the windows were open, the sound of the quick carriages and of the linkmen's call came into the house. The affair had rather glittered; a sense of festal things was in the heavy air: not only the influence of that particular entertainment, but the suggestion of the wide hurry of pleasure which in London on summer nights fills so many of the happier quarters of the complicated town. Gradually Mrs St George's drawing-room emptied itself; Paul was left alone with his hostess, to whom he explained the motive of his waiting. 'Ah yes, some intellectual, some *professional*, talk,' she leered; 'at this season doesn't one miss it? Poor dear Henry, I'm so glad!' The young man looked out of the window a moment, at the called hansoms that lurched up, at the smooth broughams that rolled away. When he turned round Mrs St George had disappeared; her husband's voice rose to him from below – he was laughing and talking, in the portico, with some lady who awaited her carriage. Paul had solitary possession, for some minutes, of the warm deserted rooms where the covered tinted lamplight was soft, the seats had been pushed about and the odour of flowers lingered. They were large, they were pretty, they contained objects of value; everything in the picture told of a 'good house.' At the end of five minutes a servant came in with a request from the Master that he would join him downstairs; upon which, descending, he followed his conductor through a long passage to an apartment thrown out, in the rear of the habitation, for the special requirements, as he guessed, of a busy man of letters.

St George was in his shirt-sleeves in the middle of a large high room – a room without windows, but with a wide skylight at the top, that of a place of exhibition. It was furnished as a library, and the serried bookshelves rose to the ceiling, a surface of incomparable tone produced by dimly-gilt 'backs' interrupted here and there by the suspension of old prints and drawings. At the end furthest from the door of admission was a tall desk, of great extent, at which the person using it could write only in the erect posture of a clerk in a counting-house; and stretched from the entrance to this structure was a wide plain band of crimson cloth, as straight as a garden-path and almost as long, where, in his mind's eye, Paul at once beheld the Master pace to and fro during vexed hours, that is, of admirable composition. The servant gave him a coat, an old jacket with a hang of experience, from a cupboard in the wall, retiring afterwards with the garment he had taken off. Paul Overt welcomed the coat; it was a coat for talk, it promised confidences – having visibly received so many – and had tragic literary elbows. 'Ah we're practical – we're practical!' St George said as he saw his visitor look the place over. 'Isn't it a good big cage for going round and round? My wife invented it and she locks me up here every morning.'

Our young man breathed – by way of tribute – with a certain oppression. 'You don't miss a window – a place to look out?'

'I did at first awfully; but her calculation was just. It saves time, it has saved me many months in these ten years. Here I stand, under the eye of day – in London of course, very often, it's rather a bleared old eye – walled in to my trade. I can't get away – so the room's a fine lesson in concentration. I've learnt the lesson, I think; look at that big bundle of proof and acknowledge it.' He pointed to a fat roll of papers, on one of the tables, which had not been undone.

'Are you bringing out another –?' Paul asked in a tone the fond deficiencies of which he didn't recognise till his companion burst out laughing, and indeed scarce even then.

'You humbug, you humbug!' – St George appeared to enjoy caressing him, as it were, with that opprobrium. 'Don't I know what you think of them?' he asked, standing there with his hands in his pockets and with a new kind of smile. It was as if he were going to let his young votary see him all now.

'Upon my word in that case you know more than I do!' the latter ventured to respond, revealing a part of the torment of being able neither clearly to esteem nor distinctly to renounce him.

'My dear fellow,' said the more and more interesting Master, 'don't imagine I talk about my books specifically, they're not a decent subject – il ne manquerait plus que ça!'[19] I'm not so bad as you may apprehend. About myself, yes, a little, if you like; though it wasn't for that I brought you down here. I want to ask you something – very much indeed; I value this chance. Therefore sit down. We're practical, but there *is* a sofa, you see – for she does humour my poor bones so far. Like all really great administrators and disciplinarians she knows when wisely to relax.' Paul sank into the corner of a deep leathern couch, but his friend remained standing and explanatory. 'If you don't mind, in this room, this is my habit. From the door to the desk and from the desk to the door. That shakes up my imagination gently; and don't you see what a good thing it is that there's no window for her to fly out of? The eternal standing as I write (I stop at that bureau and put it down, when anything comes, and so we go on) was rather wearisome at first, but we adopted it with an eye to the long run: you're in better order – if your legs don't break down! – and you can keep it up for more years. Oh we're practical – we're practical!' St George repeated, going to the table and taking up all mechanically the bundle of proofs. But, pulling off the wrapper, he had a change of attention that appealed afresh to our hero. He lost himself a moment examining the sheets of his new book, while the younger man's eyes wandered over the room again.

'Lord, what good things I should do if I had such a charming place as this to do them in!' Paul reflected. The outer world, the world of accident and ugliness, was so successfully excluded, and within the rich protecting square, beneath the patronising sky, the dream-figures, the summoned company, could hold their particular revel. It was a fond prevision of Overt's rather than an observation on actual data, for which occasions had been too few, that the Master thus more closely viewed would have the quality, the charming gift, of flashing out, all surprisingly, in personal intercourse and at moments of suspended or perhaps even of diminished expectation. A happy relation with him would be a thing proceeding by jumps, not by traceable stages.

'Do you read them – really?' he asked, laying down the proofs on Paul's enquiring of him how soon the work would be published. And when the young man answered 'Oh yes, always,' he was moved to mirth again by something he caught in his manner of saying that. 'You go to see your grandmother on her birthday – and very proper it is, especially as she won't last for ever. She has lost every faculty and every sense; she neither sees, nor hears, nor speaks; but all customary pieties and kindly habits are respectable. Only you're strong if you *do* read 'em! *I* couldn't, my dear fellow. You *are* strong, I know; and that's just a part of what I wanted to say to you. You're very strong indeed. I've been going into your other things – they've interested me immensely. Some one ought to have told me about them before – some one I could believe. But whom can one believe? You're wonderfully on the right road – it's awfully decent work. Now do you mean to keep it up? – that's what I want to ask you.'

'Do I mean to do others?' Paul asked, looking up from his sofa at his erect inquisitor and feeling partly like a happy little boy when the schoolmaster is gay, and partly like some pilgrim of old who might have consulted a world-famous oracle. St George's own performance had been infirm, but as an adviser he would be infallible.

'Others – others? Ah the number won't matter; one other would do, if we were really a further step – a throb of the same effort. What I mean is have you it in your heart to go in for some sort of decent perfection?'

'Ah decency, ah perfection –!' the young man sincerely sighed. 'I talked of them the other Sunday with Miss Fancourt.'

It produced on the Master's part a laugh of odd acrimony. 'Yes, they'll "talk" of them as much as you like! But they'll do little to help one to them. There's no obligation of course; only you strike me as capable,' he went on. 'You must have thought it all over. I can't believe you're without a plan. That's the sensation you give me, and it's so rare that it really stirs one up – it makes you remarkable. If you haven't a plan, if you *don't* mean to keep it up, surely you're within your rights; it's nobody's business, no one can force you, and not more than two or three people will notice you don't go straight. The others – *all* the rest, every blest soul in England, will think you do – will think you *are* keeping it up: upon my honour they will! I shall be one of the two or three who know better. Now the question is whether you can do it for two or three. Is that the stuff you're made of?'

It locked his guest a minute as in closed throbbing arms. 'I could do it for one, if you were the one.'

'Don't say that; I don't deserve it; it scorches me,' he protested with eyes suddenly grave and glowing. 'The "one" is of course one's self, one's conscience, one's idea, the singleness of one's aim. I think of that pure spirit as a man thinks of a woman he has in some detested hour of his youth loved and forsaken. She haunts him with reproachful eyes, she lives for ever before him. As an artist, you know, I've married for money.' Paul stared and even blushed a little, confounded by this avowal; whereupon his host, observing the expression of his face, dropped a quick laugh and pursued: 'You don't follow my figure. I'm not speaking of my dear wife, who had a small fortune – which, however was not my bribe. I fell in love with her, as many other people have done. I refer to the mercenary muse whom I led to the altar of literature. Don't, my boy, put your nose into *that* yoke. The awful jade will lead you a life!'

Our hero watched him, wondering and deeply touched. 'Haven't you been happy?'

'Happy? It's a kind of hell.'

'There are things I should like to ask you,' Paul said after a pause.

'Ask me anything in all the world. I'd turn myself inside out to save you.'

'To "save" me?' he quavered.

'To make you stick to it – to make you see it through. As I said to you the other night at Summersoft, let my example be vivid to you.'

'Why your books are not so bad as that,' said Paul, fairly laughing and feeling that if ever a fellow had breathed the air of art –!

'So bad as what?'

'Your talent's so great that it's in everything you do, in what's less good as well as in what's best. You've some forty volumes to show for it – forty volumes of wonderful life, of rare observation, of magnificent ability.'

'I'm very clever, of course I know that' – but it was a thing, in fine, this author made nothing of. 'Lord, what rot they'd all be if I hadn't been! I'm a successful charlatan,' he went on – 'I've been able to pass off my system. But do you know what it is? It's *carton-pierre*.'[20]

'*Carton-pierre*?' Paul was struck, and gaped.

'Lincrusta-Walton!'[21]

'Ah don't say such things – you make me bleed!' the younger man protested. 'I see you in a beautiful fortunate home, living in comfort and honour.'

'Do you call it honour?' – his host took him up with an intonation that often comes back to him. 'That's what I want *you* to go in for. I mean the real thing. This is brummagem.'[22]

'Brummagem?' Paul ejaculated while his eyes wandered, by a movement natural at the moment, over the luxurious room.

'Ah they make it so well today – it's wonderfully deceptive!'

Our friend thrilled with the interest and perhaps even more with the pity of it. Yet he wasn't afraid to seem to patronise when he could still so far envy. 'Is it deceptive that I find you living with every appearance of domestic felicity – blest with a devoted, accomplished wife, with children whose acquaintance I haven't yet had the pleasure of making, but who *must* be delightful young people, from what I know of their parents?'

St George smiled as for the candour of his question. 'It's all excellent, my dear fellow – heaven forbid I should deny it. I've made a great deal of money; my wife has known how to take care of it, to use it without wasting it, to put a good bit of it by, to make it fructify. I've got a loaf on the shelf; I've got everything in fact but the great thing.'

'The great thing?' Paul kept echoing.

'The sense of having done the best – the sense which is the real life of the artist and the absence of which is his death, of having drawn from his intellectual instrument the finest music that nature had hidden in it, of having played it as it should be played. He either does that or he doesn't – and if he doesn't he isn't worth speaking of. Therefore, precisely, those who really know *don't* speak of him. He may still hear a great chatter, but what he hears most is the incorruptible silence of Fame. I've squared her, you may say, for my little hour – but what's my little hour? Don't imagine for a moment,' the Master pursued, 'that I'm such a cad as to have brought you down here to abuse or to complain of my wife to you. She's a woman of distinguished qualities, to whom my obligations are immense; so that, if you please, we'll say nothing about her. My boys – my children are all boys – are straight and strong, thank God, and have no poverty of growth about them, no penury of needs. I receive periodically the most satisfactory attestation from Harrow, from Oxford, from Sandhurst[23] – oh we've done the best for them! – of their eminence as living thriving consuming organisms.'

'It must be delightful to feel that the son of one's loins is at Sandhurst,' Paul remarked enthusiastically.

'It is – it's charming. Oh I'm a patriot!'

The young man then could but have the greater tribute of questions to pay. 'Then what did you mean – the other night at Summersoft – by saying that children are a curse?'

'My dear youth, on what basis are we talking?' and St George dropped upon the sofa at a short distance from him. Sitting a little sideways he leaned back against the opposite arm with his hands raised and interlocked behind his head. 'On the supposition that a certain perfection's possible and even desirable – isn't it so? Well, all I say is that one's

children interfere with perfection. One's wife interferes.
Marriage interferes.'

'You think then the artist shouldn't marry?'

'He does so at his peril – he does so at his cost.'

'Not even when his wife's in sympathy with his work?'

'She never is – she can't be! Women haven't a conception
of such things.'

'Surely they on occasion work themselves,' Paul objected.

'Yes, very badly indeed. Oh of course, often, they think
they understand, they think they sympathise. Then it is
they're most dangerous. Their idea is that you shall do a
great lot and get a great lot of money. Their great nobleness
and virtue, their exemplary conscientiousness as British
females, is in keeping you up to that. My wife makes all my
bargains with my publishers for me, and has done so for
twenty years. She does it consummately well – that's why
I'm really pretty well off. Aren't you the father of their
innocent babes, and will you withhold from them their
natural sustenance? You asked me the other night if they're
not an immense incentive. Of course they are – there's no
doubt of that!'

Paul turned it over: it took, from eyes he had never felt
open so wide, so much looking at. 'For myself I've an idea
I need incentives.'

'Ah well then, n'en parlons plus!'[24] his companion handsomely smiled.

'*You* are an incentive, I maintain,' the young man went
on. 'You don't affect me in the way you'd apparently like
to. Your great success is what I see – the pomp of Ennismore
Gardens'

'Success?' – St George's eyes had a cold fine light. 'Do you
call it success to be spoken of as you'd speak of me if
you were sitting here with another artist – a young man
intelligent and sincere like yourself? Do you call it success
to make you blush – as you *would* blush! – if some foreign

critic (some fellow, of course I mean, who should know what he was talking about and should have shown you he did, as foreign critics like to show it) were to say to you: "He's the one, in this country, whom they consider the most perfect, isn't he?" Is it success to be the occasion of a young Englishman's having to stammer as you would have to stammer at such a moment for old England? No, no; success is to have made people wriggle to another tune. Do try it!'

Paul continued all gravely to glow. 'Try what?'

'Try to do some really good work.'

'Oh I want to, heaven knows!'

'Well, you can't do it without sacrifices – don't believe that for a moment,' the Master said. 'I've made none. I've had everything. In other words I've missed everything.'

'You've had the full rich masculine human general life, with all the responsibilities and duties and burdens and sorrows and joys – all the domestic and social initiations and complications. They must be immensely suggestive, immensely amusing,' Paul anxiously submitted.

'Amusing?'

'For a strong man – yes.'

'They've given me subjects without number, if that's what you mean; but they've taken away at the same time the power to use them. I've touched a thousand things, but which one of them have I turned into gold? The artist has to do only with that – he knows nothing of any baser metal. I've led the life of the world, with my wife and my progeny; the clumsy conventional expensive materialised vulgarised brutalised life of London. We've got everything handsome, even a carriage – we're perfect Philistines and prosperous hospitable eminent people. But, my dear fellow, don't try to stultify yourself and pretend you don't know what we *haven't* got. It's bigger than all the rest. Between artists – come!' the Master wound up. 'You know as well as you sit there that you'd put a pistol-ball into your brain if you had written my books!'

It struck his listener that the tremendous talk promised by him at Summersoft had indeed come off, and with a promptitude, a fulness, with which the latter's young imagination had scarcely reckoned. His impression fairly shook him and he throbbed with the excitement of such deep soundings and such strange confidences. He throbbed indeed with the conflict of his feelings – bewilderment and recognition and alarm, enjoyment and protest and assent, all commingled with tenderness (and a kind of shame in the participation) for the sores and bruises exhibited by so fine a creature, and with a sense of the tragic secret nursed under his trappings. The idea of *his*, Paul Overt's, becoming the occasion of such an act of humility made him flush and pant, at the same time that his consciousness was in certain directions too much alive not to swallow – and not intensely to taste – every offered spoonful of the revelation. It had been his odd fortune to blow upon the deep waters, to make them surge and break in waves of strange eloquence. But how couldn't he give out a passionate contradiction of his host's last extravagance, how couldn't he enumerate to him the parts of his work he loved, the splendid things he had found in it, beyond the compass of any other writer of the day? St George listened a while, courteously; then he said, laying his hand on his visitor's: 'That's all very well; and if your idea's to do nothing better there's no reason you shouldn't have as many good things as I – as many human and material appendages, as many sons or daughters, a wife with as many gowns, a house with as many servants, a stable with as many horses, a heart with as many aches.' The Master got up when he had spoken thus – he stood a moment – near the sofa looking down on his agitated pupil. 'Are you possessed of any property?' it occurred to him to ask.

'None to speak of.'

'Oh well then there's no reason why you shouldn't make a goodish income – if you set about it the right way. Study *me* for that – study me well. You may really have horses.'

Paul sat there some minutes without speaking. He looked straight before him – he turned over many things. His friend had wandered away, taking up a parcel of letters from the table where the roll of proofs had lain. 'What was the book Mrs St George made you burn – the one she didn't like?' our young man brought out.

'The book she made me burn – how did you know that?' The Master looked up from his letters quite without the facial convulsion the pupil had feared.

'I heard her speak of it at Summersoft.'

'Ah yes – she's proud of it. I don't know – it was rather good.'

'What was it about?'

'Let me see.' And he seemed to make an effort to remember. 'Oh yes – it was about myself.' Paul gave an irrepressible groan for the disappearance of such a production, and the elder man went on: 'Oh but *you* should write it – *you* should do me.' And he pulled up – from the restless motion that had come upon him; his fine smile a generous glare. 'There's a subject, my boy: no end of stuff in it!'

Again Paul was silent, but it was all tormenting. 'Are there no women who really understand – who can take part in a sacrifice?'

'How can they take part? They themselves are the sacrifice. They're the idol and the altar and the flame.'

'Isn't there even *one* who sees further?' Paul continued.

For a moment St George made no answer; after which, having torn up his letters, he came back to the point all ironic. 'Of course I know the one you mean. But not even Miss Fancourt.'

'I thought you admired her so much.'

'It's impossible to admire her more. Are you in love with her?' St George asked.

'Yes,' Paul Overt presently said.

'Well then give it up.'

Paul stared. 'Give up my "love"?'

'Bless me, no. Your idea.' And then as our hero but still gazed: 'The one you talked with her about. The idea of a decent perfection.'

'She'd help it – she'd help it!' the young man cried.

'For about a year – the first year, yes. After that she'd be as a millstone round its neck.'

Paul frankly wondered. 'Why she has a passion for the real thing, for good work – for everything you and I care for most.'

'"You and I" is charming, my dear fellow!' his friend laughed. 'She has it indeed, but she'd have a still greater passion for her children – and very proper too. She'd insist on everything's being made comfortable, advantageous, propitious for them. That isn't the artist's business.'

'The artist – the artist! Isn't he a man all the same?'

St George had a grand grimace. 'I mostly think not. You know as well as I what he has to do: the concentration, the finish, the independence he must strive for from the moment he begins to wish his work really decent. Ah my young friend, his relation to women, and especially to the one he's most intimately concerned with, is at the mercy of the damning fact that whereas he can in the nature of things have but one standard, they have about fifty. That's what makes them so superior,' St George amusingly added. 'Fancy an artist with a change of standards as you'd have a change of shirts or of dinner-plates. To *do* it – to do it and make it divine – is the only thing he has to think about. "Is it done or not?" is his only question. Not "Is it done as well as a proper solicitude for my dear little family will allow?" He has nothing to do with the relative – he has only to do with the absolute; and a dear little family may represent a dozen relatives.'

'Then you don't allow him the common passions and affections of men?' Paul asked.

'Hasn't he a passion, an affection, which includes all the rest? Besides, let him have all the passions he likes – if he only keeps his independence. He must be able to be poor.'

Paul slowly got up. 'Why then did you advise me to make up to her?'

St George laid a hand on his shoulder. 'Because she'd make a splendid wife! And I hadn't read you then.'

The young man had a strained smile. 'I wish you had left me alone!'

'I didn't know that that wasn't good enough for you,' his host returned.

'What a false position, what a condemnation of the artist, that he's a mere disfranchised monk and can produce his effect only by giving up personal happiness. What an arraignment of art!' Paul went on with a trembling voice.

'Ah you don't imagine by chance that I'm defending art? "Arraignment" – I should think so! Happy the societies in which it hasn't made its appearance, for from the moment it comes they have a consuming ache, they have an incurable corruption, in their breast. Most assuredly is the artist in a false position! But I thought we were taking him for granted. Pardon me,' St George continued: '"Ginistrella" made me!'

Paul stood looking at the floor – one o'clock struck, in the stillness, from a neighbouring church-tower. 'Do you think she'd ever look at me?' he put to his friend at last.

'Miss Fancourt – as a suitor? Why shouldn't I think it? That's why I've tried to favour you – I've had a little chance or two of bettering your opportunity.'

'Forgive my asking you, but do you mean by keeping away yourself?' Paul said with a blush.

'I'm an old idiot – my place isn't there,' St George stated gravely.

'I'm nothing yet, I've no fortune; and there must be so many others,' his companion pursued.

The Master took this considerably in, but made little of it. 'You're a gentleman and a man of genius. I think you might do something.'

'But if I must give that up – the genius?'

'Lots of people, you know, think I've kept mine,' St George wonderfully grinned.

'You've a genius for mystification!' Paul declared, but grasping his hand gratefully in attenuation of this judgement.

'Poor dear boy, I do worry you! But try, try, all the same. I think your chances are good and you'll win a great prize.'

Paul held fast the other's hand a minute; he looked into the strange deep face. 'No, I *am* an artist – I can't help it!'

'Ah show it then!' St George pleadingly broke out. 'Let me see before I die the thing I most want, the thing I yearn for: a life in which the passion – ours – is really intense. If you can be rare don't fail of it! Think what it is – how it counts – how it lives!'

They had moved to the door and he had closed both his hands over his companion's. Here they paused again and our hero breathed deep. 'I want to live!'

'In what sense?'

'In the greatest.'

'Well then stick to it – see it through.'

'With your sympathy – your help?'

'Count on that – you'll be a great figure to me. Count on my highest appreciation, my devotion. You'll give me satisfaction – if that has any weight with you!' After which, as Paul appeared still to waver, his host added: 'Do you remember what you said to me at Summersoft?'

'Something infatuated, no doubt!'

'"I'll do anything in the world you tell me." You said that.'

'And you hold me to it?'

'Ah what am I?' the Master expressively sighed.

'Lord, what things I shall have to do!' Paul almost moaned as he departed.

VI

'It goes on too much abroad – hang abroad!' These or something like them had been the Master's remarkable words in relation to the action of 'Ginistrella'; and yet, though they had made a sharp impression on the author of that work, like almost all spoken words from the same source, he a week after the conversation I have noted left England for a long absence and full of brave intentions. It is not a perversion of the truth to pronounce that encounter the direct cause of his departure. If the oral utterance of the eminent writer had the privilege of moving him deeply it was especially on his turning it over at leisure, hours and days later, that it appeared to yield him its full meaning and exhibit its extreme importance. He spent the summer in Switzerland and, having in September begun a new task, determined not to cross the Alps till he should have made a good start. To this end he returned to a quiet corner he knew well, on the edge of the Lake of Geneva and within sight of the towers of Chillon: a region and a view for which he had an affection that sprang from old associations and was capable of mysterious revivals and refreshments. Here he lingered late, till the snow was on the nearer hills, almost down to the limit to which he could climb when his stint, on the shortening afternoons, was performed. The autumn was fine, the lake was blue and his book took form and direction. These felicities, for the time, embroidered his life, which he suffered to cover him with its mantle. At the end of six weeks he felt he had learnt St George's lesson by heart, had tested and proved its doctrine. Nevertheless he did a very inconsistent thing: before crossing the Alps he wrote to Marian Fancourt. He was aware of the perversity of this act, and it was only as a luxury, an amusement, the reward of a strenuous autumn, that he justified it. She had asked of him no such favour when, shortly before he left London, three days after their dinner in Ennismore Gardens, he went to take leave of her. It was true she had had no ground – he hadn't named his intention of absence. He had kept his counsel for want of due assurance: it was that particular visit that was, the next thing, to settle the matter. He had paid the visit to see how much he really cared for her, and quick departure, without so much as an explicit farewell, was the sequel to this enquiry, the answer to which had created within him a deep yearning. When he wrote her from Clarens he noted that he owed her an explanation (more than three months after!) for not having told her what he was doing.

She replied now briefly but promptly, and gave him a striking piece of news: that of the death, a week before, of Mrs St George. This exemplary woman had succumbed, in the country, to a violent attack of inflammation of the lungs – he would remember that for a long time she had been delicate. Miss Fancourt added that she believed her husband overwhelmed by the blow; he would miss her too terribly – she had been everything in life to him. Paul Overt, on this, immediately wrote to St George. He would from the day of their parting have been glad to remain in communication with him, but had hitherto lacked the right excuse for troubling so busy a man. Their long nocturnal talk came back to him in every detail, but this was no bar to an expression of proper sympathy with the head of the profession, for hadn't that very talk made it clear that the late accomplished lady was the influence that ruled his life?

What catastrophe could be more cruel than the extinction of such an influence? This was to be exactly the tone taken by St George in answering his young friend upwards of a month later. He made no allusion of course to their important discussion. He spoke of his wife as frankly and generously as if he had quite forgotten that occasion, and the feeling of deep bereavement was visible in his words. 'She took everything off my hands – off my mind. She carried on our life with the greatest art, the rarest devotion, and I was free, as few men can have been, to drive my pen, to shut myself up with my trade. This was a rare service – the highest she could have rendered me. Would I could have acknowledged it more fitly!'

A certain bewilderment, for our hero, disengaged itself from these remarks: they struck him as a contradiction, a retraction, strange on the part of a man who hadn't the excuse of witlessness. He had certainly not expected his correspondent to rejoice in the death of his wife, and it was perfectly in order that the rupture of a tie of more than twenty years should have left him sore. But if she had been so clear a blessing what in the name of consistency had the dear man meant by turning *him* upside down that night – by dosing him to that degree, at the most sensitive hour of his life, with the doctrine of renunciation? If Mrs St George was an irreparable loss, then her husband's inspired advice had been a bad joke and renunciation was a mistake. Overt was on the point of rushing back to London to show that, for his part, he was perfectly willing to consider it so, and he went so far as to take the manuscript of the first chapters of his new book out of his table-drawer and insert it into a pocket of his portmanteau. This led to his catching a glimpse of certain pages he hadn't looked at for months, and that accident, in turn, to his being struck with the high promise they revealed – a rare result of such retrospections, which it was his habit to avoid as much as possible: they usually brought home to him that the glow of composition might be a purely subjective and misleading emotion. On this occasion a certain belief in himself disengaged itself whimsically from the serried erasures of his first draft, making him think it best after all to pursue his present trial to the end. If he could write so well under the rigour of privation it might be a mistake to change the conditions before that spell had spent itself. He would go back to London of course, but he would go back only when he should have finished his book. This was the vow he privately made, restoring his manuscript to the table-drawer. It may be added that it took him a long time to finish his book, for the subject was as difficult as it was fine, and he was literally embarrassed by the fulness of his notes. Something within him warned him he must make it supremely good – otherwise he should lack, as regards his private behaviour, a handsome excuse. He had a horror of this deficiency and found himself as firm as need be on the question of the lamp and the file. He crossed the Alps at last and spent the winter, the spring, the ensuing summer, in Italy, where still, at the end of a twelvemonth, his task was unachieved. 'Stick to it – see it through': this general injunction of St George's was good also for the particular case. He applied it to the utmost, with the result that when in its slow order the summer had come round again he felt he had given all that was in him. This time he put his papers into his portmanteau, with the address of his publisher attached, and took his way northward.

He had been absent from London for two years; two years which, seeming to count as more, had made such a difference in his own life – through the production of a novel far stronger, he believed, than 'Ginistrella' – that he turned out into Piccadilly, the morning after his arrival, with a vague expectation of changes, of finding great things had happened. But there were few transformations in Piccadilly – only three or four big red houses where there had been low black ones – and the brightness of the end of June peeped through the rusty railings of the Green Park and glittered in the varnish of the rolling carriages as he had seen it in other, more cursory Junes. It was a greeting he appreciated; it seemed friendly and pointed, added to the exhilaration of his finished book, of his having his own country and the huge oppressive amusing city that suggested everything, that contained everything, under his hand again. 'Stay at home and do things here – do subjects we can measure,' St George had said; and now it struck him he should ask nothing better than to stay at home for ever. Late in the afternoon he took his way to Manchester Square, looking out for a number he hadn't forgotten. Miss Fancourt, however, was not at home, so that he turned rather dejectedly from the door. His movement brought him face to face with a gentleman just approaching it and recognised on another glance as Miss Fancourt's father. Paul saluted this personage, and the General returned the greeting with his customary good manner – a manner so good, however, that you could never tell whether it meant he placed you. The disappointed caller felt the impulse to address him, then, hesitating, became both aware of having no particular remark to make, and convinced that though the old soldier remembered him he remembered him wrong. He therefore went his way without computing the irresistible effect his own evident recognition would have on the General, who never neglected a chance to gossip. Our young man's face was expressive, and observation seldom let it pass. He hadn't taken ten steps before he heard himself called after with a friendly semi-articulate 'Er – I beg your pardon!' He turned round and the General, smiling at him from the porch, said: 'Won't you come in? I won't leave you the advantage of me!' Paul declined to come in, and then felt regret, for Miss Fancourt, so late in the afternoon, might return at any moment. But her father gave him no second chance; he appeared mainly to wish not to have struck him as ungracious. A further look at the visitor had recalled something, enough at least to enable him to say: 'You've come back, you've come back?' Paul was on the point of replying that he had come back the night before, but he suppressed, the next instant, this strong light on the immediacy of his visit and, giving merely a general assent, alluded to the young lady he deplored not having found. He had come late in the hope she would be in. 'I'll tell her – I'll tell her,' said the old man; and then he added quickly, gallantly: 'You'll be giving us something new? It's a long time, isn't it?' Now he remembered him right.

'Rather long. I'm very slow,' Paul explained. 'I met you at Summersoft a long time ago.'

'Oh yes – with Henry St George. I remember very well. Before his poor wife –' General Fancourt paused a moment, smiling a little less. 'I dare say you know.'

'About Mrs St George's death? Certainly – I heard at the time.'

'Oh no, I mean – I mean he's to be married.'

'Ah I've not heard that!' But just as Paul was about to add 'To whom?' the General crossed his intention.

'When did you come back? I know you've been away – by my daughter. She was very sorry. You ought to give her something new.'

'I came back last night,' said our young man, to whom something had occurred which made his speech for the moment a little thick.

'Ah most kind of you to come so soon. Couldn't you turn up at dinner?'

'At dinner?' Paul just mechanically repeated, not liking to ask whom St George was going to marry, but thinking only of that.

'There are several people, I believe. Certainly St George.

Or afterwards if you like better. I believe my daughter expects –' He appeared to notice something in the visitor's raised face (on his steps he stood higher) which led him to interrupt himself, and the interruption gave him a momentary sense of awkwardness, from which he sought a quick issue. 'Perhaps then you haven't heard she's to be married.'

Paul gaped again. 'To be married?'

'To Mr St George – it has just been settled. Odd marriage, isn't it?' Our listener uttered no opinion on this point: he only continued to stare. 'But I dare say it will do – she's so awfully literary!' said the General.

Paul had turned very red. 'Oh, it's a surprise – very interesting, very charming! I'm afraid I can't dine – so many thanks!'

'Well, you must come to the wedding!' cried the General. 'Oh I remember that day at Summersoft. He's a great man, you know.'

'Charming – charming!' Paul stammered for retreat. He shook hands with the General and got off. His face was red and he had the sense of its growing more and more crimson. All the evening at home – he went straight to his rooms and remained there dinnerless – his cheek burned at intervals as if it had been smitten. He didn't understand what had happened to him, what trick had been played him, what treachery practised. 'None, none,' he said to himself. 'I've nothing to do with it. I'm out of it – it's none of my business.' But that bewildered murmur was followed again and again by the incongruous ejaculation: 'Was it a plan – was it a plan?' Sometimes he cried to himself, breathless, 'Have I been duped, sold, swindled?' If at all, he was an absurd, an abject victim. It was as if he hadn't lost her till now. He had renounced her, yes; but that was another affair – that was a closed but not a locked door. Now he seemed to see the door quite slammed in his face. Did he expect her to wait – was she to give him his time like that: two years at a stretch?

He didn't know what he had expected – he only knew what he hadn't. It wasn't this – it wasn't this. Mystification bitterness and wrath rose and boiled in him when he thought of the deference, the devotion, the credulity with which he had listened to St George. The evening wore on and the light was long; but even when it had darkened he remained without a lamp. He had flung himself on the sofa, where he lay through the hours with his eyes either closed or gazing at the gloom, in the attitude of a man teaching himself to bear something, to bear having been made a fool of. He had made it too easy – that idea passed over him like a hot wave. Suddenly, as he heard eleven o'clock strike, he jumped up, remembering what General Fancourt had said about his coming after dinner. He'd go – he'd see her at least; perhaps he should see what it meant. He felt as if some of the elements of a hard sum had been given him and the others were wanting: he couldn't do his sum till he had got all his figures.

He dressed and drove quickly, so that by half-past eleven he was at Manchester Square. There were a good many carriages at the door – a party was going on; a circumstance which at the last gave him a slight relief, for now he would rather see her in a crowd. People passed him on the staircase; they were going away, going 'on' with the hunted herdlike movement of London society at night. But sundry groups remained in the drawing-room, and it was some minutes, as she didn't hear him announced, before he discovered and spoke to her. In this short interval he had seen St George talking to a lady before the fireplace; but he at once looked away, feeling unready for an encounter, and therefore couldn't be sure the author of 'Shadowmere' noticed him. At all events he didn't come over; though Miss Fancourt did as soon as she saw him – she almost rushed at him, smiling rustling radiant beautiful. He had forgotten what her head, what her face offered to the sight; she was in white, there were gold figures on her dress and her hair was a casque of gold. He saw in a single moment that she was happy, happy with an aggressive splendour. But she wouldn't speak to him of that, she would speak only of himself.

'I'm so delighted; my father told me. How kind of you to come!' She struck him as so fresh and brave, while his eyes moved over her, that he said to himself irresistibly: 'Why to *him*, why not to youth, to strength, to ambition, to a future? Why, in her rich young force, to failure, to abdication, to superannuation?' In his thought at that sharp moment he blasphemed even against all that had been left of his faith in the peccable master. 'I'm so sorry I missed you,' she went on. 'My father told me. How charming of you to have come so soon!'

'Does that surprise you?' Paul Overt asked.

'The first day? No, from you – nothing that's nice.' She was interrupted by a lady who bade her good night, and he seemed to read that it cost her nothing to speak to him in that tone; it was her old liberal lavish way, with a certain added amplitude that time had brought; and if this manner began to operate on the spot, at such a juncture in her history, perhaps in the other days too it had meant just as little or as much – a mere mechanical charity, with the difference now that she was satisfied, ready to give but in want of nothing. Oh she was satisfied – and why shouldn't she be? Why shouldn't she have been surprised at his coming the first day – for all the good she had ever got from him? As the lady continued to hold her attention Paul turned from her with a strange irritation in his complicated artistic soul and a sort of disinterested disappointment. She was so happy that it was almost stupid – a disproof of the extraordinary intelligence he had formerly found in her. Didn't she know how bad St George could be, hadn't she recognised the awful thinness –? If she didn't she was nothing, and if she did why such an insolence of serenity?

This question expired as our young man's eyes settled at last on the genius who had advised him in a great crisis. St George was still before the chimney-piece, but now he was alone – fixed, waiting, as if he meant to stop after every one – and he met the clouded gaze of the young friend so troubled as to the degree of his right (the right his resentment would have enjoyed) to regard himself as a victim. Somehow the ravage of the question was checked by the Master's radiance. It was as fine in its way as Marian Fancourt's, it denoted the happy human being; but also it represented to Paul Overt that the author of 'Shadowmere' had now definitely ceased to count – ceased to count as a writer. As he smiled a welcome across the place he was almost *banal*, was almost smug. Paul fancied that for a moment he hesitated to make a movement, as if, for all the world, he *had* his bad conscience; then they had already met in the middle of the room and had shaken hands – expressively, cordially on St George's part. With which they had passed back together to where the elder man had been standing, while St George said: 'I hope you're never going away again. I've been dining here; the General told me.' He was handsome, he was young, he looked as if he had still a great fund of life. He bent the friendliest, most unconfessing eyes on his disciple of a couple of years before; asked him about everything, his health, his plans, his late occupations, the new book. 'When will it be out – soon, soon, I hope? Splendid, eh? That's right; you're a comfort, you're a luxury! I've read you all over again these last six months.' Paul waited to see if he'd tell him what the General had told him in the afternoon and what Miss Fancourt, verbally, at least, of course hadn't. But as it didn't come out he at last put the question. 'Is it true, the great news I hear – that you're to be married?'

'Ah you *have* heard it then?'

'Didn't the General tell you?' Paul asked.

The Master's face was wonderful. 'Tell me what?'

'That he mentioned it to me this afternoon?'

'My dear fellow, I don't remember. We've been in the midst of people. I'm sorry, in that case, that I lose the pleasure, myself, of announcing to you a fact that touches me so nearly. It *is* a fact, strange as it may appear. It has only just become one. Isn't it ridiculous?' St George made this speech without confusion, but on the other hand, so far as our friend could judge, without latent impudence. It struck his interlocutor that, to talk so comfortably and coolly, he must simply have forgotten what had passed between them. His next words, however, showed he hadn't, and they produced, as an appeal to Paul's own memory, an effect which would have been ludicrous if it hadn't been cruel. 'Do you recall the talk we had at my house that night, into which Miss Fancourt's name entered? I've often thought of it since.'

'Yes; no wonder you said what you did' – Paul was careful to meet his eyes.

'In the light of the present occasion? Ah but there was no light then. How could I have foreseen this hour?'

'Didn't you think it probable?'

'Upon my honour, no,' said Henry St George. 'Certainly I owe you that assurance. Think how my situation has changed.'

'I see – I see,' our young man murmured.

His companion went on as if, now that the subject had been broached, he was, as a person of imagination and tact, quite ready to give every satisfaction – being both by his genius and his method so able to enter into everything another might feel. 'But it's not only that; for honestly, at my age, I never dreamed – a widower with big boys and with so little else! It has turned out differently from anything one could have dreamed, and I'm fortunate beyond all measure. She has been so free, and yet she consents. Better than any one else perhaps – for I remember how you liked her before you went away, and how she liked you – you can intelligently congratulate me.'

'She has been so free!' Those words made a great impression on Paul Overt, and he almost writhed under that irony in them as to which it so little mattered whether it was designed or casual. Of course she had been free, and appreciably perhaps by his own act; for wasn't the Master's allusion to her having liked him a part of the irony too? 'I thought that by your theory you disapproved of a writer's marrying.'

'Surely – surely. But you don't call me a writer?'

'You ought to be ashamed,' said Paul.

'Ashamed of marrying again?'

'I won't say that – but ashamed of your reasons.'

The elder man beautifully smiled. 'You must let me judge of them, my good friend.'

'Yes; why not? For you judged wonderfully of mine.'

The tone of these words appeared suddenly, for St George, to suggest the unsuspected. He stared as if divining a bitterness. 'Don't you think I've been straight?'

'You might have told me at the time perhaps.'

'My dear fellow, when I say I couldn't pierce futurity –!'

'I mean afterwards.'

The Master wondered. 'After my wife's death?'

'When this idea came to you.'

'Ah never, never! I wanted to save you, rare and precious as you are.'

Poor Overt looked hard at him. 'Are you marrying Miss Fancourt to save me?'

'Not absolutely, but it adds to the pleasure. I shall be the making of you,' St George smiled. 'I was greatly struck, after our talk, with the brave devoted way you quitted the country, and still more perhaps with your force of character in remaining abroad. You're very strong – you're wonderfully strong.'

Paul tried to sound his shining eyes; the strange thing was that he seemed sincere – not a mocking fiend. He turned away, and as he did so heard the Master say something about his giving them all the proof, being the joy of his old age. He faced him again, taking another look. 'Do you mean to say you've stopped writing?'

'My dear fellow, of course I have. It's too late. Didn't I tell you?'

'I can't believe it!'

'Of course you can't – with your own talent! No, no; for the rest of my life I shall only read *you*.'

'Does she know that – Miss Fancourt?'

'She will – she will.' Did he mean this, our young man wondered, as a covert intimation that the assistance he should derive from that young lady's fortune, moderate as it was, would make the difference of putting it in his power to cease to work ungratefully an exhausted vein? Somehow, standing there in the ripeness of his successful manhood, he didn't suggest that any of his veins were exhausted. 'Don't you remember the moral I offered myself to you that night as pointing?' St George continued. 'Consider at any rate the warning I am at present.'

This was too much – he *was* the mocking fiend. Paul turned from him with a mere nod for good night and the sense in a sore heart that he might come back to him and his easy grace, his fine way of arranging things, some time in the far future, but couldn't fraternise with him now. It was necessary to his soreness to believe for the hour in the intensity of his grievance – all the more cruel for its not being a legal one. It was doubtless in the attitude of hugging this wrong that he descended the stairs without taking leave of Miss Fancourt, who hadn't been in view at the moment

he quitted the room. He was glad to get out into the honest
dusky unsophisticating night, to move fast, to take his way
home on foot. He walked a long time, going astray, paying
no attention. He was thinking of too many other things.
His steps recovered their direction, however, and at the end
of an hour he found himself before his door in the small
inexpensive empty street. He lingered, questioning himself
still before going in, with nothing around and above him
but moonless blackness, a bad lamp or two and a few far-
away dim stars. To these last faint features he raised his
eyes; he had been saying to himself that he should have
been 'sold' indeed, diabolically sold, if now, on his new
foundation, at the end of a year, St George were to put forth
something of his prime quality – something of the type of
'Shadowmere' and finer than his finest. Greatly as he admired his talent Paul literally hoped such an incident
wouldn't occur; it seemed to him just then that he shouldn't
be able to bear it. His late adviser's words were still in his
ears – 'You're very strong, wonderfully strong.' Was he
really? Certainly he would have to be, and it might a little
serve for revenge. *Is* he? the reader may ask in turn, if his
interest has followed the perplexed young man so far. The
best answer to that perhaps is that he's doing his best, but
that it's too soon to say. When the new book came out
in the autumn Mr and Mrs St George found it really
magnificent. The former still has published nothing, but
Paul doesn't even yet feel safe. I may say for him, however,
that if this event were to occur he would really be the very
first to appreciate it: which is perhaps a proof that the
Master was essentially right and that Nature had dedicated
him to intellectual, not to personal passion.

THE PRIVATE LIFE

✤

THE PRIVATE LIFE

We talked of London face to face with a great bristling primeval glacier. The hour and the scene were one of those impressions that make up a little in Switzerland for the modern indignity of travel – the promiscuities and vulgarities, the station and the hotel, the gregarious patience, the struggle for a scrappy attention, the reduction to a numbered state. The high valley was pink with the mountain rose, the cool air as fresh as if the world were young. There was a faint flush of afternoon on undiminished snows, and the fraternising tinkle of the unseen cattle came to us with a cropped and sun-warmed odour. The balconied inn stood on the very neck of the sweetest pass in the Oberland, and for a week we had had company and weather. This was felt to be great luck, for one would have made up for the other had either been bad.

The weather certainly would have made up for the company; but it wasn't subjected to this tax, for we had by a happy chance the *fleur des pois*:[1] Lord and Lady Mellifont, Clare Vawdrey, the greatest (in the opinion of many) of our literary glories, and Blanche Adney, the greatest (in the opinion of all) of our theatrical. I mention these first because they were just the people whom in London, at that time, people tried to 'get'. People endeavoured to 'book' them six weeks ahead, yet on this occasion we had come in for them, we had all come in for each other, without the least wire-pulling. A turn of the game had pitched us together the last of August, and we recognised our luck by remaining so, under protection of the barometer. When the golden days were over – that would come soon enough – we should wind down opposite sides of the pass and disappear over the crest of surrounding heights. We were of the same general communion, chalk-marked for recognition by signs from the same alphabet. We met, in London, with irregular frequency; we were more or less governed by the laws and the language, the traditions and the shibboleths of the same dense social state. I think all of us, even the ladies, 'did' something, though we pretended we didn't when it was mentioned. Such things aren't mentioned indeed in London, but it was our innocent pleasure to be different here. There had to be some way to show the difference, inasmuch as we were under the impression that this was our annual holiday. We felt at any rate that the conditions were more human than in London, or at least that we ourselves were. We were frank about this, we talked about it: it was what we were talking about as we looked at the flushing glacier, just as some one called attention to the prolonged absence of Lord Mellifont and Mrs Adney. We were seated on the terrace of the inn, where there were benches and little tables, and those of us most bent on showing with what a rush we had returned to nature were, in the queer Germanic fashion, having coffee before meat.

The remark about the absence of our two companions was not taken up, not even by Lady Mellifont, not even by little Adney, the fond composer; for it had been dropped only in the briefest intermission of Clare Vawdrey's talk. (This celebrity was 'Clarence' only on the title-page.) It was just that revelation of our being after all human that was his theme. He asked the company whether, candidly, every one hadn't been tempted to say to every one else: 'I had no idea you were really so nice.' I had had, for my part, an idea that *he* was, and even a good deal nicer, but that was too complicated to go into then; besides it's exactly my story.

There was a general understanding among us that when Vawdrey talked we should be silent, and not, oddly enough, because he at all expected it. He didn't, for of all copious talkers he was the most undesigning, the least greedy and professional. It was rather the religion of the host, of the hostess, that prevailed among us; it was their own idea, but they always looked for a listening circle when the great novelist dined with them. On the occasion I allude to there was probably no one present with whom in London he hadn't dined, and we felt the force of this habit. He had dined even with me; and on the evening of that dinner, as on this Alpine afternoon, I had been at no pains to hold my tongue, absorbed as I inveterately was in a study of the question that always rose before me to such a height in his fair square strong stature.

This question was all the more tormenting that I'm sure he never suspected himself of imposing it, any more than he had ever observed that every day of his life every one listened to him at dinner. He used to be called 'subjective and introspective' in the weekly papers, but if that meant he was avid of tribute no distinguished man could in society have been less so. He never talked about himself; and this was an article on which, though it would have been tremendously worthy of him, he apparently never even reflected. He had his hours and his habits, his tailor and his hatter, his hygiene and his particular wine, but all these things together never made up an attitude. Yet they constituted the only one he ever adopted, and it was easy for him to refer to our being 'nicer' abroad than at home. *He* was exempt from variations, and not a shade either less or more nice in one place than in another. He differed from other people, but never from himself – save in the extraordinary sense I shall throw my light upon – and he struck me as having neither moods nor sensibilities nor preferences. He might have been always in the same company, so far as he recognised any influence from age or condition or sex: he addressed himself to women exactly as he addressed himself to men, and gossiped with all men alike, talking no better to clever folk than to dull. I used to wail to myself over his way of liking one subject – so far as I could tell – precisely as much as another: there were some I hated so myself. I never found him anything but loud and liberal and cheerful, and I never heard him utter a paradox or express a shade or play with an idea. That fancy about our being 'human' was, in his conversation, quite an exceptional flight. His opinions were sound and second-rate, and of his perceptions it was too mystifying to think. I envied him his magnificent health.

Vawdrey had marched with his even pace and his perfectly good conscience into the flat country of anecdote, where stories are visible from afar like windmills and sign-posts; but I observed after a little that Lady Mellifont's attention wandered. I happened to be sitting next her. I noticed that her eyes rambled a little anxiously over the lower slopes of the mountains. At last, after looking at her watch, she said to me: 'Do you know where they went?'

'Do you mean Mrs Adney and Lord Mellifont?'

'Lord Mellifont and Mrs Adney.' Her ladyship's speech seemed – unconsciously indeed – to correct me, but it didn't occur to me that this might be an effect of jealousy. I imputed to her no such vulgar sentiment: in the first place because I liked her, and in the second because it would always occur to one rather quickly to put Lord Mellifont, whatever the connexion, first. He *was* first – extraordinarily first. I don't say greatest or wisest or most renowned, but essentially at the top of the list and the head of the table. That's a position by itself, and his wife was naturally accustomed to see him in it. My phrase had sounded as if Mrs Adney had taken him; but it was not possible for him to be taken – he only took. No one, in the nature of things, could know this better than Lady Mellifont. I had originally been rather afraid of her, thinking her, with her stiff silences and the extreme blackness of almost everything that made up her person, somewhat hard, even a little saturnine. Her paleness seemed slightly grey and her glossy black hair metallic, even as the brooches and bands and combs with which it was inveterately adorned. She was in perpetual mourning and wore numberless ornaments of jet and onyx, a thousand clicking chains and bugles² and beads. I had heard Mrs Adney call her the Queen of Night, and the term was descriptive if you took the night for cloudy. She had a secret, and if you didn't find it out as you knew her better you at least felt sure she was gentle unaffected and limited, as well as rather submissively sad. She was like a woman with a painless malady. I told her that I had merely seen her husband and his companion stroll down the glen together about an hour before, and suggested that Mr Adney would perhaps know something of their intentions.

Vincent Adney, who, though fifty years old, looked like a good little boy on whom it had been impressed that children shouldn't talk in company, acquitted himself with remarkable simplicity and taste of the position of husband of a great exponent of comedy. When all was said about her making it easy for him one couldn't help admiring the charmed affection with which he took everything for granted. It's difficult for a husband not on the stage, or at least in the theatre, to be graceful about a wife so conspicuous there; but Adney did more than carry it off, the awkwardness – he taught it ever so oddly to make *him* interesting. He set his beloved to music; and you remember how genuine his music could be – the only English compositions I ever saw a foreigner care for. His wife was in them somewhere always; they were a free rich translation of the impression she produced. She seemed, as one listened, to pass laughing, with loosened hair and the gait of a wood-nymph, across the scene. He had been only a little fiddler at her theatre, always in his place during the acts; but she had made him something rare and brave and misunderstood. Their superiority had become a kind of partnership, and their happiness was a part of the happiness of their friends. Adney's one discomfort was that he couldn't write a play for his wife, and the only way he meddled with her affairs was by asking impossible people if *they* couldn't.

Lady Mellifont, after looking across at him a moment, remarked to me that she would rather not put any question to him. She added the next minute: 'I had rather people shouldn't see I'm nervous.'

'*Are* you nervous?'

'I always become so if my husband's away from me for any time.'

'Do you imagine something has happened to him?'

'Yes, always. Of course I'm used to it.'

'Do you mean his tumbling over precipices – that sort of thing?'

'I don't know exactly *what* I fear: it's the general sense that he'll never come back.'

She said so much and withheld so much that the only way to treat her idiosyncrasy seemed the jocular. 'Surely he'll never forsake you!' I laughed.

She looked at the ground a moment. 'Oh at bottom I'm easy.'

'Nothing can ever happen to a man so accomplished, so infallible, so armed at all points,' I went on in the same spirit.

'Oh you don't know how he's armed!' she returned with such an odd quaver that I could account for it only by her being nervous. This idea was confirmed by her moving just afterwards, changing her seat rather pointlessly, not as if to cut our conversation short, but because she was worried. I could scarcely enter into her feeling, though I was presently relieved to see Mrs Adney come towards us. She had in her hand a big bunch of wild flowers, but was not closely attended by Lord Mellifont. I quickly saw, however, that she had no disaster to announce; yet as I knew there was a question Lady Mellifont would like to hear answered, without wishing to ask it, I expressed to her at once the hope that his lordship hadn't remained in a crevasse.

'Oh no; he left me but three minutes ago. He has gone into the house.' Blanche Adney rested her eyes on mine an instant – a mode of intercourse to which no man, for himself, could ever object. The interest on this occasion was quickened by the particular thing the eyes happened to say. What they usually said was only: 'Oh yes, I'm charming, I know, but don't make a fuss about it. I only want a new part – I do, I do, I do!' At present they added dimly, surreptitiously and of course sweetly – since that was the way they did everything: 'It's all right, but something did happen. Perhaps I'll tell you later.' She turned to Lady Mellifont, and the transition to simple gaiety suggested her mastery of her profession. 'I've brought him safe. We had a charming walk.'

'I'm so very glad,' said Lady Mellifont with her faint smile; continuing vaguely, as she got up: 'He must have gone to dress for dinner. Isn't it rather near?' She moved away to the hotel in her leave-taking simplifying fashion, and the rest of us, at the mention of dinner, looked at each other's watches as if to shift the responsibility for such grossness. The head-waiter, essentially, like all head-waiters, a man of the world, allowed us hours and places of our own, so that in the evening, apart under the lamp, we formed a compact, an indulged little circle. But it was only the Mellifonts who 'dressed' and as to whom it was recognised that they naturally *would* dress: she exactly in the same manner as on any other evening of her ceremonious existence – she wasn't a woman whose habits could take account of anything so mutable as fitness – and he, on the other hand, with remarkable adjustment and suitability. He was almost as much a man of the world as the head-waiter, and spoke almost as many languages; but he abstained from courting a comparison of dress-coats and white waistcoats, analysing the occasion in a much finer way – into black velvet and blue velvet and brown velvet, for instance, into delicate harmonies of necktie and subtle laxities of shirt. He had a costume for every function and a moral for every costume; and his functions and costumes and morals were ever a part of the amusement of life – a part at any rate of its beauty and romance – for an immense circle of spectators. For his particular friends indeed these things were more than an amusement; they were a topic, a social support and of course in addition a constant theme for speculative suspense. If his wife hadn't been present before dinner they were what the rest of us probably would have been putting our heads together about.

Clare Vawdrey had a fund of anecdote on the whole question: he had known Lord Mellifont almost from the beginning. It was a peculiarity of this nobleman that there could be no conversation about him that didn't instantly take the form of anecdote, and a still further distinction that there could apparently be no anecdote that wasn't on the whole to his honour. At whatever moment he came into a room people might say frankly: 'Of course we were telling stories about you!' As consciences go, in London, the general conscience would have been good. Moreover it would have been impossible to imagine his taking such a tribute otherwise than amiably, for he was always as unperturbed as an actor with the right cue. He had never in his life needed the prompter – his very embarrassments had been rehearsed. For myself, when he was talked about I had always had a sense of our speaking of the dead: it had the mark of that peculiar accumulation of relish. His reputation was a kind of gilded obelisk,[3] as if he had been buried beneath it; the body of legend and reminiscence of which he was to be the subject had crystallised in advance.

This ambiguity sprang, I suppose, from the fact that the mere sound of his name and air of his person, the general expectation he created, had somehow a pitch so romantic and abnormal. The experience of his urbanity always came later; the prefigurement, the legend paled then before the reality. I remember that on the evening I refer to the reality struck me as supreme. The handsomest man of his period could never have looked better, and he sat among us like a bland conductor controlling by an harmonious play of arm an orchestra still a little rough. He directed the conversation by gestures as irresistible as they were vague; one felt as if without him it wouldn't have had anything to call a tone. This was essentially what he contributed to any occasion – what he contributed above all to English public life. He pervaded it, he coloured it, he embellished it, and without him it would have lacked, comparatively speaking, a vocabulary. Certainly it wouldn't have had a style, for a style was what it had in having Lord Mellifont. He *was* a style. I was freshly struck with it as, in the *salle-à-manger*[4] of the little Swiss inn, we resigned ourselves to inevitable veal. Confronted with *his* high form – I must parenthesise that it wasn't confronted much – Clare Vawdrey's talk suggested the reporter contrasted with the bard. It was interesting to watch the shock of characters from which of an evening so much would be expected. There was however no concussion – it was all muffled and minimised in Lord Mellifont's tact. It was rudimentary with him to find the solution of such a problem in playing the host, assuming responsibilities that carried with them their sacrifice. He had indeed never been a guest in his life; he was the host, the patron, the moderator at every board. If there was a defect in his manner – and I suggest this under my breath – it was that he had a little more art than any conjunction, even the most complicated, could possibly require. At any rate one made one's reflexions in noticing how the accomplished peer handled the case and how the sturdy man of letters hadn't a suspicion that the case – and least of all he himself as part of it – was handled. Lord Mellifont expended treasures of tact, and Clare Vawdrey never dreamed he was doing it.

Vawdrey had no suspicion of any such precaution even when Blanche Adney asked him if he really didn't see by this time his third act – an enquiry into which she introduced a subtlety of her own. She had settled it for him that he was to write her a play and that the heroine, should he but do his duty, would be the part for which she had immemorially longed. She was forty years old – this could be no secret to those who had admired her from the first – and might now reach out her hand and touch her uttermost goal. It gave a shade of tragic passion – perfect actress of comedy as she was – to her desire not to miss the great thing. The years had passed, and still she had missed it; none of the things she had done was the thing she had dreamed of, so that at present she had no more time to lose. This was the canker in the rose, the ache beneath the smile. It made her touching – made her melancholy more arch than her mirth. She had done the old English and the new French,[5] and had charmed for a while her generation; but she was haunted by the vision of a bigger chance, of something truer to the conditions that lay near her. She was tired of Sheridan[6] and she hated Bowdler;[7] she called for a canvas of a finer grain. The worst of it, to my sense, was that she would never extract her modern comedy from the great mature novelist, who was as incapable of producing it as he was of threading a needle. She coddled him, she talked to him, she made love to him, as she frankly proclaimed; but she dwelt in illusions – she would have to live and die with Bowdler.

It is difficult to be cursory over this charming woman, who was beautiful without beauty and complete with a dozen deficiencies. The perspective of the stage made her over, and in society she was like the model off the pedestal. She was the picture walking about, which to the artless social mind was a perpetual surprise – a miracle. People thought she told them the secrets of the pictorial nature, in return for which they gave her relaxation and tea. She told them nothing and she drank the tea; but they had all the same the best of the bargain. Vawdrey was really at work on a play; but if he had begun it because he liked her I think he let it drag for the same reason. He secretly felt the atrocious difficulty and hung off, for illusion's sake, from the point of tests and tribulations. In spite of which nothing could be so agreeable as to have such a question open with Blanche Adney, and from time to time he doubtless put something very good into the play. If he deceived Mrs Adney it was only because in her despair she was determined to be deceived. To her appeal about their third act he replied that before dinner he had written a splendid passage.

'Before dinner?' I said. 'Why, *cher grand maître*,[8] before dinner you were holding us all spell-bound on the terrace.'

My words were a joke, because I thought his had been; but for the first time that I could remember I noted in his face a shade of confusion. He looked at me hard, throwing back his head quickly, the least bit like a horse who has been pulled up short. 'Oh it was before that,' he returned naturally enough.

'Before that you were playing billiards with *me*,' Lord Mellifont threw off.

'Then it must have been yesterday,' said Vawdrey.

But he was in a tight place. 'You told me this morning you did nothing yesterday,' Blanche objected.

'I don't think I really know when I do things.' He looked vaguely, without helping himself, at a dish just offered him.

'It's enough if *we* know,' smiled Lord Mellifont.

'I don't believe you've written a line,' said Blanche Adney.

'I think I could repeat you the scene.' And Vawdrey took refuge in *haricots verts.*'

'Oh do – oh do!' two or three of us cried.

'After dinner, in the salon, it will be a high *régal*,'[10] Lord Mellifont declared.

'I'm not sure, but I'll try,' Vawdrey went on.

'Oh you lovely sweet man!' exclaimed the actress, who was practising what she believed to be Americanisms and was resigned even to an American comedy.

'But there must be this condition,' said Vawdrey: 'you must make your husband play.'

'Play while you're reading? Never!'

'I've too much vanity,' said Adney.

The direction of Lord Mellifont's fine eyes distinguished him. 'You must give us the overture before the curtain rises. That's a peculiarly delightful moment.'

'I shan't read – I shall just speak,' said Vawdrey.

'Better still, let me go and get your manuscript,' Blanche suggested.

Vawdrey replied that the manuscript didn't matter; but an hour later, in the salon, we wished he might have had it. We sat expectant, still under the spell of Adney's violin. His wife, in the foreground, on an ottoman, was all impatience and profile, and Lord Mellifont, in the chair – it was always *the* chair, Lord Mellifont's – made our grateful little group feel like a social science congress or a distribution of prizes. Suddenly, instead of beginning, our tame lion began to roar out of tune – he had clean forgotten every word. He was very sorry, but the lines absolutely wouldn't come to him; he was utterly ashamed, but his memory was a blank. He didn't look in the least ashamed – Vawdrey had never looked ashamed in his life; he was only imperturbably and merrily natural. He protested that he had never expected to make such a fool of himself, but we felt that this wouldn't prevent the incident's taking its place among his jolliest reminiscences. It was only *we* who were humiliated, as if he had played us a premeditated trick. This was an occasion, if ever, for Lord Mellifont's tact, which descended on us all like balm: he told us, in his charming artistic way, his way of bridging over arid intervals (he had a *débit*[11] – there was nothing to approach it in England – like the actors of the Comédie Française) of his own collapse on a momentous occasion, the delivery of an address to a mighty multitude, when, finding he had forgotten his memoranda, he fumbled, on the terrible platform, the cynosure of every eye, fumbled vainly in irreproachable pockets for indispensable notes. But the point of his story was finer than that of our other entertainer's easy fiasco; for he sketched with a few light gestures the brilliancy of a performance which had risen superior to embarrassment, had resolved itself, we were left to divine, into an effort recognised at the moment as not absolutely a blot on what the public was so good as to call his reputation.

'Play up – play up!' cried Blanche Adney, tapping her husband and remembering how on the stage a *contretemps* is always drowned in music. Adney threw himself upon his fiddle, and I said to Clare Vawdrey that his mistake could easily be corrected by his sending for the manuscript. If he'd tell me where it was I'd immediately fetch it from his room. To this he replied: 'My dear fellow, I'm afraid there *is* no manuscript.'

'Then you've not written anything?'

'I'll write it tomorrow.'

'Ah you trifle with us!' I said in much mystification.

He seemed at this to think better of it. 'If there *is* anything you'll find it on my table.'

One of the others, at the moment, spoke to him, and Lady Mellifont remarked audibly, as to correct gently our want of consideration, that Mr Adney was playing something very beautiful. I had noticed before how fond she appeared of music; she always listened to it in a hushed transport. Vawdrey's attention was drawn away, but it didn't seem to me the words he had just dropped constituted a definite permission to go to his room. Moreover I wanted to speak to Blanche Adney; I had something to ask her. I had to await my chance, however, as we remained silent a while for her husband, after which the conversation became general. It was our habit to go early to bed, but a little of the evening was still left. Before it quite waned I found an opportunity to tell Blanche that Vawdrey had given me leave to put my hand on his manuscript. She adjured me, by all I held sacred, to bring it at once, to give it to her; and her insistence was proof against my suggestion that it would now be too late for him to begin to read: besides which the charm was broken – the others wouldn't care. It wasn't, she assured me, too late for *her* to begin; therefore I was to possess myself without more delay of the precious pages. I told her she should be obeyed in a moment, but I wanted her first to satisfy my just curiosity. What had happened before dinner, while she was on the hills with Lord Mellifont?

'How do you know anything happened?'

'I saw it in your face when you came back.'

'And they call me an actress!' my friend cried.

'What do they call *me*?' I asked.

'You're a searcher of hearts – that frivolous thing an observer.'

'I wish you'd let an observer write you a play!' I broke out.

'People don't care for what you write: you'd break any run of luck.'

'Well, I see plays all round me,' I declared; 'the air is full of them tonight.'

'The air? Thank you for nothing! I only wish my table-drawers were.'

'Did he make love to you on the glacier?' I went on.

She stared – then broke into the graduated ecstasy of her laugh. 'Lord Mellifont, poor dear? What a funny place! It would indeed be the place for *our* love!'

'Did he fall into a crevasse?' I continued.

Blanche Adney looked at me again as she had done – so unmistakably though briefly – when she came up before dinner with her hands full of flowers. 'I don't know into what he fell. I'll tell you tomorrow.'

'He did come down then?'

'Perhaps he went up,' she laughed. 'It's really strange.'

'All the more reason you should tell me tonight.'

'I must think it over; I must puzzle it out.'

'Oh if you want conundrums I'll throw in another,' I said. 'What's the matter with the Master?'

'The master of what?'

'Of every form of dissimulation. Vawdrey hasn't written a line.'

'Go and get his papers and we'll see.'

'I don't like to expose him,' I said.

'Why not, if I expose Lord Mellifont?'

'Oh I'd do anything for that,' I allowed. 'But why should Vawdrey have made a false statement? It's very curious.'

'It's very curious,' Blanche Adney repeated with a musing air and her eyes on Lord Mellifont. Then rousing herself she added: 'Go and look in his room.'

'In Lord Mellifont's?'

She turned to me quickly. '*That* would be a way!'

'A way to what?'

'To find out – to find out!' She spoke gaily and excitedly, but suddenly checked herself. 'We're talking awful nonsense.'

'We're mixing things up, but I'm struck with your idea. Get Lady Mellifont to let you.'

'Oh *she* has looked!' Blanche brought out with the oddest dramatic expression. Then after a movement of her beautiful uplifted hand, as if to brush away a fantastic vision, she added imperiously: 'Bring me the scene – bring me the scene!'

'I go for it,' I answered; 'but don't tell me I can't write a play.'

She left me, but my errand was arrested by the approach of a lady who had produced a birthday-book – we had been threatened with it for several evenings – and who did me the honour to solicit my autograph. She had been asking the others and couldn't decently leave me out. I could usually remember my name, but it always took me long to recall my date, and even when I had done so I was never very sure. I hesitated between two days, remarking to my petitioner that I would sign on both if it would give her any satisfaction. She opined that I had surely been born but once, and I replied of course that on the day I made her acquaintance I had been born again. I mention the feeble joke only to show that, with the obligatory inspection of the other autographs, we gave some minutes to this transaction. The lady departed with her book, and I then found the company had scattered. I was alone in the little salon that had been appropriated to our use. My first impression was one of disappointment: if Vawdrey had gone to bed I didn't wish to disturb him. While I hesitated however I judged that my friend must still be afoot. A window was open and the sound of voices outside came in to me: Blanche was on the terrace with her dramatist and they were talking about the stars. I went to the window for a glimpse – the Alpine night was splendid. My friends had stepped out together; Mrs Adney had picked up a cloak; she looked as I had seen her look in the wing of the theatre. They were silent a while, and I heard the roar of a neighbouring torrent. I turned back into the room, and its quiet lamplight gave me an idea. Our companions had dispersed – it was late for a pastoral country – and we three should have the place to ourselves. Clare Vawdrey had written his scene, which couldn't but be splendid; and his reading it to us there at such an hour would be a thing always to remember. I'd bring down his manuscript and meet the two with it as they came in.

I quitted the salon for this purpose; I had been in his room and knew it was on the second floor, the last in a long corridor. A minute later my hand was on the knob of the door, which I naturally pushed open without knocking. It was equally natural that in the absence of its occupant the room should be dark; the more so as, the end of the corridor being at that hour unlighted, the obscurity was not immediately diminished by the opening of the door. I was only aware at first that I had made no mistake and that, the window-curtains not being drawn, I had before me a couple of vague star-lighted apertures. Their aid, however, was not sufficient to enable me to find what I had come for, and my hand, in my pocket, was already on the little box of matches that I always carried for cigarettes. Suddenly I withdrew it with a start, uttering an ejaculation, an apology. I had entered the wrong room; a glance prolonged for three seconds showed me a figure seated at a table near one of the windows – a figure I had at first taken for a travelling-rug thrown over a chair. I retreated with a sense of intrusion; but as I did so I took in more rapidly than it takes me to express it, first that this was Vawdrey's room and second that, surprisingly, its occupant himself sat before me. Checking myself on the threshold I was briefly bewildered, but before I knew it I had called out: 'Hullo, is that you, Vawdrey?'

He neither turned nor answered me, but my question received an immediate and practical reply in the opening of a door on the other side of the passage. A servant with a candle had come out of the opposite room, and in this flitting illumination I definitely recognised the man whom an instant before I had to the best of my belief left below in

conversation with Mrs Adney. His back was half-turned to
me and he bent over the table in the attitude of writing, but
I took in at every pore his identity. 'I beg your pardon – I
thought you were downstairs,' I said; and as the person
before me gave no sign of hearing I added: 'If you're busy I
won't disturb you.' I backed out, closing the door – I had
been in the place, I suppose, less than a minute. I had a sense
of mystification which however deepened infinitely the next
instant. I stood there with my hand still on the knob of
the door, overtaken by the oddest impression of my life.
Vawdrey was seated at his table, and it was a very natural
place for him; but why was he writing in the dark and why
hadn't he answered me? I waited a few seconds for the sound
of some movement, to see if he wouldn't rouse himself from
his abstraction – a fit conceivable in a great writer – and call
out 'Oh my dear fellow, is it you?' But I heard only the
stillness, I felt only the star-lighted dusk of the room, with
the unexpected presence it enclosed. I turned away, slowly
retracing my steps, and came confusedly downstairs. The
lamp still burned in the salon, but the room was empty. I
passed round to the door of the hotel and stepped out. Empty
too was the terrace. Blanche Adney and the gentleman with
her had apparently come in. I hung about five minutes –
then I went to bed.

II

I slept badly, for I was agitated. On looking back at these
queer occurrences (you'll see presently *how* queer!) I perhaps
suppose myself more affected than in fact; for great anom-
alies are never so great at first as after we've reflected on
them. It takes us time to use up explanations. I was vaguely
nervous – I had been sharply startled; but there was nothing
I couldn't clear up by asking Blanche Adney, the first thing
in the morning, who had been with her on the terrace. Oddly

enough, however, when the morning dawned – it dawned admirably – I felt less desire to satisfy myself on this point than to escape, to brush away the shadow of my stupefaction. I saw the day would be splendid, so that the fancy took me to spend it, as I had spent happy days of youth, in a lonely mountain ramble. I dressed early, partook of conventional coffee, put a big roll into one pocket and a small flask into the other, and, with a stout stick in my hand, went forth into the high places. My story isn't closely concerned with the charming hours I passed there – hours of the kind that make intense memories. If I roamed away half of them on the shoulders of the hills, I lay on the sloping grass for the other half and, with my cap pulled over my eyes – save a peep for immensities of view – listened, in the bright stillness, to the mountain bee and felt most things sink and dwindle. Clare Vawdrey grew small, Blanche Adney grew dim, Lord Mellifont grew old, and before the day was over I forgot I had ever been puzzled. When in the late afternoon I made my way down to the inn there was nothing I wanted so much to learn as that dinner was at hand. Tonight I dressed, in a manner, and by the time I was presentable they were all at table.

In their company again my little problem came back to me, so that I was curious to see if Vawdrey wouldn't look at me with a certain queerness. But he didn't look at me at all; which gave me a chance both to be patient and to wonder why I should hesitate to ask him my question across the table. I did hesitate, and with the consciousness of doing so came back a little of the agitation I had left behind me, or below me, during the day. I wasn't ashamed of my scruple, however: it was only a fine discretion. What I vaguely felt was that a public enquiry wouldn't have been fair. Lord Mellifont was there, of course, to mitigate with his perfect manner all consequences; but I think it was present to me that with these particular elements his lordship wouldn't be at home. The moment we got up therefore I approached Mrs Adney, asking her whether, as the evening was lovely, she wouldn't take a turn with me outside.

'You've walked a hundred miles; hadn't you better be quiet?' she replied.

'I'd walk a hundred miles more to get you to tell me something.'

She looked at me an instant with a little of the odd consciousness I had sought, but hadn't found, in Clare Vawdrey's eyes. 'Do you mean what became of Lord Mellifont?'

'Of Lord Mellifont?' With my new speculation I had lost that thread.

'Where's your memory, foolish man? We talked of it last evening.'

'Ah yes!' I cried, recalling; 'we shall have lots to discuss.' I drew her out to the terrace and, before we had gone three steps, said to her: 'Who was with you here last night?'

'Last night?' – she was as wide of the mark as I had been.

'At ten o'clock – just after our company broke up. You came out here with a gentleman. You talked about the stars.'

She stared a moment, then gave her laugh. 'Are you jealous of dear Vawdrey?'

'Then it was he?'

'Certainly it was he.'

'And how long did he stay?'

She laughed again. 'You have it badly! He stayed about a quarter of an hour – perhaps rather more. We walked some distance. He talked about his play. There you have it all. That is the only witchcraft I have used.'

Well, it wasn't enough for me; so 'What did Vawdrey do afterwards?' I continued.

'I haven't the least idea. I left him and went to bed.'

'At what time did you go to bed?'

'At what time did *you*? I happen to remember that I parted from Mr Vawdrey at ten twenty-five,' said Mrs Adney. 'I came back into the salon to pick up a book, and I noticed the clock.'

'In other words you and Vawdrey distinctly lingered here from about five minutes past ten till the hour you mention?'

'I don't know how distinct we were, but we were very jolly. Où voulez-vous en venir?'[12] Blanche Adney asked.

'Simply to this, dear lady: that at the time your companion was occupied in the manner you describe he was also engaged in literary composition in his own room.'

She stopped short for it, and her eyes had a sheen in the darkness. She wanted to know if I challenged her veracity; and I replied that on the contrary I backed it up – it made the case so interesting. She returned that this would only be if she should back up mine; which however I had no difficulty in persuading her to do after I had related to her circumstantially the incident of my quest of the manuscript – the manuscript which at the time, for a reason I could now understand, appeared to have passed so completely out of her own head.

'His talk made me forget it – I forgot I sent you for it. He made up for his fiasco in the salon: he declaimed me the scene,' said Blanche. She had dropped on a bench to listen to me and, as we sat there, had briefly cross-examined me. Then she broke out into fresh laughter. 'Oh the eccentricities of genius!'

'Yes indeed! They seem greater even than I supposed.'

'Oh the mysteries of greatness!'

'You ought to know all about them, but they take me by surprise,' I declared.

'Are you absolutely certain it was Vawdrey?' my companion asked.

'If it wasn't he who in the world was it? That a strange gentleman, looking exactly like him and of like literary pursuits, should be sitting in his room at that hour of the night and writing at his table *in the dark*,' I insisted, 'would be practically as wonderful as my own contention.'

'Yes, why in the dark?' my friend mused.

'Cats can see in the dark,' I said.

She smiled at me dimly. 'Did it look like a cat?'

'No, dear lady, but I'll tell you what it did look like – it looked like the author of Vawdrey's admirable works. It looked infinitely more like him than our friend does himself,' I pronounced.

'Do you mean it was somebody he gets to do them?'

'Yes, while he dines out and disappoints you.'

'Disappoints me?' she murmured artlessly.

'Disappoints *me* – disappoints every one who looks in him for the genius that created the pages they adore. Where is it in his talk?'

'Ah last night he was splendid,' said the actress.

'He's always splendid, as your morning bath is splendid, or a sirloin of beef, or the railway-service to Brighton. But he's never rare.'

'I see what you mean.'

I could have hugged her – and perhaps I did. 'That's what makes you such a comfort to talk to. I've often wondered – now I know. There are two of them.'

'What a delightful idea!'

'One goes out, the other stays at home. One's the genius, the other's the bourgeois, and it's only the bourgeois whom we personally know. He talks, he circulates, he's awfully popular, he flirts with you –'

'Whereas it's the genius *you* are privileged to flirt with!' Mrs Adney broke in. 'I'm much obliged to you for the distinction.'

I laid my hand on her arm. 'See him yourself. Try it, test it, go to his room.'

'Go to his room? It wouldn't be proper!' she cried in the manner of her best comedy.

'Anything's proper in such an enquiry. If you see him it settles it.'

'How charming – to settle it!' She thought a moment, then sprang up. 'Do you mean *now*?'

'Whenever you like.'

'But suppose I should find the wrong one?' she said with an exquisite effect.

'The wrong one? Which one do you call the right?'

'The wrong one for a lady to go and see. Suppose I shouldn't find – the genius?'

'Oh I'll look after the other,' I returned. Then as I had happened to glance about me I added: 'Take care – here comes Lord Mellifont.'

'I wish you'd look after *him*,' she said with a drop of her voice.

'What's the matter with him?'

'That's just what I was going to tell you.'

'Tell me now. He's not coming.'

Blanche looked a moment. Lord Mellifont, who appeared to have emerged from the hotel to smoke a meditative cigar, had paused at a distance from us and stood admiring the wonders of the prospect, discernible even in the dusk. We strolled slowly in another direction, and she presently resumed: 'My idea's almost as droll as yours.'

'I don't call mine droll: it's beautiful.'

'There's nothing so beautiful as the droll,' Mrs Adney returned.

'You take a professional view. But I'm all ears.' My curiosity was indeed alive again.

'Well then, my dear friend, if Clare Vawdrey's double – and I'm bound to say I think that the more of him the better – his lordship there has the opposite complaint: he isn't even whole.'

We stopped once more, simultaneously. 'I don't understand.'

'No more do I. But I've a fancy that if there are two of Mr Vawdrey, there isn't so much as one, all told, of Lord Mellifont.'

I considered a moment, then I laughed out. 'I think I see what you mean!'

'That's what makes *you* a comfort.' She didn't, alas, hug me, but she promptly went on. 'Did you ever see him alone?'

I tried to remember. 'Oh yes – he has been to see me.'

'Ah then he wasn't alone.'

'And I've been to see *him* – in his study.'

'Did he know you were there?'

'Naturally – I was announced.'

She glared at me like a lovely conspirator. 'You mustn't *be* announced!' With this she walked on.

I rejoined her, breathless. 'Do you mean one must come upon him when he doesn't know it?'

'You must take him unawares. You must go to his room – that's what you must do.'

If I was elated by the way our mystery opened out I was also, pardonably, a little confused. 'When I know he's not there?'

'When you know he *is*.'

'And what shall I see?'

'You won't see anything!' she cried as we turned round.

We had reached the end of the terrace and our movement brought us face to face with Lord Mellifont, who, addressing himself again to his walk, had now, without indiscretion, overtaken us. The sight of him at that moment was illuminating, and it kindled a great backward train, connecting itself with one's general impression of the personage. As he stood there smiling at us and waving a practised hand into

the transparent night – he introduced the view as if it had
been a candidate and 'supported' the very Alps – as he rose
before us in the delicate fragrance of his cigar and all
his other delicacies and fragrances, with more perfections
somehow heaped on his handsome head than one had ever
seen accumulated before or elsewhere, he struck me as
so essentially, so conspicuously and uniformly the public
character that I read in a flash the answer to Blanche's
riddle. He was all public and had no corresponding private
life, just as Clare Vawdrey was all private and had no
corresponding public. I had heard only half my companion's
tale, yet as we joined Lord Mellifont – he had followed us,
liking Mrs Adney, but it was always to be conceived of him
that he accepted society rather than sought it – as we
participated for half an hour in the distributed wealth of his
discourse I felt with unabashed duplicity that we had, as it
were, found him out. I was even more deeply diverted by
that whisk of the curtain to which the actress had just
treated me than I had been by my own discovery; and if I
wasn't ashamed of my share of her secret any more than of
having divided my own with her – though my own was, of
the two mysteries, the more glorious for the personage
involved – this was because there was no cruelty in my
advantage, but on the contrary an extreme tenderness and
a positive compassion. Oh he was safe with me, and I felt
moreover rich and enlightened, as if I had suddenly got the
universe into my pouch. I had learned what an affair of the
spot and the moment a great appearance may be. It would
doubtless be too much to say that I had always suspected
the possibility, in the background of his lordship's being, of
some such beautiful instance; but it's at least a fact that,
patronising as such words may sound, I had been conscious
of a certain reserve of indulgence for him. I had secretly
pitied him for the perfection of his performance, had wondered what blank face such a mask had to cover, what was

left to him for the immitigable hours in which a man sits down with himself, or, more serious still, with that intenser self his lawful wife. How was he at home and what did he do when he was alone? There was something in Lady Mellifont that gave a point to these researches – something that suggested how even to her he must have been still the public character and she beset with similar questionings. She had never cleared them up: that was her eternal trouble. We therefore knew more than she did, Blanche Adney and I; but we wouldn't tell her for the world, nor would she probably thank us for doing so. She preferred the relative grandeur of uncertainty. She wasn't at home with him, so she couldn't say; and with her he wasn't alone, so he couldn't show her. He represented to his wife and was a hero to his servants, and what one wanted to arrive at was what really became of him when no eye could see – and *a fortiori* no soul admire. He relaxed and rested presumably; but how utter a blank mustn't it take to repair such a plenitude of presence! – how intense an *entr'acte* to make possible more such performances! Lady Mellifont was too proud to pry, and as she had never looked through a keyhole she remained dignified and unrelieved.

It may have been a fancy of mine that Mrs Adney drew out our companion, or it may be that the practical irony of our relation to him at such a moment made me see him more vividly: at any rate he never had struck me as so dissimilar from what he would have been if we hadn't offered him a reflexion of his image. We were only a concourse of two, but he had never been more public. His perfect manner had never been more perfect, his remarkable tact never more remarkable, his one conceivable *raison d'être*, the absolute singleness of his identity, never more attested. I had a tacit sense that it would all be in the morning papers, with a leader, and also a secretly exhilarating one that I knew something that wouldn't be, that never could be, though any enterprising journal would give me a fortune for it. I must add, however, that in spite of my enjoyment – it was almost sensual, like that of a consummate dish or an unprecedented pleasure – I was eager to be alone again with Mrs Adney, who owed me an anecdote. This proved impossible that evening, for some of the others came out to see what he found so absorbing; and then Lord Mellifont bespoke a little music from the fiddler, who produced his violin and played to us divinely, on our platform of echoes, face to face with the ghosts of the mountains. Before the concert was over I missed our actress and, glancing into the window of the salon, saw her established there with Vawdrey, who was reading out from a manuscript. The great scene had apparently been achieved and was doubtless the more interesting to Blanche from the new lights she had gathered about its author. I judged discreet not to disturb them, and went to bed without seeing her again. I looked out for her betimes the next morning and, as the promise of the day was fair, proposed to her that we should take to the hills, reminding her of the high obligation she had incurred. She recognised the obligation and gratified me with her company, but before we had strolled ten yards up the pass she broke out with intensity: 'My dear friend, you've no idea how it works in me! I can think of nothing else.'

'Than your theory about Lord Mellifont?'

'Oh bother Lord Mellifont! I allude to yours about Mr Vawdrey, who's much the more interesting person of the two. I'm fascinated by that vision of his – what-do-you-call-it?'

'His alternate identity?'

'His other self: that's easier to say.'

'You accept it then, you adopt it?'

'Adopt it? I rejoice in it! It became tremendously vivid to me last evening.'

'While he read to you there?'

'Yes, as I listened to him, watched him. It simplified everything, explained everything.'

I rose to my triumph. 'That's indeed the blessing of it. Is the scene very fine?'

'Magnificent, and he reads beautifully.'

'Almost as well as the other one writes!' I laughed.

This made her stop a moment, laying her hand on my arm. 'You utter my very impression! I felt he was reading me the work of another.'

'In a manner that was such a service to the other,' I concurred.

'Such a totally different person,' said Blanche. We talked of this difference as we went on, and of what a wealth it constituted, what a resource for life, such a duplication of character.

'It ought to make him live twice as long as other people,' I made out.

'Ought to make which of them?'

'Well, both; for after all they're members of a firm, and one of them would never be able to carry on the business without the other. Moreover mere survival would be dreadful for either.'

She was silent a little; after which she exclaimed: 'I don't know – I wish he *would* survive!'

'May I on my side enquire which?'

'If you can't guess I won't tell you.'

'I know the heart of woman. You always prefer the other.'

She halted again, looking round her. 'Off here, away from my husband, I *can* tell you. I'm in love with him!'

'Unhappy woman, he has no passions,' I answered.

'That's exactly why I adore him. Doesn't a woman with my history know the passions of others for insupportable? An actress, poor thing, can't care for any love that's not all on *her* side; she can't afford to be repaid. My marriage proves that: a pretty one, a lucky one like ours, is ruinous.

Do you know what was in my mind last night and all the while Mr Vawdrey read me those beautiful speeches? An insane desire to see the author.' And dramatically, as if to hide her shame, Blanche Adney passed on.

'We'll manage that,' I returned. 'I want another glimpse of him myself. But meanwhile please remember that I've been waiting more than forty-eight hours for the evidence that supports your sketch, intensely suggestive and plausible, of Lord Mellifont's private life.'

'Oh Lord Mellifont doesn't interest me.'

'He did yesterday,' I said.

'Yes, but that was before I fell in love. You blotted him out with *your* story.'

'You'll make me sorry I told it. Come,' I pleaded, 'if you don't let me know how your idea came into your head I shall imagine you simply made it up.'

'Let me recollect then, while we wander in this velvet gorge.'

We stood at the entrance of a charming crooked valley, a portion of the level floor of which formed the bed of a stream that was smooth with swiftness. We turned into it, and the soft walk beside the clear torrent drew us on and on; till suddenly, as we continued and I waited for my companion to remember, a bend of the ravine showed us Lady Mellifont coming towards us. She was alone, under the canopy of her parasol, drawing her sable train over the turf; and in this form, on the devious ways, she was a sufficiently rare apparition. She mostly took out a footman, who marched behind her on the highroads and whose livery was strange to the rude rustics. She blushed on seeing us, as if she ought somehow to justify her being there; she laughed vaguely and described herself as abroad but for a small early stroll. We stood together thus, exchanging platitudes, and then she told us how she had counted a little on finding her husband.

'Is he in this quarter?' I asked.

'I supposed he would be. He came out an hour ago to sketch.'

'Have you been looking for him?' Mrs Adney put to her.

'A little; not very much,' said Lady Mellifont.

Each of the women rested her eyes with some intensity, as it seemed to me, on the eyes of the other. 'We'll look for him *for* you, if you like,' said Blanche.

'Oh it doesn't matter. I thought I'd join him.'

'He won't make his sketch if you don't,' my companion hinted.

'Perhaps he will if *you* do,' said Lady Mellifont.

'Oh I dare say he'll turn up,' I interposed.

'He certainly will if he knows we're here!' Blanche retorted.

'Will you wait while we search?' I asked of Lady Mellifont.

She repeated that it was of no consequence; upon which Mrs Adney went on: 'We'll go into the matter for our own pleasure.'

'I wish you a pleasant excursion,' said her ladyship, and was turning away when I sought to know if we should inform her husband she was near. 'That I've followed him?' She demurred a moment and then jerked out oddly: 'I think you had better not.' With this she took leave of us, floating a little stiffly down the gorge.

My companion and I watched her retreat; after which we exchanged a stare and a light ghost of a laugh rippled from the actress's lips. 'She might be walking in the shrubberies at Mellifont!'

I had my view. 'She suspects it, you know.'

'And she doesn't want him to guess it. There won't be any sketch.'

'Unless we overtake him,' I suggested. 'In that case we shall find him producing one, in the very most graceful and established attitude, and the queer thing is that it will be brilliant.'

'Let us leave him alone – he'll have to come home without it,' my friend contributed.

'He'd rather never come home. Oh he'll find a public!'

'Perhaps he'll do it for the cows,' Blanche risked; and as I was on the point of rebuking her profanity she went on: 'That's simply what I happened to discover.'

'What are you speaking of?'

'The incident of day before yesterday.'

I jumped at it. 'Ah let's have it at last!'

'That's all it was – that I was like Lady Mellifont: I couldn't find him.'

'Did you lose him?'

'He lost *me* – that appears to be the way of it. He supposed me gone. And then –!' But she paused, looking – that is smiling – volumes.

'You did find him, however,' I said as I wondered, 'since you came home with him.'

'It was he who found *me*. That again is what must happen. He's there from the moment he knows somebody else is.'

'I understand his intermissions,' I returned on short reflection, 'but I don't quite seize the law that governs them.'

Ah Blanche had quite mastered it! 'It's a fine shade, but I caught it at that moment. I had started to come home, I was tired and had insisted on his not coming back with me. We had found some rare flowers – those I brought home – and it was he who had discovered almost all of them. It amused him very much, and I knew he wanted to get more; but I was weary and I quitted him. He let me go – where else would have been his tact? – and I was too stupid then to have guessed that from the moment I wasn't there no flower would be – *could* be – gathered. I started homeward, but at the end of three minutes I found I had brought away his penknife – he had lent it to me to trim a branch – and I knew

he'd need it. I turned back a few steps to call him, but before I spoke I looked about for him. You can't understand
what happened then without having the scene before
you.'

'You must take me there,' I said.

'We may see the wonder here. The place was simply one
that offered no chance for concealment – a great gradual
hillside without obstructions or cavities or bushes or trees.
There were some rocks below me, behind which I myself had
disappeared, but from which on coming back I immediately
emerged again.'

'Then he must have seen you.'

'He was too absent, too utterly gone, as gone as a candle
blown out; for some reason best known to himself. It was
probably some moment of fatigue – he's getting on, you
know, so that with the sense of returning solitude the
reaction had been proportionately great, the extinction
proportionately complete. At any rate the stage was as bare
as your hand.'

'Couldn't he have been somewhere else?'

'He couldn't have been, in the time, anywhere but just
where I had left him. Yet the place was utterly empty – as
empty as this stretch of valley in front of us. He had
vanished – he had ceased to be. But as soon as my voice rang
out – I uttered his name – he rose before me like the rising
sun.'

'And where did the sun rise?'

'Just where it ought to – just where he would have been
and where I should have seen him had he been like other
people.'

I had listened with the deepest interest, but it was my
duty to think of objections. 'How long a time elapsed
between the moment you were sure of his absence and the
moment you called?'

'Oh but a few seconds. I don't pretend it was long.'

'Long enough for you to be really certain?' I said.

'Certain he wasn't there?'

'Yes, and that you weren't mistaken, weren't the victim of some hocus-pocus of your eyesight.'

'I may have been mistaken – but I feel too strongly I wasn't. At any rate that's just why I want you to look in his room.'

I thought a moment. 'How *can* I – when even his wife doesn't dare to?'

'She *wants* to; propose it to her. It wouldn't take much to make her. She does suspect.'

I thought another moment. 'Did he seem to know?'

'That I had missed him and might have immensely wondered? So it struck me – but with it too that he probably thought he had been quick enough. He has, you see, to think that – to take it mostly for granted.'

Ah – I lost myself – who could say? 'But did you speak at least of his disappearance?'

'Heaven forbid – *y pensez-vous?*[13] It seemed to me too strange.'

'Quite right. And how did he look?'

Trying to think it out again and reconstitute her miracle, Blanche Adney gazed abstractedly up the valley. Suddenly she brought out: 'Just as he looks now!' and I saw Lord Mellifont stand before us with his sketch-block. I took in as we met him that he appeared neither suspicious nor blank: he simply stood there, as he stood always everywhere, for the principal feature of the scene. Naturally he had no sketch to show us, but nothing could better have rounded off our actual conception of him than the way he fell into position as we approached. He had been selecting his point of view – he took possession of it with a flourish of the pencil. He leaned against a rock; his beautiful little box of water-colours reposed on a natural table beside him, a ledge of the bank which showed how inveterately nature

ministered to his convenience. He painted while he talked
and he talked while he painted; and if the painting was as
miscellaneous as the talk, the talk would equally have graced
an album. We stayed while the exhibition went on, and the
conscious profiles of the peaks might to our apprehension
have been interested in his success. They grew as black as
silhouettes in paper, sharp against a livid sky from which,
however, there would be nothing to fear till Lord Mellifont's
sketch should be finished. All nature deferred to him and
the very elements waited. Blanche Adney communed with
me dumbly, and I could read the language of her eyes: 'Oh
if *we* could only do it as well as that! He fills the stage in a
way that beats us.' We could no more have left him than we
could have quitted the theatre till the play was over; but in
due time we turned round with him and strolled back to the
inn, before the door of which his lordship, glancing again
at his picture, tore the fresh leaf from the block and presented
it with a few happy words to our friend. Then he went into
the house; and a moment later, looking up from where we
stood, we saw him, above, at the window of his sitting-
room – he had the best apartments – watching the signs of
the weather.

'He'll have to rest after this,' Blanche said, dropping her
eyes on her water-colour.

'Indeed he will!' I raised mine to the window: Lord
Mellifont had vanished. 'He's already reabsorbed.'

'Reabsorbed?' I could see the actress was now thinking
of something else.

'Into the immensity of things. He has lapsed again. The
entr'acte has begun.'

'It ought to be long.' She surveyed the terrace and as at
that moment the head-waiter appeared in the doorway
she suddenly turned to address him. 'Have you seen Mr
Vawdrey lately?'

The man immediately approached. 'He left the house five

minutes ago – for a walk, I think. He went down the pass; he had a book.'

I was watching the ominous clouds. 'He had better have had an umbrella.'

The waiter smiled. 'I recommended him to take one.'

'Thank you,' Blanche said; and the Oberkellner withdrew. Then she went on abruptly: 'Will you do me a favour?'

'Yes, if you'll do *me* one. Let me see if your picture's signed.'

She glanced at the sketch before giving it to me. 'For a wonder it isn't.'

'It ought to be, for full value. May I keep it a while?'

'Yes, if you'll do what I ask. Take an umbrella and go after Mr Vawdrey.'

'To bring him to Mrs Adney?'

'To keep him out – as long as you can.'

'I'll keep him as long as the rain holds off.'

'Oh never mind the rain!' my companion cried.

'Would you have us drenched?'

'Without remorse.' Then with a strange light in her eyes: 'I'm going to try.'

'To try?'

'To see the real one. Oh if I can get at him!' she broke out with passion.

'Try, try!' I returned. 'I'll keep our friend all day.'

'If I can get at the one who does it' – and she paused with shining eyes – 'if I can have it out with him I shall get another act, I shall have my part!'

'I'll keep Vawdrey for ever!' I called after her as she passed quickly into the house.

Her audacity was communicable and I stood there in a glow of excitement. I looked at Lord Mellifont's watercolour and I looked at the gathering storm; I turned my eyes again to his lordship's windows and then I bent them on my watch. Vawdrey had so little the start of me that I should

have time to overtake him, time even if I should take five
minutes to go up to Lord Mellifont's sitting-room – where
we had all been hospitably received – and say to him, as a
messenger, that Mrs Adney begged he would bestow on his
sketch the high consecration of his signature. As I again
considered this work of art I noted there was something it
certainly did lack: what else then but so noble an autograph?
It was my duty without loss of time to make the deficiency
good, and in accordance with this view I instantly re-entered
the hotel. I went up to Lord Mellifont's apartments; I
reached the door of his salon. Here, however, I was met by
a difficulty with which my extravagance hadn't counted. If
I were to knock I should spoil everything; yet was I prepared
to dispense with this ceremony? I put myself the question
and it embarrassed me; I turned my little picture round and
round, but it gave me no answer I wanted. I wanted it to
say 'Open the door gently, gently, without a sound, yet very
quickly: then you'll see what you'll see.' I had gone so far
as to lay my hand on the knob when I became aware (having
my wits so about me) that exactly in the manner I was
thinking of – gently, gently, without a sound – another door
had moved, and on the opposite side of the hall. At the same
instant I found myself smiling rather constrainedly at Lady
Mellifont, who, seeing me, had checked herself by the
threshold of her room. For a moment, as she stood there,
we exchanged two or three ideas that were the more singular
for being so unspoken. We had caught each other hovering
and to that extent understood each other; but as I stepped
over to her – so that we were separated from the sitting-
room by the width of the hall – her lips formed the almost
soundless entreaty: 'Don't!' I could see in her conscious eyes
everything the word expressed – the confession of her own
curiosity and the dread of the consequences of mine. *'Don't!'*
she repeated as I stood before her. From the moment my
experiment could strike her as an act of violence I was ready

to renounce it; yet I thought I caught from her frightened face a still deeper betrayal – a possibility of disappointment if I should give way. It was as if she had said: 'I'll let you do it if you'll take the responsibility. Yes, with some one else I'd surprise him. But it would never do for him to think it was I.'

'We soon found Lord Mellifont,' I observed in allusion to our encounter with her an hour before, 'and he was so good as to give this lovely sketch to Mrs Adney, who has asked me to come up and beg him to put in the omitted signature.'

Lady Mellifont took the drawing from me, and I could guess the struggle that went on in her while she looked at it. She waited to speak; then I felt all her delicacies and dignities, all her old timidities and pieties obstruct her great chance. She turned away from me and, with the drawing, went back to her room. She was absent for a couple of minutes, and when she reappeared I could see she had vanquished her temptation, that even with a kind of resurgent horror she had shrunk from it. She had deposited the sketch in the room. 'If you'll kindly leave the picture with me I'll see that Mrs Adney's request is attended to,' she said with great courtesy and sweetness, but in a manner that put an end to our colloquy.

I assented, with a somewhat artificial enthusiasm perhaps, and then, to ease off our separation, remarked that we should have a change of weather.

'In that case we shall go – we shall go immediately,' the poor lady returned. I was amused at the eagerness with which she made this declaration: it appeared to represent a coveted flight into safety, an escape with her threatened secret. I was the more surprised therefore when, as I was turning away, she put out her hand to take mine. She had the pretext of bidding me farewell, but as I shook hands with her on this supposition I felt that what the movement really conveyed was: 'I thank you for the help you'd have given me, but it's better as it is. If I should know, who would help me then?' As I went to my room to get my umbrella I said to myself: 'She's sure, but she won't put it to the proof.'

A quarter of an hour later I had overtaken Clare Vawdrey in the pass, and shortly after this we found ourselves looking for refuge. The storm hadn't only completely gathered, but had broken at the last with extraordinary force. We scrambled up a hillside to an empty cabin, a rough structure that was hardly more than a shed for the protection of cattle. It was a tolerable shelter however, and it had fissures through which we could see the show, watch the grand rage of nature. Our entertainment lasted an hour – an hour that has remained with me as full of odd disparities. While the lightning played with the thunder and the rain gushed in on our umbrellas, I said to myself that Clare Vawdrey was disappointing. I don't know exactly what I should have predicated of a great author exposed to the fury of the elements, I can't say what particular Manfred[14] attitude I should have expected my companion to assume, but it struck me somehow that I shouldn't have looked to him to regale me in such a situation with stories – which I had already heard – about the celebrated Lady Ringrose. Her ladyship formed the subject of Vawdrey's conversation during this prodigious scene, though before it was quite over he had launched out on Mr Chafer, the scarcely less notorious reviewer. It broke my heart to hear a man like Vawdrey talk of reviewers. The lightning projected a hard clearness upon the truth, familiar to me for years, to which the last day or two had added transcendent support – the irritating certitude that for personal relations this admirable genius thought his second-best good enough. It *was*, no doubt, as society was made, but there was a contempt in the distinction which couldn't fail to be galling to an admirer. The world was vulgar and stupid, and the real man would have been a fool to come out for it when he could gossip and dine by deputy. None the less my heart sank as I felt him practise this economy. I don't know exactly what I wanted; I suppose I wanted him to make an exception for *me* – for me all alone, and all handsomely and tenderly, in the vast horde of the dull. I almost believed he would have done so had he known how I worshipped his talent. But I had never been able to translate this to him, and his application of his principle was relentless. At any rate I was more than ever sure that at such an hour his chair at home at least wasn't empty: *there* was the Manfred attitude, *there* were the responsive flashes. I could only envy Mrs Adney her presumable enjoyment of them.

The weather drew off at last and the rain abated sufficiently to allow us to emerge from our asylum and make our way back to the inn, where we found on our arrival that our prolonged absence had produced some agitation. It was judged apparently that the storm had placed us in a predicament. Several of our friends were at the door, who seemed just disconcerted to note we were only drenched. Clare Vawdrey, for some reason, had had the greater soaking, and he took a straight course to his room. Blanche Adney was among the persons collected to look out for us, but as the subject of our speculation came towards her she shrank from him without a greeting; with a movement that I measured as almost one of coldness she turned her back on him and went quickly into the salon. Wet as I was I went in after her; on which she immediately flung round and faced me. The first thing I saw was that she had never been so beautiful. There was a light of inspiration in her, and she broke out to me in the quickest whisper, which was at the same time the loudest cry I have ever heard: 'I've got my *part*!'

'You went to his room – I was right?'

'Right?' Blanche Adney repeated. 'Ah my dear fellow!' she murmured.

'He was there – you saw him?'

'He saw *me*. It was the hour of my life!'

'It must have been the hour of his, if you were half as lovely as you are at this moment.'

'He's splendid,' she pursued as if she didn't hear me. 'He *is* the one who does it!' I listened, immensely impressed, and she added: 'We understood each other.'

'By flashes of lightning?'

'Oh I didn't see the lightning then!'

'How long were you there?' I asked with admiration.

'Long enough to tell him I adore him.'

'Ah that's what I've never been able to tell him!' I quite wailed.

'I shall have my part – I shall have my part!' she continued with triumphant indifference; and she flung round the room with the joy of a girl, only checking herself to say: 'Go and change your clothes.'

'You shall have Lord Mellifont's signature,' I said.

'Oh hang Lord Mellifont's signature! He's far nicer than Mr Vawdrey,' she went on irrelevantly.

'Lord Mellifont?' I pretended to enquire.

'Confound Lord Mellifont!' And Blanche Adney, in her elation, brushed by me, whisking again through the open door. Just outside of it she came upon her husband; whereupon with a charming cry of 'We're talking of *you*, my love!' she threw herself upon him and kissed him.

I went to my room and changed my clothes, but I remained there till the evening. The violence of the storm had passed over us, but the rain had settled down to a drizzle. On descending to dinner I saw the change in the weather had already broken up our party. The Mellifonts had departed in a carriage and four, they had been followed by others, and several vehicles had been bespoken for the morning.

Blanche Adney's was one of them, and on the pretext that she had preparations to make she quitted us directly after dinner. Clare Vawdrey asked me what was the matter with her – she suddenly appeared to dislike him. I forget what answer I gave, but I did my best to comfort him by driving away with him the next day. Blanche had vanished when we came down; but they made up their quarrel in London, for he finished his play, which she produced. I must add that she is still nevertheless in want of the great part. I've a beautiful one in my head, but she doesn't come to see me to stir me up about it. Lady Mellifont always drops me a kind word when we meet, but that doesn't console me.

THE MIDDLE YEARS

❖

THE MIDDLE YEARS

THE MIDDLE YEARS

130   The Middle Years

The April day was soft and bright, and poor Dencombe,
happy in the conceit of reasserted strength, stood in the
garden of the hotel, comparing, with a deliberation in which
however there was still something of languor, the attractions
of easy strolls. He liked the feeling of the south so far as you
could have it in the north, he liked the sandy cliffs and the
clustered pines, he liked even the colourless sea.
'Bournemouth as a health-resort' had sounded like a mere
advertisement, but he was thankful now for the commonest
conveniences. The sociable country postman, passing
through the garden, had just given him a small parcel which
he took out with him, leaving the hotel to the right and
creeping to a bench he had already haunted, a safe recess in
the cliff. It looked to the south, to the tinted walls of the
Island,[1] and was protected behind by the sloping shoulder
of the down. He was tired enough when he reached it, and
for a moment was disappointed; he was better of course,
but better, after all, than what? He should never again, as
at one or two great moments of the past, be better than
himself. The infinite of life was gone, and what remained
of the dose a small glass scored like a thermometer by the
apothecary. He sat and stared at the sea, which appeared
all surface and twinkle, far shallower than the spirit of man.
It was the abyss of human illusion that was the real, the
tideless deep. He held his packet, which had come by book-
post, unopened on his knee, liking, in the lapse of so many
joys – his illness had made him feel his age – to know it was

there, but taking for granted there could be no complete renewal of the pleasure, dear to young experience, of seeing one's self 'just out'. Dencombe, who had a reputation, had come out too often and knew too well in advance how he should look.

His postponement associated itself vaguely, after a little, with a group of three persons, two ladies and a young man, whom, beneath him, straggling and seemingly silent, he could see move slowly together along the sands. The gentleman had his head bent over a book and was occasionally brought to a stop by the charm of this volume, which, as Dencombe could perceive even at a distance, had a cover alluringly red. Then his companions, going a little further, waited for him to come up, poking their parasols into the beach, looking around them at the sea and sky and clearly sensible of the beauty of the day. To these things the young man with the book was still more clearly indifferent; lingering, credulous, absorbed, he was an object of envy to an observer from whose connexion with literature all such artlessness had faded. One of the ladies was large and mature; the other had the spareness of comparative youth and of a social situation possibly inferior. The large lady carried back Dencombe's imagination to the age of crinoline; she wore a hat of the shape of a mushroom, decorated with a blue veil, and had the air, in her aggressive amplitude, of clinging to a vanished fashion or even a lost cause. Presently her companion produced from under the folds of a mantle a limp portable chair which she stiffened out and of which the large lady took possession. This act, and something in the movement of either party, at once characterised the performers – they performed for Dencombe's reaction – as opulent matron and humble dependent. Where moreover was the virtue of an approved novelist if one couldn't establish a relation between such figures? the clever theory for instance that the young man was the son of the opulent matron and that the humble dependent, the daughter of a clergyman or an officer, nourished a secret passion for him. Was that not visible from the way she stole behind her protectress to look back at him? – back to where he had let himself come to a full stop when his mother sat down to rest. His book was a novel, it had the catchpenny binding;[2] so that while the romance of life stood neglected at his side he lost himself in that of the circulating library.[3] He moved mechanically to where the sand was softer and ended by plumping down in it to finish his chapter at his ease. The humble dependent, discouraged by his remoteness, wandered with a martyred droop of the head in another direction, and the exorbitant lady, watching the waves, offered a confused resemblance to a flying-machine that had broken down.

When his drama began to fail Dencombe remembered that he had after all another pastime. Though such promptitude on the part of the publisher was rare he was already able to draw from its wrapper his 'latest', perhaps his last. The cover of 'The Middle Years' was duly meretricious, the smell of the fresh pages the very odour of sanctity; but for the moment he went no further – he had become conscious of a strange alienation. He had forgotten what his book was about. Had the assault of his old ailment, which he had so fallaciously come to Bournemouth to ward off, interposed utter blankness as to what had preceded it? He had finished the revision of proof before quitting London, but his subsequent fortnight in bed had passed the sponge over colour.[4] He couldn't have chanted to himself a single sentence, couldn't have turned with curiosity or confidence to any particular page. His subject had already gone from him, leaving scarce a superstition behind. He uttered a low moan as he breathed the chill of this dark void, so desperately it seemed to represent the completion of a sinister process. The tears filled his mild eyes; something precious had passed away. This was the pang that had been sharpest during the last few years – the sense of ebbing time, of shrinking opportunity; and now he felt not so much that his last chance was going as that it was gone indeed. He had done all he should ever do, and yet hadn't done what he wanted. This was the laceration – that practically his career was over: it was as violent as a grip at his throat. He rose from his seat nervously – a creature hunted by a dread; then he fell back in his weakness and nervously opened his book. It was a single volume; he preferred single volumes and aimed at a rare compression. He began to read and, little by little, in this occupation, was pacified and reassured. Everything came back to him, but came back with a wonder, came back above all with a high and magnificent beauty. He read his own prose, he turned his own leaves, and had as he sat there with the spring sunshine on the page an emotion peculiar and intense. His career was over, no doubt, but it was over, when all was said, with *that*.

He had forgotten during his illness the work of the previous year; but what he had chiefly forgotten was that it was extraordinarily good. He dived once more into his story and was drawn down, as by a siren's hand, to where, in the dim underworld of fiction, the great glazed tank of art,⁵ strange silent subjects float. He recognised his motive and surrendered to his talent. Never probably had that talent, such as it was, been so fine. His difficulties were still there, but what was also there, to his perception, though probably, alas! to nobody's else, was the art that in most cases had surmounted them. In his surprised enjoyment of this ability he had a glimpse of a possible reprieve. Surely its force wasn't spent – there was life and service in it yet. It hadn't come to him easily, it had been backward and roundabout. It was the child of time, the nursling of delay; he had struggled and suffered for it, making sacrifices not to be counted, and now that it was really mature was it to cease to yield, to confess itself brutally beaten? There was an infinite charm for Dencombe in feeling as he had never felt before that diligence *vincit omnia*.[6] The result produced in his little book was somehow a result beyond his conscious intention: it was as if he had planted his genius, had trusted his method, and they had grown up and flowered with this sweetness. If the achievement had been real, however, the process had been painful enough. What he saw so intensely today, what he felt as a nail driven in, was that only now, at the very last, had he come into possession. His development had been abnormally slow, almost grotesquely gradual. He had been hindered and retarded by experience, he had for long periods only groped his way. It had taken too much of his life to produce too little of his art. The art had come, but it had come after everything else. At such a rate a first existence was too short – long enough only to collect material; so that to fructify, to use the material, one should have a second age, an extension. This extension was what poor Dencombe sighed for. As he turned the last leaves of his volume he murmured 'Ah for another go, ah for a better chance!'

The three persons drawing his attention to the sands had vanished and then reappeared; they had now wandered up a path, an artificial and easy ascent, which led to the top of the cliff. Dencombe's bench was halfway down, on a sheltered ledge, and the large lady, a massive heterogeneous person with bold black eyes and kind red cheeks, now took a few moments to rest. She wore dirty gauntlets and immense diamond ear-rings; at first she looked vulgar, but she contradicted this announcement in an agreeable off-hand tone. While her companions stood waiting for her she spread her skirts on the end of Dencombe's seat. The young man had gold spectacles, through which, with his finger still in his red-covered book, he glanced at the volume, bound in the same shade of the same colour, lying on the lap of the original occupant of the bench. After an instant Dencombe felt him struck with a resemblance; he had recognised the gilt stamp on the crimson cloth, was reading 'The Middle Years' and now noted that somebody else had kept pace with him. The stranger was startled, possibly even a little ruffled, to find himself not the only person favoured with an early copy. The eyes of the two proprietors met a moment, and Dencombe borrowed amusement from the expression of those of his competitor, those, it might even be inferred, of his admirer. They confessed to some resentment – they seemed to say: 'Hang it, has he got it *already*? Of course he's a brute of a reviewer!' Dencombe shuffled his copy out of sight while the opulent matron, rising from her repose, broke out: 'I feel already the good of this air!'

'I can't say I do,' said the angular lady. 'I find myself quite let down.'

'I find myself horribly hungry. At what time did you order luncheon?' her protectress pursued.

The young person put the question by. 'Doctor Hugh always orders it.'

'I ordered nothing today – I'm going to make you diet,' said their comrade.

'Then I shall go home and sleep. *Qui dort dine!*'[7]

'Can I trust you to Miss Vernham?' asked Doctor Hugh of his elder companion.

'Don't I trust *you*?' she archly enquired.

'Not too much!' Miss Vernham, with her eyes on the ground, permitted herself to declare. 'You must come with us at least to the house,' she went on while the personage on whom they appeared to be in attendance began to mount higher. She had got a little out of ear-shot; nevertheless Miss Vernham became, so far as Dencombe was concerned, less distinctly audible to murmur to the young man: 'I don't think you realise all you owe the Countess!'

Absently, a moment, Doctor Hugh caused his gold-rimmed spectacles to shine at her. 'Is that the way I strike you? I see – I see!'

'She's awfully good to us,' continued Miss Vernham, compelled by the lapse of the other's motion to stand there in spite of his discussion of private matters. Of what use would it have been that Dencombe should be sensitive to shades hadn't he detected in that arrest a strange influence from the quiet old convalescent in the great tweed cape? Miss Vernham appeared suddenly to become aware of some such connection, for she added in a moment: 'If you want to sun yourself here you can come back after you've seen us home.'

Doctor Hugh, at this, hesitated, and Dencombe, in spite of a desire to pass for unconscious, risked a covert glance at him. What his eyes met this time, as happened, was, on the part of the young lady, a queer stare, naturally vitreous, which made her remind him of some figure – he couldn't name it – in a play or a novel, some sinister governess or tragic old maid. She seemed to scan him, to challenge him, to say out of general spite: 'What have you got to do with us?' At the same instant the rich humour of the Countess reached them from above: 'Come, come, my little lambs; you should follow your old *bergère*!'[8] Miss Vernham turned away for it, pursuing the ascent, and Doctor Hugh, after another mute appeal to Dencombe and a minute's evident demur, deposited his book on the bench as if to keep his place, or even as a gauge of earnest return, and bounded without difficulty up the rougher part of the cliff.

Equally innocent and infinite are the pleasures of observation and the resources engendered by the trick of analysing life. It amused poor Dencombe, as he dawdled in his tepid air-bath, to believe himself awaiting a revelation of something at the back of a fine young mind. He looked hard at the book on the end of the bench, but wouldn't have touched it for the world. It served his purpose to have a theory that shouldn't be exposed to refutation. He already felt better of his melancholy; he had, according to his old formula, put his head at the window. A passing Countess could draw off the fancy when, like the elder of the ladies who had just retreated, she was as obvious as the giantess of a caravan.' It was indeed general views that were terrible; short ones, contrary to an opinion sometimes expressed, were the refuge, were the remedy. Doctor Hugh couldn't possibly be anything but a reviewer who had understandings for early copies with publishers or with newspapers. He reappeared in a quarter of an hour with visible relief at finding Dencombe on the spot and the gleam of white teeth in an embarrassed but generous smile. He was perceptibly disappointed at the eclipse of the other copy of the book; it made a pretext the less for speaking to the quiet gentleman. But he spoke notwithstanding; he held up his own copy and broke out pleadingly: '*Do* say, if you have occasion to speak of it, that it's the best thing he has done yet!'

Dencombe responded with a laugh: 'Done yet' was so amusing to him, made such a grand avenue of the future. Better still, the young man took *him* for a reviewer. He pulled out 'The Middle Years' from under his cape, but instinctively concealed any telltale look of fatherhood. This was partly because a person was always a fool for insisting to others on his work. 'Is that what you're going to say yourself?' he put to his visitor.

'I'm not quite sure I shall write anything. I don't, as a regular thing – I enjoy in peace. But it's awfully fine.'

Dencombe just debated. If the young man had begun to abuse him he would have confessed on the spot to his identity, but there was no harm in drawing out any impulse to praise. He drew it out with such success that in a few moments his new acquaintance, seated by his side, was confessing candidly that the works of the author of the volumes before them were the only ones he could read a second time. He had come the day before from London, where a friend of his, a journalist, had lent him his copy of the last, the copy sent to the office of the journal and already the subject of a 'notice' which, as was pretended there – but one had to allow for 'swagger' – it had taken a full quarter of an hour to prepare. He intimated that he was ashamed for his friend, and in the case of a work demanding and repaying study, of such inferior manners; and, with his fresh appreciation and his so irregular wish to express it, he speedily became for poor Dencombe a remarkable, a delightful apparition. Chance had brought the weary man of letters face to face with the greatest admirer in the new generation of whom it was supposable he might boast. The admirer in truth was mystifying, so rare a case was it to find a bristling young doctor – he looked like a German physiologist – enamoured of literary form. It was an accident, but happier than most accidents, so that Dencombe, exhilarated as well as confounded, spent half an hour in making his visitor talk while he kept himself quiet. He explained his premature possession of 'The Middle Years' by an allusion to the friendship of the publisher, who, knowing he was at Bournemouth for his health, had paid him this graceful attention. He allowed he had been ill, for Doctor Hugh would infallibly have guessed it; he even went so far as to wonder if he mightn't look for some hygienic 'tip' from a personage combining so bright an enthusiasm with a presumable knowledge of the remedies now in vogue. It would shake his faith a little perhaps to have to take a doctor seriously who could take *him* so seriously, but he enjoyed this gushing modern youth and felt with an acute pang that there would still be work to do in a world in which such odd combinations were presented. It wasn't true, what he had tried for renunciation's sake to believe, that all the combinations were exhausted. They weren't by any means – they were infinite: the exhaustion was in the miserable artist.

Doctor Hugh, an ardent physiologist, was saturated with the spirit of the age – in other words he had just taken his degree; but he was independent and various, he talked like a man who would have preferred to love literature best. He would fain have made fine phrases, but nature had denied him the trick. Some of the finest in 'The Middle Years' had struck him inordinately, and he took the liberty of reading them to Dencombe in support of his plea. He grew vivid, in the balmy air, to his companion, for whose deep refreshment he seemed to have been sent; and was particularly ingenuous in describing how recently he had become acquainted, and how instantly infatuated, with the only man who had put flesh between the ribs of an art that was starving on superstitions. He hadn't yet written to him – he was deterred by a strain of respect. Dencombe at this moment rejoiced more inwardly than ever that he had never answered the photographers. His visitor's attitude promised him a luxury of intercourse, though he was sure a due freedom from Doctor Hugh would depend not a little on the Countess. He learned without delay what type of Countess was involved, mastering as well the nature of the tie that united the curious trio. The large lady, an Englishwoman by birth and the daughter of a celebrated baritone, whose taste *minus* his talent she had inherited, was the widow of a French noble-man and mistress of all that remained of the handsome fortune, the fruit of her father's earnings, that had consti-tuted her dower. Miss Vernham, an odd creature but an accomplished pianist, was attached to her person at a salary. The Countess was generous, independent, eccentric; she travelled with her minstrel and her medical man. Ignorant and passionate she had nevertheless moments in which she was almost irresistible. Dencombe saw her sit for her portrait in Doctor Hugh's free sketch, and felt the picture of his young friend's relation to her frame itself in his mind. This young friend, for a representative of the new psychology,[10] was himself easily hypnotised, and if he became abnormally communicative it was only a sign of his real subjection. Dencombe did accordingly what he wanted with him, even without being known as Dencombe.

Taken ill on a journey in Switzerland the Countess had picked him up at an hotel, and the accident of his happening to please her had made her offer him, with her imperious liberality, terms that couldn't fail to dazzle a practitioner without patients and whose resources had been drained dry by his studies. It wasn't the way he would have proposed to spend his time, but it was time that would pass quickly, and meanwhile she was wonderfully kind. She exacted perpetual attention, but it was impossible not to like her. He gave details about his queer patient, a 'type' if there ever was one, who had in connexion with her flushed obesity, and in addition to the morbid strain of a violent and aimless will, a grave organic disorder; but he came back to his loved novelist, whom he was so good as to pronounce more essentially a poet than many of those who went in for verse, with a zeal excited, as all his indiscretion had been excited, by the happy chance of Dencombe's sympathy and the coincidence of their occupation. Dencombe had confessed to a slight personal acquaintance with the author of 'The Middle Years' but had not felt himself as ready as he could have wished when his companion, who had never yet encountered a being so privileged, began to be eager for particulars. He even divined in Doctor Hugh's eye at that moment a glimmer of suspicion. But the young man was too inflamed to be shrewd and repeatedly caught up the book to exclaim: 'Did you notice this?' or 'Weren't you immensely struck with that?' 'There's a beautiful passage towards the end,' he broke out; and again he laid his hand on the volume. As he turned the pages he came upon something else, while Dencombe saw him suddenly change colour. He had taken up as it lay on the bench Dencombe's copy instead of his own, and his neighbour at once guessed the reason of his start. Doctor Hugh looked grave an instant; then he said: 'I see you've been altering the text!' Dencombe was a passionate corrector, a fingerer of style; the last thing he ever arrived at was a form final for himself. His ideal would have been to publish secretly, and then, on the published text, treat himself to the terrified revise, sacrificing always a first edition and beginning for posterity and even for the collectors, poor dears, with a second. This morning, in 'The Middle Years', his pencil had pricked a dozen lights.[11] He was amused at the effect of the young man's reproach; for an instant it made him change colour. He stammered at any rate ambiguously, then through a blur of ebbing consciousness saw Doctor Hugh's mystified eyes. He only had time to feel he was about to be ill again – that emotion, excitement, fatigue, the heat of the sun, the solicitation of the air, had combined to play him a trick, before, stretching out a hand to his visitor with a plaintive cry, he lost his senses altogether.

Later he knew he had fainted and that Doctor Hugh had got him home in a Bath-chair,[12] the conductor of which, prowling within hail for custom, had happened to remember seeing him in the garden of the hotel. He had recovered his perception on the way, and had, in bed that afternoon, a vague recollection of Doctor Hugh's young face, as they went together, bent over him in a comforting laugh and expressive of something more than a suspicion of his identity. That identity was ineffaceable now, and all the more that he was rueful and sore. He had been rash, been stupid, had gone out too soon, stayed out too long. He oughtn't to have exposed himself to strangers, he ought to have taken his servant. He felt as if he had fallen into a hole too deep to descry any little patch of heaven. He was confused about the time that had passed – he pieced the fragments together. He had seen his doctor, the real one, the one who had treated him from the first and who had again been very kind. His servant was in and out on tiptoe, looking very wise after the fact. He said more than once something about the sharp young gentleman. The rest was vagueness in so far as it wasn't despair. The vagueness, however, justified itself by dreams, dozing anxieties from which he finally emerged to the consciousness of a dark room and a shaded candle.

'You'll be all right again – I know all about you now,' said a voice near him that he felt to be young. Then his meeting with Doctor Hugh came back. He was too discouraged to joke about it yet, but made out after a little that the interest was intense for his visitor. 'Of course I can't attend you professionally – you've got your own man, with whom I've talked and who's excellent,' Doctor Hugh went on. 'But you must let me come to see you as a good friend. I've just looked in before going to bed. You're doing beautifully, but it's a good job I was with you on the cliff. I shall come in early tomorrow. I want to do something for you. I want to do everything. You've done a tremendous lot for me.' The young man held his hand, hanging over him, and poor Dencombe, weakly aware of this living pressure, simply lay there and accepted his devotion. He couldn't do anything less – he needed help too much.

The idea of the help he needed was very present to him that night, which he spent in a lucid stillness, an intensity of thought that constituted a reaction from his hours of stupor. He was lost, he was lost – he was lost if he couldn't be saved. He wasn't afraid of suffering, of death, wasn't even in love with life; but he had had a deep demonstration of desire. It came over him in the long quiet hours that only with 'The Middle Years' had he taken his flight; only on that day, visited by soundless processions, had he recognised his kingdom. He had had a revelation of his range. What he dreaded was the idea that his reputation should stand on the unfinished. It wasn't with his past but with his future that it should properly be concerned. Illness and age rose before him like spectres with pitiless eyes: how was he to bribe such fates to give him the second chance? He had had the one chance that all men have – he had had the chance of life. He went to sleep again very late, and when he awoke Doctor Hugh was sitting at hand. There was already by this time something beautifully familiar in him.

'Don't think I've turned out your physician,' he said; 'I'm acting with his consent. He has been here and seen you. Somehow he seems to trust me. I told him how we happened to come together yesterday, and he recognises that I've a peculiar right.'

Dencombe felt his own face pressing. 'How have you squared the Countess?'

The young man blushed a little, but turned it off. 'Oh never mind the Countess!'

'You told me she was very exacting.'

Doctor Hugh had a wait. 'So she is.'

'And Miss Vernham's an *intrigante*.'[13]

'How do you know that?'

'I know everything. One *has* to, to write decently!'

'I think she's mad,' said limpid Doctor Hugh.

'Well, don't quarrel with the Countess – she's a present help to you.'

'I don't quarrel,' Doctor Hugh returned. 'But I don't get on with silly women.' Presently he added: 'You seem very much alone.'

'That often happens at my age. I've outlived, I've lost by the way.'

Doctor Hugh faltered; then surmounting a soft scruple: 'Whom have you lost?'

'Every one.'

'Ah no,' the young man breathed, laying a hand on his arm.

'I once had a wife – I once had a son. My wife died when

my child was born, and my boy, at school, was carried off by typhoid.'

'I wish I'd been there!' cried Doctor Hugh.

'Well – if you're here!' Dencombe answered with a smile that, in spite of dimness, showed how he valued being sure of his companion's whereabouts.

'You talk strangely of your age. You're not old.'

'Hypocrite – so early!'

'I speak physiologically.'

'That's the way I've been speaking for the last five years, and it's exactly what I've been saying to myself. It isn't till we *are* old that we begin to tell ourselves we're not.'

'Yet I know I myself am young,' Doctor Hugh returned.

'Not so well as I!' laughed his patient, whose visitor indeed would have established the truth in question by the honesty with which he changed the point of view, remarking that it must be one of the charms of age – at any rate in the case of high distinction – to feel that one has laboured and achieved. Doctor Hugh employed the common phrase about earning one's rest, and it made poor Dencombe for an instant almost angry. He recovered himself, however, to explain, lucidly enough, that if, ungraciously, he knew nothing of such a balm, it was doubtless because he had wasted inestimable years. He had followed literature from the first, but he had taken a lifetime to get abreast of her. Only today at last had he begun to *see*, so that all he had hitherto shown was a movement without a direction. He had ripened too late and was so clumsily constituted that he had had to teach himself by mistakes.

'I prefer your flowers then to other people's fruit, and your mistakes to other people's successes,' said gallant Doctor Hugh. 'It's for your mistakes I admire you.'

'You're happy – you don't know,' Dencombe answered.

Looking at his watch the young man had got up; he named the hour of the afternoon at which he would return.

Dencombe warned him against committing himself too deeply, and expressed again all his dread of making him neglect the Countess – perhaps incur her displeasure.

'I want to be like you – I want to learn by mistakes!' Doctor Hugh laughed.

'Take care you don't make too grave a one! But do come back,' Dencombe added with the glimmer of a new idea.

'You should have had more vanity!' His friend spoke as if he knew the exact amount required to make a man of letters normal

'No, no – I only should have had more time. I want another go.'

'Another go?'

'I want an extension.'

'An extension?' Again Doctor Hugh repeated Dencombe's words, with which he seemed to have been struck.

'Don't you know? – I want to what they call "live".'

The young man, for good-bye, had taken his hand, which closed with a certain force. They looked at each other hard. 'You *will* live,' said Doctor Hugh.

'Don't be superficial. It's too serious!'

'You *shall* live!' Dencombe's visitor declared, turning pale.

'Ah that's better!' And as he retired the invalid, with a troubled laugh, sank gratefully back.

All that day and all the following night he wondered if it mightn't be arranged. His doctor came again, his servant was attentive, but it was to his confident young friend that he felt himself mentally appeal. His collapse on the cliff was plausibly explained and his liberation, on a better basis, promised for the morrow; meanwhile, however, the intensity of his meditations kept him tranquil and made him indifferent. The idea that occupied him was none the less absorbing because it was a morbid fancy. Here was a clever son of the age, ingenious and ardent, who happened to have set him up for connoisseurs to worship. This servant of his altar had all the new learning in science and all the old reverence in faith; wouldn't he therefore put his knowledge at the disposal of his sympathy, his craft at the disposal of his love? Couldn't he be trusted to invent a remedy for a poor artist to whose art he had paid a tribute? If he couldn't the alternative was hard: Dencombe would have to surrender to silence unvindicated and undivined. The rest of the day and all the next he toyed in secret with this sweet futility. Who would work the miracle for him but the young man who could combine such lucidity with such passion? He thought of the fairy-tales of science and charmed himself into forgetting that he looked for a magic that was not of this world. Doctor Hugh was an apparition, and that placed him above the law. He came and went while his patient, who now sat up, followed him with supplicating eyes. The interest of knowing the great author had made the young man begin 'The Middle Years' afresh and would help him to find a richer sense between its covers. Dencombe had told him what he 'tried for'; with all his intelligence, on a first perusal, Doctor Hugh had failed to guess it. The baffled celebrity wondered then who in the world *would* guess it: he was amused once more at the diffused massive weight that could be thrown into the missing of an intention. Yet he wouldn't rail at the general mind today – consoling as that ever had been: the revelation of his own slowness had seemed to make all stupidity sacred.

Doctor Hugh, after a little, was visibly worried, confessing, on enquiry, to a source of embarrassment at home. 'Stick to the Countess – don't mind me,' Dencombe said repeatedly; for his companion was frank enough about the large lady's attitude. She was so jealous that she had fallen ill – she resented such a breach of allegiance. She paid so much for his fidelity that she must have it all: she refused him the right to other sympathies, charged him with scheming to

make her die alone, for it was needless to point out how
little Miss Vernham was a resource in trouble. When Doctor
Hugh mentioned that the Countess would already have left
Bournemouth if he hadn't kept her in bed, poor Dencombe
held his arm tighter and said with decision: 'Take her
straight away.' They had gone out together, walking back
to the sheltered nook in which, the other day, they had met.
The young man, who had given his companion a personal
support, declared with emphasis that his conscience was
clear – he could ride two horses at once. Didn't he dream
for his future of a time when he should have to ride five
hundred? Longing equally for virtue, Dencombe replied
that in that golden age no patient would pretend to have
contracted with him for his whole attention. On the part of
the Countess wasn't such an avidity lawful? Doctor Hugh
denied it, said there was no contract, but only a free
understanding, and that a sordid servitude was impossible
to a generous spirit; he liked moreover to talk about art,
and that was the subject on which, this time, as they sat
together on the sunny bench, he tried most to engage the
author of 'The Middle Years'. Dencombe, soaring again a
little on the weak wings of convalescence and still haunted
by that happy notion of an organised rescue, found another
strain of eloquence to plead the cause of a certain splendid
'last manner', the very citadel, as it would prove, of his
reputation, the stronghold into which his real treasure
would be gathered. While his listener gave up the morning
and the great still sea ostensibly waited he had a wondrous
explanatory hour. Even for himself he was inspired as he
told what his treasure would consist of; the precious metals
he would dig from the mine, the jewels rare, strings of
pearls, he would hang between the columns of his temple.
He was wondrous for himself, so thick his convictions
crowded, but still more wondrous for Doctor Hugh, who
assured him none the less that the very pages he had just

published were already encrusted with gems. This admirer, however, panted for the combinations to come and, before the face of the beautiful day, renewed to Dencombe his guarantee that his profession would hold itself responsible for such a life. Then he suddenly clapped his hand upon his watch-pocket and asked leave to absent himself for half an hour. Dencombe waited there for his return, but was at last recalled to the actual by the fall of a shadow across the ground. The shadow darkened into that of Miss Vernham, the young lady in attendance on the Countess; whom Dencombe, recognising her, perceived so clearly to have come to speak to him that he rose from his bench to acknowledge the civility. Miss Vernham indeed proved not particularly civil; she looked strangely agitated, and her type was not unmistakable.

'Excuse me if I do ask,' she said, 'whether it's too much to hope that you may be induced to leave Doctor Hugh alone.' Then before our poor friend, greatly disconcerted, could protest: 'You ought to be informed that you stand in his light – that you may do him a terrible injury.'

'Do you mean by causing the Countess to dispense with his services?'

'By causing her to disinherit him.' Dencombe stared at this, and Miss Vernham pursued, in the gratification of seeing she could produce an impression: 'It has depended on himself to come into something very handsome. He has had a grand prospect, but I think you've succeeded in spoiling it.'

'Not intentionally, I assure you. Is there no hope the accident may be repaired?' Dencombe asked.

'She was ready to do anything for him. She takes great fancies, she lets herself go – it's her way. She has no relations, she's free to dispose of her money, and she's very ill,' said Miss Vernham for a climax.

'I'm very sorry to hear it,' Dencombe stammered.

'Wouldn't it be possible for you to leave Bournemouth? That's what I've come to see about.'

He sank to his bench. 'I'm very ill myself, but I'll try!'

Miss Vernham still stood there with her colourless eyes and the brutality of her good conscience. 'Before it's too late, please!' she said; and with this she turned her back, in order, quickly, as if it had been a business to which she could spare but a precious moment, to pass out of his sight.

Oh yes, after this Dencombe was certainly very ill. Miss Vernham had upset him with her rough fierce news; it was the sharpest shock to him to discover what was at stake for a penniless young man of fine parts. He sat trembling on his bench, staring at the waste of waters, feeling sick with the directness of the blow. He was indeed too weak, too unsteady, too alarmed; but he would make the effort to get away, for he couldn't accept the guilt of interference and his honour was really involved. He would hobble home, at any rate, and then think what was to be done. He made his way back to the hotel and, as he went, had a characteristic vision of Miss Vernham's great motive. The Countess hated women of course – Dencombe was lucid about that; so the hungry pianist had no personal hopes and could only console herself with the bold conception of helping Doctor Hugh in order to marry him after he should get his money or else induce him to recognise her claim for compensation and buy her off. If she had befriended him at a fruitful crisis he would really, as a man of delicacy – and she knew what to think of that point – have to reckon with her.

At the hotel Dencombe's servant insisted on his going back to bed. The invalid had talked about catching a train and had begun with orders to pack; after which his racked nerves had yielded to a sense of sickness. He consented to see his physician, who immediately was sent for, but he wished it to be understood that his door was irrevocably closed to Doctor Hugh. He had his plan, which was so fine that he rejoiced in it after getting back to bed. Doctor Hugh, suddenly finding himself snubbed without mercy, would, in natural disgust and to the joy of Miss Vernham, renew his allegiance to the Countess. When his physician arrived Dencombe learned that he was feverish and that this was very wrong: he was to cultivate calmness and try, if possible, not to think. For the rest of the day he wooed stupidity; but there was an ache that kept him sentient, the probable sacrifice of his 'extension', the limit of his course. His medical adviser was anything but pleased; his successive relapses were ominous. He charged this personage to put out a strong hand and take Doctor Hugh off his mind – it would contribute so much to his being quiet. The agitating name, in his room, was not mentioned again, but his security was a smothered fear, and it was not confirmed by the receipt, at ten o'clock that evening, of a telegram which his servant opened and read him and to which, with an address in London, the signature of Miss Vernham was attached. 'Beseech you to use all influence to make our friend join us here in the morning. Countess much the worse for dreadful journey, but everything may still be saved.' The two ladies had gathered themselves up and had been capable in the afternoon of a spiteful revolution. They had started for the capital, and if the elder one, as Miss Vernham had announced, was very ill, she had wished to make it clear that she was proportionately reckless. Poor Dencombe, who was not reckless and who only desired that everything should indeed be 'saved', sent this missive straight off to the young man's lodging and had on the morrow the pleasure of knowing that he had quitted Bournemouth by an early train.

Two days later he pressed in with a copy of a literary journal in his hand. He had returned because he was anxious and for the pleasure of flourishing the great review of 'The

Middle Years'. Here at least was something adequate – it rose to the occasion; it was an acclamation, a reparation, a critical attempt to place the author in the niche he had fairly won. Dencombe accepted and submitted; he made neither objection nor enquiry, for old complications had returned and he had had two dismal days. He was convinced not only that he should never again leave his bed, so that his young friend might pardonably remain, but that the demand he should make on the patience of beholders would be of the most moderate. Doctor Hugh had been to town, and he tried to find in his eyes some confession that the Countess was pacified and his legacy clinched; but all he could see there was the light of his juvenile joy in two or three of the phrases of the newspaper. Dencombe couldn't read them, but when his visitor had insisted on repeating them more than once he was able to shake an unintoxicated head. 'Ah no – but they would have been true of what I *could* have done!'

'What people "could have done" is mainly what they've in fact done,' Doctor Hugh contended.

'Mainly, yes; but I've been an idiot!' Dencombe said.

Doctor Hugh did remain; the end was coming fast. Two days later his patient observed to him, by way of the feeblest of jokes, that there would now be no question whatever of a second chance. At this the young man stared; then he exclaimed: 'Why it has come to pass – it has come to pass! The second chance has been the public's – the chance to find the point of view, to pick up the pearl!'

'Oh the pearl!' poor Dencombe uneasily sighed. A smile as cold as a winter sunset flickered on his drawn lips as he added: 'The pearl is the unwritten – the pearl is the unalloyed, the *rest*, the lost!'

From that hour he was less and less present, heedless to all appearance of what went on round him. His disease was definitely mortal, of an action as relentless, after the short

arrest that had enabled him to fall in with Doctor Hugh, as
a leak in a great ship. Sinking steadily, though this visitor,
a man of rare resources, now cordially approved by his
physician, showed endless art in guarding him from pain,
poor Dencombe kept no reckoning of favour or neglect,
betrayed no symptom of regret or speculation. Yet towards
the last he gave a sign of having noticed how for two days
Doctor Hugh hadn't been in his room, a sign that consisted
of his suddenly opening his eyes to put a question. Had he
spent those days with the Countess?

'The Countess is dead,' said Doctor Hugh. 'I knew that
in a particular contingency she wouldn't resist. I went to
her grave.'

Dencombe's eyes opened wider. 'She left you "something
handsome"?'

The young man gave a laugh almost too light for a
chamber of woe. 'Never a penny. She roundly cursed me.'

'Cursed you?' Dencombe wailed.

'For giving her up. I gave her up for *you*. I had to choose,'
his companion explained.

'You chose to let a fortune go?'

'I chose to accept, whatever they might be, the consequences of my infatuation,' smiled Doctor Hugh. Then as
a larger pleasantry: 'The fortune be hanged! It's your own
fault if I can't get your things out of my head.'

The immediate tribute to his humour was a long bewildered moan; after which, for many hours, many days,
Dencombe lay motionless and absent. A response so absolute, such a glimpse of a definite result and such a sense of
credit, worked together in his mind and, producing a strange
commotion, slowly altered and transfigured his despair.
The sense of cold submersion left him – he seemed to
float without an effort. The incident was extraordinary as
evidence, and it shed an intenser light. At the last he signed
to Doctor Hugh to listen and, when he was down on his

knees by the pillow, brought him very near. 'You've made me think it all a delusion.'

'Not your glory, my dear friend,' stammered the young man.

'Not my glory – what there is of it! It *is* glory – to have been tested, to have had our little quality and cast our little spell. The thing is to have made somebody care. You happen to be crazy of course, but that doesn't affect the law.'

'You're a great success!' said Doctor Hugh, putting into his young voice the ring of a marriage-bell.

Dencombe lay taking this in; then he gathered strength to speak once more. 'A second chance – *that's* the delusion. There never was to be but one. We work in the dark – we do what we can – we give what we have. Our doubt is our passion and our passion is our task. The rest is the madness of art.'

'If you've doubted, if you've despaired, you've always "done" it,' his visitor subtly argued.

'We've done something or other,' Dencombe conceded.

'Something or other is everything. It's the feasible. It's *you*!'

'Comforter!' poor Dencombe ironically sighed.

'But it's true,' insisted his friend.

'It's true. It's frustration that doesn't count.'

'Frustration's only life,' said Doctor Hugh.

'Yes, it's what passes.' Poor Dencombe was barely audible, but he had marked with the words the virtual end of his first and only chance.

THE DEATH OF THE LION

THE DEATH OF THE
LION

THE DEATH OF THE LION

I

I had simply, I suppose, a change of heart, and it must have begun when I received my manuscript back from Mr Pinhorn. Mr Pinhorn was my 'chief', as he was called in the office: he had accepted the high mission of bringing the paper up. This was a weekly periodical, which had been supposed to be almost past redemption when he took hold of it. It was Mr Deedy who had let the thing down so dreadfully: he was never mentioned in the office now save in connexion with that misdemeanour. Young as I was I had been in a manner taken over from Mr Deedy, who had been owner as well as editor; forming part of a promiscuous lot, mainly plant and office-furniture, which poor Mrs Deedy, in her bereavement and depression, parted with at a rough valuation. I could account for my continuity but on the supposition that I had been cheap. I rather resented the practice of fathering all flatness on my late protector, who was in his unhonoured grave; but as I had my way to make I found matter enough for complacency in being on a 'staff'. At the same time I was aware of my exposure to suspicion as a product of the old lowering system. This made me feel I was doubly bound to have ideas, and had doubtless been at the bottom of my proposing to Mr Pinhorn that I should lay my lean hands on Neil Paraday. I remember how he looked at me – quite, to begin with, as if he had never heard of this celebrity, who indeed at that moment was by no means in the centre of the heavens; and even when I had knowingly explained he expressed but little confidence in the demand for any such stuff. When I had reminded him that the great principle on which we were supposed to work was just to create the demand we required, he considered a moment and then returned: 'I see – you want to write him up.'

'Call it that if you like.'

'And what's your inducement?'

'Bless my soul – my admiration!'

Mr Pinhorn pursed up his mouth. 'Is there much to be done with him?'

'Whatever there is we should have it all to ourselves, for he hasn't been touched.'

This argument was effective and Mr Pinhorn responded. 'Very well, touch him.' Then he added: 'But where can you do it?'

'Under the fifth rib!'

Mr Pinhorn stared. 'Where's that?'

'You want me to go down and see him?' I asked when I had enjoyed his visible search for the obscure suburb I seemed to have named.

'I don't "want" anything – the proposal's your own. But you must remember that that's the way we do things *now*,' said Mr Pinhorn with another dig at Mr Deedy.

Unregenerate as I was I could read the queer implications of this speech. The present owner's superior virtue as well as his deeper craft spoke in his reference to the late editor as one of that baser sort who deal in false representations. Mr Deedy would as soon have sent me to call on Neil Paraday as he would have published a 'holiday-number'; but such scruples presented themselves as mere ignoble thrift to his successor, whose own sincerity took the form of ringing door-bells and whose definition of genius was the art of finding people at home. It was as if Mr Deedy had published reports without his young men's having, as Pinhorn would have said, really been there. I was unregenerate, as I have hinted, and couldn't be concerned to straighten out the journalistic morals of my chief, feeling them indeed to be an abyss over the edge of which it was better not to peer. Really to be there this time moreover was a vision that made the idea of writing something subtle about Neil Paraday only the more inspiring. I would be as considerate as even Mr Deedy could have wished, and yet I should be as present as only Mr Pinhorn could conceive. My allusion to the sequestered manner in which Mr Paraday lived – it had formed part of my explanation, though I knew of it only by hearsay – was, I could divine, very much what had made Mr Pinhorn nibble. It struck him as inconsistent with the success of his paper that any one should be so sequestered as that. And then wasn't an immediate exposure of everything just what the public wanted? Mr Pinhorn effectually called me to order by reminding me of the promptness with which I had met Miss Braby at Liverpool on her return from her fiasco in the States. Hadn't we published, while its freshness and flavour were unimpaired, Miss Braby's own version of that great international episode? I felt somewhat uneasy at this lumping of the actress and the author, and I confess that after having enlisted Mr Pinhorn's sympathies I procrastinated a little. I had succeeded better than I wished, and I had, as it happened, work nearer at hand. A few days later I called on Lord Crouchley and carried off in triumph the most unintelligible statement that had yet appeared of his lordship's reasons for his change of front. I thus set in motion in the daily papers columns of virtuous verbiage. The following week I ran down to Brighton for a chat, as Mr Pinhorn called it, with Mrs Bounder, who gave me, on the subject of her divorce, many curious particulars that had not been articulated in court. If ever an article flowed from the primal fount it was that article on Mrs Bounder. By this time, however, I became aware that Neil Paraday's new book was on the point of appearing and that its

approach had been the ground of my original appeal to Mr
Pinhorn, who was now annoyed with me for having lost so
many days. He bundled me off – we would at least not
lose another. I've always thought his sudden alertness a
remarkable example of the journalistic instinct. Nothing
had occurred, since I first spoke to him, to create a visible
urgency, and no enlightenment could possibly have reached
him. It was a pure case of professional *flair* – he had smelt
the coming glory as an animal smells its distant prey.

II

I may as well say at once that this little record pretends in
no degree to be a picture either of my introduction to Mr
Paraday or of certain proximate steps and stages. The
scheme of my narrative allows no space for these things,
and in any case a prohibitory sentiment would hang about
my recollection of so rare an hour. These meagre notes are
essentially private, so that if they see the light the insidious
forces that, as my story itself shows, make at present for
publicity will simply have overmastered my precautions.
The curtain fell lately enough on the lamentable drama. My
memory of the day I alighted at Mr Paraday's door is a fresh
memory of kindness, hospitality, compassion, and of the
wonderful illuminating talk in which the welcome was
conveyed. Some voice of the air had taught me the right
moment, the moment of his life at which an act of unexpected young allegiance might most come home to him. He had
recently recovered from a long, grave illness. I had gone to
the neighbouring inn for the night, but I spent the evening
in his company, and he insisted the next day on my sleeping
under his roof. I hadn't an indefinite leave: Mr Pinhorn
supposed us to put our victims through on the gallop. It was
later, in the office, that the rude motions of the jig were set
to music. I fortified myself, however, as my training had

taught me to do, by the conviction that nothing could be more advantageous for my article than to be written in the very atmosphere. I said nothing to Mr Paraday about it, but in the morning, after my removal from the inn, while he was occupied in his study, as he had notified me he should need to be, I committed to paper the main heads of my impression. Then thinking to commend myself to Mr Pinhorn by my celerity, I walked out and posted my little packet before luncheon. Once my paper was written I was free to stay on, and if it was calculated to divert attention from my levity in so doing I could reflect with satisfaction that I had never been so clever. I don't mean to deny of course that I was aware it was much too good for Mr Pinhorn; but I was equally conscious that Mr Pinhorn had the supreme shrewdness of recognising from time to time the cases in which an article was not too bad only because it was too good. There was nothing he loved so much as to print on the right occasion a thing he hated. I had begun my visit to the great man on a Monday, and on the Wednesday his book came out. A copy of it arrived by the first post, and he let me go out into the garden with it immediately after breakfast. I read it from beginning to end that day, and in the evening he asked me to remain with him the rest of the week and over the Sunday.

That night my manuscript came back from Mr Pinhorn, accompanied with a letter the gist of which was the desire to know what I meant by trying to fob off on him such stuff. That was the meaning of the question, if not exactly its form, and it made my mistake immense to me. Such as this mistake was I could now only look it in the face and accept it. I knew where I had failed, but it was exactly where I couldn't have succeeded. I had been sent down to be personal and then in point of fact hadn't been personal at all: what I had dispatched to London was just a little finicking feverish study of my author's talent. Anything less relevant to Mr

Pinhorn's purpose couldn't well be imagined, and he was
visibly angry at my having (at his expense, with a second-
class ticket) approached the subject of our enterprise only
to stand off so helplessly. For myself, I knew but too well
what had happened, and how a miracle – as pretty as some
old miracle of legend – had been wrought on the spot to
save me. There had been a big brush of wings, the flash of
an opaline robe, and then, with a great cool stir of the air,
the sense of an angel's having swooped down and caught
me to his bosom. He held me only till the danger was over,
and it all took place in a minute. With my manuscript back
on my hands I understood the phenomenon better, and the
reflections I made on it are what I meant, at the beginning
of this anecdote, by my change of heart. Mr Pinhorn's note
was not only a rebuke decidedly stern, but an invitation
immediately to send him – it was the case to say so – the
genuine article, the revealing and reverberating sketch to
the promise of which, and of which alone, I owed my
squandered privilege. A week or two later I recast my
peccant paper and, giving it a particular application to Mr
Paraday's new book, obtained for it the hospitality of
another journal, where, I must admit, Mr Pinhorn was so
far vindicated as that it attracted not the least attention.

III

I was frankly, at the end of three days, a very prejudiced
critic, so that one morning when, in the garden, my great
man had offered to read me something I quite held my
breath as I listened. It was the written scheme of another
book – something put aside long ago, before his illness, but
that he had lately taken out again to reconsider. He had
been turning it round when I came down on him, and it had
grown magnificently under this second hand. Loose liberal
confident, it might have passed for a great gossiping eloquent

letter – the overflow into talk of an artist's amorous plan.
The theme I thought singularly rich, quite the strongest he
had yet treated; and this familiar statement of it, full too of
fine maturities, was really, in summarised splendour, a mine
of gold, a precious independent work.[1] I remember rather
profanely wondering whether the ultimate production could
possibly keep at the pitch. His reading of the fond epistle,
at any rate, made me feel as if I were, for the advantage of
posterity, in close correspondence with him – were the
distinguished person to whom it had been affectionately
addressed. It was a high distinction simply to be told such
things. The idea he now communicated had all the freshness,
the flushed fairness, of the conception untouched and un-
tried: it was Venus rising from the sea and before the airs
had blown upon her. I had never been so throbbingly present
at such an unveiling. But when he had tossed the last bright
word after the others, as I had seen cashiers in banks,
weighing mounds of coin, drop a final sovereign into the
tray, I knew a sudden prudent alarm.

'My dear master, how, after all, are you going to do it?
It's infinitely noble, but what time it will take, what patience
and independence, what assured, what perfect conditions!
Oh for a lone isle in a tepid sea!'

'Isn't this practically a lone isle, and aren't you, as an
encircling medium, tepid enough?' he asked, alluding with
a laugh to the wonder of my young admiration and the
narrow limits of his little provincial home. 'Time isn't what
I've lacked hitherto: the question hasn't been to find it, but
to use it. Of course my illness made, while it lasted, a great
hole – but I dare say there would have been a hole at any
rate. The earth we tread has more pockets than a billiard-
table. The great thing is now to keep on my feet.'

'That's exactly what I mean.'

Neil Paraday looked at me with eyes – such pleasant eyes
as he had – in which, as I now recall their expression, I seem

to have seen a dim imagination of his fate. He was fifty years old, and his illness had been cruel, his convalescence slow. 'It isn't as if I weren't all right.'

'Oh if you weren't all right I wouldn't look at you!' I tenderly said.

We had both got up, quickened as by this clearer air, and he had lighted a cigarette. I had taken a fresh one, which with an intenser smile, by way of answer to my exclamation, he applied to the flame of his match. 'If I weren't better I shouldn't have thought of *that*!' He flourished his script in his hand.

'I don't want to be discouraging, but that's not true,' I returned. 'I'm sure that during the months you lay here in pain you had visitations sublime. You thought of a thousand things. You think of more and more all the while. That's what makes you, if you'll pardon my familiarity, so respectable. At a time when so many people are spent you come into your second wind. But, thank God, all the same, you're better! Thank God too you're not, as you were telling me yesterday, "successful." If *you* weren't a failure what would be the use of trying? That's my one reserve on the subject of your recovery – that it makes you "score," as the newspapers say. It looks well in the newspapers, and almost anything that does that's horrible. "We are happy to announce that Mr Paraday, the celebrated author, is again in the enjoyment of excellent health." Somehow I shouldn't like to see it.'

'You won't see it; I'm not in the least celebrated – my obscurity protects me. But couldn't you bear even to see I was dying or dead?' my host enquired.

'Dead – *passe encore*;[2] there's nothing so safe. One never knows what a living artist may do – one has mourned so many. However, one must make the worst of it. You must be as dead as you can.'

'Don't I meet that condition in having just published a book?'

'Adequately, let us hope; for the book's verily a masterpiece.'

At this moment the parlour-maid appeared in the door that opened from the garden: Paraday lived at no great cost, and the frisk of petticoats, with a timorous 'Sherry, sir?' was about his modest mahogany. He allowed half his income to his wife, from whom he had succeeded in separating without redundancy of legend. I had a general faith in his having behaved well, and I had once, in London, taken Mrs Paraday down to dinner. He now turned to speak to the maid, who offered him, on a tray, some card or note, while, agitated, excited, I wandered to the end of the precinct. The idea of his security became supremely dear to me, and I asked myself if I were the same young man who had come down a few days before to scatter him to the four winds. When I retraced my steps he had gone into the house, and the woman – the second London post had come in – had placed my letters and a newspaper on a bench. I sat down there to the letters, which were a brief business, and then, without heeding the address, took the paper from its envelope. It was the journal of highest renown, *The Empire* of that morning. It regularly came to Paraday, but I remembered that neither of us had yet looked at the copy already delivered. This one had a great mark on the 'editorial' page, and, uncrumpling the wrapper, I saw it to be directed to my host and stamped with the name of his publishers. I instantly divined that *The Empire* had spoken of him, and I've not forgotten the odd little shock of the circumstance. It checked all eagerness and made me drop the paper a moment. As I sat there conscious of a palpitation I think I had a vision of what was to be. I had also a vision of the letter I would presently address to Mr Pinhorn, breaking, as it were, with

Mr Pinhorn. Of course, however, the next minute the voice of *The Empire* was in my ears.

The article wasn't, I thanked heaven, a review; it was a 'leader', the last of three, presenting Neil Paraday to the human race. His new book, the fifth from his hand, had been but a day or two out, and *The Empire*, already aware of it, fired, as if on the birth of a prince, a salute of a whole column. The guns had been booming these three hours in the house without our suspecting them. The big blundering newspaper had discovered him, and now he was proclaimed and anointed and crowned. His place was assigned him as publicly as if a fat usher with a wand had pointed to the topmost chair; he was to pass up and still up, higher and higher, between the watching faces and the envious sounds – away up to the dais and the throne. The article was 'epoch-making', a landmark in his life; he had taken rank at a bound, waked up a national glory. A national glory was needed, and it was an immense convenience he was there. What all this meant rolled over me, and I fear I grew a little faint – it meant so much more than I could say 'yea' to on the spot. In a flash, somehow, all was different; the tremendous wave I speak of had swept something away. It had knocked down, I suppose, my little customary altar, my twinkling tapers and my flowers, and had reared itself into the likeness of a temple vast and bare. When Neil Paraday should come out of the house he would come out a contemporary. That was what had happened: the poor man was to be squeezed into his horrible age. I felt as if he had been overtaken on the crest of the hill and brought back to the city. A little more and he would have dipped down the short cut to posterity and escaped.

IV

When he came out it was exactly as if he had been in custody, for beside him walked a stout man with a big black beard, who, save that he wore spectacles, might have been a policeman, and in whom at a second glance I recognised the highest contemporary enterprise.

'This is Mr Morrow,' said Paraday, looking, I thought, rather white: 'he wants to publish heaven knows what about me.'

I winced as I remembered that this was exactly what I myself had wanted. 'Already?' I cried with a sort of sense that my friend had fled to me for protection.

Mr Morrow glared, agreeably, through his glasses: they suggested the electric headlights of some monstrous modern ship, and I felt as if Paraday and I were tossing terrified under his bows. I saw his momentum was irresistible. 'I was confident that I should be the first in the field. A great interest is naturally felt in Mr Paraday's surroundings,' he heavily observed.

'I hadn't the least idea of it,' said Paraday, as if he had been told he had been snoring.

'I find he hasn't read the article in *The Empire*,' Mr Morrow remarked to me. 'That's so very interesting – it's something to start with,' he smiled. He had begun to pull off his gloves, which were violently new, and to look encouragingly round the little garden. As a 'surrounding' I felt how I myself had already been taken in; I was a little fish in the stomach of a bigger one. 'I represent,' our visitor continued, 'a syndicate of influential journals, no less than thirty-seven, whose public – whose publics, I may say – are in peculiar sympathy with Mr Paraday's line of thought. They would greatly appreciate any expression of his views on the subject of the art he so nobly exemplifies. In addition to my connexion with the syndicate just mentioned I hold a particular commission from *The Tatler*, whose most prominent department, "Smatter and Chatter" – I dare say you've often enjoyed it – attracts such attention. I was honoured only last week, as a representative of *The Tatler*, with the confidence of Guy Walsingham, the brilliant author of "Obsessions". She pronounced herself thoroughly pleased with my sketch of her method; she went so far as to say that I had made her genius more comprehensible even to herself.'

Neil Paraday had dropped on the garden-bench and sat there at once detached and confounded; he looked hard at a bare spot in the lawn, as if with an anxiety that had suddenly made him grave. His movement had been interpreted by his visitor as an invitation to sink sympathetically into a wicker chair that stood hard by, and while Mr Morrow so settled himself I felt he had taken official possession and that there was no undoing it. One had heard of unfortunate people's having 'a man in the house',[3] and this was just what *we* had. There was a silence of a moment, during which we seemed to acknowledge in the only way that was possible the presence of universal fate; the sunny stillness took no pity, and my thought, as I was sure Paraday's was doing, performed within the minute a great distant revolution. I saw just how emphatic I should make my rejoinder to Mr Pinhorn, and that having come, like Mr Morrow, to betray, I must remain as long as possible to save. Not because I had brought my mind back, but because our visitor's last words were in my ear, I presently enquired with gloomy irrelevance if Guy Walsingham were a woman.

'Oh yes, a mere pseudonym – rather pretty, isn't it? – and convenient, you know, for a lady who goes in for the larger latitude.[4] "Obsessions, by Miss So-and-so," would look a little odd, but men are more naturally indelicate. Have you peeped into "Obsessions"?' Mr Morrow continued sociably to our companion.

Paraday, still absent, remote, made no answer, as if he hadn't heard the question: a form of intercourse that appeared to suit the cheerful Mr Morrow as well as any other. Imperturbably bland, he was a man of resources – he only needed to be on the spot. He had pocketed the whole poor place while Paraday and I were wool-gathering, and I could imagine that he had already got his 'heads'.[5] His system, at any rate, was justified by the inevitability with which I replied, to save my friend the trouble: 'Dear no – he hasn't read it. He doesn't read such things!' I unwarily added.

'Things that are *too* far over the fence, eh?' I was indeed a godsend to Mr Morrow. It was the psychological moment; it determined the appearance of his note-book, which, however, he at first kept slightly behind him, even as the dentist approaching his victim keeps the horrible forceps. 'Mr Paraday holds with the good old proprieties – I see!' And thinking of the thirty-seven influential journals, I found myself, as I found poor Paraday, helplessly assisting at the promulgation of this ineptitude. 'There's no point on which distinguished views are so acceptable as on this question – raised perhaps more strikingly than ever by Guy Walsingham – of the permissibility of the larger latitude. I've an appointment, precisely in connexion with it, next week, with Dora Forbes, author of "The Other Way Round", which everybody's talking about. Has Mr Paraday glanced at "The Other Way Round"?' Mr Morrow now frankly appealed to me. I took on myself to repudiate the supposition, while our companion, still silent, got up nervously and walked away. His visitor paid no heed to his withdrawal, but opened out the note-book with a more fatherly pat. 'Dora Forbes, I gather, takes the ground, the same as Guy Walsingham's, that the larger latitude has simply got to come. He holds that it has got to be squarely faced. Of course his sex makes him a less prejudiced witness. But an authoritative word from Mr Paraday – from the point of view of *his* sex, you know – would go right round the globe. He takes the line that we *haven't* got to face it?'

I was bewildered: it sounded somehow as if there were three sexes. My interlocutor's pencil was poised, my private responsibility great. I simply sat staring, none the less, and only found presence of mind to say: 'Is this Miss Forbes a gentleman?'

Mr Morrow had a subtle smile. 'It wouldn't be "Miss" – there's a wife!'

'I mean is she a man?'

'The wife?' – Mr Morrow was for a moment as confused as myself. But when I explained that I alluded to Dora Forbes in person he informed me, with visible amusement at my being so out of it, that this was the 'pen-name' of an indubitable male – he had a big red moustache. 'He goes in for the slight mystification because the ladies are such popular favourites. A great deal of interest is felt in his acting on that idea – which *is* clever, isn't it? – and there's every prospect of its being widely imitated.' Our host at this moment joined us again, and Mr Morrow remarked invitingly that he should be happy to make a note of any observation the movement in question, the bid for success under a lady's name, might suggest to Mr Paraday. But the poor man, without catching the allusion, excused himself, pleading that, though greatly honoured by his visitor's interest, he suddenly felt unwell and should have to take leave of him – have to go and lie down and keep quiet. His young friend might be trusted to answer for him, but he hoped Mr Morrow didn't expect great things even of his young friend. His young friend, at this moment, looked at Neil Paraday with an anxious eye, greatly wondering if he were doomed to be ill again; but Paraday's own kind face met his question reassuringly, seemed to say in a glance intelligible enough: 'Oh I'm not ill, but I'm scared; get him out of the house as quietly as possible.' Getting newspaper-men out of the house was odd business for an emissary of Mr Pinhorn, and I was so exhilarated by the idea of it that

I called after him as he left us: 'Read the article in *The Empire* and you'll soon be all right!'

V

'Delicious my having come down to tell him of it!' Mr Morrow ejaculated. 'My cab was at the door twenty minutes after *The Empire* had been laid on my breakfast-table. Now what have you got for me?' he continued, dropping again into his chair, from which, however, he the next moment eagerly rose. 'I was shown into the drawing-room but there must be more to see – his study, his literary sanctum, the little things he has about, or other domestic objects and features. He wouldn't be lying down on his study-table? There's a great interest always felt in the scene of an author's labours. Sometimes we're favoured with very delightful peeps. Dora Forbes showed me all his table-drawers, and almost jammed my hand into one into which I made a dash! I don't ask that of you, but if we could talk things over right there where he sits I feel as if I should get the keynote.'

I had no wish whatever to be rude to Mr Morrow, I was much too initiated not to tend to more diplomacy; but I had a quick inspiration, and I entertained an insurmountable, an almost superstitious objection to his crossing the threshold of my friend's little lonely shabby consecrated workshop. 'No, no – we shan't get at his life that way,' I said. 'The way to get at his life is to – But wait a moment!' I broke off and went quickly into the house, whence I in three minutes reappeared before Mr Morrow with the two volumes of Paraday's new book. 'His life's here,' I went on, 'and I'm so full of this admirable thing that I can't talk of anything else. The artist's life's his work, and this is the place to observe him. What he has to tell us he tells us with *this* perfection. My dear sir, the best interviewer's the best reader.'

Mr Morrow good-humouredly protested. 'Do you mean to say that no other source of information should be open to us?'

'None other till this particular one – by far the most copious – has been quite exhausted. Have you exhausted it, my dear sir? Had you exhausted it when you came down here? It seems to me in our time almost wholly neglected, and something should surely be done to restore its ruined credit. It's the course to which the artist himself at every step, and with such pathetic confidence, refers us. This last book of Mr Paraday's is full of revelations.'

'Revelations?' panted Mr Morrow, whom I had forced again into his chair.

'The only kind that count. It tells you with a perfection that seems to me quite final all the author thinks, for instance, about the advent of the "larger latitude." '

'Where does it do that?' asked Mr Morrow, who had picked up the second volume and was insincerely thumbing it.

'Everywhere – in the whole treatment of his case. Extract the opinion, disengage the answer – those are the real acts of homage.'

Mr Morrow, after a minute, tossed the book away. 'Ah but you mustn't take me for a reviewer.'

'Heaven forbid I should take you for anything so dreadful! You came down to perform a little act of sympathy, and so, I may confide to you, did I. Let us perform our little act together. These pages overflow with the testimony we want: let us read them and taste them and interpret them. You'll of course have perceived for yourself that one scarcely does read Neil Paraday till one reads him aloud; he gives out to the ear an extraordinary full tone, and it's only when you expose it confidently to that test that you really get near his style. Take up your book again and let me listen, while you pay it out, to that wonderful fifteenth chapter. If you feel you can't do it justice, compose yourself to attention while I produce for you – I think I can! – this scarcely less admirable ninth.'

Mr Morrow gave me a straight look which was as hard as a blow between the eyes; he had turned rather red, and a question had formed itself in his mind which reached my sense as distinctly as if he had uttered it: 'What sort of a damned fool are *you*?' Then he got up, gathering together his hat and gloves, buttoning his coat, projecting hungrily all over the place the big transparency of his mask. It seemed to flare over Fleet Street and somehow made the actual spot distressingly humble: there was so little for it to feed on unless he counted the blisters of our stucco or saw his way to do something with the roses. Even the poor roses were common kinds. Presently his eyes fell on the manuscript from which Paraday had been reading to me and which still lay on the bench. As my own followed them I saw it looked promising, looked pregnant, as if it gently throbbed with the life the reader had given it. Mr Morrow indulged in a nod at it and a vague thrust of his umbrella. 'What's that?'

'Oh it's a plan – a secret.'

'A secret!' There was an instant's silence, and then Mr Morrow made another movement. I may have been mistaken, but it affected me as the translated impulse of the desire to lay hands on the manuscript, and this led me to indulge in a quick anticipatory grab which may very well have seemed ungraceful, or even impertinent, and which at any rate left Mr Paraday's two admirers very erect, glaring at each other while one of them held a bundle of papers well behind him. An instant later Mr Morrow quitted me abruptly, as if he had really carried something off with him. To reassure myself, watching his broad back recede, I only grasped my manuscript the tighter. He went to the back door of the house, the one he had come out from, but on trying the handle he appeared to find it fastened. So he

passed round into the front garden, and by listening intently
enough I could presently hear the outer gate close behind him
with a bang. I thought again of the thirty-seven influential
journals and wondered what would be his revenge. I hasten
to add that he was magnanimous: which was just the most
dreadful thing he could have been. *The Tatler* published a
charming chatty familiar account of Mr Paraday's 'Home-
life', and on the wings of the thirty-seven influential journals
it went, to use Mr Morrow's own expression, right round
the globe.

VI

A week later, early in May, my glorified friend came up to
town, where, it may be veraciously recorded, he was the
king of the beasts of the year. No advancement was ever
more rapid, no exaltation more complete, no bewilderment
more teachable. His book sold but moderately, though the
article in *The Empire* had done unwonted wonders for it;
but he circulated in person to a measure that the libraries
might well have envied. His formula had been found – he
was a 'revelation'. His momentary terror had been real, just
as mine had been – the overclouding of his passionate desire
to be left to finish his work. He was far from unsociable,
but he had the finest conception of being let alone that I've
ever met. For the time, none the less, he took his profit where
it seemed most to crowd on him, having in his pocket the
portable sophistries about the nature of the artist's task.
Observation too was a kind of work and experience a kind
of success; London dinners were all material and London
ladies were fruitful toil. 'No one has the faintest conception
of what I'm trying for,' he said to me, 'and not many have
read three pages that I've written; but I must dine with them
first – they'll find out why when they've time.' It was rather
rude justice perhaps; but the fatigue had the merit of being

a new sort, while the phantasmagoric town was probably after all less of a battlefield than the haunted study. He once told me that he had had no personal life to speak of since his fortieth year, but had had more than was good for him before. London closed the parenthesis and exhibited him in relations; one of the most inevitable of these being that in which he found himself to Mrs Weeks Wimbush, wife of the boundless brewer and proprietress of the universal menagerie. In this establishment, as everybody knows, on occasions when the crush is great, the animals rub shoulders freely with the spectators and the lions sit down for whole evenings with the lambs.

It had been ominously clear to me from the first that in Neil Paraday this lady, who, as all the world agreed, was tremendous fun, considered that she had secured a prime attraction, a creature of almost heraldic oddity. Nothing could exceed her enthusiasm over her capture, and nothing could exceed the confused apprehensions it excited in me. I had an instinctive fear of her which I tried without effect to conceal from her victim, but which I let her notice with perfect impunity. Paraday heeded it, but she never did, for her conscience was that of a romping child. She was a blind violent force to which I could attach no more idea of responsibility than to the creaking of a sign in the wind. It was difficult to say what she conduced to but circulation. She was constructed of steel and leather, and all I asked of her for our tractable friend was not to do him to death. He had consented for a time to be of india-rubber, but my thoughts were fixed on the day he should resume his shape or at least get back into his box. It was evidently all right, but I should be glad when it was well over. I had a special fear – the impression was ineffaceable of the hour when, after Mr Morrow's departure, I had found him on the sofa in his study. That pretext of indisposition had not in the least been meant as a snub to the envoy of *The Tatler* – he had gone to lie down in very truth. He had felt a pang of his old pain, the result of the agitation wrought in him by this forcing open of a new period. His old programme, his old ideal even had to be changed. Say what one would, success was a complication and recognition had to be reciprocal. The monastic life, the pious illumination of the missal in the convent-cell were things of the gathered past. It didn't engender despair, but at least it required adjustment. Before I left him on that occasion we had passed a bargain, my part of which was that I should make it my business to take care of him. Let whoever would represent the interest in his presence (I must have had a mystical prevision of Mrs Weeks Wimbush) I should represent the interest in his work – or otherwise expressed in his absence. These two interests were in their essence opposed; and I doubt, as youth is fleeting, if I shall ever again know the intensity of joy with which I felt that in so good a cause I was willing to make myself odious.

One day in Sloane Street I found myself questioning Paraday's landlord, who had come to the door in answer to my knock. Two vehicles, a barouche and a smart hansom, were drawn up before the house.

'In the drawing-room, sir? Mrs Weeks Wimbush.'

'And in the dining-room?'

'A young lady, sir – waiting: I think a foreigner.'

It was three o'clock, and on days when Paraday didn't lunch out he attached a value to these appropriated hours. On which days, however, didn't the dear man lunch out? Mrs Wimbush, at such a crisis, would have rushed round immediately after her own repast. I went into the dining-room first, postponing the pleasure of seeing how, upstairs, the lady of the barouche would, on my arrival, point the moral of my sweet solicitude. No one took such an interest as herself in his doing only what was good for him, and she was always on the spot to see that he did it. She made appointments with him to discuss the best means of economising his time and protecting his privacy. She further made his health her special business, and had so much sympathy with my own zeal for it that she was the author of pleasing fictions on the subject of what my devotion had led me to give up. I gave up nothing (I don't count Mr Pinhorn) because I had nothing, and all I had as yet achieved was to find myself also in the menagerie. I had dashed in to save my friend, but I had only got domesticated and wedged; so that I could do little more for him than exchange with him over people's heads looks of intense but futile intelligence.

VII

The young lady in the dining-room had a brave face, black hair, blue eyes, and in her lap a big volume. 'I've come for his autograph,' she said when I had explained to her that I was under bonds to see people for him when he was occupied. 'I've been waiting half an hour, but I'm prepared to wait all day.' I don't know whether it was this that told me she was American, for the propensity to wait all day is not in general characteristic of her race. I was enlightened probably not so much by the spirit of the utterance as by some quality of its sound. At any rate I saw she had an individual patience and a lovely frock, together with an expression that played among her pretty features like a breeze among flowers. Putting her book on the table she showed me a massive album, showily bound and full of autographs of price. The collection of faded notes, of still more faded 'thoughts', of quotations, platitudes, signatures, represented a formidable purpose.

I could only disclose my dread of it. 'Most people apply to Mr Paraday by letter, you know.'

'Yes, but he doesn't answer. I've written three times.'

'Very true,' I reflected; 'the sort of letter you mean goes straight into the fire.'

'How do you know the sort I mean?' My interlocutress had blushed and smiled, and in a moment she added: 'I don't believe he gets many like them!'

'I'm sure they're beautiful, but he burns without reading.' I didn't add that I had convinced him he ought to.

'Isn't he then in danger of burning things of importance?'

'He would perhaps be so if distinguished men hadn't an infallible nose for nonsense.'

She looked at me a moment – her face was sweet and gay. 'Do *you* burn without reading too?' – in answer to which I assured her that if she'd trust me with her repository I'd see that Mr Paraday should write his name in it.

She considered a little. 'That's very well, but it wouldn't make me see him.'

'Do you want very much to see him?' It seemed ungracious to catechise so charming a creature, but somehow I had never yet taken my duty to the great author so seriously.

'Enough to have come from America for the purpose.'

I stared. 'All alone?'

'I don't see that that's exactly your business, but if it will make me more seductive I'll confess that I'm quite by myself. I had to come alone or not come at all.'

She was interesting; I could imagine she had lost parents, natural protectors – could conceive even she had inherited money. I was at a pass of my own fortunes when keeping hansoms at doors seemed to me pure swagger. As a trick of this bold and sensitive girl, however, it became romantic – a part of the general romance of her freedom, her errand, her innocence. The confidence of young Americans was notorious, and I speedily arrived at a conviction that no impulse could have been more generous than the impulse that had operated here. I foresaw at that moment that it would make her my peculiar charge, just as circumstances had made Neil Paraday. She would be another person to look after, so that one's honour would be concerned in guiding her straight. These things became clearer to me later on; at the instant I had scepticism enough to observe to her, as I turned the pages of her volume, that her net had all the same caught many a big fish. She appeared to have had fruitful access to the great ones of the earth; there were people moreover whose signatures she had presumably secured without a personal interview. She couldn't have worried George Washington and Friedrich Schiller and Hannah More.⁶ She met this argument, to my surprise, by throwing up the album without a pang. It wasn't even her own; she was responsible for none of its treasures. It belonged to a girl-friend in America, a young lady in a western city. This young lady had insisted on her bringing it, to pick up more autographs: she thought they might like to see, in Europe, in what company they would be. The 'girl-friend', the western city, the immortal names, the curious errand, the idyllic faith, all made a story as strange to me, and as beguiling, as some tale in the Arabian Nights. Thus it was that my informant had encumbered herself with the ponderous tome; but she hastened to assure me that this was the first time she had brought it out. For her visit to Mr Paraday it had simply been a pretext. She didn't really care a straw that he should write his name; what she did want was to look straight into his face.

I demurred a little. 'And why do you require to do that?'

'Because I just love him!' Before I could recover from the agitating effect of this crystal ring my companion had continued: 'Hasn't there ever been any face that *you've* wanted to look into?'

How could I tell her so soon how much I appreciated the opportunity of looking into hers? I could only assent in general to the proposition that there were certainly for every one such yearnings, and even such faces; and I felt the crisis demand all my lucidity, all my wisdom. 'Oh yes, I'm a student of physiognomy. Do you mean,' I pursued, 'that you've a passion for Mr Paraday's books?'

'They've been everything to me and a little more beside – I know them by heart. They've completely taken hold of me. There's no author about whom I'm in such a state as I'm in about Neil Paraday.'

'Permit me to remark then,' I presently returned, 'that you're one of the right sort.'

'One of the enthusiasts? Of course I am!'

'Oh there are enthusiasts who are quite of the wrong. I mean you're one of those to whom an appeal can be made.'

'An appeal?' Her face lighted as if with the chance of some great sacrifice.

If she was ready for one it was only waiting for her, and in a moment I mentioned it. 'Give up this crude purpose of seeing him. Go away without it. That will be far better.'

She looked mystified, then turned visibly pale. 'Why, hasn't he any personal charm?' The girl was terrible and laughable in her bright directness.

'Ah that dreadful word "personal"!' I wailed; 'we're dying of it, for you women bring it out with murderous effect. When you meet with a genius as fine as this idol of ours let him off the dreary duty of being a personality as well. Know him only by what's best in him and spare him for the same sweet sake.'

My young lady continued to look at me in confusion and mistrust, and the result of her reflection on what I had just said was to make her suddenly break out: 'Look here, sir – what's the matter with him?'

'The matter with him is that if he doesn't look out people will eat a great hole in his life.'

She turned it over. 'He hasn't any disfigurement?'

'Nothing to speak of!'

'Do you mean that social engagements interfere with his occupations?'

'That but feebly expresses it.'

'So that he can't give himself up to his beautiful imagination?'

'He's beset, badgered, bothered – he's pulled to pieces on the pretext of being applauded. People expect him to give them his time, his golden time, who wouldn't themselves give five shillings for one of his books.'

'Five? I'd give five thousand!'

'Give your sympathy – give your forbearance. Two thirds of those who approach him only do it to advertise themselves.'

'Why it's too bad!' the girl exclaimed with the face of an angel. 'It's the first time I was ever called crude!' she laughed.

I followed up my advantage. 'There's a lady with him now who's a terrible complication, and who yet hasn't read, I'm sure, ten pages he ever wrote.'

My visitor's wide eyes grew tenderer. 'Then how does she talk –?'

'Without ceasing. I only mention her as a single case. Do you want to know how to show a superlative consideration? Simply avoid him.'

'Avoid him?' she despairingly breathed.

'Don't force him to have to take account of you; admire him in silence, cultivate him at a distance and secretly appropriate his message. Do you want to know,' I continued, warming to my idea, 'how to perform an act of homage really sublime?' Then as she hung on my words: 'Succeed in never seeing him at all!'

'Never at all?' – she suppressed a shriek for it.

'The more you get into his writings the less you'll want to, and you'll be immensely sustained by the thought of the good you're doing him.'

She looked at me without resentment or spite, and at the

truth I had put before her with candour, credulity, pity. I was afterwards happy to remember that she must have gathered from my face the liveliness of my interest in herself. 'I think I see what you mean.'

'Oh I express it badly, but I should be delighted if you'd let me come to see you – to explain it better.'

She made no response to this, and her thoughtful eyes fell on the big album, on which she presently laid her hands as if to take it away. 'I did use to say out West that they might write a little less for autographs – to all the great poets, you know – and study the thoughts and style a little more.'

'What do they care for the thoughts and style? They didn't even understand you. I'm not sure,' I added, 'that I do myself, and I dare say that you by no means make me out.'

She had got up to go, and though I wanted her to succeed in not seeing Neil Paraday I wanted her also, inconsequently, to remain in the house. I was at any rate far from desiring to hustle her off. As Mrs Weeks Wimbush, upstairs, was still saving our friend in her own way, I asked my young lady to let me briefly relate, in illustration of my point, the little incident of my having gone down into the country for a profane purpose and been converted on the spot to holiness. Sinking again into her chair to listen she showed a deep interest in the anecdote. Then thinking it over gravely she returned with her odd intonation: 'Yes, but you do see him!' I had to admit that this was the case; and I wasn't so prepared with an effective attenuation as I could have wished. She eased the situation off, however, by the charming quaintness with which she finally said: 'Well, I wouldn't want him to be lonely!' This time she rose in earnest, but I persuaded her to let me keep the album to show Mr Paraday. I assured her I'd bring it back to her myself. 'Well, you'll find my address somewhere in it on a paper!' she sighed all resignedly at the door.

VIII

I blush to confess it, but I invited Mr Paraday that very day to transcribe into the album one of his most characteristic passages. I told him how I had got rid of the strange girl who had brought it – her ominous name was Miss Hurter and she lived at an hotel; quite agreeing with him moreover as to the wisdom of getting rid with equal promptitude of the book itself. This was why I carried it to Albemarle Street no later than on the morrow. I failed to find her at home, but she wrote to me and I went again: she wanted so much to hear more about Neil Paraday. I returned repeatedly, I may briefly declare, to supply her with this information. She had been immensely taken, the more she thought of it, with that idea of mine about the act of homage: it had ended by filling her with a generous rapture. She positively desired to do something sublime for him, though indeed I could see that, as this particular flight was difficult, she appreciated the fact that my visits kept her up. I had it on my conscience to keep her up; I neglected nothing that would contribute to it, and her conception of our cherished author's independence became at last as fine as his very own. 'Read him, read him – *that* will be an education in decency,' I constantly repeated; while, seeking him in his works even as God in nature, she represented herself as convinced that, according to my assurance, this was the system that had, as she expressed it, weaned her. We read him together when I could find time, and the generous creature's sacrifice was fed by our communion. There were twenty selfish women about whom I told her and who stirred her to a beautiful rage. Immediately after my first visit her sister, Mrs Milsom, came over from Paris, and the two ladies began to present, as they called it, their letters. I thanked our stars that none had been presented to Mr Paraday. They received invitations and dined out, and some of these occasions enabled Fanny

Hurter to perform, for consistency's sake, touching feats of submission. Nothing indeed would now have induced her even to look at the object of her admiration. Once, hearing his name announced at a party, she instantly left the room by another door and then straightway quitted the house. At another time when I was at the opera with them – Mrs Milsom had invited me to their box – I attempted to point Mr Paraday out to her in the stalls. On this she asked her sister to change places with her and, while that lady devoured the great man through a powerful glass, presented, all the rest of the evening, her inspired back to the house. To torment her tenderly I pressed the glass upon her, telling her how wonderfully near it brought our friend's handsome head. By way of answer she simply looked at me in charged silence, letting me see that tears had gathered in her eyes. These tears, I may remark, produced an effect on me of which the end is not yet. There was a moment when I felt it my duty to mention them to Neil Paraday, but I was deterred by the reflexion that there were questions more relevant to his happiness.

These questions indeed, by the end of the season, were reduced to a single one – the question of reconstituting so far as might be possible the conditions under which he had produced his best work. Such conditions could never all come back, for there was a new one that took up too much place; but some perhaps were not beyond recall. I wanted above all things to see him sit down to the subject he had, on my making his acquaintance, read me that admirable sketch of. Something told me there was no security but in his doing so before the new factor, as we used to say at Mr Pinhorn's, should render the problem incalculable. It only half-reassured me that the sketch itself was so copious and so eloquent that even at the worst there would be the making of a small but complete book, a tiny volume which, for the faithful, might well become an object of adoration. There would even not be wanting critics to declare, I foresaw, that the plan was a thing to be more thankful for than the structure to have been reared on it. My impatience for the structure, none the less, grew and grew with the interruptions. He had on coming up to town begun to sit for his portrait to a young painter, Mr Rumble, whose little game, as we also used to say at Mr Pinhorn's, was to be the first to perch on the shoulders of renown. Mr Rumble's studio was a circus in which the man of the hour, and still more the woman, leaped through the hoops of his showy frames almost as electrically as they burst into telegrams and 'specials'.[7] He pranced into the exhibitions on their back; he was the reporter on canvas, the Vandyke[8] up to date, and there was one roaring year in which Mrs Bounder and Miss Braby, Guy Walsingham and Dora Forbes proclaimed in chorus from the same pictured walls that no one had yet got ahead of him.

Paraday had been promptly caught and saddled, accepting with characteristic good humour his confidential hint that to figure in his show was not so much a consequence as a cause of immortality. From Mrs Wimbush to the last 'representative' who called to ascertain his twelve favourite dishes, it was the same ingenuous assumption that he would rejoice in the repercussion. There were moments when I fancied I might have had more patience with them if they hadn't been so fatally benevolent. I hated at all events Mr Rumble's picture, and had my bottled resentment ready when, later on, I found my distracted friend had been stuffed by Mrs Wimbush into the mouth of another cannon. A young artist in whom she was intensely interested, and who had no connexion with Mr Rumble, was to show how far he could make him go. Poor Paraday, in return, was naturally to write something somewhere about the young artist. She played her victims against each other with admirable ingenuity, and her establishment was a huge machine in which the tiniest and the biggest wheels went round to the same treadle. I had a scene with her in which I tried to express that the function of such a man was to exercise his genius – not to serve as a hoarding for pictorial posters. The people I was perhaps angriest with were the editors of magazines who had introduced what they called new features, so aware were they that the newest feature of all would be to make him grind their axes by contributing his views on vital topics and taking part in the periodical prattle about the future of fiction. I made sure that before I should have done with him there would scarcely be a current form of words left me to be sick of; but meanwhile I could make surer still of my animosity to bustling ladies for whom he drew the water that irrigated their social flower-beds.

I had a battle with Mrs Wimbush over the artist she protected, and another over the question of a certain week, at the end of July, that Mr Paraday appeared to have contracted to spend with her in the country. I protested against this visit; I intimated that he was too unwell for hospitality without a *nuance*, for caresses without imagination; I begged he might rather take the time in some restorative way. A sultry air of promises, of ponderous parties, hung over his August, and he would greatly profit by the interval of rest. He hadn't told me he was ill again – that he had had a warning; but I hadn't needed this, for I found his reticence his worst symptom. The only thing he said to me was that he believed a comfortable attack of something or other would set him up: it would put out of the question everything but the exemptions he prized. I'm afraid I shall have presented him as a martyr in a very small cause if I fail to explain that he surrendered himself much more liberally than I surrendered him. He filled his lungs, for the most part, with the comedy of his queer fate: the tragedy was in the spectacles through which I chose to look. He was conscious of inconvenience, and above all of a great renouncement; but how could he have heard a mere dirge in the bells of his accession? The sagacity and the jealousy were mine, and his the impressions and the harvest. Of course, as regards Mrs Wimbush, I was worsted in my encounters, for wasn't the state of his health the very reason for his coming to her at Prestidge? Wasn't it precisely at Prestidge that he was to be coddled, and wasn't the dear Princess coming to help her to coddle him? The dear Princess, now on a visit to England, was of a famous foreign house, and, in her gilded cage, with her retinue of keepers and feeders, was the most expensive specimen in the good lady's collection. I don't think her august presence had had to do with Paraday's consenting to go, but it's not impossible he had operated as a bait to the illustrious stranger. The party had been made up for him, Mrs Wimbush averred, and every one was counting on it, the dear Princess most of all. If he was well enough he was to read them something absolutely fresh, and it was on that particular prospect the Princess had set her heart. She was so fond of genius in *any* walk of life, and was so used to it and understood it so well: she was the greatest of Mr Paraday's admirers, she devoured everything he wrote. And then he read like an angel. Mrs Wimbush reminded me that he had again and again given her, Mrs Wimbush, the privilege of listening to him.

I looked at her a moment. 'What has he read to you?' I crudely enquired.

For a moment too she met my eyes, and for the fraction of a moment she hesitated and coloured. 'Oh all sorts of things!'

I wondered if this were an imperfect recollection or only a perfect fib, and she quite understood my unuttered comment on her measure of such things. But if she could forget Neil Paraday's beauties she could of course forget my rudeness, and three days later she invited me, by telegraph, to join the party at Prestidge. This time she might indeed

have had a story about what I had given up to be near
the master. I addressed from that fine residence several
communications to a young lady in London, a young lady
whom, I confess, I quitted with reluctance and whom the
reminder of what she herself could give up was required to
make me quit at all. It adds to the gratitude I owe her on
other grounds that she kindly allows me to transcribe from
my letters a few of the passages in which that hateful sojourn
is candidly commemorated.

IX

'I suppose I ought to enjoy the joke of what's going on here,'
I wrote, 'but somehow it doesn't amuse me. Pessimism on
the contrary possesses me and cynicism deeply engages. I
positively feel my own flesh sore from the brass nails in Neil
Paraday's social harness. The house is full of people who
like him, as they mention, awfully, and with whom his talent
for talking nonsense has prodigious success. I delight in his
nonsense myself; why is it therefore that I grudge these
happy folk their artless satisfaction? Mystery of the human
heart – abyss of the critical spirit! Mrs Wimbush thinks she
can answer that question, and as my want of gaiety has at
last worn out her patience she has given me a glimpse of her
shrewd guess. I'm made restless by the selfishness of the
insincere friend – I want to monopolise Paraday in order
that he may push me on. To be intimate with him's a feather
in my cap; it gives me an importance that I couldn't naturally
pretend to, and I seek to deprive him of social refreshment
because I fear that meeting more disinterested people may
enlighten him as to my real motive. All the disinterested
people here are his particular admirers and have been
carefully selected as such. There's supposed to be a copy of
his last book in the house, and in the hall I come upon ladies,
in attitudes, bending gracefully over the first volume. I

discreetly avert my eyes, and when I next look round the precarious joy has been superseded by the book of life. There's a sociable circle or a confidential couple, and the relinquished volume lies open on its face and as dropped under extreme coercion. Somebody else presently finds it and transfers it, with its air of momentary desolation, to another piece of furniture. Every one's asking every one about it all day, and every one's telling every one where they put it last. I'm sure it's rather smudgy about the twentieth page. I've a strong impression too that the second volume is lost – has been packed in the bag of some departing guest; and yet everybody has the impression that somebody else has read to the end. You see therefore that the beautiful book plays a great part in our existence. Why should I take the occasion of such distinguished honours to say that I begin to see deeper into Gustave Flaubert's doleful refrain about the hatred of literature? I refer you again to the perverse constitution of man.

'The Princess is a massive lady with the organisation of an athlete and the confusion of tongues of a *valet de place*.' She contrives to commit herself extraordinarily little in a great many languages, and is entertained and conversed with in detachments and relays, like an institution which goes on from generation to generation or a big building contracted for under a forfeit. She can't have a personal taste any more than, when her husband succeeds, she can have a personal crown, and her opinion on any matter is rusty and heavy and plain – made, in the night of ages, to last and be transmitted. I feel as if I ought to "tip" some *custode*[10] for my glimpse of it. She has been told everything in the world and has never perceived anything, and the echoes of her education respond awfully to the rash footfall – I mean the casual remark – in the cold Valhalla of her memory. Mrs Wimbush delights in her wit and says there's nothing so charming as to hear Mr Paraday draw it out.

He's perpetually detailed for this job, and he tells me it has a peculiarly exhausting effect. Every one's beginning – at the end of two days – to sidle obsequiously away from her, and Mrs Wimbush pushes him again and again into the breach. None of the uses I have yet seen him put to infuriate me quite so much. He looks very fagged and has at last confessed to me that his condition makes him uneasy – has even promised me he'll go straight home instead of returning to his final engagements in town. Last night I had some talk with him about going today, cutting his visit short; so sure am I that he'll be better as soon as he's shut up in his lighthouse. He told me that this is what he would like to do; reminding me, however, that the first lesson of his greatness has been precisely that he can't do what he likes. Mrs Wimbush would never forgive him if he should leave her before the Princess has received the last hand. When I hint that a violent rupture with our hostess would be the best thing in the world for him he gives me to understand that if his reason assents to the proposition his courage hangs woefully back. He makes no secret of being mortally afraid of her, and when I ask what harm she can do him that she hasn't already done he simply repeats: "I'm afraid, I'm afraid! Don't enquire too closely," he said last; "only believe that I feel a sort of terror. It's strange, when she's so kind! At any rate, I'd as soon overturn that piece of priceless Sèvres[11] as tell her I must go before my date." It sounds dreadfully weak, but he has some reason, and he pays for his imagination, which puts him (I should hate it) in the place of others and makes him feel, even against himself, their feelings, their appetites, their motives. It's indeed inveterately against himself that he makes his imagination act. What a pity he has such a lot of it! He's too beastly intelligent. Besides, the famous reading's still to come off, and it has been postponed a day to allow Guy Walsingham to arrive. It appears this eminent lady's staying at a house a few miles off, which means of course that Mrs Wimbush has forcibly annexed her. She's to come over in a day or two – Mrs Wimbush wants her to hear Mr Paraday.

'Today's wet and cold, and several of the company, at the invitation of the Duke, have driven over to luncheon at Bigwood. I saw poor Paraday wedge himself, by command, into the little supplementary seat of a brougham in which the Princess and our hostess were already ensconced. If the front glass isn't open on his dear old back perhaps he'll survive. Bigwood, I believe, is very grand and frigid, all marble and precedence, and I wish him well out of the adventure. I can't tell you how much more and more *your* attitude to him, in the midst of all this, shines out by contrast. I never willingly talk to these people about him, but see what a comfort I find it to scribble to you! I appreciate it – it keeps me warm; there are no fires in the house. Mrs Wimbush goes by the calendar, the temperature goes by the weather, the weather goes by God knows what, and the Princess is easily heated. I've nothing but my acrimony to warm me, and have been out under an umbrella to restore my circulation. Coming in an hour ago I found Lady Augusta Minch rummaging about the hall. When I asked her what she was looking for she said she had mislaid something that Mr Paraday had lent her. I ascertained in a moment that the article in question is a manuscript, and I've a foreboding that it's the noble morsel he read me six weeks ago. When I expressed my surprise that he should have bandied about anything so precious (I happen to know it's his only copy – in the most beautiful hand in all the world) Lady Augusta confessed to me that she hadn't had it from himself, but from Mrs Wimbush, who had wished to give her a glimpse of it as a salve for her not being able to stay and hear it read.

'"Is that the piece he's to read," I asked, "when Guy Walsingham arrives?"

'"It's not for Guy Walsingham they're waiting now, it's

for Dora Forbes," Lady Augusta said. "She's coming, I believe, early tomorrow. Meanwhile Mrs Wimbush has found out about *him*, and is actively wiring to him. She says he also must hear him."

'"You bewilder me a little," I replied; "in the age we live in one gets lost among the genders and the pronouns. The clear thing is that Mrs Wimbush doesn't guard such a treasure so jealously as she might."

'"Poor dear, she has the Princess to guard! Mr Paraday lent her the manuscript to look over."

'"She spoke, you mean, as if it were the morning paper?"

'Lady Augusta stared – my irony was lost on her. "She didn't have time, so she gave me a chance first; because unfortunately I go tomorrow to Bigwood."

'"And your chance has only proved a chance to lose it?"

'"I haven't lost it. I remember now – it was very stupid of me to have forgotten. I told my maid to give it to Lord Dorimont – or at least to his man."

'"And Lord Dorimont went away directly after luncheon."

'"Of course he gave it back to my maid – or else his man did," said Lady Augusta. "I dare say it's all right."

'The conscience of these people is like a summer sea. They haven't time to "look over" a priceless composition; they've only time to kick it about the house. I suggested that the "man", fired with a noble emulation, had perhaps kept the work for his own perusal; and her ladyship wanted to know whether, if the thing shouldn't reappear for the grand occasion appointed by our hostess, the author wouldn't have something else to read that would do just as well. Their questions are too delightful! I declared to Lady Augusta briefly that nothing in the world can ever do so well as the thing that does best; and at this she looked a little disconcerted. But I added that if the manuscript had gone astray our little circle would have the less of an effort of attention to make. The piece in question was very long – it would keep them three hours.

'"Three hours! Oh the Princess will get up!" said Lady Augusta.

'"I thought she was Mr Paraday's greatest admirer."

'"I dare say she is – she's so awfully clever. But what's the use of being a Princess –"

'"If you can't dissemble your love?" I asked as Lady Augusta was vague. She said at any rate that she'd question her maid; and I'm hoping that when I go down to dinner I shall find the manuscript has been recovered.'

X

'It has *not* been recovered,' I wrote early the next day, 'and I'm moreover much troubled about our friend. He came back from Bigwood with a chill and, being allowed to have a fire in his room, lay down a while before dinner. I tried to send him to bed and indeed thought I had put him in the way of it; but after I had gone to dress Mrs Wimbush came up to see him, with the inevitable result that when I returned I found him under arms and flushed and feverish, though decorated with the rare flower she had brought him for his button-hole. He came down to dinner, but Lady Augusta Minch was very shy of him. Today he's in great pain, and the advent of *ces dames*[12] – I mean of Guy Walsingham and Dora Forbes – doesn't at all console me. It does Mrs Wimbush, however, for she has consented to his remaining in bed so that he may be all right tomorrow for the listening circle. Guy Walsingham's already on the scene, and the doctor for Paraday also arrived early. I haven't yet seen the author of "Obsessions", but of course I've had a moment by myself with the Doctor. I tried to get him to say that our invalid must go straight home – I mean tomorrow or next day; but he quite refuses to talk about the future. Absolute quiet and warmth and the regular administration of an important remedy are the points he mainly insists on. He returns this afternoon, and I'm to go back to see the patient at one o'clock, when he next takes his medicine. It consoles me a little that he certainly won't be able to read – an exertion he was already more than unfit for. Lady Augusta went off after breakfast, assuring me her first care would be to follow up the lost manuscript. I can see she thinks me a shocking busybody and doesn't understand my alarm, but she'll do what she can, for she's a good-natured woman. "So are they all honourable men." That was precisely what made her give the thing to Lord Dorimont and made Lord Dorimont bag it. What use *he* has for it God only knows. I've the worst forebodings, but somehow I'm strangely without passion – desperately calm. As I consider the unconscious, the well-meaning ravages of our appreciative circle I bow my head in submission to some great natural, some universal accident; I'm rendered almost indifferent, in fact quite gay (ha-ha!) by the sense of immitigable fate. Lady Augusta promises me to trace the precious object and let me have it through the post by the time Paraday's well enough to play his part with it. The last evidence is that her maid did give it to his lordship's valet. One would suppose it some thrilling number of *The Family Budget*. Mrs Wimbush, who's aware of the accident, is much less agitated by it than she would doubtless be were she not for the hour inevitably engrossed with Guy Walsingham.'

Later in the day I informed my correspondent, for whom indeed I kept a loose diary of the situation, that I had made the acquaintance of this celebrity and that she was a pretty little girl who wore her hair in what used to be called a crop. She looked so juvenile and so innocent that if, as Mr Morrow had announced, she was resigned to the larger latitude, her superiority to prejudice must have come to her early. I spent most of the day hovering about Neil Paraday's room, but it was communicated to me from below that Guy Walsingham, at Prestidge, was a success. Towards evening I became conscious somehow that her superiority was contagious, and by the time the company separated for the night I was sure the larger latitude had been generally accepted. I thought of Dora Forbes and felt that he had no time to lose. Before dinner I received a telegram from Lady Augusta Minch. 'Lord Dorimont thinks he must have left bundle in train – enquire.' How could I enquire – if I was to take the word as a command? I was too worried and now too alarmed about Neil Paraday. The Doctor came back, and it was an immense satisfaction to me to be sure he was wise and interested. He was proud of being called to so distinguished a patient, but he admitted to me that night that my friend was gravely ill. It was really a relapse, a recrudescence of his old malady. There could be no question of moving him: we must at any rate see first, on the spot, what turn his condition would take. Meanwhile, on the morrow, he was to have a nurse. On the morrow the dear man was easier, and my spirits rose to such cheerfulness that I could almost laugh over Lady Augusta's second telegram: 'Lord Dorimont's servant been to station – nothing found. Push enquiries.' I did laugh, I'm sure, as I remembered this to be the mystic scroll I had scarcely allowed poor Mr Morrow to point his umbrella at. Fool that I had been: the thirty-seven influential journals wouldn't have destroyed it, they'd only have printed it. Of course I said nothing to Paraday.

When the nurse arrived she turned me out of the room, on which I went downstairs. I should premise that at breakfast the news that our brilliant friend was doing well excited universal complacency, and the Princess graciously remarked that he was only to be commiserated for missing the society of Miss Collop. Mrs Wimbush, whose social gift never shone brighter than in the dry decorum with which she accepted this fizzle in her fireworks, mentioned to me that Guy Walsingham had made a very favourable impression on her Imperial Highness. Indeed I think every one did so, and that, like the money-market or the national honour, her Imperial Highness was constitutionally sensitive. There was a certain gladness, a perceptible bustle in the air, however, which I thought slightly anomalous in a house where a great author lay critically ill. 'Le roy est mort — vive le roy':[13] I was reminded that another great author had already stepped into his shoes. When I came down again after the nurse had taken possession I found a strange gentleman hanging about the hall and pacing to and fro by the closed door of the drawing-room. This personage was florid and bald; he had a big red moustache and wore showy knickerbockers — characteristics all that fitted to my conception of the identity of Dora Forbes. In a moment I saw what had happened: the author of 'The Other Way Round' had just alighted at the portals of Prestidge, but had suffered a scruple to restrain him from penetrating further. I recognised his scruple when, pausing to listen at his gesture of caution, I heard a shrill voice lifted in a sort of rhythmic uncanny chant. The famous reading had begun, only it was the author of 'Obsessions' who now furnished the sacrifice. The new visitor whispered to me that he judged something was going on he oughtn't to interrupt.

'Miss Collop arrived last night,' I smiled, 'and the Princess has a thirst for the *inédit*.'[14]

Dora Forbes raised his bushy brows. 'Miss Collop?'

'Guy Walsingham, your distinguished confrère — or shall I say your formidable rival?'

'Oh!' growled Dora Forbes. Then he added: 'Shall I spoil it if I go in?'

'I should think nothing could spoil it!' I ambiguously laughed.

Dora Forbes evidently felt the dilemma; he gave an

irritated crook to his moustache. '*Shall* I go in?' he presently asked.

We looked at each other hard a moment; then I expressed something bitter that was in me, expressed it in an infernal 'Do!' After this I got out into the air, but not so fast as not to hear, when the door of the drawing-room opened, the disconcerted drop of Miss Collop's public manner: she must have been in the midst of the larger latitude. Producing with extreme rapidity, Guy Walsingham has just published a work in which amiable people who are not initiated have been pained to see the genius of a sister-novelist held up to unmistakable ridicule; so fresh an exhibition does it seem to them of the dreadful way men have always treated women. Dora Forbes, it's true, at the present hour, is immensely pushed by Mrs Wimbush and has sat for his portrait to the young artists she protects, sat for it not only in oils but in monumental alabaster.

What happened at Prestidge later in the day is of course contemporary history. If the interruption I had whimsically sanctioned was almost a scandal, what is to be said of that general scatter of the company which, under the Doctor's rule, began to take place in the evening? His rule was soothing to behold, small comfort as I was to have at the end. He decreed in the interest of his patient an absolutely soundless house and a consequent break-up of the party. Little country practitioner as he was, he literally packed off the Princess. She departed as promptly as if a revolution had broken out, and Guy Walsingham emigrated with her. I was kindly permitted to remain, and this was not denied even to Mrs Wimbush. The privilege was withheld indeed from Dora Forbes; so Mrs Wimbush kept her latest capture temporarily concealed. This was so little, however, her usual way of dealing with her eminent friends that a couple of days of it exhausted her patience and she went up to town with him in great publicity. The sudden turn for the worse

her afflicted guest had, after a brief improvement, taken on
the third night raised an obstacle to her seeing him before
her retreat; a fortunate circumstance doubtless, for she was
fundamentally disappointed in him. This was not the kind
of performance for which she had invited him to Prestidge,
let alone invited the Princess. I must add that none of the
generous acts marking her patronage of intellectual and
other merit have done so much for her reputation as her
lending Neil Paraday the most beautiful of her numerous
homes to die in. He took advantage to the utmost of the
singular favour. Day by day I saw him sink, and I roamed
alone about the empty terraces and gardens. His wife never
came near him, but I scarcely noticed it: as I paced there
with rage in my heart I was too full of another wrong. In
the event of his death it would fall to me perhaps to bring
out in some charming form, with notes, with the tenderest
editorial care, that precious heritage of his written project.
But where *was* that precious heritage, and were both the
author and the book to have been snatched from us? Lady
Augusta wrote me she had done all she could and that poor
Lord Dorimont, who had really been worried to death, was
extremely sorry. I couldn't have the matter out with Mrs
Wimbush, for I didn't want to be taunted by her with
desiring to aggrandise myself by a public connection with
Mr Paraday's sweepings. She had signified her willingness
to meet the expense of all advertising, as indeed she was
always ready to do. The last night of the horrible series, the
night before he died, I put my ear closer to his pillow.

'That thing I read you that morning, you know.'

'In your garden that dreadful day? Yes!'

'Won't it do as it is?'

'It would have been a glorious book.'

'It *is* a glorious book,' Neil Paraday murmured. 'Print it
as it stands – beautifully.'

'Beautifully!' I passionately promised.

It may be imagined whether, now that he's gone, the promise seems to me less sacred. I'm convinced that if such pages had appeared in his lifetime the Abbey would hold him today. I've kept the advertising in my own hands, but the manuscript has not been recovered. It's impossible, and at any rate intolerable, to suppose it can have been wantonly destroyed. Perhaps some hazard of a blind hand, some brutal fatal ignorance has lighted kitchen-fires with it. Every stupid and hideous accident haunts my meditations. My undiscourageable search for the lost treasure would make a long chapter. Fortunately I've a devoted associate in the person of a young lady who has every day a fresh indignation and a fresh idea, and who maintains with intensity that the prize will still turn up. Sometimes I believe her, but I've quite ceased to believe myself. The only thing for us at all events is to go on seeking and hoping together, and we should be closely united by this firm tie even were we not at present by another.

THE NEXT TIME

✤

THE NEXT TIME

THE NEXT TIME

I

Mrs Highmore's errand this morning was odd enough to
deserve commemoration: she came to ask me to write a
notice of her great forthcoming work. Her great works have
come forth so frequently without my assistance that I was
sufficiently entitled on this occasion to open my eyes; but
what really made me stare was the ground on which her
request reposed, and what prompts a note of the matter is
the train of memory lighted by that explanation. Poor Ray
Limbert, while we talked, seemed to sit there between us:
she reminded me that my acquaintance with him had begun,
eighteen years ago, with her having come in, precisely as
she came today before luncheon, to bespeak my charity for
him. If she didn't know then how little my charity was
worth she's at least enlightened now, and this is just what
makes the drollery of her visit. As I hold up the torch to the
dusky years – by which I mean as I cipher up with a
pen that stumbles and stops the figured column of my
reminiscences – I see that Limbert's public hour, or at least
my small apprehension of it, is rounded by those two
occasions. It was *finis*, with a little moralising flourish, that
Mrs Highmore seemed to trace today at the bottom of the
page. 'One of the most voluminous writers of the time,' she
has often repeated this sign; but never, I dare say, in spite
of her professional command of appropriate emotion, with
an equal sense of that mystery and that sadness of things
which to people of imagination generally hover over the
close of human histories. This romance at any rate is

bracketed by her early and her late appeal; and when its melancholy protrusions had caught the declining light again from my half-hour's talk with her I took a private vow to recover while that light still lingers something of the delicate flush, to pick out with a brief patience the perplexing lesson.

It was wonderful to see how for herself Mrs Highmore had already done so: she wouldn't have hesitated to announce to me what was the matter with Ralph Limbert, or at all events to give me a glimpse of the high admonition she had read in his career. There could have been no better proof of the vividness of this parable, which we were really in our pleasant sympathy quite at one about, than that Mrs Highmore, of all hardened sinners, should have been converted. It wasn't indeed news to me: she impressed on me that for the last ten years she had wanted to do something artistic, something as to which she was prepared not to care a rap whether or no it should sell. She brought home to me further that it had been mainly seeing what her brother-in-law did and how he did it that had wedded her to this perversity. As *he* didn't sell, dear soul, and as several persons, of whom I was one, thought highly of that, the fancy had taken her – taken her even quite early in her prolific course – of reaching, if only once, the same heroic eminence. She yearned to be, like Limbert, but of course only once, an exquisite failure. There was something a failure was, a failure in the market, that a success somehow wasn't. A success was as prosaic as a good dinner: there was nothing more to be said about it than that you had had it. Who but vulgar people, in such a case, made gloating remarks about the courses? It was often by such vulgar people that a success was attested. It made, if you came to look at it, nothing but money; that is it made so much that any other result showed small in comparison. A failure now could make – oh with the aid of immense talent of course, for there were failures and failures – such a reputation! She did me the honour – she had often done it – to intimate that what she meant by reputation was seeing *me* toss a flower. If it took a failure to catch a failure I was by my own admission well qualified to place the laurel. It was because she had made so much money and Mr Highmore had taken such care of it that she could treat herself to an hour of pure glory. She perfectly remembered that as often as I had heard her heave that sigh I had been prompt with my declaration that a book sold might easily be as glorious as a book unsold. Of course she knew this, but she knew also that it was the age of trash triumphant and that she had never heard me speak of anything that had 'done well' exactly as she had sometimes heard me speak of something that hadn't – with just two or three words of respect which, when I used them, seemed to convey more than they commonly stood for, seemed to hush the discussion up a little, as for the very beauty of the secret.

I may declare in regard to these allusions that, whatever I then thought of myself as a holder of the scales,[1] I had never scrupled to laugh out at the humour of Mrs Highmore's pursuit of quality at any price. It had never rescued her even for a day from the hard doom of popularity, and though I never gave her my word for it there was no reason at all why it should. The public *would* have her, as her husband used roguishly to remark; not indeed that, making her bargains, standing up to her publishers, and even in his higher flights to her reviewers, he ever had a glimpse of her attempted conspiracy against her genius, or rather, as I may say, against mine. It wasn't that when she tried to be what she called subtle (for wasn't Limbert subtle, and wasn't I?) her fond consumers, bless them, didn't suspect the trick nor show what they thought of it: they straightway rose on the contrary to the morsel she had hoped to hold too high, and, making but a big cheerful bite of it, wagged their great collective tail artlessly for more. It was not given to her not to please, not granted even to her best refinements to affright. I had always respected the mystery of those humiliations, but I was fully aware this morning that they were practically the reason why she had come to me. Therefore when she said with the flush of a bold joke in her kind coarse face, 'What I feel is, you know, that *you* could settle me if you only would,' I knew quite well what she meant. She meant that of old it had always appeared to be the fine blade (as some one had hyperbolically called it) of my particular opinion that snapped the silken thread by which Limbert's chance in the market was wont to hang. She meant that my favour was compromising, that my praise indeed was fatal. I had cultivated the queer habit of seeing nothing in certain celebrities, of seeing overmuch in an occasional nobody, and of judging from a point of view that, say what I would for it (and I had a monstrous deal to say), mostly remained perverse and obscure. Mine was in short the love that killed, for my subtlety, unlike Mrs Highmore's, produced no tremor of the public tail. She hadn't forgotten how, towards the end, when his case was worst, Limbert would absolutely come to me with an odd shy pathos in his eyes and say: 'My dear fellow, I think I've done it this time, if you'll only keep quiet.' If my keeping quiet in those days was to help him to appear to have hit the usual taste, for the want of which he was starving, so now my breaking-out was to help Mrs Highmore to appear to have hit the unusual.

The moral of all this was that I had frightened the public too much for our late friend, but that as she was not starving this was exactly what her grosser reputation required. And then, she good-naturedly and delicately intimated, there would always be, if further reasons were wanting, the price of my clever little article. I think she gave that hint with a flattering impression – spoiled child of the booksellers as she is – that the offered fee for my clever little articles is heavy. Whatever it is, at any rate, she had evidently reflected that poor Limbert's anxiety for his own profit used to involve my sacrificing mine. Any inconvenience that my obliging her might entail would not in fine be pecuniary. Her appeal, her motive, her fantastic thirst for quality and her ingenious theory of my influence struck me all as excellent comedy, and when I consented at hazard to oblige her she left me the sheets of her new novel. I could plead no inconvenience and have been looking them over; but I'm frankly appalled at what she expects of me. What's she thinking of, poor dear, and what has put it into her head that the muse of 'quality' has ever sat with her for so much as three minutes? Why does she suppose that she has been 'artistic'? She hasn't been anything whatever, I surmise, that she hasn't inveterately been. What does she imagine she has left out? What does she conceive she has put in? She has neither left out nor put in anything. I shall have to write her an embarrassed note. The book doesn't exist and there's nothing in life to say about it. How can there be anything but the same old faithful rush for it?

II

This rush had already begun when, early in the seventies, in the interest of her prospective brother-in-law, she approached me on the singular ground of the unencouraged sentiment I had entertained for her sister. Pretty pink Maud had cast me out, but I appear to have passed in the flurried little circle for a magnanimous youth. Pretty pink Maud, so lovely then, before her troubles, that dusky Jane was gratefully conscious of all she made up for, Maud Stannace, very literary too, very languishing and extremely bullied by her mother, had yielded, invidiously as it might have struck me, to Ray Limbert's suit, which Mrs Stannace wasn't the woman to stomach. Mrs Stannace was seldom the woman to do anything: she had been shocked at the way her children, with the grubby taint of their father's blood – he had published pale Remains or flat Conversations of *his* father – breathed the alien air of authorship. If not the daughter, nor even the niece, she was, if I'm not mistaken, the second cousin of a hundred earls and a great stickler for relationship, so that she had other views for her brilliant child, especially after her quiet one – such had been her original discreet forecast of the producer of eighty volumes – became the second wife of an ex-army-surgeon, already the father of four children. Mrs Stannace had too manifestly dreamed it would be given to pretty pink Maud to detach some one of the noble hundred, who wouldn't be missed, from the cluster. It was because she cared only for cousins that I unlearnt the way to her house, which she had once reminded me was one of the few paths of gentility I could hope to tread. Ralph Limbert, who belonged to nobody and had done nothing – nothing even at Cambridge – had only the uncanny spell he had cast on her younger daughter to recommend him; but if her younger daughter had a spark of filial feeling she wouldn't commit the indecency of deserting for his sake a deeply dependent and intensely aggravated mother.

These things I learned from Jane Highmore, who, as if her books had been babies – they remained her only ones – had waited till after marriage to show what she could do, and now bade fair to surround her satisfied spouse (he took, for some mysterious reason, a part of the credit) with a little family, in sets of triplets, which properly handled would be the support of his declining years. The young couple, neither of whom had a penny, were now virtually engaged: the thing was subject to Ralph's putting his hand on some regular employment. People more enamoured couldn't be conceived, and Mrs Highmore, honest woman, who had moreover a professional sense for a love-story, was eager to take them under her wing. What was wanted was a decent opening for Limbert, which it had occurred to her I might assist her to find, though indeed I had not yet found any such matter for myself. But it was well known that I was too particular, whereas poor Ralph, with the easy manners of genius, was ready to accept almost anything to which a salary, even a small one, was attached. If he could only for instance get a place on a newspaper the rest of his maintenance would come freely enough. It was true that his two novels, one of which she had brought to leave with me, had passed unperceived, and that to her, Mrs Highmore personally, they didn't irresistibly appeal; but she could all the same assure me that I should have only to spend ten minutes with him – and our encounter must speedily take place – to receive an impression of latent power.

Our encounter took place soon after I had read the volumes Mrs Highmore had left with me, in which I recognised an intention of a sort that I had then pretty well given up the hope of meeting. I dare say that without knowing it I had been looking out rather hungrily for an altar of sacrifice: however that may be I submitted when I came across Ralph Limbert to one of the rarest emotions of my literary life, the sense of an activity in which I could critically rest. The rest was deep and salutary, and has not been disturbed to this hour. It has been a long large surrender, the luxury of dropped discriminations. He couldn't trouble me, whatever he did, for I practically enjoyed him as much when he was worse as when he was better. It was a case, I suppose, of natural prearrangement, in which, I hasten to add, I keep excellent company. We're a numerous band, partakers of the same repose, who sit together in the shade of the tree, by the plash of the fountain, with the glare of the desert round us and no great vice that I know of but the habit perhaps of estimating people a little too much by what they think of a certain style. If it had been laid upon these few pages, none the less, to be the history of an enthusiasm,

I shouldn't have undertaken them: they're concerned with Ralph Limbert in relations to which I was a stranger or in which I participated but by sympathy. I used to talk about his work, but I seldom talk now: the brotherhood of the faith have become, like the Trappists,[2] a silent order. If to the day of his death, after mortal disenchantments, the impression he first produced always evoked the word 'ingenuous', those to whom his face was familiar can easily imagine what it must have been when it still had the light of youth. I had never seen a man of genius show so for passive, a man of experience so off his guard. At the time I made his acquaintance this freshness was all unbrushed. His foot had begun to stumble, but he was full of big intentions and of sweet Maud Stannace. Black-haired and pale, deceptively languid, he had the eyes of a clever child and the voice of a bronze bell. He saw more even than I had done in the girl he was engaged to; as time went on I became conscious that we had both, properly enough, seen rather more than there was. Our odd situation, that of the three of us, became perfectly possible from the moment I recognised how much more patience he had with her than I should have had. I was happy at not having to supply this quantity, and she, on her side, found pleasure in being able to be impertinent to me without incurring the reproach of the bad wife.

Limbert's novels appeared to have brought him no money: they had only brought him, so far as I could then make out, tributes that took up his time. These indeed brought him from several quarters some other things, and on my part at the end of three months *The Blackport Beacon*. I don't today remember how I obtained for him the London correspondence of the great northern organ, unless it was through somebody's having obtained it for myself. I seem to recall that I got rid of it in Limbert's interest, urging on the editor that he was much the better man. The better man was naturally the man who had pledged himself at the altar to provide for a charming woman. We were neither of us good, as the event proved, but he had the braver badness. *The Blackport Beacon* rejoiced in two London correspondents – one a supposed haunter of political circles, the other a votary of questions sketchily classified as literary. They were both expected to be lively, and what was held out to each was that it was honourably open to him to be livelier than the other. I recollect the political correspondent of that period and how the problem offered to Ray Limbert was to try to be livelier than Pat Moyle. He had not yet seemed to me so candid as when he undertook this exploit, which brought matters to a head with Mrs Stannace, inasmuch as her opposition to the marriage now logically fell to the ground. It's all tears and laughter as I look back upon that admirable time, in which nothing was so romantic as our intense vision of the real. No fool's paradise ever rustled such a cradle-song. It was anything but Bohemia – it was the very temple of Mrs Grundy.[3] We knew we were too critical, and that made us sublimely indulgent; we believed we did our duty or wanted to, and that made us free to dream. But we dreamed over the multiplication-table; we were nothing if not practical. Oh the long smokes and sudden happy thoughts, the knowing hints and banished scruples! The great thing was for Limbert to bring out his next book, which was just what his delightful engagement with the *Beacon* would give him leisure and liberty to do. The kind of work, all human and elastic and suggestive, was capital experience: in picking up things for his bi-weekly letter he would pick up life as well, he would pick up literature. The new publications, the new pictures, the new people – there would be nothing too novel for us and nobody too sacred. We introduced everything and everybody into Mrs Stannace's drawing-room, of which I again became a familiar.

Mrs Stannace, it was true, thought herself in strange company; she didn't particularly mind the new books, though some of them seemed queer enough, but to the new people she had decided objections. It was notorious however that poor Lady Robeck secretly wrote for one of the papers, and the thing had certainly, in its glance at the doings of the great world, a side that might be made attractive. But we were going to make every side attractive and we had everything to say about the sort of thing a paper like the *Beacon* would want. To give it what it would want and to give it nothing else was not doubtless an inspiring but was a perfectly respectable task, especially for a man with an appealing bride and a contentious mother-in-law. I thought Limbert's first letters as charming as the type allowed, though I won't deny that in spite of my sense of the importance of concessions I was just a trifle disconcerted at the way he had caught the tone. The tone was of course to be caught, but need it have been caught so in the act? The creature was even cleverer, as Maud Stannace said, than she had ventured to hope. Verily it was a good thing to have a dose of the wisdom of the serpent. If it had to be journalism – well, it *was* journalism. If he had to be 'chatty' – well, he *was* chatty. Now and then he made a hit that – it was stupid of me – brought the blood to my face. I hated him to be so personal; but still, if it would make his fortune –! It wouldn't of course directly, but the book would, practically and in the sense to which our pure ideas of fortune were confined; and these things were all for the book. The daily balm meanwhile was in what one knew of the book – there were exquisite things to know; in the quiet monthly cheques from Blackport and in the deeper rose of Maud's little preparations, which were as dainty, on their tiny scale, as if she had been a humming-bird building a nest. When at the end of three months her betrothed had fairly settled down to his correspondence – in which Mrs Highmore was the only person, so far as we could discover, disappointed, even she moreover being in this particular tortuous and possibly jealous; when the situation had assumed such a comfortable shape it was quite time to prepare. I published at that moment my first volume, mere faded ink today, a little collection of literary impressions, odds and ends of criticism contributed to a journal less remunerative but also less chatty than the *Beacon*, small ironies and ecstasies, great phrases and mistakes; and the very week it came out poor Limbert devoted half of one of his letters to it, with the happy sense this time of gratifying both himself and me as well as the Blackport breakfast-tables. I remember his saying it wasn't literature, the stuff, superficial stuff, he had to write about me; but what did that matter if it came back, as we knew, to the making for literature in the roundabout way? I had sold the thing, I recall, for ten pounds, and with the money I bought in Vigo Street a quaint piece of old silver for Maud Stannace, which I carried her with my own hand as a wedding-gift. In her mother's small drawing-room, a faded bower of photography fenced in and bedimmed by folding screens out of which sallow persons of fashion with dashing signatures looked at you from retouched eyes and little windows of plush,[4] I was left to wait long enough to feel in the air of the house a hushed vibration of disaster. When our young lady came in she was very pale and *her* eyes too had been retouched.

'Something horrid has happened,' I at once said; and having really all along but half-believed in her mother's meagre permission, I risked with an unguarded groan the introduction of Mrs Stannace's name.

'Yes, she has made a dreadful scene; she insists on our putting it off again. We're very unhappy: poor Ray has been turned off.' Her tears recommenced to flow.

I had such a good conscience that I stared. 'Turned off what?'

'Why his paper of course. The *Beacon* has given him what he calls the sack. They don't like his letters – they're not the style of thing they want.'

My blankness could only deepen. 'Then what style of thing, in God's name, *do* they want?'

'Something more chatty.'

'More?' I cried, aghast.

'More gossipy, more personal. They want "journalism". They want tremendous trash.'

'Why that's just what his letters have *been*!' I broke out.

This was strong, and I caught myself up, but the girl offered me the pardon of a beautiful wan smile. 'So Ray himself declares. He says he has stooped so low.'

'Very well – he must stoop lower. He *must* keep the place.'

'He can't!' poor Maud wailed. 'He says he has tried all he knows, has been abject, has gone on all fours, has crawled like a worm; and that if they don't like that –'

'He accepts his dismissal?' I interposed in dismay.

She gave a tragic shrug. 'What other course is open to him? He wrote to them that such work as he has done is the very worst he can do for the money.'

'Therefore,' I pressed with a flash of hope, 'they'll offer him more for worse?'

'No indeed,' she answered, 'they haven't even offered him to go on at a reduction. He isn't funny enough.'

I reflected a moment. 'But surely such a thing as his notice of my book –!'

'It was your wretched book that was the last straw! He should have treated it superficially.'

'Well, if he didn't –!' I began. Then I checked myself. 'Je vous porte malheur.'⁵

She didn't deny this; she only went on: 'What on earth is he to do?'

'He's to do better than the monkeys! He's to write!'

'But what on earth are we to marry on?'

I considered once more. 'You're to marry on "The Major Key".'

III

'The Major Key' was the new novel, and the great thing accordingly was to finish it; a consummation for which three months of the *Beacon* had in some degree prepared the way. The action of that journal was indeed a shock, but I didn't know then the worst, didn't know that in addition to being a shock it was also a symptom. It was the first hint of the difficulty to which poor Limbert was eventually to succumb. His state was the happier, of a truth, for his not immediately seeing all it meant. Difficulty was the law of life, but one could thank heaven it was quite abnormally present in that awful connection. There was the difficulty that inspired, the difficulty of 'The Major Key' to wit, which it was after all base to sacrifice to the turning of somersaults for pennies. These convictions my friend beguiled his fresh wait by blandly entertaining: not indeed, I think, that the failure of his attempt to be chatty didn't leave him slightly humiliated. If it was bad enough to have grinned through a horse-collar it was very bad indeed to have grinned in vain. Well, he would try no more grinning or at least no more horse-collars. The only success worth one's powder was success in the line of one's idiosyncrasy. Consistency was in itself distinction, and what was talent but the art of being completely whatever it was that one happened to be? One's things were characteristic or they were nothing. I look back rather fondly on our having exchanged in those days these admirable remarks and many others; on our having been very happy too, in spite of postponements and obscurities, in spite also of such occasional hauntings as could spring from our lurid glimpse of the fact that even twaddle cun-

ningly calculated was far above people's heads. It was easy
to wave away spectres by the reflection that all one had to
do was not to write for people; it was certainly not for
people that Limbert wrote while he hammered at 'The
Major Key'. The taint of literature was fatal only in a certain
kind of air, which was precisely the kind against which we
had now closed our window. Mrs Stannace rose from
her crumpled cushions as soon as she had obtained an
adjournment, and Maud looked pale and proud, quite
victorious and superior, at her having obtained nothing
more. Maud behaved well, I thought, to her mother, and
well indeed, for a girl who had mainly been taught to be
flowerlike, to every one. What she gave Ray Limbert her
fine abundant needs made him then and ever pay for; but
the gift was liberal, almost wonderful – an assertion I make
even while remembering to how many clever women, early
and late, his work has been dear. It was not only that the
woman he was to marry was in love with him, but that –
this was the strangeness – she had really seen almost better
than any one what he could do. The greatest strangeness
was that she didn't want him to do something different.
This boundless belief was indeed the main way of her
devotion; and as an act of faith it naturally asked for
miracles. She was a rare wife for a poet, if she was not
perhaps the best to have been picked out for a poor man.

Well, we were to have the miracles at all events and we
were in a perfect state of mind to receive them. There were
more of us every day, and we thought highly even of our
friend's odd jobs and pot-boilers. The *Beacon* had had
no successor, but he found some quiet corners and stray
chances. Perpetually poking the fire and looking out of the
window, he was certainly not a monster of facility, but he
was, thanks perhaps to a certain method in that madness,
a monster of certainty. It wasn't every one however who
knew him for this: many editors printed him but once. He

was getting a small reputation as a man it was well to have the first time; he created obscure apprehensions as to what might happen the second. He was good for making an impression, but no one seemed exactly to know what the impression was good for when made. The reason was simply that they had not seen yet 'The Major Key', that fiery-hearted rose as to which we watched in private the formation of petal after petal and flame after flame. Nothing mattered but this, for it had already elicited a splendid bid, much talked about in Mrs Highmore's drawing-room, where at this point my reminiscences grow particularly thick. *Her* roses bloomed all the year and her sociability increased with her row of prizes. We had an idea that we 'met every one' there – so we naturally thought when we met each other. Between our hostess and Ray Limbert flourished the happiest relation, the only cloud on which was that her husband eyed him rather askance. When he was called clever this personage wanted to know what he had to 'show'; and it was certain that he showed nothing that could compare with Jane Highmore. Mr Highmore took his stand on accomplished work and, turning up his coat-tails, warmed his rear with a good conscience at the neat bookcase in which the generations of triplets were chronologically arranged. The harmony between his companions rested on the fact that, as I have already hinted, each would have liked so much to be the other. Limbert couldn't but have a feeling about a woman who in addition to being the best creature and her sister's backer would have made, could she have condescended, such a success with the *Beacon*. On the other hand Mrs Highmore used freely to say: 'Do you know, he'll do exactly the thing that *I* want to do? I shall never do it myself, but he'll do it instead. Yes, he'll do *my* thing, and I shall hate him for it – the wretch.' Hating him was her pleasant humour, for the wretch was personally to her taste. She prevailed on her own publisher to promise to take

'The Major Key' and to engage to pay a considerable sum down, as the phrase is, on the presumption of its attracting attention. This was good news for the evening's end at Mrs Highmore's when there were only four or five left and cigarettes ran low; but there was better to come, and I have never forgotten how, as it was I who had the good fortune to bring it, I kept it back on one of those occasions, for the sake of my effect, till only the right people remained. The right people were now more and more numerous, but this was a revelation addressed only to a choice residuum – a residuum including of course Limbert himself, with whom I haggled for another cigarette before I announced that as a consequence of an interview I had had with him that afternoon, and of a subtle argument I had brought to bear, Mrs Highmore's pearl of publishers had agreed to put forth the new book as a serial. He was to 'run' it in his magazine and he was to pay ever so much for the privilege. I produced a fine gasp which presently found a more articulate relief, but poor Limbert's voice failed him once for all – he knew he was to walk away with me – and it was some one else who asked me what my subtle argument had been. I forget what florid description I then gave of it: today I've no reason not to confess that it had resided in the simple plea that the book was exquisite. I had said: 'Come, my dear friend, be original; just risk it for that!' My dear friend seemed to rise to the chance, and I followed up my advantage, permitting him honestly no illusion as to the nature of the thing. He clutched interrogatively at two or three attenuations, but I dashed them aside, leaving him face to face with the formidable truth. It was just a pure gem: was he the man not to flinch? His danger appeared to have acted on him as the anaconda acts on the rabbit; fascinated and paralysed, he had been engulfed in the long pink throat. When a week before, at my request, Limbert had left with me for a day the complete manuscript, beautifully copied out by Maud

Stannace, I had flushed with indignation at its having to be said of the author of such pages that he hadn't the common means to marry. I had taken the field in a great glow to repair this scandal, and it was therefore quite directly my fault if three months later, when 'The Major Key' began to run, Mrs Stannace was driven to the wall. She had made a condition of a fixed income, and at last a fixed income was achieved.

She had to recognise it, and after much prostration among the photographs she recognised it to the extent of accepting some of the convenience of it in the form of a project for a common household, to the expenses of which each party should proportionately contribute. Jane Highmore made a great point of her not being left alone, but Mrs Stannace herself determined the proportion, which on Limbert's side at least and in spite of many other fluctuations was never altered. His income had been 'fixed' with a vengeance: having painfully stooped to the comprehension of it Mrs Stannace rested on this effort to the end and asked no further question on the subject. 'The Major Key' in other words ran ever so long, and before it was half out Limbert and Maud had been married and the common household set up. These first months were probably the happiest in the family annals, with wedding-bells and budding laurels, the quiet assured course of the book and the friendly familiar note, round the corner, of Mrs Highmore's big guns. They gave Ralph time to block in another picture as well as to let me know after a while that he had the happy prospect of becoming a father. We had at times some dispute as to whether 'The Major Key' was making an impression, but our difference could only be futile so long as we were not agreed as to what an impression consisted of. Several persons wrote to the author and several others asked to be introduced to him: wasn't that an impression? One of the lively 'weeklies', snapping at the deadly 'monthlies', said the whole thing was 'grossly inartistic' – wasn't *that*? It was somewhere else proclaimed 'a wonderfully subtle character-study' – wasn't that too? The strongest effect doubtless was produced on the publisher when, in its lemon-coloured volumes, like a little dish of three custards, the book was at last served cold: he never got his money back and so far as I know has never got it back to this day. 'The Major Key' was rather a great performance than a great success. It converted readers into friends and friends into lovers; it placed the author, as the phrase is – placed him all too definitely; but it shrank to obscurity in the account of sales eventually rendered. It was in short an exquisite thing, but it was scarcely a thing to have published and certainly not a thing to have married on. I heard all about the matter, for my intervention had much exposed me. Mrs Highmore was emphatic as to the second volume's having given her ideas, and the ideas are probably to be found in some of her works, to the circulation of which they have even perhaps contributed. This was not absolutely yet the very thing she wanted to do – though on the way to it. So much, she informed me, she particularly perceived in the light of a critical study that I put forth in a little magazine; a thing the publisher in his advertisements quoted from profusely, and as to which there sprang up some absurd story that Limbert himself had written it. I remember that on my asking some one why such an idiotic thing had been said my interlocutor replied: 'Oh because, you know, it's just the way he *would* have written!' My spirit sank a little perhaps as I reflected that with such analogies in our manner there might prove to be some in our fate.

It was during the next four or five years that our eyes were open to what, unless something could be done, that fate, at least on Limbert's part, might be. The thing to be done was of course to write the book, the book that would make the difference, really justify the burden he had accepted and consummately express his power. For the works that followed upon 'The Major Key' he had inevitably to accept conditions the reverse of brilliant, at a time too when the strain upon his resources had begun to show sharpness. With three babies in due course, an ailing wife and a complication still greater than these, it became highly important that a man should do only his best. Whatever Limbert did was his best; so at least each time I thought and so I unfailingly said somewhere, though it was not my saying it, heaven knows, that made the desired difference. Every one else indeed said it, and there was among multiplied worries always the comfort that his position was quite assured. The two books that followed 'The Major Key' did more than anything else to assure it, and Jane Highmore was always crying out: 'You stand alone, dear Ray; you stand absolutely alone!' Dear Ray used to leave me in no doubt of how he felt the truth of this in feebly-attempted discussions with his bookseller. His sister-in-law gave him good advice into the bargain; she was a repository of knowing hints, of esoteric learning. These things were doubtless not the less valuable to him for bearing wholly on the question of how a reputation might be with a little gumption, as Mrs Highmore said, 'worked'. Save when she occasionally bore testimony to her desire to do, as Limbert did, something some day for her own very self, I never heard her speak of the literary motive as if it were distinguishable from the pecuniary. She cocked up his hat, she pricked up his prudence for him, reminding him that as one seemed to take one's self so the silly world was ready to take one. It was a fatal mistake to be too candid even with those who were all right – not to look and to talk prosperous, not at least to pretend one had beautiful sales. To listen to her you would have thought the profession of letters a wonderful game of bluff. Wherever one's idea began it ended somehow in inspired paragraphs in the newspapers. '*I* pretend, I assure you, that you're going off like wildfire – I can at least do that for you!' she often declared, prevented as she was from doing much else by Mr Highmore's insurmountable objection to *their* taking Mrs Stannace.

I couldn't help regarding the presence of this latter lady in Limbert's life as the major complication: whatever he attempted it appeared given to him to achieve as best he could in the mere margin of the space in which she swung her petticoats. I may err in the belief that she practically lived on him, for though it was not in him to follow adequately Mrs Highmore's counsel there were exasperated confessions he never made, scant domestic curtains he rattled on their rings. I may exaggerate in the retrospect his apparent anxieties, for these after all were the years when his talent was freshest and when as a writer he most laid down his line. It wasn't of Mrs Stannace nor even as time went on of Mrs Limbert that we mainly talked when I got at longer intervals a smokier hour in the little grey den from which we could step out, as we used to say, to the lawn. The lawn was the back-garden, and Limbert's study was behind the dining-room, with folding doors not impervious to the clatter of the children's tea. We sometimes took refuge from it in the depths – a bush and a half deep – of the shrubbery, where was a bench that gave us while we gossiped a view of Mrs Stannace's tiara-like headdress nodding at an upper window. Within doors and without Limbert's life was overhung by an awful region that figured in his conversation, comprehensively and with unpremeditated art, as Upstairs. It was Upstairs that the thunder gathered, that Mrs Stannace kept her accounts and her state, that Mrs Limbert had her babies and her headaches, that the bells for ever jangled at the maids, that everything imperative in short took place – everything that he had somehow, pen in hand, to meet, to deal with and dispose of, in the little room on the garden-level. I don't think he liked to go Upstairs, but no special burst of confidence was needed to make me feel that a terrible deal of service went. It was the habit of the ladies of the Stannace family to be extremely waited on, and I've never been in a house where three maids and a nursery-governess gave such an impression of a retinue. 'Oh they're so deucedly, so hereditarily fine!' – I remember how that dropped from him in some worried hour. Well, it was because Maud was so universally fine that we had both been in love with her. It was not an air moreover for the plaintive note: no private inconvenience could long outweigh for him the great happiness of these years – the happiness that sat with us when we talked and that made it always amusing to talk, the sense of his being on the heels of success, coming closer and closer, touching it at last, knowing that he should touch it again and hold it fast and hold it high. Of course when we said success we didn't mean exactly what Mrs Highmore for instance meant. He used to quote at me as a definition something from a nameless page of my own, some stray dictum to the effect that the man of his craft had achieved it when of a beautiful subject his expression was complete. Well, wasn't Limbert's in all conscience complete?

IV

It was bang upon this completeness all the same that the turn arrived, the turn I can't say of his fortune – for what was that? – but of his confidence, of his spirits and, what was more to the point, of his system. The whole occasion on which the first symptom flared out is before me as I write. I had met them both at dinner: they were diners who had reached the penultimate stage – the stage which in theory is a rigid selection and in practice a wan submission. It was late in the season and stronger spirits than theirs were broken; the night was close and the air of the banquet such as to restrict conversation to the refusal of dishes and consumption to the sniffing of a flower. It struck me all the more that Mrs Limbert was flying her flag. As vivid as a page of her husband's prose, she had one of those flickers of freshness that are the miracle of her sex and one of those expensive dresses that are the miracle of ours. She had also a neat brougham in which she had offered to rescue an old lady from the possibilities of a queer cab-horse; so that when she had rolled away with her charge I proposed a walk home with her husband, whom I had overtaken on the doorstep. Before I had gone far with him he told me he had news for me – he had accepted, of all people and of all things, an 'editorial position'. It had come to pass that very day, from one hour to another, without time for appeals or ponderations: Mr Bousefield, the proprietor of a 'high-class monthly', making, as they said, a sudden change, had dropped on him heavily out of the blue. It was all right – there was a salary and an idea, and both of them, as such things went, rather high. We took our way slowly through the vacant streets, and in the explanations and revelations that as we lingered under lamp-posts I drew from him I found with an apprehension that I tried to gulp down a foretaste of the bitter end. He told me more than he had ever told me yet. He couldn't balance accounts – that was the trouble: his expenses were too rising a tide. It was imperative he should at last make money, and now he must work only for that. The need this last year had gathered the force of a crusher: it had rolled over him and laid him on his back. He had his scheme; this time he knew what he was about; on some good occasion, with leisure to talk it over, he would tell me the blest whole. His editorship would help him, and for the rest he must help himself. If he couldn't they would have to do something fundamental – change their life altogether, give up London, move into the country, take a house at thirty pounds a year, send their children to the Board-school.[6] I saw he was excited, and he admitted he was: he had waked out of a trance. He had been on the wrong tack; he had piled mistake on mistake. It was the vision of his remedy that now excited him: ineffably, grotesquely simple, it had yet come to him only within a day or two. No, he wouldn't tell me what it was; he would give me the night to guess, and if I shouldn't guess it would be because I was as big an ass as himself. However, a lone man might be an ass: he had room in his life for his ears. Ray had a burden that demanded a back: the back must therefore now be properly instituted. As to the editorship, it was simply heaven-sent, being not at all another case of *The Blackport Beacon* but a case of the very opposite. The proprietor, the great Mr Bousefield, had approached him precisely because his name, which was to be on the cover, *didn't* represent the chatty. The whole thing was to be – oh on fiddling little lines of course – a protest against the chatty. Bousefield wanted him to be himself; it was for himself Bousefield had picked him out. Wasn't it beautiful and brave of Bousefield? He wanted literature, he saw the great reaction coming, the way the cat was going to jump. 'Where will you get literature?' I woefully asked; to which he replied with a laugh that what he had to get was not literature but only what Bousefield would take for it.

In that single phrase I without more ado discovered his famous remedy. What was before him for the future was not to do his work but to do what somebody else would take for it. I had the question out with him on the next opportunity, and of all the lively discussions into which we had been destined to drift it lingers in my mind as the liveliest. This was not, I hasten to add, because I disputed his conclusions: it was an effect of the very force with which, when I had fathomed his wretched premisses, I took them to my soul. It was very well to talk with Jane Highmore about his standing alone: the eminent relief of this position had brought him to the verge of ruin. Several persons admired his books – nothing was less contestable; but they appeared to have a mortal objection to acquiring them by subscription or by purchase: they begged or borrowed or stole, they delegated one of the party perhaps to commit the volumes to memory and repeat them, like the bards of old, to listening multitudes. Some ingenious theory was required at any rate to account for the inexorable limits of his circulation. It wasn't a thing for five people to live on; therefore either the objects circulated must change their nature or the organisms to be nourished must. The former change was perhaps the easier to consider first. Limbert considered it with sovereign ingenuity from that time on, and the ingenuity, greater even than any I had yet had occasion to admire in him, made the whole next stage of his career rich in curiosity and suspense.

'I've been butting my skull against a wall,' he had said in those hours of confidence; 'and, to be as sublime a block-head, if you'll allow me the word, you, my dear fellow, have kept sounding the charge. We've sat prating here of "success," heaven help us, like chanting monks in a cloister, hugging the sweet delusion that it lies somewhere in the work itself, in the expression, as you said, of one's subject or the intensification, as somebody else somewhere says, of one's note. One has been going on in short as if the only thing to do were to accept the law of one's talent, and thinking that if certain consequences didn't follow it was only because one wasn't logical enough. My disaster has served me right – I mean for using that ignoble word at all. It's a mere distributor's, a mere hawker's word. What *is* "success" anyhow? When a book's right it's right – shame to it surely if it isn't. When it sells it sells – it brings money like potatoes or beer. If there's dishonour one way and inconvenience the other, it certainly is comfortable, but it as certainly isn't glorious, to have escaped them. People of delicacy don't brag either about their probity or about their luck. Success be hanged! – I want to sell. It's a question of life and death. I must study the way. I've studied too much the other way – I know the other way now, every inch of it. I must cultivate the market – it's a science like another. I must go in for an infernal cunning. It will be very amusing, I foresee that; I shall lead a dashing life and drive a roaring trade. I haven't been obvious – I must *be* obvious. I haven't been popular – I must *be* popular. It's another art – or perhaps it isn't an art at all. It's something else; one must find out *what* it is. Is it something awfully queer? – you blush! – something barely decent? All the greater incentive to curiosity! Curiosity's an immense motive; we shall have tremendous sport. "They all do it" – doesn't somebody sing at a music hall? – it's only a question of how. Of course I've everything to unlearn; but what's life, as Jane Highmore says, but a lesson? I must get all I can, all she can give me, from Jane. She can't explain herself much; she's all intuition; her processes are obscure; it's the spirit that swoops down and catches her up. But I must study her reverently in her works. Yes, you've defied me before, but now my loins are girded: I declare I'll *read* one of them – I really will; I'll put it through if I perish!'

I won't pretend he made all these remarks at once; but there wasn't one that he didn't make at one time or another, for suggestion and occasion were plentiful enough, his life being now given up altogether to his new necessity. It wasn't a question of his having or not having, as they say, my intellectual sympathy: the brute force of the pressure left no room for judgement; it made all emotion a mere recourse to the spy-glass. I watched him as I should have watched a long race or a long chase, irresistibly siding with him, yet much occupied with the calculation of odds. I confess indeed that my heart, for the endless stretch he covered so fast, was often in my throat. I saw him peg away over the sun-dappled plain, I saw him double and wind and gain and lose; and all the while I secretly entertained a conviction. I wanted him to feed his many mouths, but at the bottom of all things was my sense that if he should succeed in doing so in this particular way I should think less well of him. Now I had an absolute terror of that. Meanwhile so far as I could I backed him up, I helped him: all the more that I had warned him immensely at first, smiled with a compassion it was very good of him not to have found exasperating over the complacency of his assumption that a man could escape from himself. Ray Limbert at all events would certainly never escape; but one could make believe for him, make believe very hard – an undertaking in which at first Mr Bousefield was visibly a blessing. Ralph was delightful on the business of this being at last my chance too – my chance, so miraculously vouchsafed, to appear with a certain luxuriance. He didn't care how often he printed me, for wasn't it exactly in my direction Mr Bousefield held the cat was going to jump? This was the least he could do for me. I might write on anything I liked – on anything at least but Mr Limbert's second manner. He didn't wish attention strikingly called to his second manner; it was to operate insidiously; people were to be left to believe they had discovered it long ago. 'Ralph Limbert? Why when did we ever live without him?' – that's what he wanted them to say. Besides, they hated manners – let sleeping dogs lie. His understanding with Mr Bousefield – on which he had had not at all to insist; it was the excellent man who insisted – was that he should run one of his beautiful stories in the magazine. As to the beauty of his story, however, Limbert was going to be less admirably straight than as to the beauty of everything else. That was another reason why I mustn't write about his new line: Mr Bousefield was not to be too definitely warned that such a periodical was exposed to prostitution.

By the time he should find it out for himself the public – *le gros public*[7] – would have bitten, and then perhaps he would be conciliated and forgive. Everything else would be literary in short, and above all *I* would be; only Ralph Limbert wouldn't – he'd chuck up the whole thing sooner. He'd be vulgar, he'd be vile, he'd be abject: he'd be elaborately what he hadn't been before.

I duly noticed that he had more trouble in making 'everything else' literary than he had at first allowed for; but this was largely counteracted by the ease with which he was able to obtain that his mark shouldn't be overshot. He had taken well to heart the old lesson of the *Beacon*; he remembered that he was after all there to keep his contributors down much rather than to keep them up. I thought at times that he kept them down a trifle too far, but he assured me that I needn't be nervous: he had his limit – his limit was inexorable. He would reserve pure vulgarity for his serial, over which he was sweating blood and water; elsewhere it should be qualified by the prime qualification, the mediocrity that attaches, that endears. Bousefield, he allowed, was proud, was difficult: nothing was really good enough for him but the middling good; he himself, however, was prepared for adverse comment, resolute for his noble course. Hadn't Limbert moreover in the event of a charge of laxity from headquarters the great strength of being able to point to my contributions? Therefore I must let myself go, I must abound in my peculiar sense, I must be a resource in case of accidents. Limbert's vision of accidents hovered mainly over the sudden awakening of Mr Bousefield to the stuff that in the department of fiction his editor was palming off. He would then have to confess in all humility that this was not what the old boy wanted, but I should be all the more there as a salutary specimen. I would cross the scent with something showily impossible, splendidly unpopular – I must be sure to have something on hand. I always had plenty on hand – poor Limbert needn't have worried: the magazine was forearmed each month by my care with a retort to any possible accusation of trifling with Mr Bousefield's standard. He had admitted to Limbert, after much consideration indeed, that he was prepared to be perfectly human; but he had added that he was not prepared for an abuse of this admission. The thing in the world I think I least felt myself was an abuse, even though – as I had never mentioned to my friendly editor – I too had my project for a bigger reverberation. I dare say I trusted mine more than I trusted Limbert's; at all events the golden mean in which, for the special case, he saw his salvation as an editor was something I should be most sure of were I to exhibit it myself. I exhibited it month after month in the form of a monstrous levity, only praying heaven that my editor might now not tell me, as he had so often told me, that my result was awfully good. I knew what that would signify – it would signify, sketchily speaking, disaster. What he did tell me heartily was that it was just what his game required: his new line had brought with it an earnest assumption – earnest save when we privately laughed about it – of the locutions proper to real bold enterprise. If I tried to keep him in the dark even as he kept Mr Bousefield there was nothing to show that I wasn't tolerably successful: each case therefore presented a promising analogy for the other. He never noticed my descent, and it was accordingly possible Mr Bousefield would never notice his. But would nobody notice it at all? – that was a question that added a prospective zest to one's possession of a critical sense. So much depended upon it that I was rather relieved than otherwise not to know the answer too soon. I waited in fact a year – the trial-year for which Limbert had cannily engaged with Mr Bousefield; the year as to which, through the same sharpened shrewdness, it had been conveyed in the agreement between them that Mr Bousefield wasn't to intermeddle. It had been

Limbert's general prayer that we would during this period let him quite alone. His terror of my direct rays was a droll dreadful force that always operated: he explained it by the fact that I understood him too well, expressed too much of his intention, saved him too little from himself. The less he was saved the more he didn't sell: I positively interpreted, and that was simply fatal.

I held my breath accordingly; I did more – I closed my eyes, I guarded my treacherous ears. He induced several of us to do that – of such devotions we were capable – so that, not even glancing at the thing from month to month and having nothing but his shamed anxious silence to go by, I participated only vaguely in the little hum that surrounded his act of sacrifice. It was blown about the town that the public would be surprised; it was hinted, it was printed, that he was making a desperate bid. His new work was spoken of as 'more calculated for general acceptance'. These tidings produced in some quarters much reprobation, and nowhere more, I think, than on the part of certain persons who had never read a word of him, or assuredly had never spent a shilling on him, and who hung for hours over the other attractions of the newspaper that announced his abasement. So much asperity cheered me a little – seemed to signify that he might really be doing something. On the other hand I had a distinct alarm; some one sent me for some alien reason an American journal – containing frankly more than that source of affliction – in which was quoted a passage from our friend's last instalment. The passage – I couldn't for my life help reading it – was simply superb. Ah he *would* have to move to the country if that was the worst he could do! It gave me a pang to see how little after all he had improved since the days of his competition with Pat Moyle. There was nothing in the passage quoted in the American paper that Pat would for a moment have owned.

During the last weeks, as the opportunity of reading

the complete thing drew near, one's suspense was barely endurable, and I shall never forget the July evening on which I put it to rout. Coming home to dinner I found the two volumes on my table, and I sat up with them half the night, dazed, bewildered, rubbing my eyes, wondering at the monstrous joke. *Was* it a monstrous joke, his second manner – was *this* the new line, the desperate bid, the scheme for more general acceptance and the remedy for material failure? Had he made a fool of all his following, or had he most injuriously made a still bigger fool of himself? Obvious? – where the deuce was it obvious? Popular? – how on earth could it be popular? The thing was charming with all his charm and powerful with all his power: it was an unscrupulous, an unsparing, a shameless merciless masterpiece. It was, no doubt, like the old letters to the *Beacon*, the worst he could do; but the perversity of the effort, even though heroic, had been frustrated by the purity of the gift. Under what illusion had he laboured, with what wavering treacherous compass had he steered? His honour was inviolable, his measurements were all wrong. I was thrilled with the whole impression and with all that came crowding in its train. It was too grand a collapse – it was too hideous a triumph; I exulted almost with tears – I lamented with a strange delight. Indeed as the short night waned and, threshing about in my emotion, I fidgeted to my high-perched window for a glimpse of the summer dawn, I became at last aware that I was staring at it out of eyes that had compassionately and admiringly filled. The eastern sky, over the London house-tops, had a wonderful tragic crimson. That was the colour of his magnificent mistake.

V

If something less had depended on my impression I dare say I should have communicated it as soon as I had swallowed my breakfast; but the case was so embarrassing that I spent the first half of the day in reconsidering it, dipping into the book again, almost feverishly turning its leaves, and trying to extract from them, for my friend's benefit, some symptom of reassurance, some ground for felicitation. This rash challenge had consequences merely dreadful; the wretched volumes, imperturbable and impeccable, with their shyer secrets and their second line of defence, were like a beautiful woman more denuded or a great symphony on a new hearing. There was something quite sinister in the way they stood up to me. I couldn't however be dumb – that was to give the wrong tinge to my disappointment; so that later in the afternoon, taking my courage in both hands, I approached with a vain tortuosity poor Limbert's door. A smart victoria waited before it, in which, from the bottom of the street, I saw that a lady who had apparently just issued from the house was settling herself. I recognised Jane Highmore and instantly paused till she should drive down to me. She soon met me halfway and directly she saw me stopped her carriage in agitation. This was a relief – it postponed a moment the sight of that pale fine face of our friend's fronting me for the right verdict. I gathered from the flushed eagerness with which Mrs Highmore asked me if I had heard the news that a verdict of some sort had already been rendered.

'What news? – about the book?'

'About that horrid magazine. They're shockingly upset. He has lost his position – he has had a fearful flare-up with Mr Bousefield.'

I stood there blank, but not unaware in my blankness of how history repeats itself. There came to me across the years Maud's announcement of their ejection from the *Beacon*, and dimly, confusedly, the same explanation was in the air. This time however I had been on my guard; I had

had my suspicion. 'He has made it too flippant?' I found breath after an instant to enquire.

Mrs Highmore's vacuity exceeded my own. 'Too "flippant"? He has made it too oracular; Mr Bousefield says he has killed it.' Then perceiving my stupefaction: 'Don't you know what has happened?' she pursued; 'isn't it because in his trouble, poor love, he has sent for you that you've come? You've heard nothing at all? Then you had better know before you see them. Get in here with me – I'll take you a turn and tell you.' We were close to the Park, the Regent's, and when with extreme alacrity I had placed myself beside her and the carriage had begun to enter it she went on: 'It was what I feared, you know. It reeked with culture. He keyed it up too high.'

I felt myself sinking in the general collapse. 'What are you talking about?'

'Why about that beastly magazine. They're all on the streets. I shall have to take mamma.'

I pulled myself together. 'What on earth then did Bousefield want? He said he wanted intellectual power.'

'Yes, but Ray overdid it.'

'Why Bousefield said it was a thing he *couldn't* overdo.'

'Well, Ray managed: he took Mr Bousefield too literally. It appears the thing has been doing dreadfully, but the proprietor couldn't say anything, because he had covenanted to leave the editor quite free. He describes himself as having stood there in a fever and seen his ship go down. A day or two ago the year was up, so he could at last break out. Maud says he did break out quite fearfully – he came to the house and let poor Ray have it. Ray gave it him back – he reminded him of his own idea of the way the cat was going to jump.'

I gasped with dismay. 'Has Bousefield abandoned that idea. *Isn't* the cat going to jump?'

Mrs Highmore hesitated. 'It appears she doesn't seem in

a hurry. Ray at any rate has jumped too far ahead of her. He should have temporised a little, Mr Bousefield says; but I'm beginning to think, you know,' said my companion, 'that Ray *can't* temporise.' Fresh from my emotion of the previous twenty-four hours I was scarcely in a position to disagree with her. 'He published too much pure thought.'

'Pure thought?' I cried. 'Why it struck me so often – certainly in a due proportion of cases – as pure drivel!'

'Oh you're more keyed up than he! Mr Bousefield says that of course he wanted things that were suggestive and clever, things that he could point to with pride. But he contends that Ray didn't allow for human weakness. He gave everything in too stiff doses.'

Sensibly, I fear, to my neighbour, I winced at her words – I felt a prick that made me meditate. Then I said: 'Is that, by chance, the way he gave *me*?' Mrs Highmore remained silent so long that I had somehow the sense of a fresh pang; and after a minute, turning in my seat, I laid my hand on her arm, fixed my eyes on her face and pursued pressingly: 'Do you suppose it to be to my "Occasional Remarks" that Mr Bousefield refers?'

At last she met my look. 'Can you bear to hear it?'

'I think I can bear anything now.'

'Well then, it was really what I wanted to give you an inkling of. It's largely over you that they've quarrelled. Mr Bousefield wants him to chuck you.'

I grabbed her arm again. 'And our friend *won't*?'

'He seems to cling to you. Mr Bousefield says no magazine can afford you.'

I gave a laugh that agitated the very coachman. 'Why, my dear lady, has he any idea of my price?'

'It isn't your price – he says you're dear at any price: you do so much to sink the ship. Your "Remarks" are called "Occasional", but nothing could be more deadly regular;

you're there month after month and you're never anywhere else. And you supply no public want.'

'I supply the most delicious irony.'

'So Ray appears to have declared. Mr Bousefield says that's not in the least a public want. No one can make out what you're talking about and no one would care if he could. I'm only quoting *him*, mind.'

'Quote, quote – if Ray holds out. I think I must leave you now, please: I must rush back to express to him what I feel.'

'I'll drive you to his door. That isn't all,' said Mrs Highmore. And on the way, when the carriage had turned, she communicated the rest. 'Mr Bousefield really arrived with an ultimatum: it had the form of something or other by Minnie Meadows.'

'Minnie Meadows?' I was stupefied.

'The new lady-humourist every one seems talking about. It's the first of a series of screaming sketches for which poor Ray was to find a place.'

'Is *that* Mr Bousefield's idea of literature?'

'No, but he says it's the public's, and you've got to take *some* account of the public. Aux grands maux les grands remèdes.⁸ They had a tremendous lot of ground to make up, and no one would make it up like Minnie. She would be the best concession they could make to human weakness; she would strike at least this note of showing that it wasn't going to be quite all – well, all *you*. Now Ray draws the line at Minnie; he won't stoop to Minnie; he declines to touch, to look at Minnie. When Mr Bousefield – rather imperiously, I believe – made Minnie a *sine quâ non* of his retention of his post he said something rather violent, told him to go to some unmentionable place and take Minnie with him. That of course put the fat on the fire. They had really a considerable scene.'

'So had he with the *Beacon* man,' I musingly replied. 'Poor dear, he seems born for considerable scenes! It's on

Minnie then they've really split?' Mrs Highmore exhaled her despair in a sound which I took for an assent, and when we had rolled a little further I rather inconsequently and to her visible surprise broke out of my reverie. 'It will never do in the world – he *must* stoop to Minnie!'

'It's too late – and what I've told you still isn't all. Mr Bousefield raises another objection.'

'What other pray?'

'Can't you guess?'

I wondered. 'No more of Ray's fiction?'

'Not a line. That's something else no magazine can stand. Now that his novel has run its course Mr Bousefield's distinctly disappointed.'

I fairly bounded in my place. 'Then it may do?'

Mrs Highmore looked bewildered. 'Why so, if he finds it too dull?'

'Dull? Ralph Limbert? He's as fine as the spray of a lawn-irrigator.'

'It comes to the same thing, when your lawn's as coarse as a turnipfield. Mr Bousefield had counted on something that *would* do, something that would have a wider accept-ance. Ray says he wants gutter-pipes and slop-buckets.' I collapsed again; my flicker of elation dropped to a throb of quieter comfort; and after a moment's silence I asked my neighbour if she had herself read the work our friend had just put forth. 'No,' she returned, 'I gave him my word at the beginning, on his urgent request, that I wouldn't.'

'Not even as a book?'

'He begged me never to look at it at all. He said he was trying a low experiment. Of course I knew what he meant and I entreated him to let me just for curiosity take a peep. But he was firm, he declared he couldn't bear the thought that a woman like me should see him in the depths.'

'He's only, thank God, in the depths of distress,' I an-swered. 'His experiment's nothing worse than a failure.'

'Then Bousefield *is* right – his circulation won't budge?'

'It won't move one, as they say in Fleet Street. The book has extraordinary beauty.'

'Poor duck – after trying so hard!' Jane Highmore sighed with real tenderness. 'What *will* then become of them?'

I was silent an instant. 'You must take your mother.'

She was silent too. 'I must speak of it to Cecil!' she presently said. Cecil is Mr Highmore, who then entertained, I knew, strong views on the inadjustability of circumstances in general to the idiosyncrasies of Mrs Stannace. He held it supremely happy that in an important relation she should have met her match. Her match was Ray Limbert – not much of a writer but a practical man. 'The dear things still think, you know,' my companion continued, 'that the book will be the beginning of their fortune. Their illusion, if you're right, will be rudely dispelled.'

'That's what makes me dread to face them. I've just spent with his volumes an unforgettable night. His illusion has lasted because so many of us have been pledged till this moment to turn our faces the other way. We haven't known the truth and have therefore had nothing to say. Now that we do know it indeed we have practically quite as little. I hang back from the threshold. How can I follow up with a burst of enthusiasm such a catastrophe as Mr Bousefield's visit?'

As I turned uneasily about my neighbour more comfortably snuggled. 'Well, I'm glad then I haven't read him and have nothing unpleasant to say!' We had come back to Limbert's door, and I made the coachman stop short of it. 'But he'll try again, with that determination of his: he'll build his hopes on the next time.'

'On what else has he built them from the very first? It's never the present for him that bears the fruit; that's always postponed and for somebody else: there has always to be another try. I admit that his idea of a "new line" has made him try harder than ever. It makes no difference,' I brooded, still timorously lingering; 'his achievement of his necessity, his hope of a market, will continue to attach itself to the future. But the next time will disappoint him as each last time has done – and then the next and the next and the next!'

I found myself seeing it all with a clearness almost inspired: it evidently cast a chill on Mrs Highmore. 'Then what on earth will become of him?' she plaintively repeated.

'I don't think I particularly care what may become of *him*,' I returned with a conscious reckless increase of my exaltation; 'I feel it almost enough to be concerned with what may become of one's enjoyment of him. I don't know in short what will become of his circulation; I'm only quite at my ease as to what will become of his work. It will simply keep all its quality. He'll try again for the common with what he'll believe to be a still more infernal cunning, and again the common will fatally elude him, for his infernal cunning will have been only his genius in an ineffectual disguise.' We sat drawn up by the pavement, facing poor Limbert's future as I saw it. It relieved me in a manner to know the worst, and I prophesied with an assurance which as I look back upon it strikes me as rather remarkable. 'Que voulez-vous?'' I went on; 'you can't make a sow's ear of a silk purse! It's grievous indeed if you like – there are people who can't be vulgar for trying. *He* can't – it wouldn't come off, I promise you, even once. It takes more than trying – it comes by grace. It happens not to be given to Limbert to fall. He belongs to the heights – he breathes there, he lives there, and it's accordingly to the heights I must ascend,' I said as I took leave of my conductress, 'to carry him this wretched news from where *we* move!'

VI

A few months were sufficient to show how right I had been about his circulation. It didn't move one, as I had said; it stopped short in the same place, fell off in a sheer descent, like some precipice gaped up at by tourists. The public in other words drew the line for him as sharply as he had drawn it for Minnie Meadows. Minnie has skipped with a flouncing caper over his line, however; whereas the mark traced by a lustier cudgel has been a barrier insurmountable to Limbert. Those next times I had spoken of to Jane Highmore, I see them simplified by retrocession. Again and again he made his desperate bid – again and again he tried to. His rupture with Mr Bousefield caused him in professional circles, I fear, to be thought impracticable, and I'm perfectly aware, to speak candidly, that no sordid advantage ever accrued to him from such public patronage of my performances as he had occasionally been in a position to offer. I reflect for my comfort that any injury I may have done him by untimely application of a faculty of analysis which could point to no converts gained by honourable exercise was at least equalled by the injury he did himself. More than once, as I have hinted, I held my tongue at his request, but my frequent plea that such favours weren't politic never found him, when in other connections there was an opportunity to give me a lift, anything but indifferent to the danger of the association. He let them have me, in a word, whenever he could; sometimes in periodicals in which he had credit, sometimes only at dinner. He talked about me when he couldn't get me in, but it was always part of the bargain that I shouldn't make him a topic. 'How can I successfully serve you if you do?' he used to ask: he was more afraid than I thought he ought to have been of the charge of tit for tat. I didn't care, for I never could distinguish tat from tit; but, as I've intimated, I dropped into silence really more than anything else because there was a certain fascinated observation of his course which was quite testimony enough and to which in this huddled conclusion of it he practically reduced me.

I see it all foreshortened, his wonderful remainder – see it from the end backwards, with the direction widening towards me as if on a level with the eye. The migration to the country promised him at first great things – smaller expenses, larger leisure, conditions eminently conducive on each occasion to the possible triumph of the next time. Mrs Stannace, who altogether disapproved of it, gave as one of her reasons that her son-in-law, living mainly in a village on the edge of a goose-green, would be deprived of that contact with the great world which was indispensable to the painter of manners. She had the showiest arguments for keeping him in touch, as she called it, with good society; wishing to know with some force where, from the moment he ceased to represent it from observation, the novelist could be said to be. In London fortunately a clever man was just a clever man; there were charming houses in which a person of Ray's undoubted ability, even though without the knack of making the best use of it, could always be sure of a quiet corner for watching decorously the social kaleidoscope. But the kaleidoscope of the goose-green, what in the world was that, and what such delusive thrift as drives about the land (with a fearful account for flys[10] from the inn) to leave cards on the country magnates? This solicitude for Limbert's subject-matter was the specious colour with which, deeply determined not to affront mere tolerance in a cottage, Mrs Stannace overlaid her indisposition to place herself under the heel of Cecil Highmore. She knew that he ruled Upstairs as well as down, and she clung to the fable of the association of interests in the north of London. The Highmores had a better address, they lived now in Stanhope Gardens; but Cecil was fearfully artful – he wouldn't hear of an association of interests nor treat with his mother-in-law save as a visitor. She didn't like false positions; but on the other hand she didn't like the sacrifice of everything she was accustomed to. Her universe at all events was a universe of card-leavings and charming houses, and it was fortunate that she couldn't, Upstairs, catch the sound of the doom to which, in his little grey den, describing to me his diplomacy, Limbert consigned alike the country magnates and the opportunities of London. Despoiled of every guarantee she went to Stanhope Gardens like a mere maidservant, with restrictions on her very luggage, while during the year that followed this upheaval Limbert, strolling with me on the goose-green, to which I often ran down, played extravagantly over the theme that with what he was now going in for it was a positive comfort not to have the social kaleidoscope. With a cold-blooded trick in view, what had life or manners or the best society or flys from the inn to say to the question? It was as good a place as another to play his new game. He had found a quieter corner than any corner of the great world, and a damp old house at tenpence a year, which, beside leaving him all his margin to educate his children, would allow of the supreme luxury of his frankly presenting himself as a poor man. This was a convenience that *ces dames*, as he called them, had never yet fully permitted him.

It rankled in me at first to see his reward so meagre, his conquest so mean; but the simplification effected had a charm that I finally felt: it was a forcing-house for the three or four other fine miscarriages to which his scheme was evidently condemned. I limited him to three or four, having had my sharp impression, in spite of the perpetual broad joke of the thing, that a spring had really broken in him on the occasion of that deeply disconcerting sequel to the episode of his editorship. He never lost his sense of the grotesque want, in the difference made, of adequate relation to the effort that had been the intensest of his life. He had carried from that moment a charge of shot, and it slowly worked its way to a vital part. As he met his embarrassments each year with his punctual false remedy I wondered period-

ically where he found the energy to return to the attack. He
did it every time with a rage more blanched, but it was clear
to me that the tension must finally snap the cord. We got
again and again the irrepressible work of art, but what did
he get, poor man, who wanted something so different?
There were likewise odder questions than this in the matter,
phenomena more curious and mysteries more puzzling,
which often for sympathy, if not for illumination, I intimately discussed with Mrs Limbert. She had her burdens,
dear lady: after the removal from London and a considerable
interval she twice again became a mother. Mrs Stannace
too, in a more restricted sense, exhibited afresh, in relation
to the home she had abandoned, the same exemplary character. In her poverty of guarantees at Stanhope Gardens there
had been least of all, it appeared, a proviso that she shouldn't
resentfully revert again from Goneril to Regan. She came
down to the goose-green like Lear[11] himself, with fewer
knights, or at least baronets, and the joint household was
at last patched up. It fell to pieces and was put together on
various occasions before Ray Limbert died. He was ridden
to the end by the superstition that he had broken up Mrs
Stannace's original home on pretences that had proved
hollow, and that if he hadn't given Maud what she might
have had he could at least give her back her mother. I was
always sure that a sense of the compensations he owed was
half the motive of the dogged pride with which he tried to
wake up the libraries. I believed Mrs Stannace still had
money, though she pretended that, called upon at every turn
to retrieve deficits, she had long since poured it into the
general fund. This conviction haunted me; I suspected her
of secret hoards, and I said to myself that she couldn't be
so infamous as not some day on her deathbed to leave
everything to her less opulent daughter. My compassion for
the Limberts led me to hover perhaps indiscreetly round
that closing scene, to dream of some happy time when such

an accession of means would make up a little for their
present penury.

This however was crude comfort, as in the first place I
had nothing definite to go by and in the second I held it for
more and more indicated that Ray wouldn't outlive her. I
never ventured to sound him as to what in this particular
he hoped or feared, for after the crisis marked by his leaving
London I had new scruples about suffering him to be
reminded of where he fell short. The poor man was in truth
humiliated, and there were things as to which that kept us
both silent. In proportion as he tried more fiercely for the
market the old plaintive arithmetic, fertile in jokes, dropped
from our conversation. We joked immensely still about the
process, but our treatment of the results became sparing
and superficial. He talked as much as ever, with monstrous
arts and borrowed hints, of the traps he kept setting, but
we all agreed to take merely for granted that the animal was
caught. This propriety had really dawned upon me the day
that, after Mr Bousefield's visit, Mrs Highmore put me
down at his door. Mr Bousefield at that juncture had been
served up to me anew, but after we had disposed of him we
came to the book, which I was obliged to confess I had
already rushed through. It was from this moment – the
moment at which my terrible impression of it had blinked
out at his anxious query – that the image of his scared face
was to abide with me. I couldn't attenuate then – the cat
was out of the bag; but later, each of the next times, I did,
I acknowledge, attenuate. We all did religiously, so far as
was possible; we cast ingenious ambiguities over the strong
places, the beauties that betrayed him most, and found
ourselves in the queer position of admirers banded to
mislead a confiding artist. If we stifled our cheers however,
if we dissimulated our joy, our fond hypocrisy accomplished
little, for Limbert's finger was on a pulse that told a plainer
story. It was a satisfaction to have secured a greater freedom

with his wife, who at last, much to her honour, entered into the conspiracy and whose sense of responsibility was flattered by the frequency of our united appeal to her for some answer to the marvellous riddle. We had all turned it over till we were tired of it, threshing out the question of why the note he strained every chord to pitch for common ears should invariably insist on addressing itself to the angels. Being, as it were, ourselves the angels, we had only a limited quarrel in each case with the event; but its inconsequent character, given the forces set in motion, was peculiarly baffling. It was like an interminable sum that wouldn't come straight; nobody had the time to handle so many figures. Limbert gathered, to make his pudding, dry bones and dead husks; how then was one to formulate the law that made the dish prove a feast? What was the cerebral treachery that defied his own vigilance? There was some obscure interference of taste, some obsession of the exquisite. All one could say was that genius was a fatal disturber or that the unhappy man had no effectual *flair*. When he went abroad to gather garlic he came home with heliotrope.[12]

I hasten to add that if Mrs Limbert was not directly illuminating she was yet rich in anecdote and example, having found a refuge from mystification exactly where the rest of us had found it, in a more devoted embrace and the sense of a finer glory. Her disappointments and eventually her privations had been many, her discipline severe; but she had ended by accepting the long grind of life and was now quite willing to take her turn at the mill. She was essentially one of us – she always understood. Touching and admirable at the last, when through the unmistakable change in Limbert's health her troubles were thickest, was the spectacle of the particular pride that she wouldn't have exchanged for prosperity. She had said to me once – only once, in a gloomy hour of London days when things were not going at all – that one really had to think him a very great man, since if one didn't one would be rather ashamed of him. She had distinctly felt it at first – and in a very tender place – that almost every one passed him on the road; but I believe that in these final years she would almost have been ashamed of him if he had suddenly gone into editions. It's certain indeed that her complacency was not subjected to that shock. She would have liked the money immensely, but she would have missed something she had taught herself to regard as rather rare. There's another remark I remember her making, a remark to the effect that of course if she could have chosen she would have liked him to be Shakespeare or Scott,[13] but that failing this she was very glad he wasn't – well, she named the two gentlemen, but I won't. I dare say she sometimes laughed out to escape an alternative. She contributed passionately to the capture of the second manner, foraging for him further afield than he could conveniently go, gleaning in the barest stubble, picking up shreds to build the nest and in particular, in the study of the great secret of how, as we always said, they all did it, laying waste of the circulating libraries. If Limbert had a weakness he rather broke down in his reading. It was fortunately not till after the appearance of 'The Hidden Heart' that he broke down in everything else. He had had rheumatic fever in the spring, when the book was but half-finished, and this ordeal had in addition to interrupting his work enfeebled his powers of resistance and greatly reduced his vitality. He recovered from the fever and was able to take up the book again, but the organ of life was pronounced ominously weak and it was enjoined upon him with some sharpness that he should lend himself to no worries. It might have struck me as on the cards that his worries would now be surmountable, for when he began to mend he expressed to me a conviction almost contagious that he had never yet made so adroit a bid as in the idea of 'The Hidden Heart'.

It is grimly droll to reflect that this superb little composition, the shortest of his novels but perhaps the loveliest, was planned from the first as an 'adventure-story' on approved lines. It was the way they all did the adventure-story that he had tried dauntlessly to emulate. I wonder how many readers ever divined to which of their bookshelves 'The Hidden Heart' was so exclusively addressed. High medical advice early in the summer had been quite viciously clear as to the inconvenience that might ensue to him should he neglect to spend the winter in Egypt. He was not a man to neglect anything; but Egypt seemed to us all then as unattainable as a second edition. He finished 'The Hidden Heart' with the energy of apprehension and desire, for if the book should happen to do what 'books of that class', as the publisher said, sometimes did, he might well have a fund to draw on. As soon as I read the fine deep thing I knew, as I had known in each case before, exactly how well it would do. Poor Limbert in this long business always figured to me an undiscourageable parent to whom only girls kept being born. A bouncing boy, a son and heir, was devoutly prayed for and almanacks and old wives consulted; but the spell was inveterate, incurable, and 'The Hidden Heart' proved, so to speak, but another female child. When the winter arrived accordingly Egypt was out of the question. Jane Highmore, to my knowledge, wanted to lend him money, and there were even greater devotees who did their best to induce him to lean on them. There was so marked a 'movement' among his friends that a very considerable sum would have been at his disposal; but his stiffness was invincible: it had its root, I think, in his sense, on his own side, of sacrifices already made. He had sacrificed honour and pride, and he had sacrificed them precisely to the question of money. He would evidently, should he be able to go on, have to continue to sacrifice them, but it must be all in the way to which he had now, as he considered, hardened himself. He had spent years in plotting for favour, and since on favour he must live it could only be as a bargain and a price.

He got through the early part of the season better than we feared, and I went down in great elation to spend Christmas on the goose-green. He told me late on Christmas Eve, after our simple domestic revels had sunk to rest and we sat together by the fire, how he had been visited the night before in wakeful hours by the finest fancy for a really good thing that he had ever felt descend in the darkness. 'It's just the vision of a situation that contains, upon my honour, everything,' he said, 'and I wonder I've never thought of it before.' He didn't describe it further, contrary to his common practice, and I only knew later, by Mrs Limbert, that he had begun 'Derogation' and was completely full of his subject. It was however a subject he wasn't to live to treat. The work went on for a couple of months in quiet mystery, without revelations even to his wife. He hadn't invited her to help him to get up his case – she hadn't taken the field with him as on his previous campaigns. We only knew he was at it again, but that less even than ever had been said about the impression to be made on the market. I saw him in February and thought him sufficiently at ease. The great thing was that he was immensely interested and was pleased with the omens. I got a strange stirring sense that he had not consulted the usual ones and indeed that he had floated away into a grand indifference, into a reckless consciousness of art. The voice of the market had suddenly grown faint and far: he had come back at the last, as people so often do, to one of the moods, the sincerities of his prime. Was he really, with a blurred sense of the urgent, doing something now only for himself? We wondered and waited – we felt he was a little confused. What had happened, I was afterwards satisfied, was that he had quite forgotten whether he generally sold or not. He had merely waked up one morning again in the country of the blue[14] and had stayed there with a good conscience and a great idea. He stayed till death knocked at the gate, for the pen dropped from his hand only at the moment when, from sudden failure of the heart, his eyes, as he sank back in his chair, closed for ever. 'Derogation' is a splendid fragment; it evidently would have been one of his high successes. I am not prepared to say it would have waked up the libraries.

THE FIGURE IN
THE CARPET

✤

The Figure in the Carpet

I

I had done a few things and earned a few pence – I had perhaps even had time to begin to think I was finer than was perceived by the patronising; but when I take the little measure of my course (a fidgety habit, for it's none of the longest yet) I count my real start from the evening George Corvick, breathless and worried, came in to ask me a service. He had done more things than I, and earned more pence, though there were chances for cleverness I thought he sometimes missed. I could only however that evening declare to him that he never missed one for kindness. There was almost rapture in hearing it proposed to me to prepare for *The Middle*, the organ of our lucubrations, so called from the position in the week of its day of appearance, an article for which he had made himself responsible, and of which, tied up with a stout string, he laid on my table the subject. I pounced upon my opportunity – that is on the first volume of it – and paid scant attention to my friend's explanation of his appeal. What explanation could be more to the point than my obvious fitness for the task? I had written on Hugh Vereker, but never a word in *The Middle*, where my dealings were mainly with the ladies and the minor poets. This was his new novel, an advance copy, and whatever much or little it should do for his reputation I was clear on the spot as to what it should do for mine. Moreover if I always read him as soon as I could get hold of him I had a particular reason for wishing to read him now: I had accepted an invitation to Bridges for the following Sunday, and it had been mentioned in Lady Jane's note that Mr Vereker was to be there. I was young enough for a flutter at meeting a man of his renown, and innocent enough to believe the occasion would demand the display of an acquaintance with his 'last'.

Corvick, who had promised a review of it, had not even had time to read it; he had gone to pieces in consequence of news requiring – as on precipitate reflection he judged – that he should catch the night-mail to Paris. He had had a telegram from Gwendolen Erme in answer to his letter offering to fly to her aid. I knew already about Gwendolen Erme; I had never seen her, but I had my ideas, which were mainly to the effect that Corvick would marry her if her mother would only die. That lady seemed now in a fair way to oblige him; after some dreadful mistake about a climate or a 'cure' she had suddenly collapsed on the return from abroad. Her daughter, unsupported and alarmed, desiring to make a rush for home but hesitating at the risk, had accepted our friend's assistance, and it was my secret belief that at sight of him Mrs Erme would pull round. His own belief was scarcely to be called secret, it discernibly at any rate differed from mine. He had showed me Gwendolen's photograph with the remark that she wasn't pretty but was awfully interesting; she had published at the age of nineteen a novel in three volumes, 'Deep Down', about which, in *The Middle*, he had been really splendid. He appreciated my present eagerness and undertook that the periodical in question should do no less; then at the last, with his hand on the door, he said to me: 'Of course you'll be all right, you know.' Seeing I was a trifle vague he added: 'I mean you won't be silly.'

'Silly – about Vereker! Why what do I ever find him but awfully clever?'

'Well, what's that but silly? What on earth does "awfully clever" mean? For God's sake try to get *at* him. Don't let him suffer by our arrangement. Speak of him, you know, if you can, as *I* should have spoken of him.'

I wondered an instant. 'You mean as far and away the biggest of the lot – that sort of thing?'

Corvick almost groaned. 'Oh you know, I don't put them back to back that way; it's the infancy of art! But he gives me a pleasure so rare; the sense of' – he mused a little – 'something or other.'

I wondered again. 'The sense, pray, of what?'

'My dear man, that's just what I want *you* to say!'

Even before he had banged the door I had begun, book in hand, to prepare myself to say it. I sat up with Vereker half the night; Corvick couldn't have done more than that. He was awfully clever – I stuck to that, but he wasn't a bit the biggest of the lot. I didn't allude to the lot, however; I flattered myself that I emerged on this occasion from the infancy of art. 'It's all right,' they declared vividly at the office; and when the number appeared I felt there was a basis on which I could meet the great man. It gave me confidence for a day or two – then that confidence dropped. I had fancied him reading it with relish, but if Corvick wasn't satisfied how could Vereker himself be? I reflected indeed that the heat of the admirer was sometimes grosser even than the appetite of the scribe. Corvick at all events wrote me from Paris a little ill-humouredly. Mrs Erme was pulling round, and I hadn't at all said what Vereker gave him the sense of.

II

The effect of my visit to Bridges was to turn me out for more profundity. Hugh Vereker, as I saw him there, was of a contact so void of angles that I blushed for the poverty of imagination involved in my small precautions. If he was in spirits it wasn't because he had read my review; in fact on the Sunday morning I felt sure he hadn't read it, though *The Middle* had been out three days and bloomed, I assured myself, in the stiff garden of periodicals which gave one of the ormolu tables the air of a stand at a station. The impression he made on me personally was such that I wished him to read it, and I corrected to this end with a surreptitious hand what might be wanting in the careless conspicuity of the sheet. I'm afraid I even watched the result of my manoeuvre, but up to luncheon I watched in vain.

When afterwards, in the course of our gregarious walk, I found myself for half an hour, not perhaps without another manoeuvre, at the great man's side, the result of his affability was a still livelier desire that he shouldn't remain in ignorance of the peculiar justice I had done him. It wasn't that he seemed to thirst for justice; on the contrary I hadn't yet caught in his talk the faintest grunt of a grudge – a note for which my young experience had already given me an ear. Of late he had had more recognition, and it was pleasant, as we used to say in *The Middle*, to see how it drew him out. He wasn't of course popular, but I judged one of the sources of his good humour to be precisely that his success was independent of that. He had none the less become in a manner the fashion; the critics at least had put on a spurt and caught up with him. We had found out at last how clever he was, and he had had to make the best of the loss of his mystery. I was strongly tempted, as I walked beside him, to let him know how much of that unveiling was my act; and there was a moment when I probably should have done so had not one of the ladies of our party, snatching a place at his other elbow, just then appealed to him in a spirit comparatively selfish. It was very discouraging: I almost felt the liberty had been taken with myself.

I had had on my tongue's end, for my own part, a phrase or two about the right word at the right time, but later on I was glad not to have spoken, for when on our return we clustered at tea I perceived Lady Jane, who had not been out with us, brandishing *The Middle* with her longest arm. She had taken it up at her leisure; she was delighted with what she had found, and I saw that, as a mistake in a man may often be a felicity in a woman, she would practically do for me what I hadn't been able to do for myself. 'Some sweet little truths that needed to be spoken,' I heard her declare, thrusting the paper at rather a bewildered couple by the fireplace. She grabbed it away from them again on the reappearance of Hugh Vereker, who after our walk had been upstairs to change something. 'I know you don't in general look at this kind of thing, but it's an occasion really for doing so. You *haven't* seen it? Then you must. The man has actually got *at* you, at what *I* always feel, you know.' Lady Jane threw into her eyes a look evidently intended to give an idea of what she always felt; but she added that she couldn't have expressed it. The man in the paper expressed it in a striking manner. 'Just see there, and there, where I've dashed it, how he brings it out.' She had literally marked for him the brightest patches of my prose, and if I was a little amused Vereker himself may well have been. He showed how much he was when before us all Lady Jane wanted to read something aloud. I liked at any rate the way he defeated her purpose by jerking the paper affectionately out of her clutch. He'd take it upstairs with him and look at it on going to dress. He did this half an hour later – I saw it in his hand when he repaired to his room. That was the moment at which, thinking to give her pleasure, I mentioned to Lady Jane that I was the author of the review. I did give her pleasure, I judged, but perhaps not quite so much as I had expected. If the author was 'only me' the thing didn't seem quite so remarkable. Hadn't I had the effect rather of diminishing the lustre of the article than of adding to my own? Her ladyship was subject to the most extraordinary drops. It didn't matter; the only effect I cared about was the one it would have on Vereker up there by his bedroom fire.

At dinner I watched for the signs of this impression, tried to fancy some happier light in his eyes; but to my disappointment Lady Jane gave me no chance to make sure. I had hoped she'd call triumphantly down the table, publicly demand if she hadn't been right. The party was large – there were people from outside as well, but I had never seen a table long enough to deprive Lady Jane of a triumph. I was just reflecting in truth that this interminable board would deprive *me* of one when the guest next me, dear woman – she was Miss Poyle, the vicar's sister, a robust unmodulated person – had the happy inspiration and the unusual courage to address herself across it to Vereker, who was opposite, but not directly, so that when he replied they were both leaning forward. She enquired, artless body, what he thought of Lady Jane's 'panegyric', which she had read – not connecting it however with her right-hand neighbour; and while I strained my ear for his reply I heard him, to my stupefaction, call back gaily, his mouth full of bread: 'Oh it's all right – the usual twaddle!'

I had caught Vereker's glance as he spoke, but Miss Poyle's surprise was a fortunate cover for my own. 'You mean he doesn't do you justice?' said the excellent woman.

Vereker laughed out, and I was happy to be able to do the same. 'It's a charming article,' he tossed us.

Miss Poyle thrust her chin half across the cloth. 'Oh you're so deep!' she drove home.

'As deep as the ocean! All I pretend is that the author doesn't see –' But a dish was at this point passed over his shoulder, and we had to wait while he helped himself.

'Doesn't see what?' my neighbour continued.

'Doesn't see anything.'

'Dear me – how very stupid!'

'Not a bit,' Vereker laughed again. 'Nobody does.'

The lady on his further side appealed to him and Miss Poyle sank back to myself. 'Nobody sees anything!' she cheerfully announced; to which I replied that I had often thought so too, but had somehow taken the thought for a proof on my own part of a tremendous eye. I didn't tell her the article was mine; and I observed that Lady Jane, occupied at the end of the table, had not caught Vereker's words.

I rather avoided him after dinner, for I confess he struck me as cruelly conceited, and the revelation was a pain. 'The usual twaddle' – my acute little study! That one's admiration should have had a reserve or two could gall him to that point? I had thought him placid, and he was placid enough; such a surface was the hard polished glass that encased the bauble of his vanity. I was really ruffled, and the only comfort was that if nobody saw anything George Corvick was quite as much out of it as I. This comfort however was not sufficient, after the ladies had dispersed, to carry me in the proper manner – I mean in a spotted jacket and humming an air – into the smoking-room. I took my way in some dejection to bed; but in the passage I encountered Mr Vereker, who had been up once more to change, coming out of his room. *He* was humming an air and had on a spotted jacket, and as soon as he saw me his gaiety gave a start.

'My dear young man,' he exclaimed, 'I'm so glad to lay hands on you! I'm afraid I most unwittingly wounded you by those words of mine at dinner to Miss Poyle. I learned but half an hour ago from Lady Jane that you're the author of the little notice in *The Middle*.'

I protested that no bones were broken; but he moved with me to my own door, his hand, on my shoulder, kindly feeling for a fracture; and on hearing that I had come up to bed he asked leave to cross my threshold and just tell me in three words what his qualification of my remarks had represented. It was plain he really feared I was hurt, and the sense of his

solicitude suddenly made all the difference to me. My cheap
review fluttered off into space, and the best things I had said
in it became flat enough beside the brilliancy of his being
there. I can see him there still, on my rug, in the firelight and
his spotted jacket, his fine clear face all bright with the desire
to be tender to my youth. I don't know what he had at first
meant to say, but I think the sight of my relief touched him,
excited him, brought up words to his lips from far within.
It was so these words presently conveyed to me something
that, as I afterwards knew, he had never uttered to any one.
I've always done justice to the generous impulse that made
him speak; it was simply compunction for a snub unconsciously administered to a man of letters in a position
inferior to his own, a man of letters moreover in the very
act of praising him. To make the thing right he talked to me
exactly as an equal and on the ground of what we both loved
best. The hour, the place, the unexpectedness deepened the
impression: he couldn't have done anything more intensely
effective.

III

'I don't quite know how to explain it to you,' he said, 'but
it was the very fact that your notice of my book had a spice
of intelligence, it was just your exceptional sharpness, that
produced the feeling – a very old story with me, I beg you
to believe – under the momentary influence of which I used
in speaking to that good lady the words you so naturally
resent. I don't read the things in the newspapers unless
they're thrust upon me as that one was – it's always one's
best friend who does it! But I used to read them sometimes –
ten years ago. I dare say they were in general rather stupider
then; at any rate it always struck me they missed my little
point with a perfection exactly as admirable when they
patted me on the back as when they kicked me in the shins.

Whenever since I've happened to have a glimpse of them they were still blazing away – still missing it, I mean, deliciously. *You* miss it, my dear fellow, with inimitable assurance; the fact of your being awfully clever and your article's being awfully nice doesn't make a hair's breadth of difference. It's quite with you rising young men,' Vereker laughed, 'that I feel most what a failure I am!'

I listened with keen interest; it grew keener as he talked. '*You* a failure – heavens! What then may your "little point" happen to be?'

'Have I got to *tell* you, after all these years and labours?' There was something in the friendly reproach of this – jocosely exaggerated – that made me, as an ardent young seeker for truth, blush to the roots of my hair. I'm as much in the dark as ever, though I've grown used in a sense to my obtuseness; at that moment, however, Vereker's happy accent made me appear to myself, and probably to him, a rare dunce. I was on the point of exclaiming 'Ah yes, don't tell me: for my honour, for that of the craft, don't!' when he went on in a manner that showed he had read my thoughts and had his own idea of the probability of our some day redeeming ourselves. 'By my little point I mean – what shall I call it? – the particular thing I've written my books most *for*. Isn't there for every writer a particular thing of that sort, the thing that most makes him apply himself, the thing without the effort to achieve which he wouldn't write at all, the very passion of his passion, the part of the business in which, for him, the flame of art burns most intensely? Well, it's *that*!'

I considered a moment – that is I followed at a respectful distance, rather gasping. I was fascinated – easily, you'll say; but I wasn't going after all to be put off my guard. 'Your description's certainly beautiful, but it doesn't make what you describe very distinct.'

'I promise you it would be distinct if it should dawn on

you at all.' I saw that the charm of our topic overflowed for my companion into an emotion as lively as my own. 'At any rate,' he went on, 'I can speak for myself: there's an idea in my work without which I wouldn't have given a straw for the whole job. It's the finest fullest intention of the lot, and the application of it has been, I think, a triumph of patience, of ingenuity. I ought to leave that to somebody else to say; but that nobody does say it is precisely what we're talking about. It stretches, this little trick of mine, from book to book, and every thing else, comparatively, plays over the surface of it. The order, the form, the texture of my books will perhaps some day constitute for the initiated a complete representation of it. So it's naturally the thing for the critic to look for. It strikes me,' my visitor added, smiling, 'even as the thing for the critic to find.'

This seemed a responsibility indeed. 'You call it a little trick?'

'That's only my little modesty. It's really an exquisite scheme.'

'And you hold that you've carried the scheme out?'

'The way I've carried it out is the thing in life I think a bit well of myself for.'

I had a pause. 'Don't you think you ought – just a trifle – to assist the critic?'

'Assist him? What else have I done with every stroke of my pen? I've shouted my intention in his great blank face!' At this, laughing out again, Vereker laid his hand on my shoulder to show the allusion wasn't to my personal appearance.

'But you talk about the initiated. There must therefore, you see, *be* initiation.'

'What else in heaven's name is criticism supposed to be?' I'm afraid I coloured at this too; but I took refuge in repeating that his account of his silver lining was poor in something or other that a plain man knows things by.

'That's only because you've never had a glimpse of it,' he returned. 'If you had had one the element in question would soon have become practically all you'd see. To me it's exactly as palpable as the marble of this chimney. Besides, the critic just *isn't* a plain man: if he were, pray, what would he be doing in his neighbour's garden? You're anything but a plain man yourself, and the very *raison d'être* of you all is that you're little demons of subtlety. If my great affair's a secret, that's only because it's a secret in spite of itself – the amazing event has made it one. I not only never took the smallest precaution to keep it so, but never dreamed of any such accident. If I had I shouldn't in advance have had the heart to go on. As it was, I only became aware little by little, and meanwhile I had done my work.'

'And now you quite like it?' I risked.

'My work?'

'Your secret. It's the same thing.'

'Your guessing that,' Vereker replied, 'is a proof that you're as clever as I say!' I was encouraged by this to remark that he would clearly be pained to part with it, and he confessed that it was indeed with him now the great amusement of life. 'I live almost to see if it will ever be detected.' He looked at me for a jesting challenge; something far within his eyes seemed to peep out. 'But I needn't worry – it won't!'

'You fire me as I've never been fired,' I declared; 'you make me determined to do or die.' Then I asked: 'Is it a kind of esoteric message?'

His countenance fell at this – he put out his hand as if to bid me good night. 'Ah my dear fellow, it can't be described in cheap journalese!'

I knew of course he'd be awfully fastidious, but our talk had made me feel how much his nerves were exposed. I was unsatisfied – I kept hold of his hand. 'I won't make use of the expression then,' I said, 'in the article which I shall eventually announce my discovery, though I dare say I shall have hard work to do without it. But meanwhile, just to hasten that difficult birth, can't you give a fellow a clue?' I felt much more at my ease.

'My whole lucid effort gives him the clue – every page and line and letter. The thing's as concrete there as a bird in a cage, a bait on a hook, a piece of cheese in a mouse-trap. It's stuck into every volume as your foot is stuck into your shoe. It governs every line, it chooses every word, it dots every i, it places every comma.'

I scratched my head. 'Is it something in the style or something in the thought? An element of form or an element of feeling?'

He indulgently shook my hand again, and I felt my questions to be crude and my distinctions pitiful. 'Good night, my dear boy – don't bother about it. After all, you do like a fellow.'

'And a little intelligence might spoil it?' I still detained him.

He hesitated. 'Well, you've got a heart in your body. Is that an element of form or an element of feeling? What I contend that nobody has ever mentioned in my work is the organ of life.'

'I see – it's some idea *about* life, some sort of philosophy. Unless it be,' I added with the eagerness of a thought perhaps still happier, 'some kind of game you're up to with your style, something you're after in the language. Perhaps it's a preference for the letter P!' I ventured profanely to break out. 'Papa, potatoes, prunes – that sort of thing?' He was suitably indulgent: he only said I hadn't got the right letter. But his amusement was over; I could see he was bored. There was nevertheless something else I had absolutely to learn. 'Should you be able, pen in hand, to state it clearly yourself – to name it, phrase it, formulate it?'

'Oh,' he almost passionately sighed, 'if I were only, pen in hand, one of *you* chaps!'

'That would be a great chance for you of course. But why should you despise us chaps for not doing what you can't do yourself?'

'Can't do?' He opened his eyes. 'Haven't I done it in twenty volumes? I do it in my way,' he continued. 'Go *you* and don't do it in yours.'

'Ours is so devilish difficult,' I weakly observed.

'So's mine! We each choose our own. There's no compulsion. You won't come down and smoke?'

'No. I want to think this thing out.'

'You'll tell me then in the morning that you've laid me bare?'

'I'll see what I can do; I'll sleep on it. But just one word more,' I added. We had left the room – I walked again with him a few steps along the passage. 'This extraordinary "general intention," as you call it – for that's the most vivid description I can induce you to make of it – is then, generally, a sort of buried treasure?'

His face lighted. 'Yes, call it that, though it's perhaps not for me to do so.'

'Nonsense!' I laughed. 'You know you're hugely proud of it.'

'Well, I didn't propose to tell you so; but it *is* the joy of my soul!'

'You mean it's a beauty so rare, so great?'

He waited a little again. 'The loveliest thing in the world!' We had stopped, and on these words he left me; but at the end of the corridor, while I looked after him rather yearningly, he turned and caught sight of my puzzled face. It made him earnestly, indeed I thought quite anxiously, shake his head and wave his finger. 'Give it up – give it up!'

This wasn't a challenge – it was fatherly advice. If I had had one of his books at hand I'd have repeated my recent act of faith – I'd have spent half the night with him. At three o'clock in the morning, not sleeping, remembering moreover how indispensable he was to Lady Jane, I stole down to the library with a candle. There wasn't, so far as I could discover, a line of his writing in the house.

IV

Returning to town I feverishly collected them all; I picked out each in its order and held it up to the light. This gave me a maddening month, in the course of which several things took place. One of these, the last, I may as well immediately mention, was that I acted on Vereker's advice: I renounced my ridiculous attempt. I could really make nothing of the business; it proved a dead loss. After all I had always, as he had himself noted, liked him; and what now occurred was simply that my new intelligence and vain preoccupation damaged my liking. I not only failed to run a general intention to earth, I found myself missing the subordinate intentions I had formerly enjoyed. His books didn't even remain the charming things they had been for me; the exasperation of my search put me out of conceit of them. Instead of being a pleasure the more they became a resource the less; for from the moment I was unable to follow up the author's hint I of course felt it a point of honour not to make use professionally of my knowledge of them. I *had* no knowledge – nobody had any. It was humiliating, but I could bear it – they only annoyed me now. At last they even bored me, and I accounted for my confusion – perversely, I allow – by the idea that Vereker had made a fool of me. The buried treasure was a bad joke, the general intention a monstrous *pose*.

The great point of it all is, however, that I told George Corvick what had befallen me and that my information had an immense effect on him. He had at last come back, but so, unfortunately, had Mrs Erme, and there was as yet, I could see, no question of his nuptials. He was immensely stirred up by the anecdote I had brought from Bridges; it fell in so completely with the sense he had had from the first that there was more in Vereker than met the eye. When I remarked that the eye seemed what the printed page had been expressly invented to meet he immediately accused me of being spiteful because I had been foiled. Our commerce had always that pleasant latitude. The thing Vereker had mentioned to me was exactly the thing he, Corvick, had wanted me to speak of in my review. On my suggesting at last that with the assistance I had now given him he would doubtless be prepared to speak of it himself he admitted freely that before doing this there was more he must understand. What he would have said, had he reviewed the new book, was that there was evidently in the writer's inmost art something to *be* understood. I hadn't so much as hinted at that: no wonder the writer hadn't been flattered! I asked Corvick what he really considered he meant by his own supersubtlety, and, unmistakably kindled, he replied: 'It isn't for the vulgar – it isn't for the vulgar!' He had hold of the tail of something: he would pull hard, pull it right out. He pumped me dry on Vereker's strange confidence and, pronouncing me the luckiest of mortals, mentioned half a dozen questions he wished to goodness I had had the gumption to put. Yet on the other hand he didn't want to be told too much – it would spoil the fun of seeing what would come. The failure of *my* fun was at the moment of our meeting not complete, but I saw it ahead, and Corvick saw that I saw it. I, on my side, saw likewise that one of the first things he would do would be to rush off with my story to Gwendolen.

On the very day after my talk with him I was surprised by the receipt of a note from Hugh Vereker, to whom our encounter at Bridges had been recalled, as he mentioned, by his falling, in a magazine, on some article to which my signature was attached. 'I read it with great pleasure,' he wrote, 'and remembered under its influence our lively conversation by your bedroom fire. The consequence of this has been that I begin to measure the temerity of my having saddled you with a knowledge that you may find something of a burden. Now that the fit's over I can't imagine how I came to be moved so much beyond my wont. I had never before mentioned, no matter in what state of expansion, the fact of my little secret, and I shall never speak of that mystery again. I was accidentally so much more explicit with you than it had ever entered into my game to be, that I find this game – I mean the pleasure of playing it – suffers considerably. In short, if you can understand it, I've rather spoiled my sport. I really don't want to give anybody what I believe you clever young men call the tip. That's of course a selfish solicitude, and I name it to you for what it may be worth to you. If you're disposed to humour me don't repeat my revelation. Think me demented – it's your right; but don't tell anybody why.'

The sequel to this communication was that as early on the morrow as I dared I drove straight to Mr Vereker's door. He occupied in those years one of the honest old houses in Kensington Square. He received me immediately, and as soon as I came in I saw I hadn't lost my power to minister to his mirth. He laughed out at sight of my face, which doubtless expressed my perturbation. I had been indiscreet – my compunction was great. 'I *have* told somebody,' I panted, 'and I'm sure that person will by this time have told somebody else! It's a woman, into the bargain.'

'The person you've told?'

'No, the other person. I'm quite sure he must have told her.'

'For all the good it will do her – or do *me*! A woman will never find out.'

'No, but she'll talk all over the place: she'll do just what you don't want.'

Vereker thought a moment, but wasn't so disconcerted as I had feared: he felt that if the harm was done it only served him right. 'It doesn't matter – don't worry.'

'I'll do my best, I promise you, that your talk with me shall go no further.'

'Very good; do what you can.'

'In the meantime,' I pursued, 'George Corvick's possession of the tip may, on his part, really lead to something.'

'That will be a brave day.'

I told him about Corvick's cleverness, his admiration, the intensity of his interest in my anecdote; and without making too much of the divergence of our respective estimates mentioned that my friend was already of opinion that he saw much further into a certain affair than most people. He was quite as fired as I had been at Bridges. He was moreover in love with the young lady: perhaps the two together would puzzle something out.

Vereker seemed struck with this. 'Do you mean they're to be married?'

'I dare say that's what it will come to.'

'That may help them,' he conceded, 'but we must give them time!'

I spoke of my own renewed assault and confessed my difficulties; whereupon he repeated his former advice: 'Give it up, give it up!' He evidently didn't think me intellectually equipped for the adventure. I stayed half an hour, and he was most good-natured, but I couldn't help pronouncing him a man of unstable moods. He had been free with me in a mood, he had repented in a mood, and now in a mood he had turned indifferent. This general levity helped me to believe that, so far as the subject of the tip went, there wasn't much in it. I contrived however to make him answer a few more questions about it, though he did so with visible impatience. For himself, beyond doubt, the thing we were all so blank about was vividly there. It was something, I guessed, in the primal plan; something like a complex figure in a Persian carpet. He highly approved of this image when I used it, and he used another himself. 'It's the very string,' he said, 'that my pearls are strung on!' The reason of his note to me had been that he really didn't want to give us a grain of succour – our density was a thing too perfect in its way to touch. He had formed the habit of depending on it, and if the spell was to break it must break by some force of its own. He comes back to me from that last occasion – for I was never to speak to him again – as a man with some safe preserve for sport. I wondered as I walked away where he had got *his* tip.

V

When I spoke to George Corvick of the caution I had received he made me feel that any doubt of his delicacy would be almost an insult. He had instantly told Gwendolen, but Gwendolen's ardent response was in itself a pledge of discretion. The question would now absorb them and would offer them a pastime too precious to be shared with the crowd. They appeared to have caught instinctively at Vereker's high idea of enjoyment. Their intellectual pride, however, was not such as to make them indifferent to any further light I might throw on the affair they had in hand. They were indeed of the 'artistic temperament', and I was freshly struck with my colleague's power to excite himself over a question of art. He'd call it letters, he'd call it life, but it was all one thing. In what he said I now seemed to understand that he spoke equally for Gwendolen, to whom, as soon as Mrs Erme was sufficiently better to allow her a little leisure, he made a point of introducing me. I remember our going together one Sunday in August to a huddled house in

Chelsea, and my renewed envy of Corvick's possession of a friend who had some light to mingle with his own. He could say things to her that I could never say to him. She had indeed no sense of humour and, with her pretty way of holding her head on one side, was one of those persons whom you want, as the phrase is, to shake, but who have learnt Hungarian by themselves. She conversed perhaps in Hungarian with Corvick; she had remarkably little English for his friend. Corvick afterwards told me that I had chilled her by my apparent indisposition to oblige them with the detail of what Vereker had said to me. I allowed that I felt I had given thought enough to that indication: hadn't I even made up my mind that it was vain and would lead nowhere? The importance they attached to it was irritating and quite envenomed my doubts.

That statement looks unamiable, and what probably happened was that I felt humiliated at seeing other persons deeply beguiled by an experiment that had brought me only chagrin. I was out in the cold while, by the evening fire, under the lamp, they followed the chase for which I myself had sounded the horn. They did as I had done, only more deliberately and sociably – they went over their author from the beginning. There was no hurry, Corvick said – the future was before them and the fascination could only grow; they would take him page by page, as they would take one of the classics, inhale him in slow draughts and let him sink all the way in. They would scarce have got so wound up, I think, if they hadn't been in love: poor Vereker's inner meaning gave them endless occasion to put and to keep their young heads together. None the less it represented the kind of problem for which Corvick had a special aptitude, drew out the particular pointed patience of which, had he lived, he would have given more striking and, it is to be hoped, more fruitful examples. He at least was, in Vereker's words, a little demon of subtlety. We had begun by disputing, but I

soon saw that without my stirring a finger his infatuation
would have its bad hours. He would bound off on false
scents as I had done – he would clap his hands over new
lights and see them blown out by the wind of the turned
page. He was like nothing, I told him, but the maniacs who
embrace some bedlamitical theory of the cryptic character
of Shakespeare.[1] To this he replied that if we had had
Shakespeare's own word for his being cryptic he would
at once have accepted it. The case there was altogether
different – we had nothing but the word of Mr Snooks. I
returned that I was stupefied to see him attach such importance even to the word of Mr Vereker. He wanted thereupon
to know if I treated Mr Vereker's word as a lie. I wasn't
perhaps prepared, in my unhappy rebound, to go so far as
that, but I insisted that till the contrary was proved I should
view it as too fond an imagination. I didn't, I confess, say –
I didn't at that time quite know – all I felt. Deep down, as
Miss Erme would have said, I was uneasy, I was expectant.
At the core of my disconcerted state – for my wonted
curiosity lived in its ashes – was the sharpness of a sense
that Corvick would at last probably come out somewhere.
He made, in defence of his credulity, a great point of the
fact that from of old, in his study of this genius, he had
caught whiffs and hints of he didn't know what, faint
wandering notes of a hidden music. That was just the rarity,
that was the charm: it fitted so perfectly into what I reported.

If I returned on several occasions to the little house in
Chelsea I dare say it was as much for news of Vereker as
for news of Miss Erme's ailing parent. The hours spent there
by Corvick were present to my fancy as those of a chessplayer
bent with a silent scowl, all the lamplit winter, over his
board and his moves. As my imagination filled it out the
picture held me fast. On the other side of the table was a
ghostlier form, the faint figure of an antagonist good-
humouredly but a little wearily secure – an antagonist who

leaned back in his chair with his hands in his pockets and a smile on his fine clear face. Close to Corvick, behind him, was a girl who had begun to strike me as pale and wasted and even, on more familiar view, as rather handsome, and who rested on his shoulder and hung on his moves. He would take up a chessman and hold it poised a while over one of the little squares, and then would put it back in its place with a long sigh of disappointment. The young lady, at this, would slightly but uneasily shift her position and look across, very hard, very long, very strangely, at their dim participant. I had asked them at an early stage of the business if it mightn't contribute to their success to have some closer communication with him. The special circumstances would surely be held to have given me a right to introduce them. Corvick immediately replied that he had no wish to approach the altar before he had prepared the sacrifice. He quite agreed with our friend both as to the delight and as to the honour of the chase – he would bring down the animal with his own rifle. When I asked him if Miss Erme were as keen a shot he said after thinking: 'No, I'm ashamed to say she wants to set a trap. She'd give anything to see him; she says she requires another tip. She's really quite morbid about it. But she must play fair – she *shan't* see him!' he emphatically added. I wondered if they hadn't even quarrelled a little on the subject – a suspicion not corrected by the way he more than once exclaimed to me: 'She's quite incredibly literary, you know – quite fantastically!' I remember his saying of her that she felt in italics and thought in capitals. 'Oh when I've run him to earth,' he also said, 'then, you know, I shall knock at his door. Rather – I beg you to believe. I'll have it from his own lips: "Right you are, my boy; you've done it this time!" He shall crown me victor – with the critical laurel.'

Meanwhile he really avoided the chances London life might have given him of meeting the distinguished novelist;

a danger, however, that disappeared with Vereker's leaving England for an indefinite absence, as the newspapers announced – going to the south for motives connected with the health of his wife, which had long kept her in retirement. A year – more than a year – had elapsed since the incident at Bridges, but I had had no further sight of him. I think I was at bottom rather ashamed – I hated to remind him that, though I had irremediably missed his point, a reputation for acuteness was rapidly overtaking me. This scruple led me a dance; kept me out of Lady Jane's house, made me even decline, when in spite of my bad manners she was a second time so good as to make me a sign, an invitation to her beautiful seat. I once became aware of her under Vereker's escort at a concert, and was sure I was seen by them, but I slipped out without being caught. I felt, as on that occasion I splashed along in the rain, that I couldn't have done anything else; and yet I remember saying to myself that it was hard, was even cruel. Not only had I lost the books, but I had lost the man himself: they and their author had been alike spoiled for me. I knew too which was the loss I most regretted. I had taken to the man still more than I had ever taken to the books.

VI

Six months after our friend had left England George Corvick, who made his living by his pen, contracted for a piece of work which imposed on him an absence of some length and a journey of some difficulty, and his undertaking of which was much of a surprise to me. His brother-in-law had become editor of a great provincial paper, and the great provincial paper, in a fine flight of fancy, had conceived the idea of sending a 'special commissioner' to India. Special commissioners had begun, in the 'metropolitan press,' to be the fashion, and the journal in question must have felt it had passed too long for a mere country cousin. Corvick had no hand, I knew, for the big brush of the correspondent, but that was his brother-in-law's affair, and the fact that a particular task was not in his line was apt to be with himself exactly a reason for accepting it. He was prepared to out-Herod the metropolitan press;[2] he took solemn precautions against priggishness, he exquisitely outraged taste. Nobody ever knew it – that offended principle was all his own. In addition to his expenses he was to be conveniently paid, and I found myself able to help him, for the usual fat book, to a plausible arrangement with the usual fat publisher. I naturally inferred that his obvious desire to make a little money was not unconnected with the prospect of a union with Gwendolen Erme. I was aware that her mother's opposition was largely addressed to his want of means and of lucrative abilities, but it so happened that, on my saying the last time I saw him something that bore on the question of his separation from our young lady, he brought out with an emphasis that startled me: 'Ah I'm not a bit engaged to her, you know!'

'Not overtly,' I answered, 'because her mother doesn't like you. But I've always taken for granted a private understanding.'

'Well, there *was* one. But there isn't now.' That was all he said save something about Mrs Erme's having got on her feet again in the most extraordinary way – a remark pointing, as I supposed, the moral that private understandings were of little use when the doctor didn't share them. What I took the liberty of more closely inferring was that the girl might in some way have estranged him. Well, if he had taken the turn of jealousy for instance it could scarcely be jealousy of me. In that case – over and above the absurdity of it – he wouldn't have gone away just to leave us together.

For some time before his going we had indulged in no allusion to the buried treasure, and from his silence, which my reserve simply emulated, I had drawn a sharp conclusion. His courage had dropped, his ardour had gone the way of mine – this appearance at least he left me to scan. More than that he couldn't do; he couldn't face the triumph with which I might have greeted an explicit admission. He needn't have been afraid, poor dear, for I had by this time lost all need to triumph. In fact I considered I showed magnanimity in not reproaching him with his collapse, for the sense of his having thrown up the game made me feel more than ever how much I at last depended on him. If Corvick had broken down I should never know; no one would be of any use if *he* wasn't. It wasn't a bit true I had ceased to care for knowledge; little by little my curiosity not only had begun to ache again, but had become the familiar torment of my days and my nights. There are doubtless people to whom torments of such an order appear hardly more natural than the contortions of disease; but I don't after all know why I should in this connection so much as mention them. For the few persons, at any rate, abnormal or not, with whom my anecdote is concerned, literature was a game of skill, and skill meant courage, and courage meant honour, and honour meant passion, meant life. The stake on the table was of a special substance and our roulette the revolving mind, but we sat round the green board as intently as the grim gamblers at Monte Carlo. Gwendolen Erme, for that matter, with her white face and her fixed eyes, was of the very type of the lean ladies one had met in the temples of chance. I recognised in Corvick's absence that she made this analogy vivid. It was extravagant, I admit, the way she lived for the art of the pen. Her passion visibly preyed on her, and in her presence I felt almost tepid. I got hold of 'Deep Down' again: it was a desert in which she had lost herself, but in which too she had dug a wonderful hole in the sand – a cavity out of which Corvick had still more remarkably pulled her.

Early in March I had a telegram from her, in consequence of which I repaired immediately to Chelsea, where the first thing she said to me was 'He has got it, he has got it!'

She was moved, as I could see, to such depths that she must mean the great thing. 'Vereker's idea?'

'His general intention. George has cabled from Bombay.'

She had the missive open there; it was emphatic though concise. 'Eureka. Immense.' That was all – he had saved the cost of the signature. I shared her emotion, but I was disappointed. 'He doesn't say what it is.'

'How could he – in a telegram? He'll write it.'

'But how does he know?'

'Know it's the real thing? Oh I'm sure that when you see it you do know. *Vera incessu patuit dea!*'[3]

'It's you, Miss Erme, who are a "dear" for bringing me such news!' – I went all lengths in my high spirits. 'But fancy finding our goddess in the temple of Vishnu! How strange of George to have been able to go into the thing again in the midst of such different and such powerful solicitations!'

'He hasn't gone into it, I know; it's the thing itself, let severely alone for six months, that has simply sprung out at him like a tigress out of the jungle. He didn't take a book with him – on purpose; indeed he wouldn't have needed to – he knows every page, as I do, by heart. They all worked in him together, and some day somewhere, when he wasn't thinking, they fell, in all their superb intricacy, into the one right combination. The figure in the carpet came out. That's the way he knew it would come and the real reason – you didn't in the least understand, but I suppose I may tell you now – why he went and why I consented to his going. We knew the change would do it – that the difference of thought, of scene, would give the needed touch, the magic shake. We had perfectly, we had admirably calculated. The elements

were all in his mind, and in the *secousse*⁴ of a new and
intense experience they just struck light.' She positively
struck light herself – she was literally, facially luminous. I
stammered something about unconscious cerebration, and
she continued: 'He'll come right home – this will bring him.'

'To see Vereker, you mean?'

'To see Vereker – and to see *me*. Think what he'll have
to tell me!'

I hesitated. 'About India?'

'About fiddlesticks! About Vereker – about the figure in
the carpet.'

'But, as you say, we shall surely have that in a letter.'

She thought like one inspired, and I remembered how
Corvick had told me long before that her face was interesting. 'Perhaps it can't be got into a letter if it's "immense".'

'Perhaps not if it's immense bosh. If he has hold of
something that can't be got into a letter he hasn't hold of
the thing. Vereker's own statement to me was exactly that
the "figure" *would* fit into a letter.'

'Well, I cabled to George an hour ago – two words,' said
Gwendolen.

'Is it indiscreet of me to ask what they were?'

She hung fire, but at last brought them out. '"Angel,
write."'

'Good!' I cried. 'I'll make it sure – I'll send him the same.'

VII

My words however were not absolutely the same – I put
something instead of 'angel'; and in the sequel my epithet
seemed the more apt, for when eventually we heard from our
traveller it was merely, it was thoroughly to be tantalised. He
was magnificent in his triumph, he described his discovery
as stupendous; but his ecstasy only obscured it – there were
to be no particulars till he should have submitted his

conception to the supreme authority. He had thrown up his commission, he had thrown up his book, he had thrown up everything but the instant need to hurry to Rapallo, on the Genoese shore, where Vereker was making a stay. I wrote him a letter which was to await him at Aden – I besought him to relieve my suspense. That he had found my letter was indicated by a telegram which, reaching me after weary days and in the absence of any answer to my laconic dispatch to him at Bombay, was evidently intended as a reply to both communications. Those few words were in familiar French, the French of the day, which Corvick often made use of to show he wasn't a prig. It had for some persons the opposite effect, but his message may fairly be paraphrased. 'Have patience; I want to see, as it breaks on you, the face you'll make!' 'Tellement envie de voir ta tête!'[5] – that was what I had to sit down with. I can certainly not be said to have sat down, for I seem to remember myself at this time as rattling constantly between the little house in Chelsea and my own. Our impatience, Gwendolen's and mine, was equal, but I kept hoping her light would be greater. We all spent during this episode, for people of our means, a great deal of money in telegrams and cabs, and I counted on the receipt of news from Rapallo immediately after the junction of the discoverer with the discovered. The interval seemed an age, but late one day I heard a hansom precipitated to my door with the crash engendered by a hint of liberality. I lived with my heart in my mouth and accordingly bounded to the window – a movement which gave me a view of a young lady erect on the footboard of the vehicle and eagerly looking up at my house. At sight of me she flourished a paper with a movement that brought me straight down, the movement with which, in melodramas, handkerchiefs and reprieves are flourished at the foot of the scaffold.

'Just seen Vereker – not a note wrong. Pressed me to bosom – keeps me a month.' So much I read on her paper while the cabby dropped a grin from his perch. In my excitement I paid him profusely and in hers she suffered it; then as he drove away we started to walk about and talk. We had talked, heaven knows, enough before, but this was a wondrous lift. We pictured the whole scene at Rapallo, where he would have written, mentioning my name, for permission to call; that is *I* pictured it, having more material than my companion, whom I felt hang on my lips as we stopped on purpose before shop-windows we didn't look into. About one thing we were clear: if he was staying on for fuller communication we should at least have a letter from him that would help us through the dregs of delay. We understood his staying on, and yet each of us saw, I think, that the other hated it. The letter we were clear about arrived; it was for Gwendolen, and I called on her in time to save her the trouble of bringing it to me. She didn't read it out, as was natural enough; but she repeated to me what it chiefly embodied. This consisted of the remarkable statement that he'd tell her after they were married exactly what she wanted to know.

'Only *then*, when I'm his wife—not before,' she explained. 'It's tantamount to saying – isn't it? – that I must marry him straight off!' She smiled at me while I flushed with disappointment, a vision of fresh delay that made me at first unconscious of my surprise. It seemed more than a hint that on me as well he would impose some tiresome condition. Suddenly, while she reported several more things from his letter, I remembered what he had told me before going away. He had found Mr Vereker deliriously interesting and his own possession of the secret a real intoxication. The buried treasure was all gold and gems. Now that it was there it seemed to grow and grow before him; it would have been, through all time and taking all tongues, one of the most wonderful flowers of literary art. Nothing, in especial, once you were face to face with it, could show for more consummately *done*. When once it came out it came out, was there with a splendour that made you ashamed; and there hadn't been, save in the bottomless vulgarity of the age, with every one tasteless and tainted, every sense stopped, the smallest reason why it should have been overlooked. It was great, yet so simple, was simple, yet so great, and the final knowledge of it was an experience quite apart. He intimated that the charm of such an experience, the desire to drain it, in its freshness, to the last drop, was what kept him there close to the source. Gwendolen, frankly radiant as she tossed me these fragments, showed the elation of a prospect more assured than my own. That brought me back to the question of her marriage, prompted me to ask if what she meant by what she had just surprised me with was that she was under an engagement.

'Of course I am!' she answered. 'Didn't you know it?' She seemed astonished, but I was still more so, for Corvick had told me the exact contrary. I didn't mention this, however; I only reminded her how little I had been on that score in her confidence, or even in Corvick's, and that moreover I wasn't in ignorance of her mother's interdict. At bottom I was troubled by the disparity of the two accounts; but after a little I felt Corvick's to be the one I least doubted. This simply reduced me to asking myself if the girl had on the spot improvised an engagement – vamped up an old one or dashed off a new – in order to arrive at the satisfaction she desired. She must have had resources of which I was destitute, but she made her case slightly more intelligible by returning presently: 'What the state of things has been is that we felt of course bound to do nothing in mamma's lifetime.'

'But now you think you'll just dispense with mamma's consent?'

'Ah it mayn't come to that!' I wondered what it might come to, and she went on: 'Poor dear, she may swallow the dose. In fact, you know,' she added with a laugh, 'she really *must*!' – a proposition of which, on behalf of every one concerned, I fully acknowledged the force.

VIII

Nothing more vexatious had ever happened to me than to become aware before Corvick's arrival in England that I shouldn't be there to put him through. I found myself abruptly called to Germany by the alarming illness of my younger brother, who, against my advice, had gone to Munich to study, at the feet indeed of a great master, the art of portraiture in oils. The near relative who made him an allowance had threatened to withdraw it if he should, under specious pretexts, turn for superior truth to Paris – Paris being somehow, for a Cheltenham aunt, the school of evil, the abyss. I deplored this prejudice at the time, and the deep injury of it was now visible – first in the fact that it hadn't saved the poor boy, who was clever frail and foolish, from congestion of the lungs, and second in the greater break with London to which the event condemned me. I'm afraid that what was uppermost in my mind during several anxious weeks was the sense that if we had only been in Paris I might have run over to see Corvick. This was actually out of the question from every point of view: my brother, whose recovery gave us both plenty to do, was ill for three months, during which I never left him and at the end of which we had to face the absolute prohibition of a return to England. The consideration of climate imposed itself, and he was in no state to meet it alone. I took him to Meran and there spent the summer with him, trying to show him by example how to get back to work and nursing a rage of another sort that I tried *not* to show him.

The whole business proved the first of a series of phenomena so strangely interlaced that, taken all together – which was how I had to take them – they form as good an illustration as I can recall of the manner in which, for the good of his soul doubtless, fate sometimes deals with a man's avidity. These incidents certainly had larger bearings than the comparatively meagre consequence we are here concerned with – though I feel that consequence also a thing to speak of with some respect. It's mainly in such a light, I confess, at any rate, that the ugly fruit of my exile is at this hour present to me. Even at first indeed the spirit in which my avidity, as I have called it, made me regard that term owed no element of ease to the fact that before coming back from Rapallo George Corvick addressed me in a way I objected to. His letter had none of the sedative action I must today profess myself sure he had wished to give it, and the march of occurrences was not so ordered as to make up for what it lacked. He had begun on the spot, for one of the quarterlies, a great last word on Vereker's writings, and this exhaustive study, the only one that would have counted, have existed, was to turn on the new light, to utter – oh so quietly! – the unimagined truth. It was in other words to trace the figure in the carpet through every convolution, to reproduce it in every tint. The result, according to my friend, would be the greatest literary portrait ever painted, and what he asked of me was just to be so good as not to trouble him with questions till he should hang up his masterpiece before me. He did me the honour to declare that, putting aside the great sitter himself, all aloft in his indifference, I was individually the connoisseur he was most working for. I was therefore to be a good boy and not try to peep under the curtain before the show was ready: I should enjoy it all the more if I sat very still.

I did my best to sit very still, but I couldn't help giving a jump on seeing in *The Times*, after I had been a week or two in Munich and before, as I knew, Corvick had reached London, the announcement of the sudden death of poor

Mrs Erme. I instantly, by letter, appealed to Gwendolen for particulars, and she wrote me that her mother had yielded to long-threatened failure of the heart. She didn't say, but I took the liberty of reading into her words, that from the point of view of her marriage and also of her eagerness, which was quite a match for mine, this was a solution more prompt than could have been expected and more radical than waiting for the old lady to swallow the dose. I candidly admit indeed that at the time – for I heard from her repeatedly – I read some singular things into Gwendolen's words and some still more extraordinary ones into her silences. Pen in hand, this way, I live the time over, and it brings back the oddest sense of my having been, both for months and in spite of myself, a kind of coerced spectator. All my life had taken refuge in my eyes, which the procession of events appeared to have committed itself to keep astare. There were days when I thought of writing to Hugh Vereker and simply throwing myself on his charity. But I felt more deeply that I hadn't fallen quite so low – besides which, quite properly, he would send me about my business. Mrs Erme's death brought Corvick straight home, and within the month he was united 'very quietly' – as quietly, I seemed to make out, as he meant in his article to bring out his *trouvaille*⁶ – to the young lady he had loved and quitted. I use this last term, I may parenthetically say, because I subsequently grew sure that at the time he went to India, at the time of his great news from Bombay, there had been no positive pledge between them whatever. There had been none at the moment she was affirming to me the very opposite. On the other hand he had certainly become engaged the day he returned. The happy pair went down to Torquay for their honeymoon, and there, in a reckless hour, it occurred to poor Corvick to take his young bride a drive. He had no command of that business: this had been brought home to me of old in a little tour we had once made together in a dog-cart. In a dog-cart he perched his companion for a rattle over Devonshire hills, on one of the likeliest of which he brought his horse, who, it was true, had bolted, down with such violence that the occupants of the cart were hurled forward and that he fell horribly on his head. He was killed on the spot; Gwendolen escaped unhurt.

I pass rapidly over the question of this unmitigated tragedy, of what the loss of my best friend meant for me, and I complete my little history of my patience and my pain by the frank statement of my having, in a postscript to my very first letter to her after the receipt of the hideous news, asked Mrs Corvick whether her husband mightn't at least have finished the great article on Vereker. Her answer was as prompt as my question: the article, which had been barely begun, was a mere heartbreaking scrap. She explained that our friend, abroad, had just settled down to it when interrupted by her mother's death, and that then, on his return, he had been kept from work by the engrossments into which that calamity was to plunge them. The opening pages were all that existed; they were striking, they were promising, but they didn't unveil the idol. That great intellectual feat was obviously to have formed his climax. She said nothing more, nothing to enlighten me as to the state of her own knowledge – the knowledge for the acquisition of which I had fancied her prodigiously acting. This was above all what I wanted to know: had *she* seen the idol unveiled? Had there been a private ceremony for a palpitating audience of one? For what else but that ceremony had the nuptials taken place? I didn't like as yet to press her, though when I thought of what had passed between us on the subject in Corvick's absence her reticence surprised me. It was therefore not till much later, from Meran, that I risked another appeal, risked it in some trepidation, for she continued to tell me nothing. 'Did you hear in those few days of your blighted bliss,' I wrote, 'what we desired so to hear?' I said 'we' as a little hint; and she showed me she could take a little hint. 'I heard everything,' she replied, 'and I mean to keep it to myself!'

IX

It was impossible not to be moved with the strongest sympathy for her, and on my return to England I showed her every kindness in my power. Her mother's death had made her means sufficient, and she had gone to live in a more convenient quarter. But her loss had been great and her visitation cruel; it never would have occurred to me moreover to suppose she could come to feel the possession of a technical tip, of a piece of literary experience, a counterpoise to her grief. Strange to say, none the less, I couldn't help believing after I had seen her a few times that I caught a glimpse of some such oddity. I hasten to add that there had been other things I couldn't help believing, or at least imagining; and as I never felt I was really clear about these, so, as to the point I here touch on, I give her memory the benefit of the doubt. Stricken and solitary, highly accomplished and now, in her deep mourning, her maturer grace and her uncomplaining sorrow, incontestably handsome, she presented herself as leading a life of singular dignity and beauty. I had at first found a way to persuade myself that I should soon get the better of the reserve formulated, the week after the catastrophe, in her reply to an appeal as to which I was not unconscious that it might strike her as mistimed. Certainly that reserve was something of a shock to me – certainly it puzzled me the more I thought of it and even though I tried to explain it (with moments of success) by an imputation of exalted sentiments, of superstitious scruples, of a refinement of loyalty. Certainly it added at the same time hugely to the price of Vereker's secret, precious as this mystery already appeared. I may as well confess abjectly that Mrs Corvick's unexpected attitude was the final tap on the nail that was to fix fast my luckless idea, convert it into the obsession of which I'm for ever conscious.

But this only helped me the more to be artful, to be adroit, to allow time to elapse before renewing my suit. There were plenty of speculations for the interval, and one of them was deeply absorbing. Corvick had kept his information from his young friend till after the removal of the last barrier to their intimacy – then only had he let the cat out of the bag. Was it Gwendolen's idea, taking a hint from him, to liberate this animal only on the basis of the renewal of such a relation? Was the figure in the carpet traceable or describable only for husbands and wives – for lovers supremely united? It came back to me in a mystifying manner that in Kensington Square, when I mentioned that Corvick would have told the girl he loved, some word had dropped from Vereker that gave colour to this possibility. There might be little in it, but there was enough to make me wonder if I should have to marry Mrs Corvick to get what I wanted. Was I prepared to offer her this price for the blessing of her knowledge? Ah that way madness lay! – so I at least said to myself in bewildered hours. I could see meanwhile the torch she refused to pass on flame away in her chamber of memory – pour through her eyes a light that shone in her lonely house. At the end of six months I was fully sure of what this warm presence made up to her for. We had talked again and again of the man who had brought us together – of his talent, his character, his personal charm, his certain career, his dreadful doom, and even of his clear purpose in that great study which was to have been a supreme literary portrait, a kind of critical Vandyke or Velasquez.[7] She had conveyed to me in abundance that she was tongue-tied by her perversity, by her piety, that she would never break the silence it had not been given to the 'right person,' as she said, to break. The hour however finally arrived. One evening when I had been sitting with her longer than usual I laid my hand firmly on her arm. 'Now at last what *is* it?'

She had been expecting me and was ready. She gave a long slow soundless headshake, merciful only in being inarticulate. This mercy didn't prevent its hurling at me the largest finest coldest 'Never!' I had yet, in the course of a life that had known denials, had to take full in the face. I took it and was aware that with the hard blow the tears had come into my eyes. So for a while we sat and looked at each other; after which I slowly rose. I was wondering if some day she would accept me; but this was not what I brought out. I said as I smoothed down my hat: 'I know what to think then. It's nothing!'

A remote disdainful pity for me gathered in her dim smile; then she spoke in a voice that I hear at this hour. 'It's my *life*!' As I stood at the door she added: 'You've insulted him!'

'Do you mean Vereker?'

'I mean the Dead!'

I recognised when I reached the street the justice of her charge. Yes, it was her life – I recognised that too; but her life none the less made room with the lapse of time for another interest. A year and a half after Corvick's death she published in a single volume her second novel, 'Overmastered,' which I pounced on in the hope of finding in it some tell-tale echo or some peeping face. All I found was a much better book than her younger performance, showing I thought the better company she had kept. As a tissue tolerably intricate it was a carpet with a figure of its own; but the figure was not the figure I was looking for. On sending a review of it to *The Middle* I was surprised to learn from the office that a notice was already in type. When the paper came out I had no hesitation in attributing this article, which I thought rather vulgarly overdone, to Drayton Deane, who in the old days had been something of a friend of Corvick's, yet had only within a few weeks made the acquaintance of his widow. I had had an early copy of the book, but Deane had evidently had an earlier. He lacked all the same the light hand with which Corvick had gilded the gingerbread – he laid on the tinsel in splotches.

X

Six months later appeared 'The Right of Way', the last chance, though we didn't know it, that we were to have to redeem ourselves. Written wholly during Vereker's sojourn abroad, the book had been heralded, in a hundred paragraphs, by the usual ineptitudes. I carried it, as early a copy as any, I this time flattered myself, straightway to Mrs Corvick. This was the only use I had for it; I left the inevitable tribute of *The Middle* to some more ingenious mind and some less irritated temper. 'But I already have it,' Gwendolen said. 'Drayton Deane was so good as to bring it to me yesterday, and I've just finished it.'

'Yesterday? How did he get it so soon?'

'He gets everything so soon! He's to review it in *The Middle*.'

'He – Drayton Deane – review Vereker?' I couldn't believe my ears.

'Why not? One fine ignorance is as good as another.'

I winced but I presently said: 'You ought to review him yourself!'

'I don't "review," ' she laughed. 'I'm reviewed!'

Just then the door was thrown open. 'Ah yes, here's your reviewer!' Drayton Deane was there with his long legs and his tall forehead: he had come to see what she thought of 'The Right of Way,' and to bring news that was singularly relevant. The evening papers were just out with a telegram on the author of that work, who, in Rome, had been ill for some days with an attack of malarial fever. It had at first not been thought grave, but had taken, in consequence of complications, a turn that might give rise to anxiety. Anxiety had indeed at the latest hour begun to be felt.

I was struck in the presence of these tidings with the fundamental detachment that Mrs Corvick's overt concern quite failed to hide: it gave me the measure of her consummate independence. That independence tested on her knowledge, the knowledge which nothing now could destroy and which nothing could make different. The figure in the carpet might take on another twist or two, but the sentence had virtually been written. The writer might go down to his grave: she was the person in the world to whom – as if she had been his favoured heir – his continued existence was least of a need. This reminded me how I had observed at a particular moment – after Corvick's death – the drop of her desire to see him face to face. She had got what she wanted without that. I had been sure that if she hadn't got it she wouldn't have been restrained from the endeavour to sound him personally by those superior reflections, more conceivable on a man's part than on a woman's, which in my case had served as a deterrent. It wasn't however, I hasten to add, that my case, in spite of this invidious comparison, wasn't ambiguous enough. At the thought that Vereker was perhaps at that moment dying there rolled over me a wave of anguish – a poignant sense of how inconsistently I still depended on him. A delicacy that it was my one compensation to suffer to rule me had left the Alps and the Apennines between us, but the sense of the waning occasion suggested that I might in my despair at last have gone to him. Of course I should really have done nothing of the sort. I remained five minutes, while my companions talked of the new book, and when Drayton Deane appealed to me for my opinion of it I made answer, getting up, that I detested Hugh Vereker and simply couldn't read him. I departed with the moral certainty that as the door closed behind me Deane would brand me for awfully superficial. His hostess wouldn't contradict *that* at least.

I continue to trace with a briefer touch our intensely odd successions. Three weeks after this came Vereker's death, and before the year was out the death of his wife. That poor lady I had never seen, but I had had a futile theory that, should she survive him long enough to be decorously accessible, I might approach her with the feeble flicker of my plea. Did she know and if she knew would she speak? It was much to be presumed that for more reasons than one she would have nothing to say; but when she passed out of all reach I felt renouncement indeed my appointed lot. I was shut up in my obsession for ever – my gaolers had gone off with the key. I find myself quite as vague as a captive in a dungeon about the time that further elapsed before Mrs Corvick became the wife of Drayton Deane. I had foreseen, through my bars, this end of the business, though there was no indecent haste and our friendship had rather fallen off. They were both so 'awfully intellectual' that it struck people as a suitable match, but I had measured better than any one the wealth of understanding the bride would contribute to the union. Never, for a marriage in literary circles – so the newspapers described the alliance – had a lady been so bravely dowered. I began with due promptness to look for the fruit of the affair – that fruit, I mean, of which the premonitory symptoms would be peculiarly visible in the husband. Taking for granted the splendour of the other party's nuptial gift, I expected to see him make a show commensurate with his increase of means. I knew what his means had been – his article on 'The Right of Way' had distinctly given one the figure. As he was now exactly in the position in which still more exactly I was not I watched from month to month, in the likely periodicals, for the heavy message poor Corvick had been unable to deliver and the responsibility of which would have fallen on his successor.

The widow and wife would have broken by the rekindled hearth the silence that only a widow and wife might break, and Deane would be as aflame with the knowledge as Corvick in his own hour, as Gwendolen in hers, had been. Well, he was aflame doubtless, but the fire was apparently not to become a public blaze. I scanned the periodicals in vain: Drayton Deane filled them with exuberant pages, but he withheld the page I most feverishly sought. He wrote on a thousand subjects, but never on the subject of Vereker. His special line was to tell truths that other people either 'funked,' as he said, or overlooked, but he never told the only truth that seemed to me in these days to signify. I met the couple in those literary circles referred to in the papers: I have sufficiently intimated that it was only in such circles we were all constructed to revolve. Gwendolen was more than ever committed to them by the publication of her third novel, and I myself definitely classed by holding the opinion that this work was inferior to its immediate predecessor. Was it worse because she had been keeping worse company? If her secret was, as she had told me, her life – a fact discernible in her increasing bloom, an air of conscious privilege that, cleverly corrected by pretty charities, gave distinction to her appearance – it had yet not a direct influence on her work. That only made one – everything only made one – yearn the more for it; only rounded it off with a mystery finer and subtler.

XI

It was therefore from her husband I could never remove my eyes: I beset him in a manner that might have made him uneasy. I went even so far as to engage him in conversation. *Didn't* he know, hadn't he come into it as a matter of course? – that question hummed in my brain. Of course he knew; otherwise he wouldn't return my stare so queerly.

His wife had told him what I wanted and he was amiably amused at my impotence. He didn't laugh – he wasn't a laugher: his system was to present to my irritation, so that I should crudely expose myself, a conversational blank as vast as his big bare brow. It always happened that I turned away with a settled conviction from these unpeopled expanses, which seemed to complete each other geographically and to symbolise together Drayton Deane's want of voice, want of form. He simply hadn't the art to use what he knew, he literally was incompetent to take up the duty where Corvick had left it. I went still further – it was the only glimpse of happiness I had. I made up my mind that the duty didn't appeal to him. He wasn't interested, he didn't care. Yes, it quite comforted me to believe him too stupid to have joy of the thing I lacked. He was as stupid after as he had been before, and that deepened for me the golden glory in which the mystery was wrapped. I had of course none the less to recollect that his wife might have imposed her conditions and exactions. I had above all to remind myself that with Vereker's death the major incentive dropped. He was still there to be honoured by what might be done – he was no longer there to give it his sanction. Who alas but he had the authority?

Two children were born to the pair, but the second cost the mother her life. After this stroke I seemed to see another ghost of a chance. I jumped at it in thought, but I waited a certain time for manners, and at last my opportunity arrived in a remunerative way. His wife had been dead a year when I met Drayton Deane in the smoking-room of a small club of which we both were members, but where for months – perhaps because I rarely entered it – I hadn't seen him. The room was empty and the occasion propitious. I deliberately offered him, to have done with the matter for ever, that advantage for which I felt he had long been looking.

'As an older acquaintance of your late wife's than even

you were,' I began, 'you must let me say to you something I have on my mind. I shall be glad to make any terms with you that you see fit to name for the information she must have had from George Corvick – the information, you know, that had come to *him*, poor chap, in one of the happiest hours of his life, straight from Hugh Vereker.'

He looked at me like a dim phrenological bust.[8] 'The information –?'

'Vereker's secret, my dear man – the general intention of his books: the string the pearls were strung on, the buried treasure, the figure in the carpet.'

He began to flush – the numbers on his bumps[9] to come out. 'Vereker's books had a general intention?'

I stared in my turn. 'You don't mean to say you don't know it?' I thought for a moment he was playing with me. 'Mrs Deane knew it; she had it, as I say, straight from Corvick, who had, after infinite search and to Vereker's own delight, found the very mouth of the cave. Where *is* the mouth? He told after their marriage – and told alone – the person who, when the circumstances were reproduced, must have told *you*. Have I been wrong in taking for granted that she admitted you, as one of the highest privileges of the relation in which you stood to her, to the knowledge of which she was after Corvick's death the sole depositary? All *I* know is that that knowledge is infinitely precious, and what I want you to understand is that if you'll in your turn admit me to it you'll do me a kindness for which I shall be lastingly grateful.'

He had turned at last very red; I dare say he had begun by thinking I had lost my wits. Little by little he followed me; on my own side I stared with a livelier surprise. Then he spoke. 'I don't know what you're talking about.'

He wasn't acting – it was the absurd truth. 'She *didn't* tell you –?'

'Nothing about Hugh Vereker.'

I was stupefied; the room went round. It had been too good even for that! 'Upon your honour?'

'Upon my honour. What the devil's the matter with you?' he growled.

'I'm astounded – I'm disappointed. I wanted to get it out of you.'

'It isn't *in* me!' he awkwardly laughed. 'And even if it were –'

'If it were you'd let me have it – oh yes, in common humanity. But I believe you. I see – I see!' I went on, conscious, with the full turn of the wheel, of my great delusion, my false view of the poor man's attitude. What I saw, though I couldn't say it, was that his wife hadn't thought him worth enlightening. This struck me as strange for a woman who had thought him worth marrying. At last I explained it by the reflection that she couldn't possibly have married him for his understanding. She had married him for something else.

He was to some extent enlightened now, but he was even more astonished, more disconcerted: he took a moment to compare my story with his quickened memories. The result of his meditation was his presently saying with a good deal of rather feeble form: 'This is the first I hear of what you allude to. I think you must be mistaken as to Mrs Drayton Deane's having had any unmentioned, and still less any unmentionable, knowledge of Hugh Vereker. She'd certainly have wished it – should it have borne on his literary character – to be used.'

'It *was* used. She used it herself. She told me with her own lips that she "lived" on it.'

I had no sooner spoken than I repented of my words; he grew so pale that I felt as if I had struck him. 'Ah "lived" –!' he murmured, turning short away from me.

My compunction was real; I laid my hand on his shoulder. 'I beg you to forgive me – I've made a mistake. You *don't* know what I thought you knew. You could, if I had been right, have rendered me a service; and I had my reasons for assuming that you'd be in a position to meet me.'

'Your reasons?' he echoed. 'What were your reasons?'

I looked at him well; I hesitated; I considered. 'Come and sit down with me here and I'll tell you.' I drew him to a sofa, I lighted another cigar and, beginning with the anecdote of Vereker's one descent from the clouds, I recited to him the extraordinary chain of accidents that had, in spite of the original gleam, kept me till that hour in the dark. I told him in a word just what I've written out here. He listened with deepening attention, and I became aware, to my surprise, by his ejaculations, by his questions, that he would have been after all not unworthy to be trusted by his wife. So abrupt an experience of her want of trust had now a disturbing effect on him; but I saw the immediate shock throb away little by little and then gather again into waves of wonder and curiosity – waves that promised, I could perfectly judge, to break in the end with the fury of my own highest tides. I may say that today as victims of unappeased desire there isn't a pin to choose between us. The poor man's state is almost my consolation, there are really moments when I feel it to be quite my revenge.

JOHN DELAVOY

JOHN DELAVOY

I

The friend who kindly took me to the first night of poor Windon's first – which was also poor Windon's last: it was removed as fast as, at an unlucky dinner, a dish of too perceptible a presence – also obligingly pointed out to me the notabilities in the house. So it was that we came round, just opposite, to a young lady in the front row of that balcony – a young lady in mourning so marked that I rather wondered to see her at a place of pleasure. I dare say my surprise was partly produced by my thinking her face, as I made it out at the distance, refined enough to aid a little the contradiction. I remember at all events dropping a word about the manners and morals of London – a word to the effect that, for the most part, elsewhere, people so bereaved as to be so becraped[1] were bereaved enough to stay at home. We recognised of course, however, during the wait, that nobody ever did stay at home; and, as my companion proved vague about my young lady, who was yet somehow more interesting than any other as directly in range, we took refuge in the several theories that might explain her behaviour. One of these was that she had a sentiment for Windon which could override superstitions; another was that her scruples had been mastered by an influence discernible on the spot. This was nothing less than the spell of a gentleman beside her, whom I had at first mentally disconnected from her on account of some visibility of difference. He was not, as it were, quite good enough to have come with her; and yet he was strikingly handsome, whereas she, on the contrary, would in all likelihood have been pronounced almost occultly so. That was what, doubtless, had led me to put a question about her; the fact of her having the kind of distinction that is quite independent of beauty. Her friend, on the other hand, whose clustering curls were fair, whose moustache and whose fixed monocular glass particularly, if indescribably, matched them, and whose expanse of white shirt and waistcoat had the air of carrying out and balancing the scheme of his large white forehead – her friend had the kind of beauty that is quite independent of distinction. That he was her friend – and very much – was clear from his easy imagination of all her curiosities. He began to show her the company, and to do much better in this line than my own companion did for me, inasmuch as he appeared even to know who we ourselves were. That gave a propriety to my finding, on the return from a dip into the lobby in the first *entr'acte*, that the lady beside me was at last prepared to identify him. I, for my part, knew too few people to have picked up anything. She mentioned a friend who had edged in to speak to her and who had named the gentleman opposite as Lord Yarracome.

Somehow I questioned the news. 'It sounds like the sort of thing that's too good to be true.'

'Too good?'

'I mean he's too much like it.'

'Like what? Like a lord?'

'Well, like the name, which is expressive, and – yes – even like the dignity. Isn't that just what lords are usually not?' I didn't, however, pause for a reply, but enquired further if his lordship's companion might be regarded as his wife.

'Dear, no. She's Miss Delavoy.'

I forget how my friend had gathered this – not from the informant who had just been with her; but on the spot I accepted it, and the younger lady became vividly interesting. 'The daughter of the great man?'

'What great man?'

'Why, the wonderful writer, the immense novelist: the one who died last year.' My friend gave me a look that led me to add: 'Did you never hear of him?' and, though she professed inadvertence, I could see her to be really so vague that – perhaps a trifle too sharply – I afterwards had the matter out with her. Her immediate refuge was in the question of Miss Delavoy's mourning. It was for *him*, then, her illustrious father; though that only deepened the oddity of her coming so soon to the theatre, and coming with a lord. My companion spoke as if the lord made it worse, and, after watching the pair a moment with her glass, observed that it was easy to see he could do anything he liked with his young lady. I permitted her, I confess, but little benefit from this diversion, insisting on giving it to her plainly that I didn't know what we were coming to and that there was in the air a gross indifference to which perhaps more almost than anything else the general density on the subject of Delavoy's genius testified. I even let her know, I am afraid, how scant, for a supposedly clever woman, I thought the grace of these *lacunae*; and I may as well immediately mention that, as I have had time to see, we were not again to be just the same allies as before my explosion. This was a brief, thin flare, but it expressed a feeling, and the feeling led me to concern myself for the rest of the evening, perhaps a trifle too markedly, with Lord Yarracome's victim. She was the image of a nearer approach, of a personal view: I mean in respect to my great artist, on whose consistent aloofness from the crowd I needn't touch, any more than on his patience in going his way and attending to his work, the most unadvertised, unreported, uninterviewed, unphotographed, uncriticised of all originals. Was he not the man of the time about whose private life we delightfully knew least? The young lady in the balcony, with the stamp of her close relation to him in her very dress, was a sudden opening into that region. I borrowed my companion's glass; I treated myself, in this direction – yes, I was momentarily gross – to an excursion of some minutes. I came back from it with the sense of something gained; I felt as if I had been studying Delavoy's own face, no portrait of which I had ever met. The result of it all, I easily recognised, would be to add greatly to my impatience for the finished book he had left behind, which had not yet seen the light, which was announced for a near date, and as to which rumour – I mean of course only in the particular warm air in which it lived at all – had already been sharp. I went out after the second act to make room for another visitor – they buzzed all over the place – and when I rejoined my friend she was primed with rectifications.

'He isn't Lord Yarracome at all. He's only Mr Beston.'

I fairly jumped; I see, as I now think, that it was as if I had read the future in a flash of lightning. 'Only –? The mighty editor?'

'Yes, of the celebrated *Cynosure*.' My interlocutress was determined this time not to be at fault. 'He's always at first nights.'

'What a chance for me, then,' I replied, 'to judge of my particular fate!'

'Does that depend on Mr Beston?' she enquired; on which I again borrowed her glass and went deeper into the subject.

'Well, my literary fortune does. I sent him a fortnight ago the best thing I've ever done. I've not as yet had a sign from him, but I can perhaps make out in his face, in the light of his type and expression, some little portent or promise.' I did my best, but when after a minute my companion asked what I discovered I was obliged to answer 'Nothing!' The next moment I added: 'He won't take it.'

'Oh, I hope so!'

'That's just what I've been doing.' I gave back the glass. 'Such a face is an abyss.'

'Don't you think it handsome?'

'Glorious. Gorgeous. Immense. Oh, I'm lost! What does Miss Delavoy think of it?' I then articulated.

'Can't you see?' My companion used her glass. 'She's under the charm – she has succumbed. How else can he have dragged her here in her state?' I wondered much, and indeed her state seemed happy enough, though somehow, at the same time, the pair struck me as not in the least matching. It was only for half a minute that my friend made them do so by going on: 'It's perfectly evident. She's not a daughter, I should have told you, by the way – she's only a sister. They've struck up an intimacy in the glow of his having engaged to publish from month to month the wonderful book that, as I understand you, her brother has left behind.'

That was plausible, but it didn't bear another look. 'Never!' I at last returned. 'Daughter or sister, that fellow won't touch him.'

'Why in the world –?'

'Well, for the same reason that, as you'll see, he won't touch *me*. It's wretched, but we're too good for him. 'My explanation did as well as another, though it had the drawback of leaving me to find another for Miss Delavoy's enslavement. I was not to find it that evening, for as poor Windon's play went on we had other problems to meet, and at the end our objects of interest were lost to sight in the general blinding blizzard. The affair was a bitter 'frost,' and if we were all in our places to the last everything else had disappeared. When I got home it was to be met by a note from Mr Beston accepting my article almost with enthusiasm, and it is a proof of the rapidity of my fond revulsion that before I went to sleep, which was not till ever so late, I had excitedly embraced the prospect of letting him have, on the occasion of Delavoy's new thing, my peculiar view of the great man. I must add that I was not a little

ashamed to feel I had made a fortune the very night Windon
had lost one.

II

Mr Beston really proved, in the event, most kind, though
his appeal, which promised to become frequent, was for
two or three quite different things before it came round to
my peculiar view of Delavoy. It in fact never addressed itself
at all to that altar and we met on the question only when,
the posthumous volume having come out, I had found
myself wound up enough to risk indiscretions. By this time
I had twice been with him and had had three or four of his
notes. They were the barest bones, but they phrased, in a
manner, a connection. This was not a triumph, however, to
bring me so near to him as to judge of the origin and nature
of his relations with Miss Delavoy. That his magazine
would, after all, publish no specimens was proved by the
final appearance of the new book at a single splendid bound.
The impression it made was of the deepest – it remains the
author's highest mark; but I heard, in spite of this, of no
emptying of table-drawers for Mr Beston's benefit. What
the book is we know still better today, and perhaps even
Mr Beston does; but there was no approach at the time to
a general rush, and I therefore of course saw that if he was
thick with the great man's literary legatee – as I, at least,
supposed her – it was on some basis independent of bringing
anything out. Nevertheless he quite rose to the idea of my
study, as I called it, which I put before him in a brief
interview.

'You ought to have something. That thing has brought
him to the front with a leap –!'

'The front? What do you call the front?'

He had laughed so good-humouredly that I could do the

same. 'Well, the front is where you and I are.' I told him my paper was already finished.

'Ah then, you must write it again.'

'Oh, but look at it first –!'

'You must write it again,' Mr Beston only repeated. Before I left him, however, he had explained a little. 'You must see his sister.'

'I shall be delighted to do that.'

'She's a great friend of mine, and my having something may please her – which, though my first, my only duty is to please my subscribers and shareholders, is a thing I should rather like to do. I'll take from you something of the kind you mention, but only if she's favourably impressed by it.'

I just hesitated, and it was not without a grain of hypocrisy that I artfully replied: 'I would much rather *you* were!'

'Well, I shall be if she is.' Mr Beston spoke with gravity. 'She can give you a good deal, don't you know? – all sorts of leads and glimpses. She naturally knows more about him than anyone. Besides, she's charming herself.'

To dip so deep could only be an enticement; yet I already felt so saturated, felt my cup so full, that I almost wondered what was left to me to learn, almost feared to lose, in greater waters, my feet and my courage. At the same time I welcomed without reserve the opportunity my patron offered, making as my one condition that if Miss Delavoy assented he would print my article as it stood. It was arranged that he should tell her that I would, with her leave, call upon her, and I begged him to let her know in advance that I was prostrate before her brother. He had all the air of thinking that he should have put us in a relation by which *The Cynosure* would largely profit, and I left him with the peaceful consciousness that if I had baited my biggest hook he had opened his widest mouth. I wondered a little, in truth, how he could care enough for Delavoy without caring more than enough, but I may at once say that I was, in

respect to Mr Beston, now virtually in possession of my
point of view. This had revealed to me an intellectual
economy of the rarest kind. There was not a thing in the
world – with a single exception, on which I shall presently
touch – that he valued for itself, and not a scrap he knew
about anything save whether or no it would do. To 'do'
with Mr Beston, was to do for *The Cynosure*. The wonder
was that he could know that of things of which he knew
nothing else whatever.

There are a hundred reasons, even in this most private
record, which, from a turn of mind so unlike Mr Beston's,
I keep exactly for a love of the fact in itself: there are a
hundred confused delicacies, operating however late, that
hold my hand from any motion to treat the question of the
effect produced on me by first meeting with Miss Delavoy.
I say there are a hundred, but it would better express my
sense perhaps to speak of them all in the singular. Certain
it is that one of them embraces and displaces the others. It
was not the first time, and I dare say it was not even the
second, that I grew sure of a shyness on the part of this
young lady greater than any exhibition in such a line that
my kindred constitution had ever allowed me to be clear
about. My own diffidence, I may say, kept me in the dark
so long that my perception of hers had to be retroactive –
to go back and put together and, with an element of relief,
interpret and fill out. It failed, inevitably, to operate in
respect to a person in whom the infirmity of which I speak
had none of the awkwardness, the tell-tale anguish, that
makes it as a rule either ridiculous or tragic. It was too deep,
too still, too general – it was perhaps even too proud. I must
content myself, however, with saying that I have in all my
life known nothing more beautiful than the faint, cool
morning-mist of confidence less and less embarrassed in
which it slowly evaporated. We have made the thing all out
since, and we understand it all now. It took her longer than

I measured to believe that a man without her particular knowledge could make such an approach to her particular love. The approach was made in my paper, which I left with her on my first visit and in which, on my second, she told me she had not an alteration to suggest. She said of it what I had occasionally, to an artist, heard said, or said myself, of a likeness happily caught: that to touch it again would spoil it, that it had 'come' and must only be left. It may be imagined that after such a speech I was willing to wait for anything; unless indeed it be suggested that there could be then nothing more to wait for. A great deal more, at any rate, seemed to arrive, and it was all in conversation about Delavoy that we ceased to be hindered and hushed. The place was still full of him, and in everything there that spoke to me I heard the sound of his voice. I read his style into everything – I read it into his sister. She was surrounded by his relics, his possessions, his books; all of which were not many, for he had worked without material reward: this only, however, made each more charged, somehow, and more personal. He had been her only devotion, and there were moments when she might have been taken for the guardian of a temple or a tomb. That was what brought me nearer than I had got even in my paper; the sense that it was he, in a manner, who had made her, and that to be with her was still to be with himself. It was not only that I could talk to him so; it was that he listened and that he also talked. Little by little and touch by touch she built him up to me; and then it was, I confess, that I felt, in comparison, the shrinkage of what I had written. It grew faint and small – though indeed only for myself; it had from the first, for the witness who counted so much more, a merit that I have ever since reckoned the great good fortune of my life, and even, I will go so far as to say, a fine case of inspiration. I hasten to add that this case had been preceded by a still finer. Miss Delavoy had made of her brother the year before his death a portrait in pencil that was precious for two rare reasons. It was the only representation of the sort in existence, and it was a work of curious distinction. Conventional but sincere, highly finished and smaller than life, it had a quality that, in any collection, would have caused it to be scanned for some signature known to the initiated. It was a thing of real vision, yet it was a thing of taste, and as soon as I learned that our hero, sole of his species, had succeeded in never, save on this occasion, sitting, least of all to a photographer, I took the full measure of what the studied strokes of a pious hand would some day represent for generations more aware of John Delavoy than, on the whole, his own had been. My feeling for them was not diminished, moreover, by learning from my young lady that Mr Beston, who had given them some attention, had signified that, in the event of his publishing an article, he would like a reproduction of the drawing to accompany it. The 'pictures' in *The Cynosure* were in general a marked chill to my sympathy: I had always held that, like good wine, honest prose needed, as it were, no bush.[2] I took them as a sign that if good wine, as we know, is more and more hard to meet, the other commodity was becoming as scarce. The bushes, at all events, in *The Cynosure*, quite planted out the text; but my objection fell in the presence of Miss Delavoy's sketch, which already, in the forefront of my study, I saw as a flower in the coat of a bridegroom.

I was obliged just after my visit to leave town for three weeks and was, in the country, surprised at their elapsing without bringing me a proof from Mr Beston. I finally wrote to ask of him an explanation of the delay; for which in turn I had again to wait so long that before I heard from him I received a letter from Miss Delavoy, who, thanking me as for a good office, let me know that our friend had asked her for the portrait. She appeared to suppose that I must have put in with him some word for it that availed more expertly than what had passed on the subject between themselves. This gave me occasion, on my return to town, to call on her for the purpose of explaining how little as yet, unfortunately, she owed me. I am not indeed sure that it didn't quicken my return. I knocked at her door with rather a vivid sense that if Mr Beston had her drawing I was yet still without my proof. My privation was the next moment to feel a sharper pinch, for on entering her apartment I found Mr Beston in possession. Then it was that I was fairly confronted with the problem given me from this time to solve. I began at that hour to look it straight in the face. What I in the first place saw was that Mr Beston was 'making up' to our hostess; what I saw in the second – what at any rate I believed I saw – was that she had come a certain distance to meet him; all of which would have been simple and usual enough had not the very things that gave it such a character been exactly the things I should least have expected. Even this first time, as my patron sat there, I made out somehow that in that position at least he was sincere and sound. Why should this have surprised me? Why should I immediately have asked myself how he would make it pay? He was there because he liked to be, and where was the wonder of his liking? There was no wonder in my own, I felt, so that my state of mind must have been already a sign of how little I supposed we could like the same things. This even strikes me, on looking back, as an implication sufficiently ungraceful of the absence on Miss Delavoy's part of direct and designed attraction. I dare say indeed that Mr Beston's subjection would have seemed to me a clearer thing if I had not had by the same stroke to account for his friend's. She liked him, and I grudged her that, though with the actual limits of my knowledge of both parties I had literally to invent reasons for its being a perversity. I could only in private treat it as one, and this in spite of Mr Beston's notorious power to please. He was the handsomest man in 'literary' London,

and, controlling the biggest circulation – a body of subscribers as vast as a conscript army – he represented in a
manner the modern poetry of numbers. He was in love
moreover, or he thought he was; that flushed with a general
glow the large surface he presented. This surface, from
my quiet corner, struck me as a huge tract, a sort of
particoloured map, a great spotted social chart. He
abounded in the names of things, and his mind was like a
great staircase at a party – you heard them bawled at the
top. He ought to have liked Miss Delavoy because *her* name,
so announced, sounded well, and I grudged him, as I grudged
the young lady, the higher motive of an intelligence of her
charm. It was a charm so fine and so veiled that if she had
been a piece of prose or of verse I was sure he would never
have discovered it. The oddity was that, as the case stood,
he had seen she would 'do.' I too had seen it, but then I was
a critic: these remarks will sadly have miscarried if they fail
to show the reader how much of one.

III

I mentioned my paper and my disappointment, but I think
it was only in the light of subsequent events that I could fix
an impression of his having, at the moment, looked a trifle
embarrassed. He smote his brow and took out his tablets;
he deplored the accident of which I complained, and promised to look straight into it. An accident it could only have
been, the result of a particular pressure, a congestion of
work. Of course he had had my letter and had fully supposed
it had been answered and acted on. My spirits revived at
this, and I almost thought the incident happy when I heard
Miss Delavoy herself put a clear question.

'It won't be for April, then, which was what I had hoped?'

It was what *I* had hoped, goodness knew, but if I had had
no anxiety I should not have caught the low, sweet ring of

her own. It made Mr Beston's eyes fix her a moment, and, though the thing has as I write it a fatuous air, I remember thinking that he must at this instant have seen in her face almost all his contributor saw. If he did he couldn't wholly have enjoyed it; yet he replied genially enough: 'I'll put it into June.'

'Oh, June!' our companion murmured in a manner that I took as plaintive – even as exquisite.

Mr Beston had got up. I had not promised myself to sit him out, much less to drive him away; and at this sign of his retirement I had a sense still dim, but much deeper, of being literally lifted by my check. Even before it was set up my article was somehow operative, so that I could look from one of my companions to the other and quite magnanimously smile. 'June will do very well.'

'Oh, if *you* say so –!' Miss Delavoy sighed and turned away.

'We must have time for the portrait; it will require great care,' Mr Beston said.

'Oh, please be sure it has the greatest!' I eagerly returned.

But Miss Delavoy took this up, speaking straight to Mr Beston. 'I attach no importance to the portrait. My impatience is all for the article.'

'The article's very neat. It's very neat,' Mr Beston repeated. 'But your drawing's our great prize.'

'Your great prize,' our young lady replied, 'can only be the thing that tells most about my brother.'

'Well, that's the case with your picture,' Mr Beston protested.

'How can you say that? My picture tells nothing in the world but that he never sat for another.'

'Which is precisely the enormous and final fact!' I laughingly exclaimed.

Mr Beston looked at me as if in uncertainty and just the least bit in disapproval; then he found his tone. 'It's the big fact for *The Cynosure*. I shall leave you in no doubt of *that*!' he added, to Miss Delavoy, as he went away.

I was surprised at his going, but I inferred that, from the pressure at the office, he had no choice; and I was at least not too much surprised to guess the meaning of his last remark to have been that our hostess must expect a handsome draft. This allusion had so odd a grace on a lover's lips that, even after the door had closed, it seemed still to hang there between Miss Delavoy and her second visitor. Naturally, however, we let it gradually drop; she only said with a kind of conscious quickness: 'I'm really very sorry for the delay.' I thought her beautiful as she spoke, and I felt that I had taken with her a longer step than the visible facts explained. 'Yes, it's a great bore. But to an editor – one doesn't show it.'

She seemed amused. 'Are they such queer fish?'

I considered. 'You know the great type.'

'Oh, I don't know Mr Beston as an editor.'

'As what, then?'

'Well, as what you call, I suppose, a man of the world. A very kind, clever one.'

'Of course *I* see him mainly in the saddle and in the charge – at the head of his hundreds of thousands. But I mustn't undermine him,' I added, smiling, 'when he's doing so much for me.'

She appeared to wonder about it. 'Is it really a great deal?'

'To publish a thing like that? Yes – as editors go. They're all tarred with the same brush.'

'Ah, but he has immense ideas. He goes in for the best in all departments. That's his own phrase. He has often assured me that he'll never stoop.'

'He wants none but "first-class stuff." That's the way he has expressed it to *me*; but it comes to the same thing. It's our great comfort. He's charming.'

'He's charming,' my friend replied; and I thought for the

moment we had done with Mr Beston. A rich reference to him, none the less, struck me as flashing from her very next words – words that she uttered without appearing to have noticed any I had pronounced in the interval. 'Does no one, then, really care for my brother?'

I was startled by the length of her flight. 'Really care?'

'No one but you? Every month your study doesn't appear is at this time a kind of slight.'

'I see what you mean. But of course *we're* serious.'

'Whom do you mean by "we"?'

'Well, you and me.'

She seemed to look us all over and not to be struck with our mass. 'And no one else? No one else is serious?'

'What I should say is that no one *feels* the whole thing, don't you know? as much.'

Miss Delavoy hesitated. 'Not even so much as Mr Beston?' And her eyes, as she named him, waited, to my surprise, for my answer.

I couldn't quite see why she returned to him, so that my answer was rather lame. 'Don't ask me too many things; else there are some *I* shall have to ask.'

She continued to look at me; after which she turned away. 'Then I won't – for I don't understand him.' She turned away, I say, but the next moment had faced about with a fresh, inconsequent question. 'Then why in the world has he cooled off?'

'About my paper? *Has* he cooled? Has he shown you that otherwise?' I asked.

'Than by his delay? Yes, by silence – and by worse.'

'What do you call worse?'

'Well, to say of it – and twice over – what he said just now.'

'That it's very "neat"? You don't think it *is*?' I laughed.

'I don't say it'; and with that she smiled. 'My brother might hear!'

Her tone was such that, while it lingered in the air, it deepened, prolonging the interval, whatever point there was in this; unspoken things therefore had passed between us by the time I at last brought out: 'He hasn't read me! It doesn't matter,' I quickly went on; 'his relation to what I may do or not do is, for his own purposes, quite complete enough without that.'

She seemed struck with this. 'Yes, his relation to almost anything is extraordinary.'

'His relation to everything!' It rose visibly before us and, as we felt, filled the room with its innumerable, indistinguishable objects. 'Oh, it's the making of him!'

She evidently recognised all this, but after a minute she again broke out: 'You say he hasn't read you and that it doesn't matter. But has he read my brother? Doesn't *that* matter?'

I waved away the thought. 'For what do you take him, and why in the world should it? He knows perfectly what he wants to do, and his postponement is quite in your interest. The reproduction of the drawing –'

She took me up. 'I hate the drawing!'

'So do I,' I laughed, 'and I rejoice in there being something on which we can feel so together!'

IV

What may further have passed between us on this occasion loses, as I try to recall it, all colour in the light of a communication that I had from her four days later. It consisted of a note in which she announced to me that she had heard from Mr Beston in terms that troubled her: a letter from Paris – he had dashed over on business – abruptly proposing that she herself should, as she quoted, give him something; something that her intimate knowledge of the subject – which was of course John Delavoy – her rare opportunities for observation and study would make precious, would make as unique as the work of her pencil. He appealed to her to gratify him in this particular, exhorted her to sit right down to her task, reminded her that to tell a loving sister's tale was her obvious, her highest duty. She confessed to mystification and invited me to explain. Was this sudden perception of her duty a result on Mr Beston's part of any difference with myself? Did he want two papers? Did he want an alternative to mine? Did he want hers as a supplement or as a substitute? She begged instantly to be informed if anything had happened to mine. To meet her request I had first to make sure and I repaired on the morrow to Mr Beston's office in the eager hope that he was back from Paris. This hope was crowned; he had crossed in the night and was in his room; so that on sending up my card I was introduced to his presence, where I promptly broke ground by letting him know that I had had even yet no proof.

'Oh, yes! about Delavoy. Well, I've rather expected you, but you must excuse me if I'm brief. My absence has put me back; I've returned to arrears. Then from Paris I meant to write to you, but even there I was up to my neck. I think, too, I've instinctively held off a little. You won't like what I have to say – you *can't*!' He spoke almost as if I might wish to prove I could. 'The fact is, you see, your thing won't do. No – not even a little.'

Even after Miss Delavoy's note it was a blow, and I felt myself turn pale. 'Not even a little? Why, I thought you wanted it so!'

Mr Beston just perceptibly braced himself. 'My dear man, we didn't want *that*! We couldn't do it. I've every desire to be agreeable to you, but we really couldn't.'

I sat staring. 'What in the world's the matter with it?'

'Well, it's impossible. That's what's the matter with it.'

'Impossible?' There rolled over me the ardent hours and a great wave of the feeling that I had put into it.

He hung back but an instant – he faced the music. 'It's indecent.'

I could only wildly echo him. 'Indecent? Why, it's absolutely, it's almost to the point of a regular chill, expository. What in the world is it but critical?'

Mr Beston's retort was prompt. 'Too critical by half! That's just where it is. It says too much.'

'But what it says is all about its subject.'

'I dare say, but I don't think we want quite so much about its subject.'

I seemed to swing in the void and I clutched, fallaciously, at the nearest thing. 'What you do want, then – what is *that* to be about?'

'That's for you to find out – it's not my business to tell you.'

It was dreadful, this snub to my happy sense that I *had* found out. 'I thought you wanted John Delavoy. I've simply stuck to him.'

Mr Beston gave a dry laugh. 'I should think you had!' Then after an instant he turned oracular. 'Perhaps we wanted him – perhaps we didn't. We didn't at any rate want indelicacy.'

'Indelicacy?' I almost shrieked. 'Why it's pure portraiture.'

'"Pure," my dear fellow, just begs the question. It's most objectionable – that's what it is. For portraiture of *such* things, at all events, there's no place in our scheme.'

I speculated. 'Your scheme for an account of Delavoy?'

Mr Beston looked as if I trifled. 'Our scheme for a successful magazine.'

'No place, do I understand you, for criticism? No place for the great figures –? If you don't want too much detail,' I went on, 'I recall perfectly that I was careful not to go into it. What I tried for was a general vivid picture – which I really supposed I arrived at. I boiled the man down – I gave the three or four leading notes. *Them* I did try to give with some intensity.'

Mr Beston, while I spoke, had turned about and, with a movement that confessed to impatience and even not a little, I thought, to irritation, fumbled on his table among a mass of papers and other objects; after which he had pulled out a couple of drawers. Finally he fronted me anew with my copy in his hand, and I had meanwhile added a word about the disadvantage at which he placed me. To have made me wait was unkind; but to have made me wait for such news – ! I ought at least to have been told it earlier. He replied to this that he had not at first had time to read me, and, on the evidence of my other things, had taken me pleasantly for granted: he had only been enlightened by the revelation of the proof. What he had fished out of his drawer was, in effect, not my manuscript, but the 'galleys'[3] that had never been sent me. The thing was all set up there, and my companion, with eyeglass and thumb, dashed back the sheets and looked up and down for places. The proof-reader, he mentioned, had so waked him up with the blue pencil[4] that he had no difficulty in finding them. They were all in his face when he again looked at me. 'Did you candidly think that we were going to print this?'

All my silly young pride in my performance quivered as if under the lash. 'Why the devil else should I have taken the trouble to write it? If you're not going to print it, why the devil did you ask me for it?'

'I didn't ask you. You proposed it yourself.'

'You jumped at it; you quite agreed you ought to have it: it comes to the same thing. So indeed you ought to have it. It's too ignoble, your not taking up such a man.'

He looked at me hard. 'I *have* taken him up. I do want

something about him, and I've got his portrait there – coming out beautifully.'

'Do you mean you've taken him up,' I enquired, 'by asking for something of his sister? Why, in that case, do you speak as if I had forced on you the question of a paper? If you want one you want one.'

Mr Beston continued to sound me. 'How do you know what I've asked of his sister?'

'I know what Miss Delavoy tells me. She let me know it as soon as she had heard from you.'

'Do you mean that you've just seen her?'

'I've not seen her since the time I met you at her house; but I had a note from her yesterday. She couldn't understand your appeal – in the face of knowing what I've done myself.'

Something seemed to tell me at this instant that she had not yet communicated with Mr Beston, but that he wished me not to know she hadn't. It came out still more in the temper with which he presently said: 'I want what Miss Delavoy can do, but I don't want this kind of thing!' And he shook my proof at me as if for a preliminary to hurling it.

I took it from him, to show I anticipated his violence, and, profoundly bewildered, I turned over the challenged pages. They grinned up at me with the proof-reader's shocks,[5] but the shocks, as my eye caught them, bloomed on the spot like flowers. I didn't feel abased – so many of my good things came back to me. 'What on earth do you seriously mean? This thing isn't bad. It's awfully good – it's beautiful.'

With an odd movement he plucked it back again, though not indeed as if from any new conviction. He had had after all a kind of contact with it that had made it a part of his stock. 'I dare say it's clever. For the kind of thing it is, it's as beautiful as you like. It's simply not *our* kind.' He seemed to break out afresh. 'Didn't you know more –?'

I waited. 'More what?'

He in turn did the same. 'More everything. More about Delavoy. The whole point was that I thought you did.'

I fell back in my chair. 'You think my article shows ignorance? I sat down to it with the sense that I knew more than anyone.'

Mr Beston restored it again to my hands. 'You've kept that pretty well out of sight then. Didn't you get anything out of *her*? It was simply for that I addressed you to her.'

I took from him with this, as well, a silent statement of what it had not been for. 'I got everything in the wide world I could. We almost worked together, but what appeared was that all her own knowledge, all her own view, quite fell in with what I had already said. There appeared nothing to subtract or to add.'

He looked hard again, not this time at me, but at the document in my hands. 'You mean she has gone into all that – seen it just as it stands there?'

'If I've still,' I replied, 'any surprise left, it's for the surprise your question implies. You put our heads together, and you've surely known all along that they've remained so. She told me a month ago that she had immediately let you know the good she thought of what I had done.'

Mr Beston very candidly remembered, and I could make out that if he flushed as he did so it was because what most came back to him was his own simplicity. 'I see. That must have been why I trusted you – sent you, without control, straight off to be set up. But now that I see you –!' he went on.

'You're surprised at her indulgence?'

Once more he snatched at the record of my rashness – once more he turned it over. Then he read out two or three paragraphs. 'Do you mean she has gone into all that?'

'My dear sir, what do you take her for? There wasn't a line we didn't thresh out, and our talk wouldn't for either of us have been a bit interesting if it hadn't been really frank. Have you to learn at this time of day,' I continued, 'what her feeling is about her brother's work? She's not a bit stupid. She has a kind of worship for it.'

Mr Beston kept his eyes on one of my pages. 'She passed her life with him and was extremely fond of him.'

'Yes, and she has the point of view and no end of ideas. She's tremendously intelligent.'

Our friend at last looked up at me, but I scarce knew what to make of his expression. 'Then she'll do me exactly what I want.'

'Another article, you mean, to replace mine?'

'Of a totally different sort. Something the public *will* stand.' His attention reverted to my proof, and he suddenly reached out for a pencil. He made a great dash against a block of my prose and placed the page before me. 'Do you pretend to me they'll stand *that*?'

'That' proved, as I looked at it, a summary of the subject, deeply interesting and treated, as I thought, with extraordinary art, of the work to which I gave the highest place in my author's array. I took it in, sounding it hard for some hidden vice, but with a frank relish, in effect, of its lucidity; then I answered: 'If they won't stand it, what will they stand?'

Mr Beston looked about and put a few objects on his table to rights. 'They won't stand anything.' He spoke with such pregnant brevity as to make his climax stronger. 'And quite right too! *I'm* right, at any rate; I can't plead ignorance. I know where I am, and I want to stay there. That single page would have cost me five thousand subscribers.'

'Why, that single page is a statement of the very essence –!'

He turned sharp around at me. 'Very essence of what?'

'Of my very topic, damn it.'

'Your very topic is John Delavoy.'

'And what's *his* very topic? Am I not to attempt to utter it? What under the sun else am I writing about?'

'You're not writing in *The Cynosure* about the relations of the sexes. With those relations, with the question of sex in any degree, I should suppose you would already have seen that we have nothing whatever to do. If you want to know what our public won't stand, there you have it.'

I seem to recall that I smiled sweetly as I took it. 'I don't know, I think, what you mean by those phrases, which strike me as too empty and too silly, and of a nature therefore to be more deplored than any, I'm positive, that I use in my analysis. I don't use a single one that even remotely resembles them. I simply try to express my author, and if your public won't stand his being expressed, mention to me kindly the source of its interest in him.'

Mr Beston was perfectly steady. 'He's all the rage with the clever people – that's the source. The interest of the public is whatever a clever article may make it.'

'I don't understand you. How can an article be clever, to begin with, and how can it make anything of anything, if it doesn't avail itself of material?'

'There *is* material, which I'd hoped you'd use. Miss Delavoy has lots of material. I don't know what she has told you, but I know what she has told *me*.' He hung fire but an instant. 'Quite lovely things.'

'And have you told *her* –?'

'Told her what?' he asked as I paused.

'The lovely things you've just told me.'

Mr Beston got up; folding the rest of my proof together, he made the final surrender with more dignity than I had looked for. 'You can do with this what you like.' Then as he reached the door with me: 'Do you suppose that I talk with Miss Delavoy on such subjects?' I answered that he could leave that to me – I shouldn't mind so doing; and I recall that before I quitted him something again passed between us on the question of her drawing. 'What we want,' he said, 'is just the really nice thing, the pleasant, right thing to go with it. That drawing's going to take!'

V

A few minutes later I had wired to our young lady that, should I hear nothing from her to the contrary, I would come to her that evening. I had other affairs that kept me out, and on going home I found a word to the effect that though she should not be free after dinner she hoped for my presence at five o'clock: a notification betraying to me that the evening would, by arrangement, be Mr Beston's hour and that she wished to see me first. At five o'clock I was there, and as soon as I entered the room I perceived two things. One of these was that she had been highly impatient, the other was that she had not heard, since my call on him, from Mr Beston, and that her arrangement with him therefore dated from earlier. The tea-service was by the fire – she herself was at the window; and I am at a loss to name the particular revelation that I drew from this fact of her being restless on general grounds. My telegram had fallen in with complications at which I could only guess; it had not found her quiet; she was living in a troubled air. But her wonder leaped from her lips. 'He does want two?'

I had brought in my proof with me, putting it in my hat and my hat on a chair. 'Oh, no – he wants only one, only yours.'

Her wonder deepened. 'He won't print –?'

'My poor old stuff! He returns it with thanks.'

'Returns it? When he had accepted it!'

'Oh, that doesn't prevent – when he doesn't like it.'

'But he does; he did. He liked it to *me*. He called it "sympathetic."'

'He only meant that *you* are – perhaps even that I myself

am. He hadn't read it then. He read it but a day or two ago, and horror seized him.'

Miss Delavoy dropped into a chair. 'Horror?'

'I don't know how to express to you the fault he finds with it.' I had gone to the fire, and I looked to where it peeped out of my hat; my companion did the same, and her face showed the pain she might have felt, in the street, at sight of the victim of an accident. 'It appears it's indecent.'

She sprang from her chair. 'To describe my brother?'

'As I've described him. That, at any rate, is how my account sins. What I've said is unprintable.' I leaned against the chimney-piece with a serenity of which, I admit, I was conscious; I rubbed it in and felt a private joy in watching my influence.

'Then what *have* you said?'

'You know perfectly. You heard my thing from beginning to end. You said it was beautiful.'

She remembered as I looked at her; she showed all the things she called back. 'It *was* beautiful.' I went over and picked it up; I came back with it to the fire. 'It was the best thing ever said about him,' she went on. 'It was the finest and truest.'

'Well, then –!' I exclaimed.

'But what have you done to it since?'

'I haven't touched it since.'

'You've put nothing else in?'

'Not a line – not a syllable. Don't you remember how you warned me against spoiling it? It's of the thing we read together, liked together, went over and over together; it's of this dear little serious thing of good sense and good faith' – and I held up my roll of proof, shaking it even as Mr Beston had shaken it – 'that he expresses that opinion.'

She frowned at me with an intensity that, though bringing me no pain, gave me a sense of her own. 'Then that's why he has asked *me* –?'

'To do something instead. But something pure. You, he hopes, won't be indecent.'

She sprang up, more mystified than enlightened; she had pieced things together, but they left the question gaping. 'Is he mad? What is he talking about?'

'Oh, *I* know – now. Has he specified what he wants of you?'

She thought a moment, all before me. 'Yes – to be very "personal."'

'Precisely. You mustn't speak of the work.'

She almost glared. 'Not speak of it?'

'That's indecent.'

'My brother's work?'

'To speak of it.'

She took this from me as she had not taken anything. 'Then how can I speak of him at all? – how can I articulate? He *was* his work.'

'Certainly he was. But that's not the kind of truth that will stand in Mr Beston's way. Don't you know what he means by wanting you to be personal?'

In the way she looked at me there was still for a moment a dim desire to spare him – even perhaps a little to save him. None the less, after an instant, she let herself go. 'Something horrible?'

'Horrible; so long, that is, as it takes the place of something more honest and really so much more clean. He wants – what do they call the stuff? anecdotes, glimpses, gossip, chat; a picture of his "home life," domestic habits, diet, dress, arrangements – all his little ways and little secrets, and even, to better it still, all your own, your relations with him, your feelings about him, his feelings about *you*: both his and yours, in short, about anything else you can think of. Don't you see what I mean?' She saw so well that, in the dismay of it, she grasped my arm an instant, half as if to steady herself, half as if to stop me. But she couldn't stop me. 'He wants you just to write round and round that portrait.'

She was lost in the reflections I had stirred, in apprehensions and indignations that slowly surged and spread, and for a moment she was unconscious of everything else. 'What portrait?'

'Why, the beautiful one you did. The beautiful one you gave him.'

'Did I give it to him? Oh, yes!' It came back to her, but this time she blushed red, and I saw what had occurred to her. It occurred, in fact, at the same instant to myself. 'Ah, *par exemple*,'⁶ she cried, 'he shan't have it!'

I couldn't help laughing. 'My dear young lady, unfortunately he *has* got it!'

'He shall send it back. He shan't use it.'

'I'm afraid he *is* using it,' I replied. 'I'm afraid he *has* used it. They've begun to work on it.'

She looked at me almost as if I were Mr Beston. 'Then they must stop working on it.' Something in her decision somehow thrilled me. 'Mr Beston must send it straight back. Indeed I'll wire to him to bring it tonight.'

'Is he coming tonight?' I ventured to enquire.

She held her head very high. 'Yes, he's coming tonight. It's most happy!' she bravely added, as if to forestall any suggestion that it could be anything else.

I thought for a moment; first about that, then about something that presently made me say: 'Oh, well, if he brings it back –!'

She continued to look at me. 'Do you mean you doubt his doing so?'

I thought again. 'You'll probably have a stiff time with him.'

She made, for a little, no answer to this but to sound me

again with her eyes; our silence, however, was carried off
by her then abruptly turning to her tea-tray and pouring me
out a cup. 'Will you do me a favour?' she asked as I took it.

'Any favour in life.'

'Will you be present?'

'Present?' – I failed at first to imagine.

'When Mr Beston comes.'

It was so much more than I had expected that I of course
looked stupid in my surprise. 'This evening – here?'

'This evening – here. Do you think my request very
strange?'

I pulled myself together. 'How can I tell when I'm so
awfully in the dark?'

'In the dark –?' She smiled at me as if I were a person who
carried such lights!

'About the nature, I mean, of your friendship.'

'With Mr Beston?' she broke in. Then in the wonderful
way that women say such things: 'It has always been so
pleasant.'

'Do you think it will be pleasant for *me*?' I laughed.

'Our friendship? I don't care whether it is or not!'

'I mean what you'll have out with him – for of course you
will have it out. Do you think it will be pleasant for *him*?'

'To find you here – or to see you come in? I don't feel
obliged to think. This is a matter in which I now care for
no one but my brother – for nothing but his honour. I stand
only on that.'

I can't say how high, with these words, she struck me as
standing, nor how the look that she gave me with them
seemed to make me spring up beside her. We were at this
elevation together a moment. 'I'll do anything in the world
you say.'

'Then please come about nine.'

That struck me as so tantamount to saying 'And please
therefore go this minute' that I immediately turned to the

door. Before I passed it, however, I gave her time to ring out clear: 'I know what I'm about!' She proved it the next moment by following me into the hall with the request that I would leave her my proof. I placed it in her hands, and if she knew what she was about I wondered, outside, what *I* was.

VI

I dare say it was the desire to make this out that, in the evening, brought me back a little before my time. Mr Beston had not arrived, and it's worth mentioning – for it was rather odd – that while we waited for him I sat with my hostess in silence. She spoke of my paper, which she had read over – but simply to tell me she had done so; and that was practically all that passed between us for a time at once so full and so quiet that it struck me neither as short nor as long. We felt, in the matter, so indivisible that we might have been united in some observance or some sanctity – to go through something decorously appointed. Without an observation we listened to the door-bell, and, still without one, a minute later, saw the person we expected stand there and show his surprise. It was at me he looked as he spoke to her.

'I'm not to see you alone?'

'Not just yet, please,' Miss Delavoy answered. 'Of what has suddenly come between us this gentleman is essentially a part, and I really think he'll be less present if we speak before him than if we attempt to deal with the question without him.' Mr Beston was amused, but not enough amused to sit down, and we stood there while, for the third time, my proof sheets were shaken for emphasis. 'I've been reading these over,' she said as she held them up.

Mr Beston, on what he had said to me of them, could only look grave; but he tried also to look pleasant, and I foresaw that, on the whole, he would really behave well. 'They're remarkably clever.'

'And yet you wish to publish instead of them something from so different a hand?'

He smiled now very kindly. 'If you'll only let me have it! *Won't* you let me have it? I'm sure you know exactly the thing I want.'

'Oh, perfectly!'

'I've tried to give her an idea of it,' I threw in.

Mr Beston promptly saw his way to make this a reproach to me. 'Then, after all, you had one yourself?'

'I think I couldn't have kept so clear of it if I hadn't had!' I laughed.

'I'll write you something,' Miss Delavoy went on, 'if you'll print this as it stands.' My proof was still in her keeping.

Mr Beston raised his eyebrows. 'Print two? Whatever do I want with two? What do I want with the wrong one if I can get the beautiful right?'

She met this, to my surprise, with a certain gaiety. 'It's a big subject – a subject to be seen from different sides. Don't you want a full, a various treatment? Our papers will have nothing in common.'

'I should hope not!' Mr Beston said good-humouredly. 'You have command, dear lady, of a point of view too good to spoil. It so happens that your brother has been really less handled than any one, so that there's a kind of obscurity about him, and in consequence a kind of curiosity, that it seems to me quite a crime not to work. There's just the perfection, don't you know? of a little sort of mystery – a tantalising *demi-jour*.'[7] He continued to smile at her as if he thoroughly hoped to kindle her, and it was interesting at that moment to get this vivid glimpse of his conception.

I could see it quickly enough break out in Miss Delavoy, who sounded for an instant almost assenting. 'And you want the obscurity and the mystery, the tantalising *demi-jour*, cleared up?'

'I want a little lovely, living thing! Don't be perverse,' he pursued, 'don't stand in your own light and in your brother's and in this young man's – in the long run, and in mine too and in every one's: just let us have him out as no one but you can bring him and as, by the most charming of chances and a particular providence, he has been kept all this time just on purpose for you to bring. Really, you know' – his vexation *would* crop up – 'one could howl to see such good stuff wasted!'

'Well,' our young lady returned, 'that holds good of one thing as well as of another. I can never hope to describe or express my brother as these pages describe and express him; but, as I tell you, approaching him from a different direction, I promise to do my very best. Only, my condition remains.'

Mr Beston transferred his eyes from her face to the little bundle in her hand, where they rested with an intensity that made me privately wonder if it represented some vain vision of a snatch defeated in advance by the stupidity of his having suffered my copy to be multiplied. 'My printing that?'

'Your printing this.'

Mr Beston wavered there between us: I could make out in him a vexed inability to keep us as distinct as he would have liked. But he was triumphantly light. 'It's impossible. Don't be a pair of fools!'

'Very well, then,' said Miss Delavoy; 'please send me back my drawing.'

'Oh dear, no!' Mr Beston laughed. 'Your drawing we must have at any rate.'

'Ah, but I forbid you to use it! This gentleman is my witness that my prohibition is absolute.'

'Was it to be your witness that you sent for the gentleman? You take immense precautions!' Mr Beston exclaimed. Before she could retort, however, he came back to his strong point. 'Do you coolly ask of me to sacrifice ten thousand subscribers?'

The number, I noticed, had grown since the morning, but Miss Delavoy faced it boldly. 'If you do, you'll be well rid of them. They must be ignoble, your ten thousand subscribers.'

He took this perfectly. 'You dispose of them easily! Ignoble or not, what I have to do is to keep them and if possible add to their number; not to get rid of them.'

'You'd rather get rid of my poor brother instead?'

'I don't get rid of him. I pay him a signal attention. Reducing it to the least, I publish his portrait.'

'His portrait – the only one worth speaking of? Why, you turn it out with horror.'

'Do you call the only one worth speaking of that misguided effort?' And, obeying a restless impulse, he appeared to reach for my tribute; not I think, with any conscious plan, but with a vague desire in some way again to point his moral with it.

I liked immensely the motion with which, in reply to this, she put it behind her: her gesture expressed so distinctly her vision of her own lesson. From that moment, somehow, they struck me as forgetting me, and I seemed to see them as they might have been alone together; even to see a little what, for each, had held and what had divided them. I remember how, at this, I almost held my breath, effacing myself to let them go, make them show me whatever they might. 'It's the only one,' she insisted, 'that tells, about its subject, anything that's anyone's business. If you really want John Delavoy, there he is. If you don't want him, don't insult him with an evasion and a pretence. Have at least the courage to say that you're afraid of him!'

I figured Mr Beston here as much incommoded; but all too simply, doubtless, for he clearly held on, smiling through flushed discomfort and on the whole bearing up. 'Do you think I'm afraid of *you*?' He might forget me, but he would have to forget me a little more to yield completely to his visible impulse to take her hand. It was visible enough to herself to make her show that she declined to meet it, and even that his effect on her was at last distinctly exasperating. Oh, how I saw at that moment that in the really touching good faith of his personal sympathy he didn't measure his effect! If he had done so he wouldn't have tried to rush it, to carry it off with tenderness. He dropped to that now so rashly that I was in truth sorry for him. 'You *could* do so gracefully, so naturally what we want. What we want, don't you see? is perfect taste. I know better than you do yourself how perfect yours would be. I always know better than people do themselves.' He jested and pleaded, getting in, benightedly, deeper. Perhaps I didn't literally hear him ask in the same accents if she didn't care for him at all, but I distinctly saw him look as if he were on the point of it, and something, at any rate, in a lower tone, dropped from him that he followed up with the statement that if she did even just a little she would help him.

VII

She made him wait a deep minute for her answer to this, and that gave me time to read into it what he accused her of failing to do. I recollect that I was startled at their having come so far, though I was reassured, after a little, by seeing that he had come much the furthest. I had now I scarce know what amused sense of knowing our hostess so much better than he. 'I think you strangely inconsequent,' she said at last. 'If you associate with – what you speak of – the idea of help, does it strike you as helping *me* to treat in that base fashion the memory I most honour and cherish?' As I was quite sure of what he spoke of I could measure the force of this challenge. 'Have you never discovered, all this time, that my brother's work is my pride and my joy?'

'Oh, my dear thing!' – and Mr Beston broke into a cry that combined in the drollest way the attempt to lighten his guilt with the attempt to deprecate hers. He let it just flash upon us that, should he be pushed, he would show as – well, scandalised.

The tone in which Miss Delavoy again addressed him offered a reflection of this gleam. 'Do you know what my brother would think of you?'

He was quite ready with his answer, and there was no moment in the whole business at which I thought so well of him. 'I don't care a hang what your brother would think!'

'Then why do you wish to commemorate him?'

'How can you ask so innocent a question? It isn't for *him*.'

'You mean it's for the public?'

'It's for the magazine,' he said with a noble simplicity.

'The magazine *is* the public,' it made me so far forget myself as to suggest.

'You've discovered it late in the day! Yes,' he went on to our companion, 'I don't in the least mind saying I don't care. I don't – I don't!' he repeated with a sturdiness in which I somehow recognised that he was, after all, a great editor. He looked at me a moment as if he even guessed what I saw, and, not unkindly, desired to force it home. 'I don't care for anybody. It's not my business to care. That's not the way to run a magazine. Except of course as a mere man!' – and he added a smile for Miss Delavoy. He covered the whole ground again. 'Your reminiscences would make a talk!'

She came back from the greatest distance she had yet reached. 'My reminiscences?'

'To accompany the head.'[8] He must have been as tender as if I had been away. 'Don't I see how you'd do them?'

She turned off, standing before the fire and looking into it; after which she faced him again. 'If you'll publish our friend here, I'll do them.'

'Why are you so awfully wound up about our friend here?'

'Read his article over – with a little intelligence – and your question will be answered.'

Mr Beston glanced at me and smiled as if with a loyal warning; then, with a good conscience, he let me have it. 'Oh, damn his article!'

I was struck with her replying exactly what I should have replied if I had not been so detached. 'Damn it as much as you like, but publish it.' Mr Beston, on this, turned to me as if to ask me if I had not heard enough to satisfy me: there was a visible offer in his face to give me more if I insisted. This amounted to an appeal to me to leave the room at least for a minute; and it was perhaps from the fear of what might pass between us that Miss Delavoy once more took him up. 'If my brother's as vile as you say –!'

'Oh, I don't say *he's* vile!' he broke in.

'You only say *I* am!' I commented.

'You've entered so into him,' she replied to me, 'that it comes to the same thing. And Mr Beston says further that out of this unmentionableness he wants somehow to make something – some money or some sensation.'

'My dear lady,' said Mr Beston, 'it's a very great literary figure!'

'Precisely. You advertise yourself with it because it's a very great literary figure, and it's a very great literary figure because it wrote very great literary things that you wouldn't for the world allow to be intelligibly or critically named. So you bid for the still more striking tribute of an intimate picture – an unveiling of God knows what! – without even having the pluck or the logic to say on what ground it is that you go in for naming him at all. Do you know, dear

Mr Beston,' she asked, 'that you make me very sick? I count on receiving the portrait,' she concluded, 'by tomorrow evening at latest.'

I felt, before this speech was over, so sorry for her interlocutor that I was on the point of asking her if she mightn't finish him without my help. But I had lighted a flame that was to consume me too, and I was aware of the scorch of it while I watched Mr Beston plead frankly, if tacitly, that, though there was something in him not to be finished, she must yet give him a moment and let him take his time to look about him at pictures and books. He took it with more coolness than I; then he produced his answer. 'You shall receive it tomorrow morning if you'll do what I asked the last time.' I could see more than he how the last time had been overlaid by what had since come up; so that, as she opposed a momentary blank, I felt almost a coarseness in his recall of it with an 'Oh, you know – you know!'

Yes, after a little she knew, and I need scarcely add that I did. I felt, in the oddest way, by this time, that she was conscious of my penetration and wished to make me, for the loss now so clearly beyond repair, the only compensation in her power. This compensation consisted of her showing me that she was indifferent to my having guessed the full extent of the privilege that, on the occasion to which he alluded, she had permitted Mr Beston to put before her. The balm for my wound was therefore to see what she resisted. She resisted Mr Beston in more ways than one. 'And if I don't do it?' she demanded.

'I'll simply keep your picture!'

'To what purpose if you don't use it?'

'To keep it *is* to use it,' Mr Beston said.

'He has only to keep it long enough,' I added, and with the intention that may be imagined, 'to bring you round, by the mere sense of privation, to meet him on the other ground.'

Miss Delavoy took no more notice of this speech than if she had not heard it, and Mr Beston showed that he had heard it only enough to show, more markedly, that he followed her example. 'I'll do anything, I'll do everything for you in life,' he declared to her, 'but publish such a thing as that.'

She gave in all decorum to this statement the minute of concentration that belonged to it; but her analysis of the matter had for sole effect to make her at last bring out, not with harshness, but with a kind of wondering pity: 'I think you're really very dreadful!'

'In what esteem then, Mr Beston,' I asked, 'do you hold John Delavoy's work?'

He rang out clear. 'As the sort of thing that's out of our purview!' If for a second he had hesitated it was partly, I judge, with just resentment at my so directly addressing him, and partly, though he wished to show our friend that he fairly faced the question, because experience had not left him in such a case without two or three alternatives. He had already made plain indeed that he mostly preferred the simplest.

'Wonderful, wonderful purview!' I quite sincerely, or at all events very musingly, exclaimed.

'Then, if you could ever have got one of his novels –?' Miss Delavoy enquired.

He smiled at the way she put it; it made such an image of the attitude of *The Cynosure*. But he was kind and explicit. 'There isn't one that wouldn't have been beyond us. We could never have run him. We could never have handled him. We could never, in fact, have touched him. We should have dropped to – oh, Lord!' He saw the ghastly figure he couldn't name – he brushed it away with a shudder.

I turned, on this, to our companion. 'I wish awfully you'd do what he asks!' She stared an instant, mystified; then I quickly explained to which of his requests I referred. 'I mean

I wish you'd do the nice familiar chat about the sweet home-life. You might make it inimitable, and, upon my word, I'd give you for it the assistance of my general lights. The thing is – don't you see? – that it would put Mr Beston in a grand position. Your position would be grand,' I hastened to add as I looked at him, 'because it would be so admirably false.' Then, more seriously, I felt the impulse even to warn him. 'I don't think you're quite aware of what you'd make it. Are you really quite conscious?' I went on with a benevolence that struck him, I was presently to learn, as a depth of fatuity.

He was to show once more that he was a rock. 'Conscious? Why should I be? Nobody's conscious.'

He was splendid; yet before I could control it I had risked the challenge of a 'Nobody?'

'Who's anybody? The public isn't!'

'Then why are you afraid of it?' Miss Delavoy demanded.

'Don't ask him that,' I answered; 'you expose yourself to his telling you that, if the public isn't anybody, that's still more the case with your brother.'

Mr Beston appeared to accept as a convenience this somewhat inadequate protection; he at any rate under cover of it again addressed us lucidly. 'There's only one false position – the one you seem so to wish to put me in.'

I instantly met him. 'That of losing –?'

'That of losing –?'

'Oh, fifty thousand – yes. And they wouldn't see anything the matter –?'

'With the position,' said Mr Beston, 'that you qualify, I neither know nor care why, as false.' Suddenly, in a different tone, almost genially, he continued; 'For what do you take them?'

For what indeed? – but it didn't signify. 'It's enough that I take *you* – for one of the masters.' It's literal that as he stood there in his florid beauty and complete command I felt his infinite force, and, with a gush of admiration, wondered how, for our young lady, there could be at such a moment another man. 'We represent different sides,' I rather lamely said. However, I picked up. 'It isn't a question of where we are, but of what. You're not on a side – you *are* a side. You're the right one. What a misery,' I pursued, 'for us not to be "on" you!'

His eyes showed me for a second that he yet saw how our not being on him did just have for it that it could facilitate such a speech; then they rested afresh on Miss Delavoy, and that brought him back to firm ground. 'I don't think you can imagine how it will come out.'

He was astride of the portrait again, and presently again she had focussed him. 'If it does come out –!' she began, poor girl; but it was not to take her far.

'Well, if it does –?'

'He means what will you do then?' I observed, as she had nothing to say.

'Mr Beston will see,' she at last replied with a perceptible lack of point.

He took this up in a flash. 'My dear young lady, it's *you* who'll see; and when you've seen you'll forgive me. Only wait till you do!' He was already at the door, as if he quite believed in what he should gain by the gain, from this moment, of time. He stood there but an instant – he looked from one of us to the other. 'It will be a ripping little thing!' he remarked; and with that he left us gaping.

VIII

The first use I made of our rebound was to say with intensity: 'What *will* you do if he does?'

'Does publish the picture?' There was an instant charm to me in the privacy of her full collapse and the sudden high tide of our common defeat. 'What *can* I? It's all very well;

but there's nothing to be done. I want never to see him again. There's only something,' she went on, 'that *you* can do.'

'Prevent him? – get it back? I'll do, be sure, my utmost; but it will be difficult without a row.'

'What do you mean by a row?' she asked.

'I mean it will be difficult without publicity. I don't think we want publicity.'

She turned this over. 'Because it will advertise him?'

'His magnificent energy. Remember what I just now told him. He's the right side.'

'And we're the wrong!' she laughed. 'We mustn't make that known – I see. But, all the same, save my sketch!'

I held her hands. 'And if I do?'

'Ah, get it back first!' she answered, ever so gently and with a smile, but quite taking them away.

I got it back, alas! neither first nor last; though indeed at the end this was to matter, as I thought and as I found, little enough. Mr Beston rose to his full height and was not to abate an inch even on my offer of another article on a subject notoriously unobjectionable. The only portrait of John Delavoy was going, as he had said, to take, and nothing was to stand in its way. I besieged his office, I waylaid his myrmidons, I haunted his path, I poisoned, I tried to flatter myself, his life; I wrote him at any rate letters by the dozen and showed him up to his friends and his enemies. The only thing I didn't do was to urge Miss Delavoy to write to her solicitors or to the newspapers. The final result, of course, of what I did and what I didn't was to create, on the subject of the sole copy of so rare an original, a curiosity that, by the time *The Cynosure* appeared with the reproduction, made the month's sale, as I was destined to learn, take a tremendous jump. The portrait of John Delavoy, prodigiously 'paragraphed' in advance and with its authorship flushing through,' was accompanied by a page or two, from an anonymous hand, of the pleasantest, liveliest comment. The press was genial, the success immense, current criticism had never flowed so full, and it was universally felt that the handsome thing had been done. The process employed by Mr Beston had left, as he had promised, nothing to be desired; and the sketch itself, the next week, arrived in safety, and with only a smutch or two, by the post. I placed my article, naturally, in another magazine, but was disappointed, I confess, as to what it discoverably did in literary circles for its subject. This ache, however, was muffled. There was a worse victim than I, and there was consolation of a sort in our having out together the question of literary circles. The great orb of *The Cynosure*, wasn't that a literary circle? By the time we had fairly to face this question we had achieved the union that – at least for resistance or endurance – is supposed to be strength.

NOTES

✤

NOTES

PREFACES TO THE NEW YORK EDITION

1 (p. 33): *recueil*. Collection, magazine.

2 (p. 36): *nouvelle*. Novella, short novel.

3 (p. 36): *Turgenieff's ... Balzac's ... Maupassant's ... Bourget's ... Kipling's*. Ivan Turgenev (1818–83), a Russian novelist greatly admired by James; Honoré de Balzac (1799–1850), the French novelist; Guy de Maupassant (1850–93), the French novelist and short-story writer; Paul Bourget (1852–1935), the French critic, poet and novelist; and Rudyard Kipling (1865–1936), poet and story-writer.

4 (p. 43): *malheureux*. The unhappy man.

5 (p. 44): *analytic projector*. i.e., the critic who forms the project of analysing him.

6 (p. 53): *Robert Browning*. The poet (1812–89) was an acquaintance of James's.

THE AUTHOR OF BELTRAFFIO

1 (p. 57): *sleeves ... sideboards*. Aestheticisim was a fashion affecting more than the fine arts. Its patrons were John Ruskin (1819–1900) and the Pre-Raphaelites, notably D. G. Rossetti (1828–82); Walter Pater (1839–94) was a potent example, and so of course was Oscar Wilde (1854–1900). Aestheticism implied an attitude of reverence for medieval and Renaissance art, a desire to unify the arts, and to endow ordinary objects with aesthetic value. The Arts and Crafts movement, which was to put these ideas to practical use, was led by William Morris (1834–96), whose decorating firm included among its partners Rossetti and Edward Burne-Jones (1833–98). Morris's influence on all kinds of decoration in furniture, hangings, wallpaper and clothes was great. The same Romantic ideas that lay behind these attitudes and activities encouraged also a certain style in the life of artists and aesthetes; John Addington Symonds (1840–93) might be taken as typical. His *Renaissance in Italy* (1875–6) was in its time a work of high importance, and his taste (though not his homosexuality) is reflected in the narrator's praise of Mark Ambient's. The fashion received a check with the trial of Oscar Wilde in 1895, but it developed into what we think

of as art nouveau, partly under the influence of Aubrey Beardsley (1872–98).

2   (p. 59): *London 'season'*. This lasted from May to July, when the fashionable congregated in London.

3   (p. 59): *cet âge est sans pitié*. This age (youth) is pitiless.

4   (p. 59): *a soft wide-awake*. A broad-brimmed hat.

5   (p. 60): *a brush of the Bohemian*. A touch of the artist.

6   (p. 61): *Quentin Durward*. A novel (1823) by Sir Walter Scott (1771–1832).

7   (p. 61): *pre-Raphaelites*. The Pre-Raphaelite Brethren, founded in 1848, included D. G. Rossetti, W. M. Rossetti (1829–1919), William Holman Hunt (1827–1910), John Millais (1829–96), Ford Madox Brown (1821–93), Edward Burne-Jones, and others. They were attacked in the press for their alleged sensuality, and defended by Ruskin.

8   (p. 61): *villa*. i.e., the Italian connotation was rather grand, the English rather suburban.

9   (p. 61): *palace of art*. An allusion to the title of Tennyson's poem (first published in 1832), which had an anti-aesthetic tone.

10   (p. 61): *genius loci*. The spirit of the place.

11   (p. 63): *Gainsborough and Romney*. Thomas Gainsborough (1727–88), the celebrated landscape and portrait painter, and his contemporary George Romney (1734–1802), the portraitist.

12   (p. 64): *Dolcino ... delightful*. The name stems from the Italian diminutive of *dolce*: 'sweet little boy'.

13   (p. 67): *suffisance*. Conceit.

14   (p. 73): *Dürer's Melancholia*. Properly 'Melencolia I', a famous engraving by Albrecht Dürer (1471–1528).

15   (p. 73): *Michael-Angelesque attitudes*. i.e., deriving from the art of Michelangelo Buonarroti (1475–1564).

16   (p. 74): *she made up ... Rossetti*. i.e., after the manner of women portrayed in the paintings of Dante Gabriel Rossetti (1828–82).

17   (p. 75): *Reynolds ... Lawrence*. Sir Joshua Reynolds (1723–92), portrait painter and first president of the Royal Academy, and Sir Thomas Lawrence (1769–1830), a distinguished successor.

18   (p. 76): *'die-away'*. Languishing.

19   (p. 78): *cinquecento*. The sixteenth century.

20   (p. 82): *prémices*. First-fruits.

21   (p. 84): *à cheval*. A stickler for.

22   (p. 84): *riguardi*. Regards, respects.

23   (p. 88): *bonnes gens*. Good people (i.e., philistine opponents).

24   (p. 93): *parterre*. A level space in a garden with ornamental flowerbeds.

25   (p. 98): *Sir Joshua*. Sir Joshua Reynolds.

26   (p. 102): *old morocco*. i.e., books bound in morocco leather.

27   (p. 103): *Elle ne s'en doute que trop!* She suspects it only too strongly.

28   (p. 108): *caro fratello mio*. My dear brother.

29   (p. 111): *Basta, basta*. Enough.

THE LESSON OF THE MASTER

1   (p. 122): *Il s'attache à ses pas*. He sticks closely to her.

2   (pp. 123–4): *his personal 'type' ... head*. In this and other tales, James makes frequent and usually jocular allusions to phrenology and the fashionable notion of types, which spread from evolutionary theory into many other spheres. The word acquired a slangy quality, as in French, where *types* came to mean nothing more than 'chaps', and it is in something like that sense that Miss Fancourt and St George later go to the park to 'look at types'.

3   (p. 130): *car*. Triumphal chariot.

4   (p. 132): *à fleur de peau*. Superficially.

5   (p. 136): *mot*. Witticism (i.e., 'St George and the Dragon').

6   (p. 137): *Italian 'subject'*. A 'genre' painting, intended to evoke admiration or talk.

7   (p. 139): *the very rustle of the laurel*. The laurel was used to crown poets, so, by extension, artists. Here this conversation is fancifully compared to the rustling of such a laurel.

8   (p. 144): *Cela s'est passé comme ça?* So that's how it happened?

9   (p. 146): *jamais de la vie!* Not a bit of it!

10   (p. 147): *victoria*. A light four-wheeled carriage for two passengers.

11   (p. 148): *a young artist in 'black-and-white'*. One after the fashionable manner of Aubrey Beardsley.

12   (p. 149): *père de famille*. Father of a family (with the implication of heavy responsibilities).

13   (p. 149): *mornes*. Gloomy.

14   (p. 151): *moeurs*. Habits.

15   (p. 151): *We're going to look at ... types*. See Note 2.

16   (p. 153): *C'est d'un trouvé*. He's a real find.

17   (p. 156): *Comment donc?* How so?

18   (p. 158): *bearskins*. The furry headgear of guardsmen.

19   (p. 162): *il ne manquerait plus que ça!* That would be the last straw!

20   (p. 166): *carton-pierre*. Papier mâché.

21   (p. 166): *Lincrusta-Walton*. A sort of paper, made of oxidized linseed oil, which, when stamped and embossed, was used as a heavy wallpaper. It was invented by a Mr Walton, who also patented linoleum.

22 (p. 166): *brummagem*. Sham or fake goods associated with Birmingham manufacture.

23 (p. 167): *Harrow ... Oxford ... Sandhurst*. An important private school, university and military academy, in that order.

24 (p. 168): *n'en parlons plus!* Let us say no more about it.

The Private Life

1 (p. 191): *fleur des pois*. The pick of the bunch.

2 (p. 195): *bugles*. Tube-shaped beads.

3 (p. 198): *gilded obelisk*. Funerary monument.

4 (p. 199): *salle-à-manger*. Dining-room.

5 (p. 200): *the old English and the new French*. The classics of the English drama, and recent imports from Paris.

6 (p. 200): *Sheridan*. Richard Brinsley Sheridan (1751-1816), dramatist, author of *The Rivals* (1775), *The School for Scandal* (1777) and *The Critic* (1779).

7 (p. 200): *Bowdler*. This is unlikely to be Thomas Bowdler (1754–1825), famous for his expurgation of Shakespeare but not himself a playwright. James seems to have borrowed the name for an imaginary nineteenth-century dramatist, perhaps suggesting an avoidance of all that might be found morally questionable.

8 (p. 201): *cher grand maître*. *Cher maître* is a respectful form of address to a senior artist or writer; the *grand* makes it more obsequious.

9 (p. 202): *haricots verts*. Green beans.

10 (p. 202): *régal*. Treat.

11 (p. 203): *débit*. Delivery.

12 (p. 211): *Où voulez-vous en venir?* What are you driving at?

13 (p. 223): *y pensez-vous?* How can you think it?

14 (p. 228): *Manfred*. Hero of the 'dramatic poem' (1817) of Lord Byron (1788–1824); in the second scene Manfred stands alone on the Jungfrau.

The Middle Years

1 (p. 235): *the Island*. The Isle of Wight.

2 (p. 237): *catchpenny binding*. Cheaply attractive cover.

3 (p. 237): *circulating library*. At this period Mudie's circulating library, from which one borrowed books for a fee, was an important element in the market for fiction.

4 (p. 237): *passed the sponge over colour*. Presumably an allusion to painters' practice when enfeebling colour.

5 (p. 238): *the great glazed tank of art*. He thinks of the novel as a tank in an aquarium.

6 (p. 239): *vincit omnia*. Conquers all (usually the subject is *amor*, love).

7 (p. 240): *Qui dort dine!* To sleep is to dine.

8 (p. 241): *bergère*. Shepherdess.

9 (p. 242): *as obvious as the giantess of a caravan*. i.e., a freak.

10 (pp. 244–5): *the new psychology*. Referring, presumably, to the therapy of hypnosis.

11 (p. 246): *pricked a dozen lights*. Made a dozen marks.

12 (p. 246): *Bath-chair*. A wheeled invalid carriage.

13 (p. 248): *intrigante*. A schemer.

THE DEATH OF THE LION

1 (pp. 266–7): *great gossiping . . . work*. James is perhaps thinking of his own notebooks, which contain examples of just such scenarios.

2 (p. 268): *passe encore*. That's bound to happen.

3 (p. 272): *having 'a man in the house'*. Being visited by bailiffs.

4 (p. 272): *the larger latitude*. A facetious euphemism for sexual candour.

5 (p. 273): *'heads'*. Headings.

6 (p. 283): *George Washington . . . Friedrich Schiller . . . Hannah More*. Washington (1732–99), Schiller (1759–1805) and More (1745-1833) were of course all dead.

7 (p. 289): *leaped through the hoops . . . telegrams and 'specials'*. His frames are likened to the hoops through which circus performers jump; they do their act with the same ease when they get into the news, and into special editions of journals.

8 (p. 289): *Vandyke*. Sir Anthony Van Dyck (1599–1641), Flemish painter, notable among other things for portraits made at the court of Charles I.

9 (p. 293): *valet de place*. An unusual term; presumably 'a guide'.

10 (p. 293): *custode*. Keeper.

11 (p. 294): *that piece of pricless Sèvres*. Fine porcelain made at Sèvres in France.

12 (p. 297): *ces dames*. These ladies.

13 (p. 300): *Le roy est mort – vive le roy*. The king is dead – long live the king.

14 (p. 300): *inédit*. Unpublished.

THE NEXT TIME

1 (p. 309): *a holder of the scales*. A dispenser of critical justice.

2 (p. 314): *Trappists*. Nickname for the Cistercians of Strict Observance,

who fast and keep silence; it derives from their monastery at La Trappe, in France.

3 (p. 315): *Bohemia ... Mrs Grundy.* 'Bohemia' stands for artists and their way of life; 'Mrs Grundy' for respectability.

4 (p. 317): *little windows of plush.* Elaborate photograph frames.

5 (p. 318): *Je vous porte malheur.* I bring you bad luck.

6 (p. 328): *Board-school.* This was what would now be called a state school, as opposed to the English public or the American 'prep' school, where fees must be paid.

7 (p. 333): *le gros public.* A derogatory expression: 'the great stupid public'.

8 (p. 340): *Aux grands maux les grands remèdes.* Great ills call for desperate remedies.

9 (p. 343): *Que voulez-vous?* What do you expect?

10 (p. 345): *flys.* A fly was a one-horse cab rented from a livery stable or, as here, an inn.

11 (p. 347): *Goneril ... Regan ... Lear.* An allusion to Shakespeare's *King Lear* (1605–6), in which the king leaves his daughter Goneril when she orders him to reduce the number of his followers, only to find that his second daughter Regan would reduce them even further.

12 (p. 349): *When he went abroad ... heliotrope.* i.e., he did his best to find something humdrum and so acceptable to the public, but couldn't help producing something rare and beautiful instead.

13 (p. 350): *Scott.* Sir Walter Scott (1771–1832), author of the *Waverley* novels.

14 (p. 353): *country of the blue.* The sense is that he had found himself again in his imaginative world, but the expression is unusual. In a marginal gloss to *The Ancient Mariner* (263ff., 1816 edition), Coleridge, speaking of the stars, says that 'everywhere the blue sky belongs to them, and is their appointed rest, and their native country ...' Possibly James's expression derives from this passage.

THE FIGURE IN THE CARPET

1 (p. 376): *maniacs who embrace some bedlamitical theory of Shakespeare.* Bedlamitical: crazy (Bedlam or Bethlehem Hospital was for the mad). Numerous writers of the time, and since, have tried, by the detection of ciphered messages in Shakespeare, to prove that his works were really by some other person such as the Earl of Oxford.

2 (p. 379): *prepared to out-Herod the metropolitan press.* i.e., to shout louder than; see *Hamlet* III, ii, 14: 'It out-Herods Herod.' (Herod was

always represented in the medieval mystery plays as a furious ranting tyrant.)

3 (p. 381): *Vera incessu patuit dea!* By her gait the true goddess is made known. A line from Virgil, *Aeneid*, i. The speaker evidently uses the old pronunciation of Latin, so that *dea* is indistinguishable from 'dear', thus permitting the pun.

4 (p. 382): *secousse*. Shock, blow.

5 (p. 383): *Tellement envie de voir ta tête!* I long to see your face!

6 (p. 388): *trouvaille*. A find.

7 (p. 389): *Velasquez*. Diego Rodríguez de Silva y Velázquez (1599–1660), Spanish painter, court painter to Philip IV.

8 (p. 398): *phrenological bust*. Model made for purposes of instruction in phrenology.

9 (p. 398): *the numbers on his bumps*. A facetious allusion to the practice of phrenology, widespread earlier in the century but now largely discredited. In diagrams of the time, areas of the head were given numbers, according to which one identified the particular function of each part.

JOHN DELAVOY

1 (p. 403): Wearing deep mourning.

2 (p. 412): *like good wine . . . no bush*. From the saying 'Good wine needs no bush' – no advertisement.

3 (p. 421): *galleys*. First proofs.

4 (p. 421): *blue pencil*. Used to mark proofs; here to indicate unacceptable passages.

5 (p. 422): *proof-reader's shocks*. Exclamation marks. (The proof-reader is suggesting that some parts of the article are too indecent to print.)

6 (p. 429): *par example*. For example; here merely an exclamation.

7 (p. 432): *demi-jour*. The half-light of dawn or dusk.

8 (p. 436): *To accompany the head*. i.e., her portrait of Delavoy.

9 (p. 442): *prodigiously 'paragraphed' in advance and with its authorship flushing through*. Given advance publicity which 'leaked' the authorship.

PENGUIN CLASSICS

www.penguinclassics.com

- *Details about every Penguin Classic*

- *Advanced information about forthcoming titles*

- *Hundreds of author biographies*

- *FREE resources including critical essays on the books and their historical background, reader's and teacher's guides.*

- *Links to other web resources for the Classics*

- *Discussion area*

- *Online review copy ordering for academics*

- *Competitions with prizes, and challenging Classics trivia quizzes*

PENGUIN CLASSICS ONLINE

READ MORE IN PENGUIN

In every corner of the world, on every subject under the sun, Penguin represents quality and variety – the very best in publishing today.

For complete information about books available from Penguin – including Puffins, Penguin Classics and Arkana – and how to order them, write to us at the appropriate address below. Please note that for copyright reasons the selection of books varies from country to country.

In the United Kingdom: Please write to *Dept. EP, Penguin Books Ltd, Bath Road, Harmondsworth, West Drayton, Middlesex UB7 0DA*

In the United States: Please write to *Consumer Services, Penguin Putnam Inc., 405 Murray Hill Parkway, East Rutherford, New Jersey 07073-2136.* VISA and MasterCard holders call 1-800-631-8571 to order Penguin titles

In Canada: Please write to *Penguin Books Canada Ltd, 10 Alcorn Avenue, Suite 300, Toronto, Ontario M4V 3B2*

In Australia: Please write to *Penguin Books Australia Ltd, 487 Maroondah Highway, Ringwood, Victoria 3134*

In New Zealand: Please write to *Penguin Books (NZ) Ltd, Private Bag 102902, North Shore Mail Centre, Auckland 10*

In India: Please write to *Penguin Books India Pvt Ltd, 11 Community Centre, Panchsheel Park, New Delhi 110017*

In the Netherlands: Please write to *Penguin Books Netherlands bv, Postbus 3507, NL-1001 AH Amsterdam*

In Germany: Please write to *Penguin Books Deutschland GmbH, Metzlerstrasse 26, 60594 Frankfurt am Main*

In Spain: Please write to *Penguin Books S. A., Bravo Murillo 19, 1°B, 28015 Madrid*

In Italy: Please write to *Penguin Italia s.r.l., Via Vittorio Emanuele 45/a, 20094 Corsico, Milano*

In France: Please write to *Penguin France, 12, Rue Prosper Ferradou, 31700 Blagnac*

In Japan: Please write to *Penguin Books Japan Ltd, Iidabashi KM-Bldg, 2-23-9 Koraku, Bunkyo-Ku, Tokyo 112-0004*

In South Africa: Please write to *Penguin Books South Africa (Pty) Ltd, P.O. Box 751093, Gardenview, 2047 Johannesburg*

READ MORE IN PENGUIN

A CHOICE OF CLASSICS

Matthew Arnold	**Selected Prose**
Jane Austen	**Emma**
	Lady Susan/The Watsons/Sanditon
	Mansfield Park
	Northanger Abbey
	Persuasion
	Pride and Prejudice
	Sense and Sensibility
William Barnes	**Selected Poems**
Mary Braddon	**Lady Audley's Secret**
Anne Brontë	**Agnes Grey**
	The Tenant of Wildfell Hall
Charlotte Brontë	**Jane Eyre**
	Juvenilia: 1829–35
	The Professor
	Shirley
	Villette
Emily Brontë	**Complete Poems**
	Wuthering Heights
Samuel Butler	**Erewhon**
	The Way of All Flesh
Lord Byron	**Don Juan**
	Selected Poems
Lewis Carroll	**Alice's Adventures in Wonderland**
	The Hunting of the Snark
Thomas Carlyle	**Selected Writings**
Arthur Hugh Clough	**Selected Poems**
Wilkie Collins	**Armadale**
	The Law and the Lady
	The Moonstone
	No Name
	The Woman in White
Charles Darwin	**The Origin of Species**
	Voyage of the Beagle
Benjamin Disraeli	**Coningsby**
	Sybil

READ MORE IN PENGUIN

A CHOICE OF CLASSICS

Charles Dickens	**American Notes for General Circulation**
	Barnaby Rudge
	Bleak House
	The Christmas Books (in two volumes)
	David Copperfield
	Dombey and Son
	Great Expectations
	Hard Times
	Little Dorrit
	Martin Chuzzlewit
	The Mystery of Edwin Drood
	Nicholas Nickleby
	The Old Curiosity Shop
	Oliver Twist
	Our Mutual Friend
	The Pickwick Papers
	Pictures from Italy
	Selected Journalism 1850–1870
	Selected Short Fiction
	Sketches by Boz
	A Tale of Two Cities
George Eliot	**Adam Bede**
	Daniel Deronda
	Felix Holt
	Middlemarch
	The Mill on the Floss
	Romola
	Scenes of Clerical Life
	Silas Marner
Fanny Fern	**Ruth Hall**
Elizabeth Gaskell	**Cranford/Cousin Phillis**
	The Life of Charlotte Brontë
	Mary Barton
	North and South
	Ruth
	Sylvia's Lovers
	Wives and Daughters

READ MORE IN PENGUIN

A CHOICE OF CLASSICS

Edward Gibbon	**The Decline and Fall of the Roman Empire** (in three volumes)
	Memoirs of My Life
George Gissing	**New Grub Street**
	The Odd Women
William Godwin	**Caleb Williams**
	Concerning Political Justice
Thomas Hardy	**Desperate Remedies**
	The Distracted Preacher and Other Tales
	Far from the Madding Crowd
	Jude the Obscure
	The Hand of Ethelberta
	A Laodicean
	The Mayor of Casterbridge
	A Pair of Blue Eyes
	The Return of the Native
	Selected Poems
	Tess of the d'Urbervilles
	The Trumpet-Major
	Two on a Tower
	Under the Greenwood Tree
	The Well-Beloved
	The Woodlanders
George Lyell	**Principles of Geology**
Lord Macaulay	**The History of England**
Henry Mayhew	**London Labour and the London Poor**
George Meredith	**The Egoist**
	The Ordeal of Richard Feverel
John Stuart Mill	**The Autobiography**
	On Liberty
	Principles of Political Economy
William Morris	**News from Nowhere and Other Writings**
John Henry Newman	**Apologia Pro Vita Sua**
Margaret Oliphant	**Miss Marjoribanks**
Robert Owen	**A New View of Society and Other Writings**
Walter Pater	**Marius the Epicurean**
John Ruskin	**Unto This Last and Other Writings**

READ MORE IN PENGUIN

A CHOICE OF CLASSICS

Walter Scott	**The Antiquary**
	Heart of Mid-Lothian
	Ivanhoe
	Kenilworth
	The Tale of Old Mortality
	Rob Roy
	Waverley
Robert Louis Stevenson	**Kidnapped**
	Dr Jekyll and Mr Hyde and Other Stories
	In the South Seas
	The Master of Ballantrae
	Selected Poems
	Weir of Hermiston
William Makepeace Thackeray	**The History of Henry Esmond**
	The History of Pendennis
	The Newcomes
	Vanity Fair
Anthony Trollope	**Barchester Towers**
	Can You Forgive Her?
	Doctor Thorne
	The Eustace Diamonds
	Framley Parsonage
	He Knew He Was Right
	The Last Chronicle of Barset
	Phineas Finn
	The Prime Minister
	The Small House at Allington
	The Warden
	The Way We Live Now
Oscar Wilde	**Complete Short Fiction**
Mary Wollstonecraft	**A Vindication of the Rights of Woman**
	Mary and **Maria** (includes Mary Shelley's **Matilda**)
Dorothy and William Wordsworth	**Home at Grasmere**

READ MORE IN PENGUIN

A CHOICE OF CLASSICS

Anton Chekhov
The Duel and Other Stories
The Kiss and Other Stories
The Fiancée and Other Stories
Lady with Lapdog and Other Stories
The Party and Other Stories
Plays (The Cherry Orchard/Ivanov/The Seagull/Uncle Vania/The Bear/The Proposal/A Jubilee/Three Sisters)

Fyodor Dostoyevsky
The Brothers Karamazov
Crime and Punishment
The Devils
The Gambler/Bobok/A Nasty Story
The House of the Dead
The Idiot
Netochka Nezvanova
The Village of Stepanchikovo
Notes from Underground/The Double

Nikolai Gogol
Dead Souls
Diary of a Madman and Other Stories

Alexander Pushkin
Eugene Onegin
The Queen of Spades and Other Stories
Tales of Belkin

Leo Tolstoy
Anna Karenin
Childhood, Boyhood, Youth
A Confession
How Much Land Does a Man Need?
Master and Man and Other Stories
Resurrection
The Sebastopol Sketches
What is Art?
War and Peace

Ivan Turgenev
Fathers and Sons
First Love
A Month in the Country
On the Eve
Rudin
Sketches from a Hunter's Album

READ MORE IN PENGUIN

A CHOICE OF CLASSICS

Thomas Wentworth Higginson	**Army Life in a Black Regiment**
William Dean Howells	**The Rise of Silas Lapham**
Gilbert Imlay	**The Emigrants**
Sarah Orne Jewett	**The Country of the Pointed Firs**
Herman Melville	**Billy Budd, Sailor and Other Stories**
	The Confidence-Man
	Moby-Dick
	Pierre
	Redburn
	Typee
Thomas Paine	**Common Sense**
	The Rights of Man
	The Thomas Paine Reader
Edgar Allan Poe	**Comedies and Satires**
	The Fall of the House of Usher
	The Narrative of Arthur Gordon Pym of Nantucket
	The Science Fiction of Edgar Allan Poe
Jacob A. Riis	**How the Other Half Lives**
Elizabeth Stoddard	**The Morgesons**
Harriet Beecher Stowe	**Uncle Tom's Cabin**
Henry David Thoreau	**Walden/Civil Disobedience**
	Week on the Concord and Merrimack
Mark Twain	**The Adventures of Huckleberry Finn**
	The Adventures of Tom Sawyer
	A Connecticut Yankee at King Arthur's Court
	Life on the Mississippi
	The Prince and the Pauper
	Pudd'nhead Wilson
	Roughing It
	Short Stories
	A Tramp Abroad
	Tales, Speeches, Essays and Sketches
Walt Whitman	**The Complete Poems**
	Leaves of Grass

READ MORE IN PENGUIN

HENRY JAMES

'He is as solitary in the history of the novel as Shakespeare in the history of poetry' Graham Greene

NOVELS

The Ambassadors

The American

The Aspern Papers *and*
  The Turn of the Screw

The Awkward Age

The Bostonians

Daisy Miller

The Europeans

The Golden Bowl

The Portrait of a Lady

The Princess Casamassima

Roderick Hudson

The Sacred Fount

The Spoils of Poynton

The Tragic Muse

Washington Square

What Maisie Knew

The Wings of the Dove

SHORT STORIES

The Figure in the Carpet
  and Other Stories

The Jolly Corner
  and Other Tales

TRAVEL AND OTHER WRITING

The American Scene

The Critical Muse: Selected Literary Criticism